NORTH of LARAMIE

NORTH of LARAMIE

A BUCK TRAMMEL WESTERN

WILLIAM W. JOHNSTONE
AND J. A. JOHNSTONE

PINNACLE BOOKS
Kensington Publishing Corp.
www.kensingtonbooks.com

PINNACLE BOOKS are published by

Kensington Publishing Corp.
119 West 40th Street
New York, NY 10018

PUBLISHER'S NOTE
Following the death of William W. Johnstone, the Johnstone family is working with a carefully selected writer to organize and complete Mr. Johnstone's outlines and many unfinished manuscripts to create additional novels in all of his series like The Last Gunfighter, Mountain Man, and Eagles, among others. This novel was inspired by Mr. Johnstone's superb storytelling.

ISBN-13: 978-0-7860-4585-3
ISBN-10: 0-7860-4585-X

First printing: May 2020

10 9 8 7 6 5 4 3 2 1

Printed in the United States of America

Electronic edition:

ISBN-13: 978-0-7860-4586-0 (e-book)
ISBN-10: 0-7860-4586-8 (e-book)

Chapter 1

"Hagen!" one of the Bowman boys yelled. "You are a drunk, a cheat, and a liar!"

From his perch in the lookout chair, Buck Trammel watched the unfolding argument between the gambler Adam Hagen and two boys from the Bowman Ranch. All of the men were still seated around the poker table, which Trammel took as a good sign. A man on his backside was often less likely to cause trouble, at least without some warning. And since all of them had checked their guns with the barman, a fistfight was the worst he could expect. Given his size, Trammel found those much easier to break up than gunfights.

Experience had taught Trammel that he was better off staying in the lookout chair and allowing the matter to unfold on its own. He looked out at the rest of the room just to make sure none of the other patrons of The Gilded Lilly saloon were preparing to take sides in the argument. A glare from him usually discouraged such decisions. The double-barreled shotgun lying across his lap helped, too. Trammel's size and reputation for violence were usually enough to keep amateurs and brawlers at bay, but the sight of a coach gun never hurt the prospects for peace.

The drunken Hagen held his cards as he laughed at William Bowman's growing rage.

The cowhand only grew that much angrier. "I called you a cheat and a liar and all you can do is giggle like an idiot?"

"No," Hagen slurred. "I giggle because I'm dumb enough to gamble with an idiot." He slapped his hands at the cards laid out in front of him. Aces and eights. A handful of nothing. "I laugh because it's the first hand I've won in an hour. I laugh because I bluffed you into building up the pot before you folded. I didn't cheat you, Billy Boy. I didn't have to. You cheated yourself by losing your nerve."

Both Bowman boys stood at the same time as the other players scrambled away from the table. Armed or not, Trammel knew every member of the Bowman clan was a brawler and not to be trifled with, especially after being called stupid.

"Get up, you drunken sot," Tyler Bowman said. "Get on your feet and repeat what you just said to Billy and me."

The sound of chair legs scraping against wood broke the silence as gamblers and drinkers moved out of the way. Some stood on chairs to get a better look at the action.

A nervous look from Lilly, the owner of the Gilded Lilly, told Trammel what he had to do. He left the shotgun in the slot on the lookout chair as he quietly climbed down. No one was paying attention to him anyway. They were waiting to see what Hagen and the Bowman boys did next.

Hagen swayed in his chair as he pulled the pile of cash toward him, but made no effort to stand.

Trammel, a full head taller than any man standing and twice as wide, eased his way through the customers craning their necks to see what would happen. It had been too quiet for too long in Wichita—nearly three days since the last killing—and the patrons were anxious for a fight.

Will Bowman shoved aside the chair he had been sitting in. "Damn you, Hagen. We're calling you out. Are you going to be a man and stand on your own, or am I going to have to rip you out of that chair?"

Trammel pushed his way through the crowd and came out behind the Bowman boys. "That's enough. You've all made your point. The game's over. Collect your guns and head on home."

Both of them turned and had to look up to face him. He knew they didn't like that. No one in the Bowman clan liked looking up at anyone. The family had enjoyed a free hand in Wichita for as long as anyone could remember, certainly long before Trammel had come to town a year before.

But Miss Lilly hadn't hired him as the bouncer at The Gilded Lilly to be popular. She had hired him to keep the peace in her place, and that's what he planned to do.

Tyler, the younger of the two, took a step toward Trammel. "This here is a private matter, boy. Best if you just climb back up in your perch and let us be."

Trammel looked at the chair that had been thrown

aside. "Your private matter's hard on our furniture and I can't have that. Game's over anyway. Take whatever money you've got left, collect your guns, and try your luck somewhere else."

But Will Bowman hadn't budged. He continued to glower down at Hagen. "Damn you, I said get up."

Hagen waved him off with a boozy hand as though he were a fly. "Mr. Trammel, I would appreciate it if you would remove these men at your earliest convenience. They are interfering with the effects of my whiskey, which I'm afraid may soon cause me to become sober."

Tyler Bowman remained between Trammel and the table. "What's it going to be, big man? You taking orders from a drunk, now?"

"I only take orders from her." Trammel nodded at Lilly, who'd been anxiously watching things from the bar at the left side of the room. "She doesn't want any trouble in here. She wants you gone, so out you go." He looked down at Tyler. "And that means all of you. Hagen included."

"We'll kill him the second we hit the street." Tyler had said it like it was supposed to be an insult to Trammel. "We'll kill him right in front of you."

"What happens outside is between you and the town sheriff." Trammel took one step closer to Tyler, making him crane his neck even more to try to maintain eye contact. "And I'm getting damned tired of repeating myself, *boy*. Everyone leaves. Right now."

"We ain't going anywhere 'til this is done." Will Bowman reached for something tucked in the back of his britches.

Trammel shoved Tyler out of the way, sending him

crashing into the poker table behind him, before grabbing Will's wrist just as it came around to the small of his back.

Will tried to break free from the bigger man's grip, but Trammel pulled up hard on his wrist until he heard the unmistakable sound of cartilage popping.

Trammel ignored Bowman's screams as he searched for what he had been grabbing for. He found a knife handle sticking out of the back of Bowman's britches. He pulled the blade free and threw it aside. He hated knives.

Still holding on to the broken arm, Trammel grabbed the screaming Bowman by the back of his shirt collar and steered him toward the door. "Out you go, boy. Best head over to Doc Freeman's. Get that arm tended to."

But Trammel stumbled when a glass bottle shattered across the back of his head.

Everything slowed. Sight and sound blurred and, for a fraction of a second, Trammel couldn't feel anything at all. Not pain. Not surprise. Not even anger.

All he could feel was rage.

He yanked Will Bowman off his feet and threw him aside as he turned around to face his assailant. Tyler. The younger man was scrambling for another whiskey bottle at another table, but Trammel launched a roundhouse right that caught Tyler square in the jaw.

From his slowed perspective, Trammel could see the jaw was as broken as the dam that had once held back his temper.

Bowman was falling, but not before a left hook from Trammel connected with Tyler's temple. The cattleman landed in a crooked heap on the floor between two card tables as men scrambled to get out of the way.

Somewhere in his mind, he could hear Lilly calling his name as he picked up a chair and brought it down hard on the fallen Bowman's back. The chair splintered into pieces. A leg landed nearby.

Trammel picked up the leg and dropped to his knees, straddling the prone man. He brought the chair leg over his head like a club, intending on bringing it down on Tyler again and again until Lilly's kind face filled his vision. The same face that graced the sign that hung over the front door, though this one bore more lines and was not as soft.

"No, Buck!" He felt her hands on his shoulders. "That's enough. Stop, please!"

Trammel let the chair leg fall behind him as his senses returned and time began to become normal. He remembered the other Bowman boy. William.

Trammel rocked back and got to his feet in one motion, remembering he had thrown him aside right after Tyler had hit him with the bottle.

Some of the patrons had gathered around the place where Will had landed, trading glances amongst themselves. They knew what Trammel could see just by looking at Bowman's neck. The twisted, unnatural angle against a broken chair only meant one thing.

"He's dead," one of the customers said. "His neck broke when he hit the chair."

"Did you see how he flew?" another said. "Hell, I only ever saw a man fly like that when he was bucked off a horse."

A cry from Lilly made Trammel look down. Her

delicate fingers were pressed against Tyler's neck, as if the Bowman boy's vacant stare wasn't proof enough for her. "He's dead, too, Buck. You've killed both of them."

"And with his bare hands, too," said someone in the saloon. "Not a hog leg or a blade on him. Killed 'em both by touch alone. Lord have mercy."

Trammel looked up when he heard the sound of clapping. It was coming from the poker table. It was Adam Hagen applauding him from behind his pile of money. "Bravo, Mr. Trammel. The citizens of Wichita salute you for the public service you've done here tonight, for the world is a far better place with two fewer Bowman boys slithering around in it."

Trammel's knuckles popped as he felt his fists ball up. Two dead men was nothing to clap about, even if it was two Bowman boys. "Someone get him out of here."

Hagen tried to sit upright in his chair. "But I live here, sir, and my luck has changed for the better." He gestured grandly at the empty chairs at the table. "Anyone care to play? We appear to have two vacancies at the moment."

Trammel started for him, but Lilly scrambled to block his way. "Someone get him up to his room before Buck kills him, too."

Three customers pulled Hagen to his feet, but not before the drunkard stuffed his winnings into his pockets. Gold and greenbacks bulged from the pockets of his coat and pants and vest.

Two men threw his arms over their shoulders as another cleared a path for them to the stairs and the rooms above. "Such service!" Hagen laughed. "Will one of you be so kind as to draw me a bath, as well?"

The man who had his right arm said, "The only thing you'll be drawing is blood if you don't keep that damned drunken mouth of yours shut."

Trammel's rage ebbed once more as he watched the men take Hagen upstairs and he realized Lilly was still holding on to him. He placed his large hands on her slender shoulders and gently eased her away. "I'm okay now, Lilly. I promise."

Lilly didn't take her eyes off him as she yelled, "Show's over, boys. Sorry for the trouble. Drinks are on the house, courtesy of your Aunt Lilly."

The patrons cheered and quickly went back to their respective games. The trouble and the dead men on the floor seemingly forgot by everyone except Trammel and Lilly.

"You're hurt, Buck." Lilly popped up on her toes to reach the wound on his head. "You're bleeding."

Trammel had nearly forgotten about the whiskey bottle that Tyler had broken over his head. He felt at the back of his head and found a shard of glass just behind his ear. He winced as he pulled it out and let it drop to the floor. He flicked other bits of glass from the wound, too, some of them falling down his collar. "It's not the first time someone's busted a bottle over my head. Doubt it'll be the last."

Lilly stepped away from him and looked at destruction all around her. "This is bad, Buck."

"No, it isn't. I'll live." He checked his hand and was surprised there wasn't more blood. "I've been through worse."

"I don't just mean you. I mean the Bowman boys.

Their people won't take kindly to you killing two of their kin, even if they had it coming."

Trammel looked down at the men on the floor. The two men he had just killed. He waited to feel something. He waited to feel anything at all. All he felt was tired. "Like I said. I've been through worse."

Chapter 2

About an hour after closing time, Trammel sat in a chair while Lilly tended to his wounds. He winced when she dabbed a rag in whiskey and put it to his cuts.

"Well, would you look at that?" She held out the bloody rag for him to see. "Looks like you're flesh and blood after all. Not some demon like some of the boys suggested. From the Old Testament, no less."

He looked back at the two dead Bowman boys on the floor. Someone had placed tablecloths over their faces, and Trammel found himself wondering where someone had found tablecloths. Must've been from another place in town. The Gilded Lilly wasn't exactly known for fine dining. "As human as the next man, I suppose. Maybe even more so."

"You just killed two men with your bare hands, Buck. That's not a human act."

"You didn't hire me to show Christian charity, Lilly. You hired me to keep things around here to a dull roar. Those boys were going to cut that drunk Hagen to pieces. If you'd wanted me to let that go, you should've said something."

"I don't care about them." She found a clean spot

on the rag and dipped it into the whiskey. It stung less this time when she touched his wound. "I care about you." She stroked his black hair. "You know that."

"I'll be fine. It was a fair fight. Everyone in the place saw it. I'm sure Marshal Meagher will see it that way, too."

"I'm not worried about how he sees it," Lilly said. "I worry about how the Bowman family will see it."

"They knew what these boys were like," Trammel said. "They won't be happy about it, but I'm sure they'll accept it once the marshal explains it to them. He's always known how to handle them before."

Lilly threw the rag on the bar. "Damn it, Buck. How long is it going to take for you to understand that not everyone is a reasonable man? Reason might've played into it back when you were a Pinkerton man, but you ain't a Pinkerton man anymore. This ain't New York City, neither, and reason don't always apply out here, especially to people like the Bowman family. They listen to Meagher because he's got a tin star on his chest and a couple of deputies willing to back him up. You don't have any star on your chest, at least not anymore, and no one to back you except me."

He smiled as he reached back and held her hand. "Don't sell yourself short. You're a formidable woman, Lilly Chase. I'm scared to death of you."

She pulled her hand free and lightly tapped his wound, causing him to yelp. "Two dead men on the floor and you're trying to sweet-talk me. You've caused yourself a lot of trouble tonight, more than I think you know. The Bowman family won't take kindly to one of their kin being killed tonight, much less two of them. They'll approve of the manner of their death even less."

Trammel took the rag from the bar and placed it on his wound himself. "I said I'll handle it. I always have before."

"Not against the likes of the Bowman clan, you haven't."

He could have used this moment to explain his life to her, to tell her more than the snippets of details he had let slip over the past year. But he chose not to do that. She had hired him when he had stepped off the stage a year ago. He had been looking for a place to lose himself for a while after his career with the Pinkerton National Detective Agency had come to an end. All she knew was that he was big, could take care of himself and had kept good order in her saloon since the day he had signed on. Most people thought twice about crossing the Big Man from Back East, as he had become known, and few people had challenged him.

Trammel had always known it would only be a matter of time before the wrong man tried to test him; to see for themselves if the big man in the lookout chair was as tough as everyone said. He hadn't thought his test would be this bad and he certainly hadn't counted on it coming from the likes of the Bowman clan.

He knew he should have been more concerned, frightened, even, about going up against the might of the Bowman family. But Trammel wasn't the least bit concerned. It just wasn't in him to be afraid of a fight.

It was the reason why he had been forced to quit the Pinkerton Agency in the first place.

"I'll handle it however you want me to handle it, Lilly. If you want me to leave, I'll leave."

He looked up when a voice from the batwing doors of the saloon said, "You're not going anywhere, Trammel. At least for a while."

Trammel recognized the lean shape of the tall man who had just pushed through the doors of The Gilded Lilly. He wasn't as tall as Trammel, but still taller than most men. His black, wide-brimmed hat was tipped forward just enough to shield his narrow eyes and thin nose. But there was no mistaking the man with the thick moustache for anyone else, even if he didn't have the deputy badge pinned to his black frock coat.

"Evening, Deputy," Trammel said. "What brings you around?"

If Deputy Wyatt Earp found any humor in Trammel's remark, he did not show it. "Heard about what happened. Came to see it for myself." He touched the brim of his hat. "Evening, Miss Lilly."

"Evening, Deputy Earp. I'm sorry you aren't here under better circumstances."

"This is Wichita, ma'am," Earp said as he paused to look down at the bodies. "No such a thing as better circumstances, just circumstances. I'd be obliged if you'd let me have a word with your man Trammel. Alone."

"Of course. Can I get you something? Whiskey, coffee?"

"No, ma'am. I won't be here that long."

Lilly squeezed Trammel's shoulder, as if trying to communicate something through her touch before she left. Whatever she was trying to say was lost on him. She disappeared into the back rooms, leaving him alone with the deputy.

He watched Earp stride into the saloon toward the body of Tyler Bowman. Trammel had seen Earp almost every day since he had come to Wichita and always noted the way he moved. He didn't shuffle along or race around like other men. He moved in a manner that one of his old bosses at the Pinkerton Agency once described as "an economy of effort." He moved neither fast nor slow, not even when there was gunplay or a fistfight to be broken up. He always moved at the same steady pace. He was as sure of himself and his movements as if he had planned and practiced every motion he would make that day before he even got out of bed that morning.

Trammel watched Earp take a knee and pull back the sheet covering Tyler Bowman's face. The dead man's gaze happened to fall exactly where Trammel was now sitting, as if the dead man had known exactly where the man who had taken his life would be hours after his death.

Earp cocked his head to the side as he studied the wounds. "Heard you did this, Trammel. Caved in his skull with one punch. That true?"

"It was a fair fight."

Earp kept looking at the body. "I didn't ask you that."

Trammel had seen Earp in action and knew that his temper, and his ferocity, matched his own. "Yeah. I did it. But it was with two punches. First was a right that broke his jaw. The second was a left to the head. Either one could've killed him."

Earp flicked the sheet back over Tyler's face, stood and moved over to the second corpse, taking a knee and moving the sheet from Will Bowman's body.

Trammel couldn't see it, but he could practically feel Earp's eyes moving over the corpse. "What happened here?"

"He got into a fight with a drunk over cards. He reached back for a knife he had tucked in his britches. I stopped him. Think I broke his elbow in the process when he put up a struggle. I was about to throw him out when Tyler over there hit me with a whiskey bottle."

Earp leaned in closer to the corpse. "Looks like his neck's broke. How'd that happen?"

"After Tyler hit me with the bottle," Trammel explained, "I threw Will to the side. He must've hit that chair as he landed."

Earp looked at him for the first time. "You threw him. From where?"

"From right around where Tyler is now."

Earp looked back and judged the distance. "You threw him that far?"

"That's right."

Trammel saw Earp's hat flinch as he placed the sheet back over Will's body and stood up. "You're a strong man."

Trammel didn't know what to say, so he said nothing. He just kept the rag against his wound.

Earp walked over to him until they were about a foot apart. Most people didn't stand that close to Trammel, given his size, but Wyatt Earp wasn't most people. "Take the rag away."

Trammel complied and lowered his head so the deputy could see the wounds for himself.

Earp had obviously seen enough. "You can put the rag back on it now."

Trammel complied again.

Earp moved and leaned against the bar next to him. "Judging by the amount of scars you've got back there, I can tell you've been hit with a bottle before."

Trammel closed his eyes. *Here come the questions.* "I have."

"You kill those men then, too?"

"Sometimes."

"They all fair fights? Just like you say this one was?"

Trammel looked up at him. "Every one of them."

"I thought so." Earp looked right back at him. "And what duty might that have been?"

Trammel looked away. The deputy was trying to get him to talk about his past. "I'd prefer not to say."

"Prefer doesn't play into it, Trammel. I'd prefer to be in bed right now, but instead, I'm here talking to you with two dead men on the floor. I'd prefer not to have to explain to Old Man Bowman how two of his kin got beaten to death in The Gilded Lilly last night. And I sure as hell would prefer not to have to deal with them when they ride into town looking to kill you for what you did to their people."

"It was a fair fight. Legal, too. You can ask anyone who was here."

"Already have," Earp said. "Got statements from ten people on my desk back at the jail right now. All of them said you were provoked. All of them saying the Bowman boys refused to leave. They all say that drunkard Hagen started it, too. That true?"

"Will and Ty said he was cheating," Trammel said. "I don't know if he was or if he wasn't. He didn't look like he was, but I wasn't watching the whole game, either, so I can't swear to it."

"You were in the lookout chair, weren't you?"

"And all I saw was Hagen get drunk and lose a lot. The boys were mad he bluffed them for the pot with nothing more than aces and eights. They accused him of cheating. I don't think he was, but like I said, I can't swear to it."

Earp considered that for a time. "Hagen lives here, doesn't he? Upstairs?"

"For the past month."

"Anyone ever accuse him of cheating before?"

"Nope." Trammel winced as he shifted the rag from one wound to the other. "He seems to win most of the time, but not enough to rankle anybody. He gets drunk mostly, and needs help up to bed, but until tonight, he's never caused any trouble. Polite enough to the girls. Pays them extra when he uses them, which is often enough. Always pays his rent bill on time, too."

"How do you know that?"

"Because I would've thrown him out on his ear if he didn't. Miss Lilly doesn't take kindly to people who owe her money."

"No, she doesn't," Earp admitted. "She's a kindly woman for the business she's in, but I've never known her to lose money without putting up a fuss." He looked at Trammel again. "You really have to beat those men to death tonight?"

Trammel had seen this line of questioning before, where the topic drifts elsewhere, only to snap back to what the questioner really wanted to know. Not too long ago, Trammel was the one on the other side of the table asking the questions.

He took the rag from his head and looked up at

Earp. "I've seen you in plenty of scrapes like this one since I've come to town. Never saw you stop to crack open a Bible and read verses at them until they saw the light."

"Never claimed to be a preacher, Trammel. But I've got the law on my side. You don't have anything except Lilly's good graces and a room somewhere out back. That's not going to be enough when the Bowman clan comes to call. I think a man of your experience knows that."

Trammel was beginning to get tired of all the talking. "You arresting me, Deputy, or running me out of town?"

"Neither." Earp crossed his arms and kept his eye on the door. "It was a fair fight, just like you said, and I've got no reason to lock you up. But there's been plenty of talk about you since you came to town, Trammel. You know that. You've kept your head down as much as you can, but that just makes people talk all the more. I've heard you were a policeman back in New York. I've heard you were a Pinkerton man, too. Some say you came here by choice. Others say you got thrown out of New York, though accounts on that score vary."

Trammel looked up at Earp, feeling the old rage beginning to stoke in his belly again. He didn't want another fight, but he could feel one might be coming. "Guess the only opinion that matters is yours, Deputy."

"What I say doesn't matter," Earp said. "But what you do next matters a hell of a lot. I know you're loyal to Miss Lilly. You should be. She's a good woman who has been good to you. Now I think the time has come for you to repay the favor. The Bowman clan is going to come looking for blood, and a lot of good people are going to die when they do."

"People like you?"

Earp smiled for the first time in the year since Trammel had known him. And it wasn't a nice smile. "No, I won't die. But others will. Some more Bowman kin. You, too."

"Not likely," Trammel said.

"They won't come at you head-on, but sideways," Earp went on. "Maybe they'll go after someone close to you, someone more vulnerable, like Miss Lilly. I wouldn't like that. And I have a feeling you'd like it even less."

Trammel put the rag back on his wound. This time he didn't wince. "No, I wouldn't like that at all."

"Which would lead to more killing," Earp said. "You get paid to enforce the peace in here, but I get paid to enforce the law everywhere. I don't have anything against the Bowman family. Their ranch is good for the town and, on the whole, they don't cause as much trouble as some people in this town. But I don't want to see them dead any more than I want to see you dead. I might not know much about you, but I think you know what you have to do next. If not for your sake, then for Miss Lilly's well-being."

Trammel knew. He had known it the second he'd realized both Bowman boys were dead. He just didn't say it because saying something had a way of making it real. He didn't want this to be real, but it was. It was as real as it got. He had to leave town. He had to leave the first real home he had ever known. "I'll be ready to leave by sunup."

Earp nodded once. "Best way all around. Just don't

tell anyone where you're going. Not me and not Miss Lilly."

Trammel wasn't going to tell anyone anything. "I know what I'm doing."

"I remember you came in here on the coach," Earp went on. "You need a horse? Provisions?"

"I've got a horse in the livery and enough money to buy what I need if the store's open in time."

"Ben Hurly opens his shop early," Earp said. "Best hit him up first. I'll tell him to expect you." He reached into his pocket, pulled out a box of cartridges, and placed them on the bar. "This is for that fancy Winchester I hear you keep in your room. You're going to need them."

Trammel already had enough ammunition, but he appreciated the gesture all the same. "Thanks."

Earp pushed himself off the bar and began walking out of the saloon, slow and easy. Over his shoulder, he said, "And you're taking Hagen with you."

Trammel stood before he realized it. "What? Why?"

"The Bowman family will want his scalp as much as they want yours. I'd arrest him for disturbing the peace and inciting violence, but the old man would only kill him as soon as I cut him loose. Best if you two ride off together. Save everyone a whole lot of trouble."

"I'm not responsible for what happens to that drunken fool!" Trammel yelled.

Earp didn't break his stride. "Well, you are now."

"Damn it, Earp. That's not . . . fair! Hell, I haven't even been to bed yet."

"This is Wichita, Trammel. Fair's got nothing to do with it. Besides, you're an old Pinkerton man, and Pinkerton men never sleep. Isn't that your motto?"

Earp pushed his way through the batwing doors and stepped out into the dark Kansas night, leaving Stephen Trammel with only a bloody rag and no options.

Trammel cursed as he threw the rag behind the bar.

CHAPTER 3

Adam Hagen woke with a gasp as a bucket of ice-cold water soaked him to the bone.

Trammel thought the gambler would have fallen out of bed if he wasn't already passed out on the floor of his room. "Time to get up, Hagen. We've got some riding to do."

"Writing? What kind of writing?" Hagen pulled himself up on his hands and knees, only to fall over on his side. "What are you babbling on about?"

"Riding, as in a horse. Not writing with a pen. Get up."

Hagen tried to sit upright but slipped on the soaked floor. "Now, see here my good man. I'm as fond of a joke as much as the next man, but it's far too early in the morning for a joke. And my head aches far too much for levity."

"And it's too late for your nonsense." Trammel grabbed him by the collar and pulled him up to a seated position onto the bed. He thought Hagen might fall over and was surprised when he didn't. "We've got to get out of town, thanks to you, and we've got to get moving. Now."

Trammel had crammed as many of Hagen's things as he could into a single bag, but doubted he'd grabbed a quarter of it. Even though Hagan was a drunk and a gambler, he had come to town with three trunks jammed with clothes. Trammel had asked Lilly to keep the rest and ship it to Hagen at the first place he could drop him off without the Bowman family finding him.

"What about all of my things?" Hagen asked. "It will take me the better part of the morning to get everything together. Now, how about you sit down and let's have a drink while we discuss this like civilized gentlemen."

"No time for that." He found a bowler and plopped it on Hagen's head before taking the gambler by the arm and pulling him off the bed. He stuck the bag into his gut, which Hagen grabbed more out of reflex than intent, and pushed him out the door. "Let's go. Now."

Hagen surprised Trammel by making it down the stairs on his own steam, only missing the last step, but managed to maintain his balance anyway. Trammel figured the old saying was true: "God looks out for drunks and babies." He hoped the same extended to the people who got stuck watching out for them.

He steered Hagen out back where he had their mounts saddled and ready. His own horse was a spirited brown roan the liveryman had told him was about four years old. She'd been a good horse to ride around the countryside on his rare days off, but he wondered how she might fare on the open trail.

In fact, Trammel wondered how *he* would fare on the open trail. He had ridden after men in the past when he had been a Pinkerton and knew something about living in the open, but his assignments had usually been confined to areas along train lines and towns and cities. And he had never been in the field alone. Not that he'd be alone with Hagen along, but given the drunkard's state of mind, he'd practically be alone until Hagen sobered up.

He tied Hagen's bag to the horse he had procured for Hagen, an old gray that the liveryman swore on his children could survive a trek down to Texas and back. Trammel had no intention of putting that claim to the test.

While the gambler slumped on the back stairs of The Gilded Lilly, Trammel checked his own rig one last time. His saddlebags were stocked with enough coffee and grain to last them three days and nights, which should give them enough time to find another town and stock up.

His brand-new Winchester '76 was in the scabbard beneath the right stirrup. He had bought the rifle more for its ornamental engravings than for its usefulness as a weapon. He hoped it shot as accurately as it was pretty. The double-barreled shotgun was in the scabbard beneath the left. He had plenty of ammunition for both and the Colt Peacemaker he had tucked in the shoulder holster beneath his brown duster. He had been a detective too long to ever become comfortable with a gun on his hip and knew, with the Bowman family likely on his trail, that this was no time for experimentation.

Satisfied his rig was as secure as it was likely to be, he decided it was time to go. The eastern sky was already beginning to brighten with the rising sun, and the Bowman clan was likely to follow soon after. Trammel went to grab Hagen, but found Lilly was already helping him get to his feet and steering him toward the gray.

Trammel held the stirrup steady for him, and was surprised when the drunkard climbed into the saddle easier than expected. "I don't need your help, damn you. I was born on a horse."

Trammel decided to leave the gambler alone, encouraged that maybe the journey would not be as one-sided as he had feared.

Lilly slipped a pint of whiskey into the pocket of Trammel's duster. "That's for him. He's liable to need it before long. Wean him off it slowly and he'll be less of a burden to you."

Trammel was ashamed of himself for not thinking of that already. It wasn't the first kindness Lilly had shown him, but it was most likely the last. He was suddenly ashamed of that and a lot of things. "I'm sorry for leaving you in the lurch, Lilly. You were always good to me, and I hate it ending like this."

"Stop it. You helped me save my saloon more times than I can count. I don't want to think about what I would've done if you hadn't stepped off that stagecoach when you did, and I owe you more than I could ever repay you."

Trammel looked away from her. "I shouldn't have killed those boys like I did. My damned temper. It sometimes—"

She placed her slender fingers over his lips. "You had no choice then, just like you don't have a choice now. Just get yourselves somewhere safe and, if you think to, send word of where you are. I'd like to know how you're doing from time to time."

She straightened his duster even though it didn't need straightening. "Maybe I could come see you after you're settled and all, especially now that you're no longer in my employ."

The words warmed him. He had thought about her as more than his boss several times since coming to work for her, but hadn't said anything about it. Because saying something made it real to him and he was afraid she might not feel the same way. For one of the first times in his life, Buck Trammel was glad he had been wrong.

"Maybe open up another Gilded Lilly somewhere else, like in—"

She covered his mouth with her soft hands again. "Don't say another word, Buck Trammel. I don't know where you're going, and I don't want to know. I just want you to get wherever it is safely and soon." She looked away as she gave him a timid shrug. "You've hung around here just about as long enough as you can. Best be on about your business."

He gently brought her small hands to his mouth and kissed them, then kissed the back of her hands. She leaned forward and he laid his cheek on top of her head. He breathed in the rosewater he knew she used to wash her hair; the same scent he had grown to love over the past year. He knew that last smell might have to hold him for a long time, perhaps for the rest of his life. However long that might be.

Lilly backed away again, wiping tears from her eyes. "Now go. Both of you. And may God be with you."

Hagen sluggishly doffed his bowler and slurred, "A lovely sentiment, m'lady, but a wasted one to be sure for, alas, God abandoned me quite some time ago."

Trammel climbed into the saddle and brought his

mount around. "Get moving, juice belly. We've got a good piece of riding ahead of us."

Hagen plopped the bowler back on his head and followed Trammel as he rode away from The Gilded Lilly for the last time.

Trammel didn't look back. He didn't dare.

CHAPTER 4

It was just after nine in the morning when the Bowman family rode into Wichita. All twenty of them rode down Main Street, four lines of five horses across.

Matt Bowman was in the lead. He wasn't an especially big man, for none of the men in the Bowman line ran big, but like his kinsmen, he was lean and solid. He had fought on the side of the Union in the late War Between the States, receiving a field commission of captain. He had brought the same leadership he had shown on the battlefield home with him after the surrender and helped his father build the BF brand into one of the most prosperous and respected in Kansas.

A man like that could not be expected to take the deaths of two of his own kindly, even if they were only cousins and troublesome cousins at that. With his father being unable to ride any more, Matt was aware that it was up to him to defend the Bowman name now. That name meant something only as long as the family was willing to fight to keep it that way. And

Matt Bowman was not known as a man to back away from a fight.

Matt brought his horse to a rough halt in front of The Gilded Lilly and tied up to the hitching post in front of the saloon. His nineteen other relatives followed his lead. He did not wait for them as he stormed up the steps and pushed his way into the saloon.

Never one given to drink or tobacco, he almost gagged on the stench of stale tobacco smoke and spilled rotgut. He swallowed the bile that rose in his throat as he looked around for any sign of the drunkard Hagen, that murdering giant Trammel or the woman who employed him, Miss Lilly.

He found most of the tables empty, with only a few old timers playing cards at the far end of the dimly lit saloon.

As his relatives began to pile in behind him, Matt yelled, "I'm here for Buck Trammel or that wench that hired him, Miss Lilly. Or the drunken gambler who goes by the name Hagen. I'll see them now, or, by God, me and mine will burn this hellhole to the ground!"

"No, you won't," came a voice from the shadows.

Matt peered in the direction from where the voice had come, but could only barely make out the outline of a man. The broad brimmed hat and the coat he wore were as dark as the shadow he sat in, but the dull glint of the star on his chest told Matt who he was. "That you, Earp?"

The man looked up from his white coffee mug. "It is. And you're interrupting my coffee."

"I don't give a damn about your coffee, boy. I came to see about my dead kin."

"You'll find William and Tyler over at the mortician

where their earthly remains are being tended to as we speak. You can collect them any time you'd like."

"There'll be time enough for the dead," Matt said. "Right now, I'm here to talk to the people who made them that way, namely that damned Trammel and that damned drunk Hagen."

Earp sipped his coffee. "They're not here. And you're disturbing the peace."

The iciness of the deputy's tone almost made him shiver. "What about Miss Lilly?"

"She's not receiving visitors at this time. She's had quite a night."

"*She's* had quite a night? What about my kin? Will and Tyler are dead."

"And they're at the mortuary waiting for you to bring them home where they belong. I already told you that. I won't tell you again. Best see about your business and leave the rest alone."

Matt took a few steps into the saloon. His relatives moved with him. "You protecting those boys, Earp?"

"Not mine to protect. They've left town."

"What?" Matt had to steady himself on a chair, his rage and sadness almost overwhelming him. "You mean you let them leave? After what they done?"

"Had nothing to hold them on. What happened here was fair and legal. I've got almost a dozen statements on my desk back at the jail attesting to that fact. I'll let you read them if you'd like, once you've had time to grieve over your losses."

"My losses?" The words hardly made sense to him. "My losses? We're not talking about a bunch of horses who've run off or have been stolen, Earp. We're talking about the murder of two young men cut down in their prime by a murdering giant and a drunken gambler."

"The gambler had nothing to do with it. And they disobeyed Trammel's order to leave. They attacked him and got killed for their trouble. Serves them right for going up against a man damned near twice their size." He brought his mug to his lips. "I told you to go collect your dead. I won't tell you again."

"Not before I've had a word with Miss Lilly."

A chair scraping against wood pierced the darkness as Earp stood. "I said no."

Matt felt his neck begin to redden. He had always tried to have respect for the law as far as it went, but in the face of his own dead, that respect didn't go far. "Now see here, Earp. You and your brother might have that old ninny Meagher buffaloed, but I'm no old ninny. You're only one against twenty and if you know what's good for you, you'll get out of the way and let us get answers on our own."

Suddenly, quietly, Earp strode out of the darkness and stood less than a foot from Matt. The rancher flinched and took a step back despite his intention to hold his ground.

Earp didn't move, not even a twitch. His flat blue eyes were locked on Matt until Bowman found himself taking still another backward step.

"I know you're grieving, so this one time, I'll repeat myself. You're not going to bother Miss Lilly. You're not going to kill Trammel or Hagen or anyone else. You're going to collect your dead and bring them home for the Christian funeral they deserve. And when you've had a chance to mourn, you'll come see me in the jail and I'll prove what happened here. Until then, you have to leave town. All of you. Right now."

Matt held his ground, his fading resolve beginning to weaken even further under Earp's glare, until his cousin Walt Bowman said, "Damn you, Earp. You can't stop us."

But Earp's eyes never left Matt's. "Looks like I already have. Go. Now."

Matt jerked his head up, trying to save some semblance of pride in front of his people. "We'll collect our dead and bury them. But someone's going to answer for this, Earp. Someone's going to answer for this damned soon."

He turned and pushed his way through his relatives. The rest of the Bowman family filed out after him, Walt last among them.

Earp stood where he was until the last of them rode away, then sat back down at the table and finished his coffee.

Chapter 5

"I need a drink." Hagen was nearly doubled over his horse as they rode the flatlands north away from Wichita. "I need it bad, Buck."

"Don't call me that." Trammel rode several yards ahead of him, hoping the distance would encourage his mount to pick up the pace a bit. He could see Hagen was hurting. He was sweating something awful, and his hands shook like a man riding at full gallop.

But Trammel also knew they needed to be farther from town than they were. Much farther. They had only a day or so to put as much space between them and the Bowman family as possible. At the rate they were riding, the family would be on them just as they reached the next town. "I only let my friends call me Buck, and you're no friend, so let's just leave it at Trammel."

"Fine!" Hagen cried out. "I'll call you anything you want, even beautiful, but I'm hurting bad and I need that drink. I need it now!"

Trammel kept riding. "You got your sip when we rested a while back. I'll give you another sip when we make camp for the night as long as we get as far as we need to. That means you picking up the pace."

Hagen sneered. "It's called a hangover for a reason, you overgrown imbecile. I didn't ask to come on this crusade of yours. I would've been just as happy to sleep it off in my room and take my chances with those Bowman idiots when I had my wits about me."

"And a belly full of whiskey, no doubt." Trammel normally didn't let such insults go unanswered, but given Hagen's current sorry state, he let it slide. "I didn't have you pegged for a brave man."

"I never said I'd fight them, but I'd be able to avoid them easily enough if I was in better shape."

Trammel figured that was the case. "Well, if it makes you feel any better, we weren't given much choice in the matter. Like I told you before, Earp pretty much ordered us out of town. Taking you with me wasn't my idea, but we're stuck with each other until we reach the next town. So the sooner you figure out how to pick up the pace, the sooner we'll be rid of each other."

Trammel noticed something he had said seemed to snap Hagen out of it. He bolted upright in the saddle, as if an iron bar had been jammed up his spine. "Music to my ears. Just where are we headed, Mr. Trammel, or have you not thought that far ahead yet?" He looked around. "We seem to be headed north."

Trammel was glad for the chance to prove to Hagen he wasn't an imbecile after all. "I let Bobby back at the livery think we were headed south. So we're headed north instead. To Newton."

"*Newton*," Hagen repeated as though the word itself was poison. He leaned over the side of his mount and spat onto the trail. "How predictable. You're more Moses than Daniel Boone, aren't you, Trammel? A real north-and-south, left-or-right man. The kind who picks out a point on a map and rides straight for it. The kind of man who gets himself killed." He spat again. "Just like a bloody copper."

"I'm not a cop, damn you." Trammel resented the insult to his logic. "You weren't exactly in any shape to give an opinion on direction when we rode out this morning, so I made the best choice I could. Newton is a solid choice, and it's got law to protect us if the Bowman family catches up to us."

"Thank God I'm beginning to regain some of my senses." Hagen winced and doubled over, no doubt from the clawing in his stomach from the lack of booze. "Fortunately, the Bowman clan are no brighter than you are and are likely to do the same thing." He looked around and saw a copse of trees just ahead. "That's exactly why we're *not* going to Newton."

Trammel resented the man's affront to his authority, until he realized he didn't have any authority. He wasn't a Pinkerton man anymore, and Hagen wasn't his prisoner. Hell, he technically wasn't even his charge. Earp had told him to bring the gambler out of town with him, and he had done that. Whatever happened to him now that they were out of town limits was out of his control. Not even a man like Earp could hold him responsible for that.

But Trammel also knew Hagen was right about him. Trammel was a straight thinker. He had picked out a spot and headed for it, just like he had always done. The Bowman family, or at least the few members he had known at The Gilded Lilly, were the same sort. They came in after a roundup to get drunk and that's what they did. They came in to gamble for high stakes at the tables and did just that. Sometimes they won and sometimes they lost.

They went straight at whatever they set their mind to, and they'd most likely do the same thing when they came after Trammel and Hagen. And he had no doubt they'd come for them and keep coming for them until they found them. It sounded like Hagen knew that, too, and might have a way around it.

"Never took instruction from a drunk before," Trammel admitted, "but I suppose there's a first time for everything. Since we've both likely got a price on our head by now, where do you think we should go?"

"A haystack where two needles like us can disappear quite nicely," Hagen said. "Come, Moses. And let me lead you to the new and eternal Jerusalem of our kind."

Trammel's mount flinched as Hagen put the spurs to his own horse and bolted for the trees. The old gray no longer moped like an old nag, and Hagen no longer rode like a drunk slumped over in the saddle. He rode upright and erect, the way he'd seen some of the army officers ride when they came to Wichita on their first day of leave. They hadn't ridden out the same way, of course, but on that first day, their poise left an impression on Trammel.

His horse bucked a bit and he could tell it was anxious to follow. He let up on the reins and let it have its head. "Okay, Mr. Hagen," Trammel said to himself. "Let's find out if you know what you're talking about."

CHAPTER 6

Ambrose Bowman's bones creaked as loudly as the floorboards of his back porch as he walked to his rocking chair. He sat down and filled the bowl of his pipe the way he had almost every night he had spent in his home. This very same home he had built decades ago with his own hands. His own sweat and labor. He saw no reason why the death of his kin should interfere with the ritual. Bowman men and women had been dying in Kansas since his father had moved the family to the wilderness long before the War Between the States. They had died since and, he reckoned, more would die before he finally passed over to whatever lie beyond. He knew not whether he would go to Heaven or Hell, but imagined that God, in His own infinite wisdom, would find a way to split the difference and plant him in Purgatory for a spell, if such a place existed. If it did not exist, he had no doubt the Almighty would create such a place if only to stick him there out of spite. His relationship with his creator had always been thus.

He struck a lucifer on the side of his chair and brought the flame to the bowl, puffing until he brought the tobacco to a decent burn before waving the match dead and flicking it over the porch railing. It was already past sunset, and he watched the purple hues of the western sky grow deeper as the sun sank farther behind the horizon.

Yet there was still enough light for him to see the family graveyard where his people lie molding, their headstones crooked and bent in the soft Kansas soil. He saw the outline of the horses in the near field and, just beyond it, the pasture where his cattle grazed.

Both herds were larger than his father and his uncles had brought with them. He was confident they would grow larger still under his son Matthew's reign. He was sure of that. His son wasn't good at much, but he knew how to raise horses and cattle. He was a Bowman, by God, and Bowman men knew how to make this land their own. They always had and, he reckoned, they always would.

He looked at the place where his own headstone stood, at the far left of the yard next to where his parents had been buried years before. It was a Bowman tradition to place the headstones of their kin within the first year of their birth, name, and birth date already etched. It was a practice that had kept the family grounded for generations, knowing that one day, they would die for one reason or another.

Two of his sons were already there. Anthony, his second eldest, and Bertram, his youngest, had both been taken from him in the war. He had mourned them in the way the Bowman family had always mourned their dead. He threw himself into building the ranch and made it even bigger.

Now, Tyler and Will would be buried beneath the stones that had stood waiting for them since their births twenty-one and twenty-five years before. They were his nephews and, in his own way, he supposed he loved them. They would join their father, Hammond, who had died in a similar fashion following an argument over a card game in the Belle Union Saloon in Newton. He judged all three men were better off where they were, more useful beneath the earth than they had ever been when they walked upon it.

But despite their shortcomings, they had been Bowman men. And that still meant something in Wichita. In Kansas. At least it would for as many days he still had before he joined them.

Ambrose Bowman looked when he heard the back door open and saw his eldest boy, Matthew, come out to join him on the porch. The sounds of the wailing and sobbing of the women inside mixed with prayers reached him. He was glad Matthew shut the door behind him to drown out their sorrow.

"Finally had enough, I reckon?" Ambrose asked his son.

"Been so long since we had a death around here," Matthew said as he pulled over a chair from the outside dining table, "that I forgot how much of show it is."

"Catholics," Ambrose said. "They do love a show, especially in mourning."

"We're Catholics too, Pa."

"As far as it goes," Ambrose said. "Too much ceremony for a hard land like this. But it pleases your mother, so I let it go. Never did much for me, though."

He heard his son's knees pop as he sat beside him. Matthew was going on fifty years of age and was no longer the young man he'd once been. *Neither am I*, Ambrose realized. He knew they called him Old Man

Bowman in town, and had for some time, just as they had called his father and his uncles before him when they had run the BF brand. The "BF" had first been struck by his father and stood for "Bowman Family." The letters had made for an easy brand and each Old Man Bowman since had done his part to make it stand for something more than it had when he had taken it over. None of them had run it for as long as Ambrose had and, as he approached his eighty-first summer, he took no small amount of pride in that. His eyes may be going and he may not be able to ride a horse for as long as he once had, but he still made a point of checking his herds on horseback daily. And despite his growing aches and pains, he thanked whatever God there was that his mind was still as sharp as ever. His father had not been given that dignity, and he hoped he'd be dead before that same fate befell him.

Matthew interrupted his thoughts by saying, "I didn't tell you what happened in town today, Pa."

"Tom told me." His second youngest was a good horseman, but an incredible gossip, a failing Ambrose decided he had inherited from his mother. "No need to relive it." He looked at his son. "No need to be ashamed of it, either."

"There were twenty of us," Matthew said. "And I let one man buffalo me. One lousy, skinny deputy."

"That deputy is the law," Ambrose said. "He's also Wyatt Earp. He's not the kind of man you cross. Not a man like you, leastways. He's buffaloed many a man and worse. Many a man better than you with a gun or their fists. Fighting him only would've gotten you killed or worse, and this family has suffered enough tragedy for one season."

But the words did not seem to soothe Matthew any. "It was his look that stopped me, Pa. A cold stare that felt like it went right through me."

"It's the kind of man he is, boy. Men like you don't go up against men like that. He's younger and meaner than you. Going against him would've been suicide. There's a place for his kind, and he's found it among the drunks and heathens he deals with in town. Put him on a horse and have him tend a herd and he wouldn't last a month. There's a place for our kind, too, and don't you forget that ever. You're a Bowman, by God, and you don't have to bow your head to any man, not even a man like Earp."

Ambrose was glad his son had decided to let it go for now. He knew the slight would eat at him for a while, but in time, it would pass. Matthew had a family of his own. A good family with three boys—Archer, Miles, and Joseph, and four daughters who were of marrying age with plenty of suitors among them. Ambrose knew he would take solace in that eventually, and the sting of his embarrassment would dull a bit more each day until he came to his senses, which he always did.

The deaths of his nephews, however, would be a different story. He knew what Matt would ask of him, but Ambrose would wait until he got around to it in his own time. For now, he was content to smoke his pipe and watch another day die in the beautiful twilight of the faraway sky.

He wasn't sure how long it had been until his son said, "I'm going after them, Pa. I'm going after them right after the burial tomorrow."

Ambrose puffed on his pipe. "You sure you want to do that, boy?"

He heard his son's chair creak as he faced him. "You don't expect me just to let Tyler and Will's deaths go unanswered, do you?"

Ambrose closed his eyes. Matthew always fell for the same trap. "I didn't say that. I asked if you were sure you wanted to do that."

Matthew turned and faced the twilight again. "I'm sure."

"You're sure you want it to happen or you're sure you want to do it?"

"I'm sure I want to do it, Pa."

"That's a different bit of business, then." Ambrose began to rock quietly, as he usually did when he was beginning to think. He had known this conversation would be coming the moment he'd heard Will and Tyler had been killed for the same reason their father had been killed twenty years before.

"I want to do what you did, Pa," Matthew went on. "I want to avenge them the way you avenged Uncle Ham."

"That was different," Ambrose said. "Ham was my brother. The man who killed him had a ranch that would've moved on our own if I hadn't killed him when I did. That death protected this family and kept those Barttleman snakes in Dodge City where they belonged."

Ambrose resumed his rocking. "Tom tells me the men responsible for Will and Tyler have moved on at Earp's urging. Might be best to let them keep going."

"They're still alive and ours are dead. I thought being a Bowman meant something."

Ambrose stopped rocking and glared at his son until the younger man looked down at his shoes rather than try to stare down his father. "It still does and always will as long as I've got breath in my lungs, boy. But they got in trouble in a place they didn't belong and went up against a man they should've known well enough to avoid. They should've done what you did with Earp today, but they didn't, and they got killed for it. That's why they're lying in boxes in my front parlor right now and you and me are still here to talk about it."

Matthew kept looking at his shoes. "I'd rather be dead than allow a slight like that to go unanswered. I aim to ride out after them tomorrow, Pa. And I'd like to have your blessing to do it."

Ambrose decided his son had endured enough humiliation for one day and went back to his rocking and his pipe. "Sounds as if your mind is already made up."

"It is," Matthew said. "It was made up the second I heard they left town. What if they head up to Newton or someplace else and brag about what they did? How long do you think it'll be before someone else tries to test one of our boys in town, only maybe they won't be drunks or thugs. Maybe they'll be cattlemen with eyes on our ranch? It'll be twice as hard to stop them then, and it'll mean more killing."

"Plenty have tried before, son. Better men than a saloon bouncer and a drunken gambler. They've always failed and always will as long as this family sticks together. And I'm not sure allowing you to ride off on some damned fool vengeance trail will do much to keep that from happening."

"That Trammel fella beat them to death, Pa. He didn't just shoot them or even knife them in a fair fight. He beat them to death, both of them, like they were dogs. Bowman men aren't dogs."

"No, we're not. And we don't run down things like dogs, either. When we do something, we do it the right way. The smart way."

"And what do you think the right way is here, Pa? Let Ma pray some rosaries and hope they break their legs in the wilderness? Pray they get struck by lightning?"

"We'll hire it done," Ambrose said. "Just like we hire cowhands to help with the herd, there are men who know how to hunt down men like this. Wichita is full of men who can do the job, men more able for it than you or me."

"None that we can trust to do it right," Matthew answered. "This is a matter of blood, Pa. This was done to Bowman men, and Bowman men have to put it right. This isn't the type of thing you pay men to do for you. You have to handle it personally, and I aim to do just that."

Ambrose rocked and smoked, but said nothing.

Matthew continued. "I know I backed down to Earp today, but I know how to fight. I fought in the war."

"This isn't war, boy. You're talking about riding out to find two men who could be anywhere by now. It could take you a year to find them, maybe more. I can't afford to have you away from the ranch for that long. And what if you happen to find them and can't beat them. What then? I can't risk losing my oldest son on a fool's errand."

Matthew sat straighter in his chair, but still didn't look at his father. "I came out here tonight to ask for your blessing, Pa. But I'm a grown man with boys of my own. I'll ride on without it if I have to."

Ambrose puffed on his pipe, quietly enjoying the mixture of emotions that were broiling in his belly.

Fear for his son, but pride in his commitment to doing what needed to be done for the sake of the family name. It had been a long time since he had heard such conviction in his voice, and it did his old heart good to hear it now, despite the consequences.

He dug into his pocket and tossed a small leather pouch to his son. "There's a thousand in gold coins in there. Enough to outfit ten men for a while. Take five men from the ranch and what you need from the ranch stores. Then go into town and hire five men to ride out with you. Ten riders ought to be enough to go up against a drunk and a bouncer, even if the man is a giant."

Matthew stood up and put the pouch in his pocket. "Me and my boys will ride out first thing after the funeral."

"Like hell you will. I'll not have your line rubbed out the way your Uncle Hammond's was. You'll take Walt with you. He's not good for much anyway, and my sister will be glad to be rid of him. That boy's been nothing but a heartache to poor Marcia since the day he came kicking and screaming into this world. You can take three hired hands with you, but not Cameron. He stays here. The rest you'll hire in town. But no more than five, understand?"

"I understand, Pa."

Ambrose Bowman stood up and faced his son. This time, Matthew didn't look away.

"Well, also understand this, boy. If you ride after these men, you'll have to kill them. I won't think any less of you if you wake up tomorrow and change your mind, but if you do it, then you're going to do it all the way. No half measures. Kill them both and come back home."

Matthew swallowed. "Don't worry, Pa. I won't change my mind."

No, Ambrose thought. *No, I don't think you will.* And that's what frightened him and pleased him all at the same time as he watched another day die in Kansas.

CHAPTER 7

Trammel dumped the last of the firewood in the center of their small encampment. He was quite pleased with himself. He had decided he had chosen a good spot to rest for the night, a space beside a small outcropping of rocks with a clear field of vision in every direction. No trees for anyone to hide behind and good grazing for the horses they had hobbled fifty feet away.

Hagen shivered beneath a blanket while Trammel did all the work. "May I have my medicine now, Mother?"

Trammel didn't want to give it to him, but he couldn't stand to see the man suffer. He usually didn't have much sympathy for drunks in his line of work, but as this drunk had helped them make greater time than he thought possible, he decided Hagen had earned a drink.

He dug the bottle out of his saddlebag. "Two pulls, no more. I don't want you drunk all over again. We need to keep up this pace tomorrow."

Hagen greedily accepted the bottle and surprised

Trammel by handing it back to him after two quick sips. "Thank you. I wouldn't have slept tonight without that, and I'd be of even less use to you tomorrow on the trail."

Trammel begrudgingly accepted his thanks and put the bottle back in the saddlebag. "You talk pretty fancy for a drunken gambler."

Hagen pulled the blanket tighter around his shoulders as his shaking seemed to subside. "That's because I'm neither a drunk nor a gambler, sir. I merely like to act like one."

Trammel began piling the wood so they could build a fire. "You're a hell of an actor, then."

"I'm not an actor, either, despite my flair for the dramatic. In fact, to use the parlance of our times, one could be forgiven for saying that I am quite loaded."

"You've been loaded since you came to Wichita, Hagen. I've seen that with my own two eyes."

"I mean loaded as in financially," Hagen clarified. "I come from money, hence all of that fancy talk you mentioned earlier."

Trammel stopped building the fire. In the dim light of dusk, he couldn't see the man's face clear enough to tell if he was lying. "Don't lie about something like that. Not now."

"I'd wager that you've heard enough lies in your time to know the truth when you hear it, Trammel. And you know I'm not lying now."

He was right. Trammel had no reason to believe him, but no reason to doubt him, either. Braggarts usually liked to talk themselves up whenever they had the chance. But in all the time Hagen had been staying at The Gilded Lilly, Trammel couldn't remember a single time when Hagen had spouted off about having money. He never spoke much about anything, really, not even when he was playing cards. He usually got drunk at the tables and had to be carried up to his room, tipping whomever had helped him after he woke the following day.

But out in the elements as he was, Trammel was in no place to take anyone at their word without a little prodding. "Where'd all this money you say you have come from?"

"It came from the same place we are headed, my new friend. My family owns one of the biggest cattle ranches in the Wyoming Territory. The Blackstone Ranch, just north of Laramie. Commonly known by its brand, the Bar H."

Trammel dropped the piece of firewood he was stacking. "The Bar H. Hagen. That's you?"

"My father," the gambler said. "Mine by right, I suppose, one day when that old sidewinder finally allows himself to die, which isn't likely." He pulled the blanket even tighter around him. "Evil never dies."

Trammel had heard about the Bar H long before he had come to Wichita. The Hagen family had employed the Pinkerton Agency on more than one occasion, though Trammel had never worked on any of their cases. But he knew they had one of the biggest ranches in the Wyoming Territory, if not the biggest.

But Trammel knew that just because this man said he was a Hagen didn't make it so. There were still plenty of details he had to know first before he believed him. "If you've got so much money, then what the hell are you doing out in Kansas, much less a place like Wichita?"

"It's a rather long story, I'm afraid, as such stories tend to be. But I'll be happy to tell it to you in broad strokes while you continue to build that fire. It's getting cold, and I'm starving."

Trammel kept building the fire as Hagen began talking. "My father and I never got along. It's probably my mother's fault as much as it was mine. She insisted on tutors and a classical education while my father wanted a son to take up the family business when his time came. He wanted a doer, not a thinker. He wanted a son who could ride and shoot and handle livestock. Trouble was I was naturally even better at all of those things, too. Much better than my brothers, Bradford and Caleb. Rather than be grateful, I think that made him resent me all the more. He figured a fancy education would ruin me, but I delighted in proving him wrong. Still, the die was cast against me and, when I was old enough, he pulled one of his many strings with his numerous friends to get me enrolled in a school in New York."

"No fooling?" Trammel looked up from the woodpile. "I'm from New York."

"Yes, I know. Lower East Side, if I'm still any judge of regional accents." Hagen quickly added, "No offense, Trammel, but one who travels as much as I have tends to develop an ear for such things."

Trammel sat back on his haunches. "I'm from Five Points. How the hell did you know that?"

The gambler smiled. "One of my many useless gifts. Anyway, I went to school and excelled in all the things both in the classroom and out of it, but my resentment of authority remained with me. I graduated at the bottom of my class despite my abilities and went on to have a mediocre career as a result."

Trammel went back to building the fire. "Which school was that?"

"A little place along the banks of the Hudson River known as West Point."

Trammel had struck a match to light the fire, but stopped. "You were in the army? As an officer?" The flame burned his fingers and he cursed as he dropped the dead match in the pile.

"Not much of one, I'm afraid," Hagen explained. "They shipped me off to Arizona to fight the Apache, probably in the hopes I'd be scalped. I acquired something of a reputation as a soldier's officer, which didn't exactly make me popular with my colleagues in rank. As soon as my stint was up, I left."

Trammel struck another match and, this time, got the fire started. "Then why didn't you go home?"

"That was my father's idea. Mother was dead by then, and King Charles had no desire to see me again. That's what they call him, though he certainly thinks of himself as American royalty. He had his people tell me he'd continue to pay for my travels for the rest of my life on the condition those travels didn't include a return to the Wyoming Territory. So, I spent time in all the places a wanderer like me would be expected to go. Manhattan and Boston and Philadelphia were nice, but too staid for my tastes. All of that ceremony and formality made me feel like I was back in the army. I had always had a knack for gambling among the officers I served with and decided to ply my trade on the long train voyages between one destination to another. Realizing city life wasn't for me; I was naturally drawn to the mighty Mississippi, where I found a home on the riverboats.

When I wore out my welcome there for a variety of reasons I don't wish to discuss, I decided to head to the one place where I thought a man could quietly drink himself to death in oblivion. Wichita, Kansas."

Trammel slowly blew on the fire, waiting for it to catch enough so he could begin to cook dinner. "If I had your kind of money, I'd buy a place in Washington Square and never leave."

"You'd get bored, especially once you've experienced life out here. The people are as petty as they are pretty. They'd never accept you and your accent, just as they never accepted me for all of my experience and money. We have the stink of the frontier about us, my friend. Me among the Apache and you among the desirables. Me from the frontier of a nation and you from the frontier of the human condition. People tend to resent what they can never understand or experience."

Trammel didn't think so, but wasn't fool enough to argue with a man who sounded like he knew what he was talking about. "I know a little more about that world than you think I do. Believe me, the money would help take plenty of sting out of whatever anyone thought of me."

"I know more about you than you think I do, Trammel."

The fire finally caught, and he could see Hagen a bit better now. Some of the color had returned to Hagen's face, and his shaking had died down by quite a bit. "You don't know a damned thing about me. You don't even remember all the times I carried you up to your room after gambling all night."

He didn't know why Hagen's words had made him

feel resentful, but they had. He forgot about it as he said, "Enough talk for one night. Time to start dinner."

He began digging the pan out of his saddlebag, along with the beans and bacon Lilly had given him before they had left.

Hagen began talking again as the food began to sizzle on the pan. "You were born in Five Points. Your father was Scottish and your mother was of some other northern European descent. Norway, I'd take it, given the high cheekbones and deep-set eyes."

Trammel dropped the pan in the fire and hardly noticed.

Hagen went on. "Your ancestry belies your large build. Highlanders and Vikings were like that. Anyway, you grew up poor in horrible conditions and, when you were old enough, you began manual labor, probably finding easy work on the docks. You thought about getting on one of those ships one day, but you were a city boy after all and didn't want to leave your aging parents in such squalor. Your size also opened other avenues to you, such as a life of crime. One might be forgiven for saying you fell in with a bad element, but people like that tend to stay in that life. No, you had a friend, maybe a cop, who looked out for you and got you to join the police. Somewhere along the way, you found the Pinkerton Agency or they found you. They're always looking for men like you and paid much better, so you joined them. Your parents were most likely dead by then, and with nothing to keep you in New York, you enjoyed life on the rails, handling cases Mr. Pinkerton doled out to you. Somewhere along the line, you either fell out of favor with the agency or they fell out of favor with you.

There's no way of knowing for sure, but like me, you wound up in Wichita to forget about your past for a while. Maybe settle down with a nice young lady, like Miss Lilly. She is nice, isn't she, Buck?"

Trammel turned on him. "Shut your mouth about her, damn you. And what makes you think you know so much about me?"

Hagen ignored the outburst. "You're comfortable enough on horseback, but hardly at ease. You know how to live somewhat on the trail, but your knowledge is rudimentary at best."

Trammel stepped toward him. "What the hell does rudimentary mean? You calling me stupid?"

"It means basic. Take that fire, for example. It's too much wood for what we need and will throw off far too much light for two men on the run. Anyone who might be following us would be able to see it for a mile or more, especially in reasonably flat country like this."

Before that day, Trammel knew he hadn't said more than ten words to Hagen since the gambler had come to live at The Gilded Lilly. There was no way he could have known so much about him. He'd never told anyone about his past, not even Lilly. Yet, here he was, having his whole life read back to him by a man he barely knew.

There was no reason for him to be angry, yet he was. He guessed Hagen had a way of getting under people's skin. It was the reason why he'd lived the life he had. It was the reason why both of them were on the run now.

He picked up the pan he had dropped. "Well, then I guess we're lucky no one's been following us, aren't we?"

"That's where you're wrong, my large friend. We *have* been followed by two men, and they're going to try to kill us. Right now."

Trammel drew his Colt from the shoulder holster and ducked just as a rifle shot rang out. A bullet ricocheted off the rocky outcropping behind Hagen.

Trammel ran for his horse and grabbed the double-barreled shotgun from the saddle before escaping into the darkness.

He crouched low with the outcropping at his back, figuring no one could get behind him that way. At least he was out of the circle of light thrown off by the growing fire. He looked for Hagen, but his blanket had been cast aside and he was nowhere to be seen.

Before the shooting had started, the gambler had said two men had been trailing them all day. How the devil had he known that? And why hadn't he said anything? Trammel decided he'd make it a point to demand some answers from him after all of this was over, assuming either of them was still alive.

Trammel realized he was holding his Colt in one hand and his shotgun in the other. Trading firepower for accuracy, he tucked the Colt under his arm and slowly thumbed back both hammers on the shotgun. He wished he had grabbed the Winchester instead, but he had no intention of going back in the light for it. Too risky.

He flinched when he heard a scream pierce the darkness.

"Hoffman!" a strange voice cried out. "You hit?"

Another scream brought another volley of rifle fire off to Trammel's right. He saw the blasts in the darkness and knew the man firing was no more than fifty feet away from him.

Trammel ran behind the flashes, raised his shotgun, and aimed in the general direction of the gunfire. Knowing Hagen was unarmed, Trammel squeezed the trigger, firing blind into the night. A fresh set of screams echoed in front of him, and he knew he must have hit someone.

"I take it that was you, my large friend," Hagen's voice rang out. "Good job. I'm heading in your direction, so don't shoot. All the bad men are done for, I assure you."

Trammel stood alone in the darkness like a damned fool, waiting for Hagen to tell him when to move.

After what felt like an eternity, he heard Hagen say, "Follow the sound of my voice, but hurry. This one's still alive, but not for long."

Trammel, indeed, followed the sound of Hagen's voice and found him standing over a man crumpled in on himself like a cat. A bloody boot knife was in his right hand.

"Drag him over to the fire so we can get a better look at him," Hagen said. "We might learn something from him before he dies on us."

Trammel ignored the wounded man's screams as he dragged him closer to the fire. Now in the light, he could see the man had caught at least one of the barrels flush in the left side. His breathing was shallow, not only from fear, but likely from the buckshot that had stuck his lungs. Either way, Trammel knew he was not long for this world.

"Who are you?" Trammel shook him. "Why are you following us?"

"Go to hell."

Hagen straddled the man and held the thin dagger against the dying man's cheek. "That's a trek you'll be taking long before us, my friend, but first you're going to tell us who sent you or the big man here will throw you on that fire."

"Name's Hoffman, damn you," the wounded man rasped. "I work the BF ranch. Walt Bowman sent me and Baxter to see where you went. He's gonna kill you scum for what you done to Tyler and Will. He's gonna kill you both."

"Perhaps," Hagen said, "but you'll never know." He placed the dagger blade next to Hoffman's throat. "Tell us how many he's bringing with him, and I'll end your suffering now. Hold your peace and I'll let your wounds take their course. Lie to me, and the fire awaits."

Hoffman said nothing. Trammel saw Hagen grin. The dancing fire cast unsettling shadows across his face. "I was hoping you were going to say that."

Trammel grabbed Hagen's hand as he drew his blade back. "Don't bother. He's dead."

The gambler placed his bloodied blade beneath Hoffman's nose. "No breath, so you appear to be right." He looked up at the big man. "You can let go of my hand now."

But Trammel didn't let go. "Not until you tell me how you knew those two were on our trail."

"I spotted them a little after we left town," Hagen said. "I thought they might be just two men heading out of town just like us. I didn't realize they were still following us until they stopped when we stopped."

Trammel's grip on his wrist tightened. "That was hours ago. Why the hell didn't you say anything then?"

"Because you would've wanted to turn back and face them on open ground. I was in no condition to fight at that time, and the odds weren't in our favor. I figured we'd wait until nightfall to see what they might do. That's why I kept talking like I did. To put them at their ease and let them think they could sneak up on us." He looked at Trammel's hand gripping his. "Now, for the last time, let go of me."

Trammel shoved him aside with enough force to send Hagen on his rump. "You could've told me when they were coming."

"The horses did that," the gambler said as he got back to his feet. "Didn't you see how they were fussing when they caught their scent on the wind? No, you didn't, because you don't know what you're doing out here. You don't know what to look for, and you don't know how to survive. So unless you've got a better plan, I highly suggest you listen to me from now on because, the next time, you're liable to get us both killed."

Trammel watched Hagen wipe his bloody blade clean on the dead man's vest before he slipped it back into his boot. "Any other demands while we're at it?"

"As a matter of fact, there are." The gambler stood and faced him. "Only one, actually. Never touch me again, do you understand? If you do, I'll kill you. Do I make myself clear?"

Trammel laughed, really laughed for the first time in as long as he could remember. He could hear the sound of his own laughter echo off the outcropping. "You'll try, little man, but it won't get you very far."

"Laugh if you want to, but I mean it. Now, help me get the boots off this one. Baxter over there has feet smaller than my sister, and my current footwear is about ready to give out."

Trammel walked toward his horse to stow the shotgun. "Do it yourself. I'm busy cooking."

Chapter 8

Matt Bowman and his cousin Walt tied up their horses to the hitching rail outside the Winter Star Saloon. Matt had known about this place for years, but had never ventured inside, as he had never been one for whoring or gambling. His nephews Will and Tyler and cousin Walt had cornered the family's market on those particular vices, and he saw no reason to contribute to it further.

He turned to his cousin, Walt, who still looked like he needed a bath despite that he had already taken one before the previous morning's burial services. "Are you sure we'll find the men we need in here?"

"If we were in the market for ranch hands or well diggers, I'd say no," Walt admitted. "But seeing as how we're looking for killers, the Star's the best place to find them."

The wind changed, and Matt caught a whiff of the stench coming out of the Star. He wondered how long he could hold his breath before passing out. He was tempted to allow his cousin to go in and hire the men he saw fit. But that temptation passed quickly when he remembered Walt was more likely to hire five of his drinking buddies than men equal to the task before them.

He turned to the three ranch hands who had volunteered to ride out with them. They had chosen to remain mounted. "You three stay out here with the pack animals. Walt and I will be out in a bit."

None of them seemed to object. Walt had already walked inside before Matt turned around.

Matt breathed in deep and bounded in after his cousin.

The inside of the Winter Star was every bit as run down and miserable as Matt had expected it to be. The green felt on the gambling tables bore years of stains that defied all description. And while no one appeared to be gambling at the moment, there was no shortage of patrons drinking their fill at the bar and the tables. It was almost ten in the morning, and none of the men were at work, a concept that defied Matt's way of thinking. All of the men were dressed as cattlemen or ranch hands. He didn't know of a single ranch within a day's ride that wasn't always looking for a few good hands to help out. How someone could prefer to drink their days away as opposed to putting in an honest day's work was beyond his capacity to comprehend. But then his father's words returned to him. Men like them aren't men like us.

His cousin beckoned him over to a table in the far corner of the saloon where five men sat around a full bottle of whiskey. Matt walked over to the table as quickly as possible, ignoring the looks he received from the drinkers and the painted ladies who fluttered around them like flies on a dung pile.

"Boys," Walt told the men at the table, "this here is

my cousin, Matt. Matt, this here is the best group of men for the kind of work we need doing."

One look at the men Walt had chosen made Matt wonder if this was a good idea. In all of his years as a rancher and a soldier, he had never seen such a ragged group of men in one place.

All of them were bearded with various amounts of hair sticking out beneath their weathered hats. Each of the men was as pale and skinny as newborn sheep. They looked like they lived on tobacco juice and whiskey, and Matt imagined that may very well be the case.

His cousin Walt began the introductions. "Matt, I'd like you to meet five of the worst men in this part of Kansas, which makes them the best men for us." He gestured to the man facing Matt, the man with the gray-streaked hair poking out from beneath a filthy brown hat. A ragged patch of leather tied around his head covered his left eye. His hands were large and deeply scarred.

"This is Lefty Hanover," Walt said, "the one you might say is the leader of this group."

"Ain't a leader," Hanover croaked. "Ain't no group, neither. Quit building us up as if we was some kind of gang or I'll split your head like a rail. We're trail hands, by God, and ain't ashamed of it."

The four others grumbled their assent, with the scrawniest among them repeating, "Ain't ashamed of it. That's a good one, Lefty. Ain't ashamed of it at all."

Undeterred, Walt pointed at the man. "This one's named Parrot Wheeler on account of how he likes to repeat everything Lefty says. Like a parrot."

Matt motioned for his cousin to get on with it. The others were a rangy man named Skinner, a pinch-faced man named Hooch, and a swarthy man named Chico. "They're not much on conversation," Walt said when the introductions were concluded, "but when it comes time to sling lead, there's no one better."

Lefty spat a stream of tobacco juice in the general direction of the spittoon, but missed badly. "Now that we're acquainted all proper-like, how about you tell me why we're acquainted at all. Never saw you in here before, Matthew."

"Yeah," Parrot said. "Never seen you in here before, Matthew."

Matt cleared his throat as he tried to ignore the smell of the five men. "You boys probably knew my nephews Tyler and Will. They were killed a couple of nights ago at The Gilded Lilly by Buck Trammel and a drunken gambler named Hagen. They've both left town before the law could catch up with them, and we aim to bring them to justice."

Skinner looked up at him. Matt only counted three teeth in his head and all of them yellow. "You mean jailing justice?"

"I mean real justice," Matt told him. "At the end of a gun or an end of a rope, whatever's handy so long as they're dead. Both of them."

He watched Lefty look around at his friends as if to take their measure. They seemed to communicate in some way by a silent vote. When he seemed satisfied, he looked up at Matt again. "How much you figure this justice of yours is worth?"

"A hundred a head when it's all said and done," Matt told him. "Five hundred in total but only when the job is done."

When Lefty sat back in his chair, Matt thought he

was insulted. He knew a hundred dollars was good money no matter the deed. At the ranch, they only paid their hands twenty-five a month and these men were being hired for just two things—to ride and kill two men.

The glare from Lefty's good eye didn't intimidate Matt, but he still felt compelled to add, "That's a damned sight more than you'll make sitting around here drinking it away. If you don't want the money, I'll find some men who can. But I need to know right now because we ride right now."

Lefty picked up the leather strap covering his eye and showed him the empty socket beneath it. "Know how I got that, mister?" He didn't wait for an answer. "Got thrown out of the Lilly one night by Trammel, but I wasn't done with my drink yet. That big galoot hit me so hard, it cost me my eye. So we'll take your lousy five hundred dollars, and gladly. But I personally would've done it for free."

Lefty stood first, then the four others got to their feet. The man was more than a head taller than Matt and his cousin. He had heard of how big Buck Trammel was, but hadn't appreciated just how big until he saw what he had done to a man of Lefty Hanover's size.

Hanover said, "Skinner, you settle up with the barkeep, and let's be on our way. We got ourselves a couple of killers to catch." He slapped Hooch on the back and laughed. "Looks like we're in the law business now, boys!"

The four men laughed with Lefty laughing loudest; a high-pitched cackle Matt hadn't expected from such a stern-looking man.

As they walked out of the Winter Star, Matt said to his cousin, "I hope you're right about these boys, Walt."

"I might not be much good at ranching, Matt, but I'm plenty good at this."

"Drinking and whoring doesn't require talent, boy. Just money."

"Tell that to Tyler and Will."

Matt couldn't argue with his cousin on that score.

CHAPTER 9

Trammel woke with a start.

He had been bone tired and realized the sun was already high in the sky by the time he awakened. They had picked up even more ground than they had the first day out of Wichita, and the journey had taken a lot more out of the big man than he had expected. He had no idea how close they were to Dodge City, but he imagined they must be close.

It took him a moment to recognize what had woken him. It was the smell of coffee. And bacon. And biscuits. But he hadn't brought along the fixings for biscuits, so he wondered if they had found themselves closer to a farmhouse or even Dodge City than he had expected.

When he lifted his head, he saw Adam Hagen over the cook fire. A pot of coffee sat on the stone next to it and a pan of biscuits and bacon over the fire.

"Morning," Hagen said. "You seemed awfully tired come sunup, so I decided to let you sleep. Hope you don't mind."

It took Trammel a moment to recognize Hagen. He remembered the gambler had changed out of his fancier clothes the previous day and had taken the gear from Baxter, the man he had knifed to death when they tried to ambush them. He no longer looked like a cardsharp but like any other man on the trail. His brown duster and floppy brown hat were more convincing than the bowler he had sported at The Gilded Lilly. He had also liberated the dead men of their money and weapons, which Trammel remembered had amounted to ten dollars, two Walker Colts, and two Winchesters with comparable ammunition.

He remembered arguing with Hagen about burying the bodies to keep them from being discovered, but with no shovels or stones about, they had no choice but to leave them to the elements.

His stomach made him forget about the dead men they had left behind. "Where the hell'd you get biscuits?"

"Same place I got that burro over there." He gestured to where they had hobbled their horses and saw a mule loaded down with sacks. "I rode into town while you were sleeping."

Trammel was fully awake now. "You rode into Dodge City?"

"It's not that far to town," Hagen said. "I told you we were close."

"But you rode in alone?"

"I've been traveling alone most of my life, Trammel," Hagen said. "Besides, it's a hell of a lot easier for a man like me to go into town than you. In case you haven't noticed yet, you don't exactly blend in, even in Dodge City. Speaking of which, I took the liberty of buying you some shaving cream and a straight razor." He ran his hands over his face. "I availed myself of a bath and a shave while I was in town, but the stream down the hill will do you just as good. Maybe even better." He frowned at the biscuits. "The girl I selected to help me was homely to say the least. But, at such an early hour, one can't be too choosy when seeking companionship."

Trammel felt his face for the first time in days. He had always had a heavy beard, but rarely let it grow this long. He hadn't seen his reflection since they had left Wichita, but imagined he was quite a sight. "Guess I could stand a little cleaning up. But why'd you go ahead and get all of those provisions for? I thought we'd part ways in Dodge City."

"You're certainly free to do that if you choose." Hagen held out the pan to him. "Here, take a biscuit. But mind that it's hot."

He plucked a biscuit from the pan and it was, indeed, hot. He dropped it on his blanket, where he decided to let it set while it cooled. Hagen surprised him by handing him a cup of coffee. "That's hot, too, but at least it has a handle."

Trammel grew suspicious. "Why the fancy treatment all of a sudden?"

"Think of it as my way of thanking you for getting me out of town and saving my life. Now, I'd like the opportunity to save yours, if you'll be kind enough to let me do it."

"From who? The Bowman family? They'll head straight on to Newton if they don't think we headed south. You said so yourself. They'll be played out after that. I don't think they'll track us all the way to Dodge."

"Matt Bowman will track us to the end of the earth as long as his money holds out." Hagen blew on the biscuit before he took one from the pan himself. "I've played a lot of poker with a lot of people who know him well. He's got a reputation for stubbornness, and he won't let the death of his nephews go unanswered. He's a proud and ruthless man when the occasion calls for it, and I'd say the death of his kin calls for it."

Hagen poured himself a cup of coffee. "Besides, he lives to impress his father, and Old Man Bowman will be mighty disappointed in his oldest son if he just lets this go."

Trammel didn't know anything about the Bowman clan except for the two he'd killed. He remembered Earp seemed to hold them in some regard, so he believed Hagen might know what he was talking about. "Think he'll come alone?"

Hagen shook his head. "My money's on him bringing his cousin Walt along. That'll be a mark in our favor. Walt Bowman is an idiot. Maybe a few others, too."

Hagen would get no argument from Trammel on that score. He'd heard of Matt, but had never met the man. He'd had a few run-ins with Walt after the boy had too much whiskey for his own good. He was the kind of drunk who thought he was more of a handful than he really was. Trammel had expected Walt to come back at him after he'd thrown him out of The Gilded Lilly, but the young man never had. He didn't know if it was because he'd found another place to drink or had found his senses floating in all that whiskey. He wished his cousins had been that smart two nights ago.

"How many do you think Matt will bring with him?"

Hagen leaned back against his saddle as he thought it over. "Between ten and twenty. Probably ten. The old man needs men to tend to the herds, so he won't spare more than that. Matt and Walt will probably hire the rest. You got many enemies in Wichita, Mr. Trammel?"

The big man sipped his coffee. "Plenty."

"Then he'll have no trouble finding a few men to follow him, especially if he pays for it, and I imagine he'll pay handsomely." He looked over at Trammel. "Still want to split up? Head out on your own?"

Trammel suddenly wasn't so sure, but he was still absorbing what Hagen had said. "I'm considering my options."

"Let me help you with that," Hagen said. "Dodge City is closest, so let's say you go there. It's a rough town, and a man like you probably won't have trouble finding a job as a bouncer or a lookout man in a saloon or house of ill repute. But it'll make you noticeable, and that'll get you killed when Bowman and his men eventually find out where you are. They're likely to have plenty of help once they get there, and as big as you are, you're not big enough to take on ten or more armed men alone."

"So I guess this really is where we part ways," Trammel said. "Me being a burden to you and all."

"Nonsense!" Hagen exclaimed. "For I have every intention of inviting you to accompany me to my family home in Wyoming."

Trammel almost spilled his coffee. "Wyoming! Hell, I can barely make the two-hundred-mile ride from Wichita to Dodge City and you want me to go all the way to Wyoming? Why the hell don't we just ride clear on up to the Yukon while we're at it?"

"It's only one hundred and fifty miles from Wichita and, besides, Wyoming is much closer and far more hospitable, especially at my family's place in Blackstone. An ominous name, don't you think? It's actually quite tranquil. Gets its name from an outcropping of black rock that bottlenecks the main road to town from Father's ranch."

"I don't care if it's called Eden," Trammel said. "It's still way up in Wyoming."

"The journey will take us a month, perhaps less." Hagen pointed his cup toward the burro. "I've made sure we have enough provisions. We have the horses of our assailants to use as fresh mounts when we need them and the will to proceed at a rapid pace. Since we're not going to Dodge City, our trail will end for them there and they'll think we most likely headed south. No one in Wichita knows I'm from Wyoming, so Bowman and his men will assume we headed back south to different climes. Maybe to Denver or New Orleans. If we keep moving and stay clear of people, we should be able to slip into Wyoming unnoticed. Once there, word of our arrival will take a year or more to reach them, if ever."

It sounded like a reasonable plan to Trammel. Maybe too reasonable. "And your father will just greet you with open arms?"

Hagen sipped his coffee. "Hopefully."

"Wyoming's a hell of a long way to ride on the promise of 'hopefully.'" Trammel may not have been a lawman for quite a while, but he still had the same instincts. Something about Hagen's story didn't fit. "He doesn't like you, does he? If he did, you wouldn't be in a place like Wichita, would you?"

"We haven't always seen eye to eye, but my brothers were young when I left, so I doubt they bear the same resentment toward me as my father does. Though Father has had an awful long time to poison their minds against me. That would be unfortunate, wouldn't it?"

"Unfortunate? Riding over a thousand miles to have a door slammed in my face isn't unfortunate. It's crazy!"

"It's barely over seven hundred miles from here," Hagen pointed out.

Trammel knew he had lived a city man's life, but seven hundred miles was a pretty long distance for a man who had almost been killed by riding about one hundred and fifty miles.

Hagen continued. "And I doubt my brothers could hold on to a grudge as long as Father has. Charles Hagen is the only man I know who can raise holding a grudge to an art form."

"Remind me to introduce you to some of my family sometime." Trammel drank more coffee. "You'd be surprised."

Hagen made no sign of hearing as he ate his biscuit. "Besides, you don't have to come with me, you know. There's something to be said for us splitting up right here and now, though I still wouldn't recommend you go to Dodge City for all of the reasons I mentioned earlier. If you want to go your own way, I would suggest you ride to Denver. I'm sure you've picked up enough from me to manage the journey by yourself in relative comfort. I'll even stake you to half of my provisions, free of charge, and you can head out after we finish breakfast."

Trammel had never considered himself to be a smart man, but he'd never been anybody's fool, either. He knew the trip to the outskirts of Dodge City would have been much worse if it hadn't been for Hagen's direction. And if they had gone straight on to Newton, they may have been tracked down and killed once they got there. Trammel may have gotten Hagen out of Wichita alive, but it was Hagen who had kept him alive.

A journey to Wyoming with Hagen would be much more than Trammel had bargained for, but it was better than taking his chances of being spotted in Dodge City, much less riding alone to Denver.

And both of them knew it.

Trammel looked over at his companion, who seemed to be grinning as he thoroughly enjoyed a biscuit. "You're a real mean-spirited rattlesnake, you know that Hagen?"

"One of my finer qualities." He held out the pan to him. "Here. Have some bacon."

CHAPTER 10

Lefty Hanover ignored Matt Bowman as he led the men north to Newton.

But that didn't prevent the rancher from talking anyway. "I don't know why we're headed north like this. The boy at the livery said Trammel and Hagen were headed south toward Texas."

"Liverymen ain't known for always being reliable," Lefty said. "It's all that time they spend in the stables, see? Makes 'em loco. Besides, these here tracks we've been following say otherwise. Chico says otherwise, too. Best tracker I ever seen, and I've seen a bunch."

But Matt persisted. "I had two men tracking them as they left town, but I don't know where they went. I think we should split up and at least take a look."

"Chico took a look at the tracks from The Gilded Lilly. They headed north, not south. Neither Trammel nor the gambler's got any call to head south along the cattle trail because neither of them are cowpunchers. They'd stick out in that crowd. Too many stragglers could see us comin' and tell us where they went. They headed north, and so are we."

But Lefty's logic failed to reach Bowman, and the old cowhand tuned him out. He and his bunch had dealt with men like Matt Bowman their entire lives; men accustomed to giving orders and not taking them. Men who thought the purse strings they held were like reins to the men they paid.

Men like Bowman just couldn't understand that they only held power for as long as the men who worked for them gave it to them. Lefty and the others hadn't ridden back down to Texas with the rest of the boys because they didn't want to, not because they didn't have a place with any of the cattle companies. They were top hands, every one of them, and better than the three Bowman had brought with him from the BF. Tending horses and cattle in a field was one thing. Driving them hundreds of miles to market took a special sort. The sort of man that Bowman thought he was, but wasn't.

And even though he hadn't been paying attention to what Bowman was saying, the noise was beginning to bother him. He could tell it was beginning to bother Skinner and the others, too, so he decided to put an end to it.

"If you want to head south, Mr. Bowman, feel free to do so, but me and mine'll continue north the way the tracks lead us. Chico's got a good bead on them, and I'm given to trusting his instinct. But before you go, you'll pay us that money you claim to have."

"Like hell I will," Bowman said. "If we split up, you'll get paid when you bring back Trammel and Hagen to the BF. Dead or alive makes no difference to us, so long as we can see they're dead with our own eyes."

Lefty looked behind him at his men. They were riding in one group, while the three BF hands brought up the rear. Walt the cousin was in between the two groups.

His men looked at him, silently telling him they'd back his play no matter what. The only one missing was Chico, who'd ridden ahead of the group a few miles to scout for them. He knew Chico wasn't the independent sort. He'd support Lefty whatever he decided to do.

"If we split," Lefty said, "we'll need money for expenses. For outfitting, see? We're out here on your dime and your say-so. You've told us you've got the money, but we ain't seen a cent of it yet. Layin' eyes on it could go a long way to settling our nerves."

"Settlin' nerves," Parrot said. "Long way."

Matt Bowman brought his horse alongside Lefty's. "Are you calling me a liar, sir?"

Lefty wouldn't look at the man and kept his pace. "Just said we ain't seen the money you claim to have is all. Layin' eyes on it would go a long way to puttin' my men at ease, not to mention makin' your talkin' that much easier to tolerate on as long a trail as this one's turning out to be."

"I've got the money, by God," Bowman said. "Right here with me. No man has ever questioned my word before and I'll be damned if I'll allow the likes of a saddle tramp like you to question it now."

Lefty had heard just about as much as he could stand of the rancher. "Then be damned."

He drew his Colt from his belly holster and fired into Matt Bowman's chest at point-blank range.

The rancher tumbled backward off his horse, his shirt aflame, and landed on the ground.

The three Bowman ranch hands at the rear of the pack bolted back down the trail, leaving the packhorses behind. Hooch, Skinner, and Parrot took off after the fleeing men without Lefty having to say a word.

Only Walt Bowman remained; man and horse frozen where they stood on the trail.

Walt said, "You shot him."

"He deserved it." Lefty turned his mount and aimed the Colt at Walt. "And so will you if you lied to us about that money, boy."

"He's got it on him," Walt said. "In his saddlebags. Saw my grandpa give it to him the night before we hired you boys."

"Unbuckle your gun belt and drop it over the left side." Lefty aimed the pistol at his head. "Do it real slow."

Walt never took his eyes off his cousin's body as he obeyed Lefty's commands, then held his hands up high. "I don't want no trouble, Lefty."

Hanover didn't think he did. "Now climb down and find them gold pieces on your cousin's person."

He kept the Colt trained on Walt as the younger Bowman stepped over his cousin's body to where the horse had trotted off and searched the saddlebags. He held the purse aloft as he grabbed the horse's bit. "Here it is, Lefty. Just like Uncle Matt said."

"Fetch it over here, now. That gelding, too, while you're at it." His own horse was played out by the long, hard ride up from Texas, and he could use a fine mount like Bowman's. The dead man wouldn't have any further use for it anyway.

He watched Walt as the boy did as he was told. He thought about whether or not he should shoot him now or keep him around. The boy hadn't done anything when Lefty had gunned down his cousin. There could be a dozen reasons why and all of them might prove useful as they ran down Trammel and the gambler. Even idiots had their purpose, as evidenced by Parrot's continued and unexplainable existence.

He took the purse Walt handed up to him. Lefty knew by the heft of it that Bowman had been telling the truth, but life had told him it paid to be cautious. Keeping the Colt on Walt, Lefty pulled open the purse strings with his teeth and looked inside. Ten gleaming coins winked back at him. One thousand dollars. The most money John "Lefty" Hanover had ever seen in his life was now in the palm of his hand.

His joy was interrupted by three gunshots echoing from somewhere down the trail.

Lefty pulled the strings closed with his teeth and tucked the purse inside his filthy shirt. "Sounds like you're the last man from the BF ranch standing."

Walt tried to put on a brave face. "Could be the other way around. Our men can handle themselves."

Lefty thumbed back the hammer on the Colt. "You really believe that, boy?"

"No. I guess I don't. And I hope I won't meet the same fate as them, Lefty. I'd like to join up with you if you'd be kind enough to have me."

Lefty grinned. "You mean you'd turn on your own kin after everything we done?"

"My kin never thought much of me, and the feeling was mutual," Walt said. "Guess I've got just as much right here as I've got waiting for me back at the BF. Maybe more. Hell, they were never going to let me run that ranch anyway."

Lefty eased back on the hammer and tucked the Colt away. Yes, maybe young Walt Bowman could be useful after all.

Lefty turned when he heard a rider coming back from the north. It was Chico, and he was smiling. "You better ride up here and take a look at this, boss man. Looks like Trammel and his friend did some of our killing for us. Got two dead men at an old campsite up ahead."

He looked down at Matt Bowman's body on the trail. "What happened here?"

Lefty stepped down from his horse and took the reins from Walt. Yes, it was a good mount indeed. "What you see here is progress, Chico. Plain, old-fashioned progress."

CHAPTER 11

After three days of good travel and harsh nights of bitter cold, Trammel and Hagen finally led their team of horses into Nebraska. Winter had already lost its grip on the land, but the air was much colder than Trammel would have liked it to be.

"So this is Nebraska," Trammel said aloud as they rode along. The land was as flat as it was plain. "By God."

"Kansas isn't exactly a bustling metropolis, my friend," Hagen said. "You'll find our passage will be quieter here, as long as we keep our heads about us."

"We been doing anything but that since we left Wichita?"

"I'm afraid more vigilance will be required of us in these parts, for there are many trials we may face on the trail to Ogallala."

"Like what?"

"Renegade Indians are always a concern," Hagen explained. "Hunters, too. Men of various ill repute and reputation are as common to these plains as the buffalo."

Sometimes all the words Hagen used to describe

one simple thing gave him a headache. "Did you always talk this way or did you learn it?"

Hagen smiled. "Why use three words when ten will do? I find language to be a poor enough form of communication, so I try to make the best of it whenever possible. Besides, it's not like there's a better way to pass the time, is there?"

Trammel saw something in the distance that made him bring his horse up short.

Hagen followed suit. "What's wrong?"

Trammel pointed to the sky over the slight rise in front of them. "See for yourself."

Both men saw a flock of buzzards circling high overhead in the near distance.

"Good eyes, Trammel," Hagen said. "I hadn't seen that."

"Too busy talking, I suppose."

"Shut up."

Trammel looked around them to see if anyone might be hiding nearby or if there was any sign that might tell them what had attracted the buzzards to whatever was just over that rise. There were no obvious clues.

"Wonder what they're circling," Trammel asked.

"Something big to attract a flock that large," Hagen explained. "Maybe a couple of buffalo carcasses left by skinners. No way of knowing until we see for ourselves. Let's hobble the horses and make our approach on foot. Safer that way."

Both men dismounted and hobbled their horses where they stood. They removed the Winchesters from their respective saddles and approached the rise at a crouch. When they got near the top, Hagen dropped to his belly and used his elbows to propel himself the rest of the way. Trammel did likewise, though far less gracefully than his companion.

When they saw what had attracted the buzzards, both men spoke at the same time.

"Good God."

With the stocks of their Winchesters on their hips, Trammel and Hagen rode their horses into the charred remains of what had once been a wagon train.

By Trammel's count, five wagons had been burned where they had formed a semicircle in an attempt to ward off some kind of an attack.

"Think it was Indians?" Trammel asked Hagen.

"Can't tell as of yet." Hagen dismounted and tied his mount off on a burned wagon wheel. "You stay mounted and keep watch. Everything's still smoldering, so whoever did this might still be close by."

Trammel figured Hagen was right. The smell of burnt wood was too strong to have been there for long.

Rather than stand stock-still in one place, he rode the horse around the wagons to get a better look at the surrounding area and the wagons themselves.

The outward sides of the charred buckboards were peppered with bullet holes. From atop his horse, Trammel could see the burnt bodies of men who had taken cover inside the wagons. Their dead hands were curled around rifles that were no longer there.

"Whoever it was took their rifles," Trammel called out. "Horses, too. Looks like they burned whatever they couldn't take."

Hagen was moving among the bodies lying inside the wagon circle. "See any women in the wagons?"

Trammel picked up his pace, fighting his horse to keep moving despite the stench of burnt flesh that hung heavy in the air. "Not a one. Think whoever did this took them?"

"Most assuredly," Hagen said, then called out. "Buck, one's still alive! Keep an eye out for anything coming our way!"

Trammel jerked his horse around to go back the way he had come. Even he knew a man on horseback was an inviting target. He didn't want to make himself any easier to hit by riding around in a predictable circle.

He saw Hagen cradle a man's head in his hands. Trammel could see the bullet wounds in his legs and arms were still bleeding. His skin had been burned, but he managed to somehow move his hand as he talked into Hagen's ear.

That same hand trembled, its fingers becoming rigid, before they went limp. Hagen slowly lowered the man's head back to the burnt ground and laid the dead man's blackened hands across his chest. Trammel couldn't swear to it, but he thought he heard the gambler praying.

"Better get in here," Hagen called out to him, "and bring the horses with you. Theys who did this hit the train only a few minutes ago and they're still around."

Trammel changed direction again and doubled back the way he'd just ridden. "You sure about that? Maybe we should just get the hell out of here?"

A rifle shot echoed as a bullet struck the ground about ten yards in front of Trammel's horse.

"You were saying?" Hagen said.

Trammel rode his own horse through the narrow gap between two burnt wagons and ran to bring the rest of the animals into the makeshift fort. Sometimes, he hated it when Hagen was right.

Trammel tossed Hagen his Winchester and a box of cartridges from the pack mule. He took his own Winchester and coach shotgun from the saddle and laid them against a wagon on the other side of the circle. Hagen would guard the eastern side and Trammel would take the west. Since they had come from the south, he figured that side was clear.

"How many are we looking at?" Trammel asked as he made sure there were two cartridges in the shotgun.

"The dead man told me ten or so." Hagen already had his Winchester at his shoulder, scanning the horizon for anything to shoot at. "Said they rode off when one of their lookouts spotted us. Five of them took the women in a wagon they'd brought with them. A couple stayed behind to scalp the survivors."

"Scalpers?" Trammel aimed the Winchester at a copse of trees in front of him. If an attack came, he figured it would come from there. "So it's Indians, then."

"No," Hagen said. "White men. That makes it worse."

Trammel gagged on the odor of charred death all around him. "Can't see as how it could be any worse."

"Indians would most likely ride on after they got what they were after," Hagen explained. "White men who'd do this will double back for our supplies, figuring there's more to be had. That shot they took at you was to find their range, probably hoping they'd hit you or the horse and cut down the odds even further in their favor."

Trammel scanned the horizon nervously. "Maybe if we ride like hell, we could get clear of them."

"They'd only run us down on the trail eventually, probably before nightfall. And in open country no less. No, there's a fight coming regardless, and I'd rather it happen here where we have cover."

Trammel wasn't so sure. "Cover didn't do these folks much good."

"True, but they were farmers. We're not."

A bloodcurdling yell echoed across the plain as the brush in front of Trammel shook before five riders came bounding straight for him. "Five on my side!" he called out.

"Same here," Hagen answered. "Hope you know how to use that Winchester."

Trammel drew a bead on the lead rider, steadied his aim, and fired. Man and horse pitched to the side and fell hard. He levered a fresh round into the chamber and aimed at a second invader. "Don't worry about me."

He heard Hagen firing, too, but was too busy with the four remaining riders to check on him.

The four riders broke apart, two splitting left while two split right. All were coming in fast. Trammel aimed at the lead rider on his left and fired. He missed but struck the man behind him in the chest. The man dropped from the saddle as his horse rode on.

He levered another round and took aim at the man he had missed. He led him a bit more this time and fired in front of him. Again, he missed the rider, but his round slammed into the horse's rear flank, causing it to rear up as the impact of the bullet caused him to spin and crash to the ground. The rider was thrown clear and landed flat on his back.

Bullets from the other riders struck the wagons all around him, but Trammel kept his focus on the thrown man. He aimed steady until the man tried to get to his feet. When he got on all fours, Trammel fired again, striking him in the side and laying him out flat.

The ground to his left rumbled and instinct made him dive for cover as another rider sped by much closer to the wagon wall, peppering the area with pistol shot. Another rider followed right behind him, almost hitting Trammel in the leg.

Trammel dropped the Winchester and scooped up the shotgun as he rose up and fired both barrels into the last rider's back. The man pitched forward on his horse amid a red cloud of his own blood.

Trammel dove behind the wagon as another rider came in at his right with a shotgun of his own. The blast obliterated the bottom of a wagon wheel behind Trammel, causing the wagon to sag.

Trammel grabbed the Winchester as he rolled onto his back and levered another round into the chamber. He brought up the rifle to his shoulder just as the shotgunner rounded the wagon. Trammel sent him to hell with a squeeze of the trigger, the bullet striking the man high in the chest.

A bullet crashed into the wagon just above Trammel's head as another shot from Hagen's Winchester rang out from the eastern side of the wagons. Another horse screamed and another thud shook the ground.

"One's on foot!" Hagen called out. "Be careful."

Trammel had just gotten to his feet when the impact of a rifle butt struck him at the base of the neck. The blow dropped him to a knee, but didn't rob him of his senses. Instinct caused his left elbow to shoot backward, catching the man in the stomach and sending him sprawling back against the wagon.

Trammel wheeled and snatched the man by the throat, pinning him against the buckboard as he slapped the man's rifle away. The man grabbed at Trammel's arm, trying to break the viselike grip on his throat. His eyes began to bulge as he his lungs could no longer get oxygen.

"Get clear of him and let me shoot him!" Hagen yelled.

But Trammel's grip held.

The rage began to wash over him again, as it always had when people struck him. His father had struck him so many times over so many years as a boy when all he could do was cower and take it.

But Buck Trammel wasn't a boy anymore.

And he would never let anyone hit him again.

"Damn it, Buck," Hagen yelled. "He's going for his gun."

But Trammel put all of his weight on the man's throat as he twisted it. A sickening pop, followed by the man falling slack. Trammel threw the body aside.

"That all of them?" Trammel asked.

Hagen didn't answer right away, but when he did, his voice was quiet. "Yes, Buck. I think so."

Trammel heard a man cry out from beyond the wagon. He looked up and saw one of the attackers pinned beneath his horse. It was the first man he'd shot. And he was still alive.

"There's still one left." Trammel pulled the Colt

from his shoulder holster and moved between two wagons to walk toward him.

Hagen scrambled after him. "What are you doing, you damned fool? There might be more of them out there."

Trammel kept walking. "Let them come. This one might know where the women are."

Hagen had to run to keep pace with the big man's stride. "They're probably long gone from here. Let's get out of here like you wanted to before."

Trammel kept the Colt at his side as he walked. "No."

He found the man's left leg pinned beneath the dead horse. The leg was crushed. The grass around him had been clawed away as the man had obviously tried to pull himself free, but to no avail. Trammel saw the man's pistol and rifle had fallen on the other side of the dead horse, well out of reach of the dying man.

Trammel stopped five yards away from the man and aimed the Colt down at him.

The man held up his hand as if it could stop a bullet. "Please, no. I'm out of the fight."

"Like hell you are." Trammel thumbed back the hammer. "Where are the women?"

"Pull me out of here and fix me up, and I promise I'll tell you."

"Say nothing and I'll let the buzzards have you. Tell me where they are, and I end it now. If not, I walk away. Your choice. Last chance."

The wounded man pointed back in the direction of the wagon arch. "We moved them back there when we saw you two coming. Tied up in a wagon just down that hill. Listen. You can still hear them screaming."

Trammel cocked his head and listened to the

wind. A slight breeze picked up from the east, and he could hear whimpering.

The same sound his mother used to make when his father came home from a night out with the boys from the docks.

"You hear that, Buck?" Hagen said. "He's telling the truth."

Trammel fired, killing the man on the ground. "So did I."

CHAPTER 12

Trammel and Hagen left the packhorses in the wagon circle while they rode to where the dead man had told them the women would be. They found all of them in an old buckboard tied together by their hands and feet, even the children. They were still cowering in the middle of the wagon while the two horses hitched to the wagon nosed the grass at their feet, oblivious to the misery behind them.

Sometimes, Trammel envied animals.

Trammel stopped about a hundred yards from the wagon. If the women saw them, they didn't show it.

"Hagen, you've got a better way about you than me. It'd be best if go down there and tend to them. Cut them loose and put them at their ease. Tell them we'll bring them to Ogallala with us where they'll be safe."

Trammel noticed Hagen had lost some of his flair for the dramatic. Maybe the shoot-out had taken some of the starch out of him. Maybe watching his companion choke a man to death with his bare hands had done that, too.

Trammel had known people to act this way around

him before. People, especially women, always liked to be around a big man until they saw what big men often had to do. It had been like that back in New York. It had been like that in the Pinkerton Agency, too. He saw no reason why Hagen should be any different.

"Of course, Buck, but you should come in with me. Help me assure them that they're safe."

"No. I'd just scare them, and they've been through enough for one day. You're more charming than I am. Tie your horse to the back of the wagon and start heading north. I'll strip the dead devils of ammunition and weapons and be along with the animals. Find a good safe place where we can make camp for a couple of days, maybe near a stream where they can wash up. We'll push on to Ogallala when they've gotten over the shock. I'll be along in a bit."

He had expected Hagen to have some kind of witty comeback or better suggestion to the contrary. He was surprised when the gambler did as Trammel had asked without saying a word. He watched him ride toward the women slowly. They screamed when they heard his approach and their fear tore into Trammel something awful.

Hagen held his hands out from his sides as his horse slowly walked toward them. "You've nothing to fear, my ladies. The worst is over, and the bad men are gone. My friend and I are here to help. Now, I would be honored if you would allow me the pleasure of doing something about those nasty ropes."

Trammel brought his horse around and rode back to strip the dead.

* * *

Hagen had chosen to make camp beside a rolling stream. By the time Trammel arrived with their horses, Hagen already had a large fire going where the women and children huddled around it for warmth. Trammel could smell coffee, beans, and bacon on the wind. He imagined they must have been from the stores the robbers had found in the wagons before they burned them.

Trammel picketed the animals outside the circle of light where there was plenty of grass to eat. He soon fed them grain from the stores Hagen had bought in Dodge City and made a bed for himself beneath an old oak tree, close enough to camp to hear anything, but far enough away so as not to bother the ladies.

He even heard a couple of them laugh as Hagen undoubtedly regaled them with one of his many stories.

About an hour later, Hagen brought him over a plate of food and a pot of coffee, which Trammel was glad to have. "How are they doing?"

"As good as you could expect, I suppose," he said as he poured two cups of coffee from the pot. "Sad, terrified, mournful. But they're strong. They're trying to be strong for the children."

Trammel shoveled a spoonful of beans into his mouth. "Children always get the worst of it."

Hagen sipped his coffee in silence while he watched his friend finish his supper. When he was done, he asked, "And how are you?"

"Fine." He set his plate aside and picked up his coffee. "Can't believe we survived a scrape like that without a scratch between us. Ever been in anything like that before? You handled yourself pretty good for a rich boy."

"A couple of times," Hagen admitted. "When I was in the army. Never outnumbered like that, though." He looked at his friend. "How *are* you, Buck?"

Trammel knew what he was getting at. "You mean about what I did to that fella who hit me?"

"The thought had crossed my mind. It was . . . unsettling to watch."

"Up-close work like that always is," Trammel said. "It's one thing to shoot a man when he's shooting back at you, but when it's just the two of you, it's a bit more personal. Guess getting hit like that has always been personal to me."

"I'm just concerned that—"

But Trammel didn't want to talk about it. "Leave it alone, Hagen. This world, the wilderness, the trail? That's your world. Killing people? Killing them like I did back there? That's my world. That's what I do best. Don't ask me how and don't ask me why. It's who I am, and it's all I am."

Hagen finished his cup of coffee and poured himself another. "There's nothing wrong with that. But it does make me wonder, though."

"Wonder what?"

"Wonder if we're doing what we're supposed to be doing after all. Think of all the winding roads both you and I have taken before Wichita and since. Think of all the different choices we could have made along the way and how it ended up right here, with us rescuing those ladies and avenging the deaths of their men. Imagine what would have happened if we hadn't come this way or decided on another path. One could be forgiven for believing we were being guided by an unseen hand."

"You mean God?" This time, Trammel did laugh.

"Don't go pulling the Almighty into this, Hagen. He's got enough on his hands with those poor women down there."

"Perhaps," Hagen allowed, "but I'd say He has a damned fine sense of humor just the same. Now, you look just about ready to fall over. Why don't you get some sleep and I'll take first watch?"

"I'm fine right here. Got a fresh pot of coffee, and I'm too keyed up to sleep anyway. Get them bedded down for the night and take a good rest for yourself. I'll come wake you when I'm feeling tired."

"And with that, I'll take my leave." He took Trammel's plate and his own cup as he stood. He paused before he left and said, "We did good work today, my friend. Have a good night."

"Yeah," Trammel admitted. "I suppose we did. Sleep well."

He waited until Hagen had some of the ladies laughing again before he eased his Winchester out of his saddle and laid it across his lap. He quietly fed rounds into it until it was full. An empty gun was no good to anyone.

And neither was a former lawman with no one to protect.

CHAPTER 13

"Nothing!" Walt yelled as he slammed down his whiskey. "A whole damned week in this miserable town and no sign of Trammel or that drunk Hagen."

Lefty Hanover ignored the boy. He knew the whiskey would kick in before long, and the loud-mouthed brat would have his head on the table, dead to the world.

Which was exactly what happened fifteen minutes later, leaving Lefty, Hooch, Parrot, Chico and Skinner practically alone once again at the back table of Mills Saloon in Dodge City.

"Never thought he'd shut up," Hooch said, grabbing for the bottle in the middle of the table. "Damned kid sure likes to talk, don't he?"

"And say nothin' while he's doin' it," Skinner added. "Complains about no action on the trail, then complains about Trammel now that we're surrounded by action." He looked over at one of the plump working girls tending to the gamblers at the other end of the saloon. "Could stand me a little action myself."

"Damned right," Chico said.

"Enough," Lefty barked. "Got enough complaining

from that damned kid to get my fill for a lifetime. I don't need the rest of you bunch pickin' up any of his bad habits."

"Yeah," Parrot said. "No bad habits."

But as much as Lefty hated Walt's griping, he knew the kid was right. Chico had lost Trammel's trail outside of Dodge City and all signs pointed to them being in town. But after a week of buying drinks for every drover and gossip they could find, no one had seen anyone resembling Trammel's description. It would be easy enough for Hagen to blend in anywhere, but a man like Trammel stood out, even in a place like Dodge City. They'd run into plenty of old friends who'd come up from Texas on the cattle trail. Some who'd come back down it from points north, too, and none of them had seen Trammel or Hagen. It was like the devils had just disappeared into the earth somewhere along the line.

He'd often wondered if that had happened. He wondered if maybe they'd been killed or captured and carted off someplace, but he knew better. The deaths of the two men Bowman had sent to track them was sign of that. They wouldn't have gone quietly, especially Trammel. If he went down, he'd take two or more with him. It would likely take a buffalo gun to stop a man like that.

It was Hooch who stirred him from his thoughts. "How much of that money we still got left?"

Lefty trusted his men only so far. They had only gone through about a hundred of the thousand they'd taken off Matt Bowman, but there was no reason for them to know that yet. "We've got plenty. Why?"

"I say we ditch the kid here and head on back

south," Hooch said. "Why the hell should we carry on a dead man's vengeance?"

The others grumbled their assent, all except Parrot, who hadn't had an original thought since Noah stepped off the ark.

Lefty knew he had to put down this kind of talk now and forever. "This was never about Bowman or his kin, boys. It's about what that big ape did to me. Remember?"

He picked up the leather strap covering his eye so all of them could take a good look at it. All of them looked away.

Skinner said, "Then what do we do next? I'm all for getting back at Trammel for what he done to you, but we don't know where he is. I say we burn through the rest of that money, have ourselves a hell of a time, then go back on the trail like we've always done. We keep our ears to the ground and ask where he lands. Someone'll hear something, and they'll tell us when they do."

"Worked pretty good all these years, I reckon," Chico said. "It's gettin' so that I'm startin' to miss Texas."

Lefty perked up when he saw the man from the telegraph office enter the saloon. He was a spindly, fretful little man Lefty had buffaloed the first day they'd arrived in Dodge City. He'd given the man twenty dollars to keep him apprised of any telegraphs involving Bowman or Trammel or Hagen. Lefty took the clerk rushing into the Mills Saloon as a good sign.

Lefty stood up and yelled, "Boy! You looking for me?"

The man scurried over between the tables full of drunks and gamblers. Lefty felt a little excitement when he saw the little man was holding an envelope.

"Yes, sir," he said when he reached the table. "Got me a telegraph here all the way from Wichita addressed to a Matt Bowman. No address given. Sent out to Newton, too. Figured you'd want to see it."

Lefty held out his hand. "Give it here."

The man eagerly handed it to him and stood where he was, waiting.

Lefty opened the envelope and realized the man was still there. He glared at him. "You waiting for a tip or a bullet, boy? I already paid you for this, now be on your way while you can."

The man turned and hurried out the door as Lefty read the telegram. Unlike the rest of the bunch, he could read fairly well and write his own name.

The others leaned forward like children listening to a campfire story. When Lefty finished reading it, he put the telegram back in the envelope and slipped it into his shirt.

"Well?" Hooch asked. "What's it say?"

"Yeah," Skinner said. "What's it all about?"

Lefty patted his shirt where the telegram was just beneath. "It's from Old Man Bowman. He sent out a blind telegram asking Matt for an update on his search for Trammel and Hagen. Says he's anxiously awaiting a reply."

Chico drank his whiskey and poured some more. "He'll be waiting a long time."

"He'll be shaking hands with him soon enough," Skinner added, "him bein' as old as he is."

But Lefty ignored the banter as an idea began to form in his mind. "We can't go back on the trail because too many in Wichita know Matt hired us. We can't leave Walt here because he'll just head back home and tell his people what we did. We'd have law on us from here to Christmas."

Hooch said, "Could just kill him here in town. Make it look like he got rolled while drunk, which ain't exactly a stretch."

"That's no good," Lefty decided. "The entire Bowman party dead and us still alive wouldn't look good. We'd be blamed for it, and Old Man Bowman would see us hang. We've always avoided crossing the law when we could, and I don't intend to stop now."

That's when that idea that had begun to form in Lefty's mind blossomed into a beautiful rose.

He got to his feet. "Time to get movin', boys. And bring old Walt with you. I've got a feelin' he might finally be good for somethin'."

Lefty Hanover had always made a practice of staying away from the law whenever possible, mostly because he wanted to avoid answering the damned fool questions lawmen tended to ask men like him. He'd never had much respect for obeying the law, but getting caught breaking it was something else entirely. It was trouble he did not need in a life already filled with as much trouble as he could handle.

That was why he squirmed a bit as Sheriff Charles Bassett glared at him from behind his big desk at the county jail.

Lefty Hanover tried to put the final shine on his story as he brought it to a dramatic close. "And that's just how it was, Sheriff. The six of us barely escaping with our lives while those mad-dog killers Buck Trammel and Adam Hagen bushwhacked us and killed our beloved employer and his men on the road to this here fine city of yours."

"Yep," Parrot said, "that's just how it happened, too, on the road here to your fine city."

Bassett's hands remained folded across his belly, only his eyes moving across the six men crammed into his office. Lefty decided the sheriff was well named as his eyes were open and honest like a basset hound's. But as wide as they were, it was clear they didn't miss much, and the quiet man seemed intent on listening more than he was on talking.

"By my estimate," the sheriff said, "you boys have been in Dodge City for more than a week. Why bring this to me now?"

Lefty kept playing the yokel. "Well, now, Sheriff, that's a right good question and I aim to give you a right good answer. See, me and the boys didn't ride into town with justice on our minds. No, sir. It was vengeance. Just about the only color any of us could see was red over the terror we met at the hands of Trammel and Hagen out there on the trail. And, although I always mean to abide by the law when I can, we sought to kill those men our own selves for what they done to us and poor Matt Bowman and the others."

He laid a fatherly hand on Walt Bowman's shoulders as the drunkard pitched forward. "Poor Walt here, Matt's own cousin, has been beside himself with grief since the moment it happened. He's been in what you might call a canonical state ever since.

Why, it was all we could do to get him here tonight in a reasonably presentable fashion."

Bassett's eyes slid toward him. "The word is 'catatonic' and, as for the rest of your words, I judge them to be equally misplaced." He leaned a few inches forward. "That means I think you're lying."

Lefty slapped the desk, feigning indignity. "Now just hold on right there, Sheriff. We was hired on, right and legal like, by Mr. Matt Bowman his own self in the main room of The Winter Star saloon back down there in Wichita. Walt here can swear to that fact, can't you Walt?"

The boy lifted his head and mumbled as he nodded, before going back to sleep.

"See that?" Lefty continued. "And you can send one of your wires down to Wichita and ask the law down there to check our story. Why, there must be a dozen or more witnesses who seen Mr. Bowman hire us on and a few dozen more who saw us ride out of town with him. Now, I'm not going to sit here before you and tell you our intentions was pure. But I hope you won't sit there and tell us we deserved to almost get killed by the men we was hired to pursue. Not to mention the dead souls those two left in the wilderness. Don't they deserve justice?"

"Justice?" Bassett repeated. "You boys were only interested in justice, eh?"

"Yes, sir, we were, on account of how we know how much of a mad dog lunatic that Trammel can be. Why, I rode into Wichita with two good eyes and lost one at the hands of that killer. All the boys here can attest to that and more can do so back in Wichita."

"Yes, I'm sure they can," Bassett said, "just as I'm

sure this mad dog Trammel attacked you while you were coming out of a church meeting one bright Sunday morning."

"Can't say that, sir, so I won't. But he took my eye, and there's no one who can say different."

"No one," Parrot said. "Took his eye, that's for sure."

Bassett groaned as he folded his hands on his desk. "I know about what happened to the Bowman boys in Wichita. I also know Trammel and Hagen were cleared of any wrongdoing and were advised by the deputies to leave town out of fear of exactly this kind of thing happening. What happened in Wichita was a matter of self-defense, however brutal that defense may have been. I'm inclined to believe that whatever happened on the trail was also in self-defense, even if it happened exactly as you say, which I sincerely doubt."

Lefty had expected this. He knew Bassett hadn't been a lawman in a place like Dodge City for so long by being a fool. He hadn't walked in there expecting the sheriff to swear out a warrant and mount up a posse just on his say-so.

No. Lefty Hanover had far less ambitious goals than that. "But I'd imagine you'd at least want to talk to Trammel and Hagen about it, wouldn't you? I mean, they ain't exactly walked in here their own selves and told you what happened, have they? And I'd wager they haven't reported it happening anywhere else, either. I ain't askin' you to take our word for it, Sheriff. I'm askin' you to ask your own questions."

His mind expressed, he sat back humbly, clutching his hat close to his chest. "With all due respect for the law and your own good judgment, of course."

Bassett closed his eyes and ran his hand across his brow. And when he opened his eyes, he looked directly at Lefty. "I'll take your statement and expect you to sign it or make your marks. All of you." He looked at Parrot. "Even that idiot there. I don't believe a word of what you've told me except that Matt Bowman and his men are likely dead. How they got that way will be determined by me. Until that happens, you and your men are remanded to town. You're not to leave unless I say so. Is that clear?"

"As clear as the Texas sun in August, your honor."

"Don't pander to me, boy. I think you had a hand in those killings, if they happened. And if I can prove it, I'll have you dancing at the end of a rope as soon as legally possible."

He dipped his pen in the inkwell and brought over a clean sheet of nice, white paper. "Now, tell it to me again and without all the flowery asides." He pointed to Parrot. "And keep that imbecile quiet or I'll lock all of you up for the duration.

Hooch slapped a hand over Parrot's mouth.

Lefty smiled. "I'll begin at the beginning, then."

CHAPTER 14

The women were just finishing up singing a hymn when Hagen brought the wagon to a stop. A cluster of jagged buildings on the distant prairie rose from the morning mist. Hagen recognized this as their new and eternal Jerusalem, at least as far as the ladies in the wagon were concerned. Ogallala, Nebraska.

Hagen looked back and watched Trammel bring the team of horses forward. He was glad he had convinced the big man to shave. He looked different this way and even more intimidating than he already did. He'd also be a bit harder to peg should anyone in town be looking for them.

Hagen knew the ladies might be happy they had reached Ogallala alive, but for him and Trammel, the danger was greater to them here than on the prairie. They ran the risk of being recognized now or remembered later on. They had no choice but to go into town now that they had to deliver the women to safety, but the way they went about it might mean the difference between life and having the Bowman family on their heels again.

A young woman in the back of the wagon named Mary Ford perked up when she saw Trammel approaching. "Good morning, Mr. Trammel. And God bless you."

The other women giggled and teased her as Trammel touched the brim of his hat. "Morning, Miss Ford. And I appreciate the sentiment, as unlikely as it may be."

Miss Ford's daily greetings had appeared to humanize Trammel some. Hagen began to wonder if it was the eager sincerity about the young woman whenever she saw a man she considered her rescuer or if politeness was closer to Trammel's true nature. Whatever the case may be, Hagen was sorry it was coming to an end now that they had reached Ogallala.

Trammel pulled his horses to a halt beside the wagon. "Why'd you stop?"

"Because I'm afraid this is where you and I must part ways," Hagen explained, "at least for a little while." He could tell the big man was confused, so he added, "Our exploits on the trail are bound to draw some attention, especially when we ride into town with a wagon filled with rescued women. Our descriptions are bound to end up in the local papers, and it's not unreasonable to believe that the Bowman family could read them and decipher our whereabouts. I think we've succeeded in throwing them off our scent for the moment, so I wouldn't want to risk that possibility because of our good deed here."

Trammel thought about it for a moment. "So you get to ride into town and get all the glory?"

"No." Hagen appreciated Trammel's suspicious nature. "I ride into town and slip into obscurity."

Mary Ford leaned forward and added, "As thanks to both of you for saving us from those brutal men, the ladies and children and I have agreed to not breathe a word about you to anyone, not even our own people, should they accept us in town. Mr. Hagen has made that point perfectly clear, and it is a humble price we are all too happy to pay. We owe you both our lives, gentlemen. Our children owe you their lives. Protecting your identities is the least we can do."

"And I have always benefited from the discretion of pious ladies." Hagen said to Trammel. "Still, we must take every precaution to not be seen together while in town. Do you have enough money to livery the horses and get a room?"

"I do, but it'll just about clean me out," Trammel said. "I wasn't counting on being a fugitive, so money's a bit tight."

"I'll reimburse you when I find you," Hagen said. "Livery the horses for a week and secure a room for yourself for the same amount of time. Don't worry about me. I'll find you after I see to the ladies."

He watched Trammel thinking it over; his lantern jaw set on edge as he thought of all the different ways he could answer. He was glad the man wasn't a gambler, because, given his open nature, he'd lose his shirt playing poker. Hagen didn't think Trammel was a stupid man by any means, but he wasn't a quick thinker, either. He moved on instinct and, so far, that instinct had saved Hagen's life and the lives of the women they had rescued. He intended on compensating the big New Yorker many times over for his kindness by the time their association came to an end.

When he was done thinking it over, Trammel simply said, "Okay. You'll find me in town."

He brought his big sorrel around and tipped his hat to the women in the wagon. "I suppose this is where we part ways, ladies. Best of luck to all of you and keep those prayers coming if you can spare the thought. Guess it can't hurt."

The ladies bid him good-bye all at once, but Miss Ford was the most enthusiastic. "Good-bye, Mr. Trammel. And thank you again for your immense kindness to us in the wilderness."

Trammel smiled. "Ma'am."

Hagen watched him swing his horses around and lead them down to Ogallala at a better clip than when he had been trailing the wagon.

He was surprised when Miss Ford leaned on his shoulder to watch Trammel ride off. "He's quite a man, isn't he, Mr. Hagen."

He imagined if Trammel had heard Miss Ford's praise, he might have actually blushed. He would've paid good money to see that.

"No argument from me on that score, Miss Ford. Now, please take your seat and allow me to take you fine ladies to your new home."

He snapped the reins and, with a great cheer from the women, headed off on the trail to town.

"How much for five days?" Trammel asked the liveryman.

The black man pulled his beard as he thought it over. Trammel saw a sign on the wall listing a price, but he wanted to see if the man would match it or try to gouge him.

The price the liveryman gave him matched the sign on the wall. Trammel plunked the coins in the liveryman's hand and hoped like hell Hagen wouldn't leave him there. He might not have counted on being a fugitive, but he hadn't counted on stabling so many horses, either. The amount may have been fair, but it put a hell of a dent in his savings. After getting a room and meals, he figured on being broke within the week. He didn't know why they just couldn't have made camp on the outskirts of town, but he'd seen enough of Hagen's actions to know the man always had a reason for doing whatever he did.

"Need a place to stay?" the liveryman asked as he led the horses to their respective stalls. "I can recommend The Old Hickory for you. It's got just about everything a man could want all under one roof. Food, whiskey, cards, women. Food's not even half bad. Tell 'em I sent you, and they'll give you a right good price for a week. Name's Sebastian."

Trammel appeared to think it over for a while. "I just might do that. And thanks."

"You're welcome, Mister . . . ? You never told me your name."

He had no intention of giving the man his real name. He already had his horses and a line on where he'd be staying. He noticed how the man watched him and, if he was like most liverymen, had a tendency to gossip. In Trammel's experience, neither barbers nor liverymen could be relied upon for their discretion.

"Ronan," Trammel said, using his cousin's name. "Jim Ronan."

The two men shook hands. "Big Jim Ronan," Sebastian said. "It suits you. Yes, sir, it suits you right down to the ground you're standing on."

Trammel hauled his saddle onto his shoulder; the rifle and the shotgun still in their scabbards. "Take care of my horses, Sebastian. I'll see you in a week."

Sebastian continued to shout pleasantries at him as Trammel walked out of the livery. He saw The Old Hickory saloon at the end of the street and walked in the opposite direction.

Instead, Trammel took a room in the Clarkson hotel. It wasn't the best place in town, but for the money, he had no complaints. The room was clean and it opened to the balcony that surrounded the second floor of the hotel. The clerk at the front desk said he could have food delivered up to his room if he wanted, though he was clear that such service was infrequent and the house made no guarantees that the food would still be warm if and when he got it.

Trammel was grateful the clerk looked too hungover to remember him if asked to describe him later. He imagined Sebastian at the livery had probably already told ten people about the big stranger named Jim Ronan.

Trammel had set his saddle on the ground and had just removed his boots for the first time in weeks when he heard a great clamor rise up from the street. In his stocking feet, he stepped out onto the balcony and saw other guests were already outside, looking for themselves.

Trammel looked down and saw Hagen in the wagon, leading the women up the street. A crowd of men and women had fallen in around them. Men tossed their hats in the air and ladies thrust flowers up to the women in the wagon.

Hagen noticed Trammel on the balcony as he passed and doffed his hat to him.

Trammel shook his head. So much for Hagen's plan to quietly slip away.

He padded back inside and shut the door behind him, making sure it was locked and the shades were pulled down. He climbed into bed and heard the springs protest under his weight.

The bed might not have been as comfortable as the one he had enjoyed at The Gilded Lilly, but he was glad to have it.

As he waited for sleep to take him, Trammel wondered if Hagen would come back for him. He wondered if he'd still plan on going to his family in Wyoming or if there was even a family at all. Hagen was a hard man to figure out, and as a gambler, he'd made a life based on bluffing other men at the card table. But the prairie was a much different place than a gambling hall, and Trammel imagined most, if not all, of what Hagen had told him on the trail was likely true.

But Ogallala was also different from the prairie. Different from Wichita, too. He hadn't seen much of the town before getting a room at the Clarkson, but he'd seen enough to know it offered all of the same vices Wichita had. Gambling and whiskey and women. The same vices that had brought Hagen to ruin the last time around. The same vices that had led to Trammel killing two men, sending them into the wilderness, as Miss Ford had said.

Trammel knew he could make a life for himself in a place like Ogallala. He'd done it in Wichita, so he could do it here. But if it was just about getting a job, he could've gotten one in Dodge City or Newton weeks ago. He reminded himself they had fled for a reason. The Bowman family was still on their trail and weren't apt to let the deaths of their relatives go unanswered. As they were a ranching family, it would be only a matter of time before they found Hagen and Trammel there.

No, Trammel decided. As much as he might've hated the rough going on the trail, they had to keep going. And he'd have to make sure Hagen didn't slip back into his bad habits and put them at risk again. They were Wyoming bound, for good or for ill. The both of them, whether Hagen liked it or not.

He felt sleep begin to pull on him as he thought of Hagen right now, in all his glory as he delivered a wagon full of widows to civilization. The words to an old hymn his mother used to sing came back to him. *I once was lost, but now am found.*

He began to dream about Miss Ford. Not the prettiest woman he had ever seen, not by a long shot, but young. Too young for his taste, nothing like Miss Lilly, but Lilly had never looked at him like that. She'd known too much of the world. Known too much about him.

Sleep took him before he had any other foolish thoughts.

CHAPTER 15

The pounding woke him.

He drew his Colt from his shoulder holster as he sat up and found himself in complete darkness. It took a few seconds for his eyes to adjust to the dim lights from behind the drawn shades for him to remember where he was in his room in the Clarkson Hotel. Ogallala, Nebraska.

He heard the pounding again and realized someone was at the door.

Realizing that he would probably be blinded by the light from the hallway if he opened the door, he cocked his pistol and aimed it at the light. "Who is it?"

"It's me." Trammel recognized it as Hagen's voice. "And I come bearing gifts. Open up."

Trammel tucked the gun back under his arm and got out of bed. He cursed as he tripped over his own boots in the darkness and fell against the door. He unlocked it and opened it, shielding his eyes from the light from the hallway.

Hagen rushed in carrying two plates of food. "God, you're living in complete darkness like some kind of bat. Leave the door open while I find a lamp."

Trammel stood on the other side of the door as he tried to rub the sleep from his eyes. He thought he had been asleep for a few minutes after lying down; maybe a half an hour at most. But he could tell he had been asleep longer than that.

"What time is it?"

"Just past nine in the evening," Hagen said as he struck a match and lit a lamp in the corner. "The day *after* we arrived in town. You've been asleep for more than a day, my friend."

"What?" Trammel shut the door. He was fully awake now. "How's that possible?"

"You're exhausted," Hagen explained. "And for good reason. But don't worry. I had the clerk open the door so I could check on you once or twice to make sure you were still among the living. Alas, you never moved, just snoring the hours away. I decided now might be a good time to wake you up."

Trammel couldn't remember a time he had ever slept so long. Drunk or sober, he'd always gotten up at first light, even back in New York. But now that he was on the trail, he was sleeping more at a time when he could ill afford to do so. "You should've woken me up."

"Why?" Hagen set the lamp on the table where he had placed the food. Two steaks spilled over the sides of the plate. A generous pile of mashed potatoes had been heaped beside them. "You needed your rest, and there was nothing for you to do, anyway. I thought it best for one of us to lie low while the other tended to business."

Trammel remembered the last time he had seen Hagen. He was leading a parade up the street with the women they had rescued. "What business? You getting your name in the papers for bringing those women in alive?"

Hagen grinned as he pulled a couple of chairs to the table. "That was entirely unintended, I assure you. Who would have thought that a wagonload of Quaker women would bring such attention? They insisted that I bring them directly to the church, and as I did, we acquired something of a following." He shrugged. "It couldn't be avoided. Now eat. Your steak is getting cold."

Trammel didn't realize how ravenous he was until he sat down and began to eat. "I hope you didn't tell anyone your real name."

"No," Hagen assured him, "but the attention was unwelcome just the same. I wasn't expecting to need an alias, so I'm afraid I gave two different reporters two different names. I can't even remember which one I gave them; a fact that didn't go unnoticed by the reporters, I'm afraid."

Trammel stopped eating. "That remark I made about the papers was supposed to be a joke."

Hagen laughed. "The funniest jokes are often the truest. I didn't want the attention, Buck. You know I didn't. But once it was foisted upon me, I had no choice but to play along. Ignoring the attention would've only made me more obvious. I didn't mention you, and the ladies refused to speak to anyone before they spoke to their parson or their preacher or whatever they call their cleric. The damage is minimal, but I'm afraid it means that we won't be able to linger in town as long as I had hoped."

Trammel was too hungry to be angry and kept

eating. "Don't tell me you've been spending all this time in church."

"Hardly," Hagen said. "I've had my share of fun. Won a couple of hands at the poker table, too. People are such suckers for celebrity. They all wanted to play with the man who delivered the women from evil." Hagen grinned. "It wasn't even fair. I cleaned them out, and they were happy for the experience. At least it gave us enough money to live on for a few weeks. Speaking of which, we're leaving town right after dinner."

Trammel kept chewing. He was too hungry to care. "Where are we going?"

"We're catching the night train to Laramie."

That was enough to break Trammel's focus on the steak. "You mean we're not riding to Wyoming?"

"On rails, but not horseback," Hagen said. "That was my surprise, Buck. I never had any intention of riding all the way to Wyoming when we can afford passage on a perfectly good train. It departs at midnight, so you can take your time with your meal. I've already arranged for our horses to be loaded. All you need to do is bring your saddle to the livery. As you're the more obvious of the two of us, I've taken the liberty of booking you a private berth. I'll be content in the dining car with the gamblers. Figure I'll keep my hand in at cards while we head back home. Money in the pocket is preferable to money on credit."

"Speaking of which . . ." Trammel started.

But Hagen waved him off. "I've already settled your account here at the hotel, too, 'Mr. Ronan.' I'll give you the money once we're on the train. I'd hoped we could have enjoyed some female companionship before we left town, but, alas, that won't be possible. Well, not for you, anyway. I met a wonderful soiled dove last night. She was—"

Trammel let him talk while he focused on eating. He had put the idea of women out of his mind since he left Lilly back in Wichita. The two of them had never been together, but he had still come to think of themselves as a sort of couple. He had never been sure if she had felt the same way, not until that morning when they had ridden out of town. He wondered if he would ever see her again. He wondered if he wanted to.

Trammel kept eating. "Don't worry about that. I'll make my own way in that regard."

"Yes, I'm sure you will," Hagen observed. "I couldn't help but noticing that you managed to catch the fancy of Miss Ford, though."

"She's a kid."

"She's eighteen, according to her mother, and ready for a husband. She's not the kind of woman that men like you and I are used to, of course, but I'm sure she'd welcome the chance for you to play the role of Moses and part her waters, to borrow a biblical term I know she would appreciate."

But Trammel appreciated the steak more than he appreciated Hagen's references. "You're the one who played Moses in leading them here, not me. And you'd damned well better hope the Bowman clan don't read papers or they'll be back on our trail worse than before."

"Our deliverance to our own promised land is only a few days away by train," Hagen said. "And then—"

The hotel door burst open and three men barged

into the room. Hagen already had his pistol out as Trammel reached for the Colt under his arm, but the sight of three Winchesters leveled at them stopped him.

The stars pinned to the men's dusters calmed him.

The man with the sheriff's star said, "You boys set your guns on the floor and come along nice and peaceful. We don't want no trouble, and I hope you don't, either."

Trammel took his hand away from the Colt and picked up his knife and fork. "I'm in the middle of my supper."

He felt Hagen look at him as the gambler set his pistol on the floor.

The sheriff took another step into the room. "Maybe you don't see too good in the lamplight, boy. Nor hear so good, neither. We're the law in this town, so if we say you move, you move. Supper or no supper."

Trammel dug into his mashed potatoes. "This is the first decent meal I've had in weeks, Sheriff, and I don't plan on having it spoiled by anyone. Law or no law. You've got questions, ask them here. If not, you can stand right there and watch me eat, and we'll join you when we're done. Otherwise, you're just going to have to shoot me and my friend here. I don't think the good people of Ogallala will take too kindly to you gunning down its latest celebrity while the brave man who delivered those holy women from the wilderness is enjoying a peaceful supper."

Hagen slid his pistol away from the table with his foot and resumed eating, too. "He's quite right, Sheriff. I'm unarmed and my large friend here is in the middle of his meal. You've got three Winchesters aimed at us and, given the exalted status I currently enjoy in these parts, I'm sure you can see your way clear to granting us certain accommodations as it pertains to your questioning. If we're anything less than truthful, you can grab us out of our chairs and bring us to jail."

With a mouthful of potatoes, Trammel added, "But I wouldn't advise it. Ask your questions, Sheriff."

Out of the corner of his eye, Trammel could see the sheriff trade glances with his deputies. The three men lowered their rifles. The sheriff motioned to the deputy on his left, who shut the broken door as best he could.

"Name's Sheriff Barnwell," he said, "and I've got a telegram from Charlie Bassett in Dodge City that says two men fitting your descriptions are wanted for questioning in the murder of five men on the trail from Wichita. Now, I know the big fella here is going by the name of Jim Ronan." He looked at Hagen. "But you're going by a couple of names you can't seem to get straight in your own mind. That's why I think you're Buck Trammel and Adam Hagen out of Wichita. You're the same two Charlie Bassett wants held for questioning."

"Out of Wichita?" Hagen gagged. "God forbid. Just because I lived there for a month doesn't mean I'm *from* that ghastly place."

Before Hagen's flowery language make things worse, Trammel said, "We didn't murder anyone, Sheriff. We shot two men who tried to kill us in camp. One said they were working for the Bowman ranch with orders to gun us down on sight. I take it you know what happened in Wichita that made us leave."

Barnwell's chin rose. "I certainly do."

"Good," Trammel said, "then you know Earp practically rode us out of town on a rail to keep the peace with the Bowman clan. We shot the two who tried to sandbag us on the way to Dodge City. You say there's five dead. That means there's five we had nothing to do with."

Hagen chimed in, "Save for the bandits we sent to hell in the service of those poor pilgrim women I brought into town yesterday. Poor lambs."

Barnwell's eyes narrowed. "You mean to tell me you didn't shoot Matt Bowman or the men riding with him?"

Trammel set down his silverware. "Matt Bowman is dead?"

Barnwell nodded. "Him and three of the men who rode with him. His cousin and the rest of their party escaped unharmed."

"The rest of their party?" Trammel repeated. "Who?"

"His cousin Walt Bowman and the men they hired to hunt you down. Leader is known as John Hanover. Goes by the name of—"

"Lefty." Trammel recognized the name. "His left eye is missing."

"So you *do* know him?" Barnwell said. His deputies gripped their rifles a little tighter.

"Of course, I know him," Trammel said. "I'm the one who cost him his eye."

"So there's bad blood between you two," Barnwell stated. "Stands to reason you'd want to kill him."

"Only if he tried killing me first," Trammel said. "I haven't seen Hanover since the night I threw him out of The Gilded Lilly on account of him getting rough with one of the girls who worked there. I threw him out and he stayed out. That was months ago. Heard he lost his eye when a cut above his eyebrow got infected. If anyone wants blood, Sheriff, it's on his side of the ledger, not mine. Besides, Hanover and his friends are saddle tramps. They've been riding the trail from Wichita to Texas since before they could walk. No one could get the jump on them, least of all a drunken gambler and a city boy like me."

"I'm not drunk," Hagen protested. "At least, not too drunk at the moment. Though I've never met this Lefty fellow. Not sure I'd want to play poker with him, though. One-eyed men are bad luck indeed. Tough to read, you know."

Trammel shook his head. Damn Hagen and his mouth. He looked up at Sheriff Barnwell. "I take it the telegraph office is still open?"

"Closed at eight, but I can get it open again. Why?"

"Because I think you should send an urgent wire to Earp in Wichita. He'll back up everything I just told you. If he doesn't, Hagen and I will come along peaceful like you said. If he does, we'll be on our way."

Barnwell traded looks with his deputies again. "You're an awfully confident man, mister. Especially with three Winchesters against you."

"You're the law, aren't you?" Trammel began cutting off another bit of steak. "No reason to be nervous around the law when you're telling the truth. Post your men at our door there and send the wire, Sheriff. You'll have your answers soon enough."

Trammel sensed some of the fight leave the sheriff. "No need, Trammel. I already did that. Bassett didn't buy Hanover's story, even though all of them, including the cousin, swore out a complaint. Bassett said he's got a shopkeeper in Dodge City who says a man fitting Hagen's description bought a lot of supplies from him a week or so *before* Lefty and his bunch came to town. Bassett thinks you boys were too far along the trail to have killed Bowman and his men the way Hanover said. Earp happens to agree."

Trammel knew the answer to his next question, but had to ask anyway. "Then why kick in the door if you already knew the answers?"

Barnwell looked down at his shoes. "Still had to put the question to you, seeing as how it was a sworn complaint and all. We've had some run-ins with Lefty Hanover ourselves here in Ogallala. Never struck us as the types who could be taken on the trail by a drunk and a tenderfoot, either, not even one as big as you."

Hagen smiled as he set his silverware aside and dabbed his mouth with his napkin. "Never have I been more comforted by my own incompetence than I am now." He bowed toward the lawman. "Thank you, Sheriff Barnwell."

Trammel saw some of the rigidity return to the sheriff. He probably didn't understand everything Hagen had just said, and Trammel knew a man like Barnwell didn't like what he didn't understand. He tried to soothe it over by saying, "We'll be happy to write out our statements right here in front of you if it'll make your job easier, Sheriff."

"I usually do that down at the jail."

Trammel decided there was no point in being coy with the man. "I'd like to keep as low a profile as I can until we board the midnight train to Laramie, Sheriff.

Someone sees us going into the jail might remember us. Word might get back to Lefty, and we've ridden too hard for too long to let them catch our trail again."

"You think Hanover's still on your tail?"

"He filed that report with Bassett to get an idea of where we were," Trammel said. "Maybe he reported it to cover his own tracks in the killings. Maybe he still plans on coming after us. Either way, I don't want to take any chances. We'll write the statements for you because you need them, and you've been good to us. We'd appreciate it if you could keep our conversation here just between you and Bassett. Maybe tell him we're not Trammel and Hagen?"

Barnwell told one of his deputies to go down to the clerk's desk and fetch some pens and paper.

"I can't promise Hanover won't pick up your scent," the sheriff said, "given that Hagen here was mentioned in the papers. Those women you rescued are likely to tell someone about you sooner rather than later. But no one will hear it from us, or where you're going, either. You've got my word on that."

Trammel hadn't met Sheriff Barnwell before he'd kicked in the door to his hotel room only a few minutes before, but he could tell the man's word meant something. "Can't ask any more than that, Sheriff."

Barnwell looked at Hagen. "And you better make sure it's written in plain American English. No fancy phrases or the like. The statement won't count if I can't understand the damned thing."

They all jumped when Hagen slapped his hand on the table. "A peaceful resolution is always good for the digestion. I should send for a bottle and celebrate this joyous occasion." He gestured toward the doorway. "If I might be permitted to summon a bottle from the bar."

"No thanks," Barnwell said. "My men and I don't drink on duty."

Hagen smiled. "Funny. The thought of offering you any never crossed my mind."

CHAPTER 16

Hagen struggled to keep up with Trammel's long strides as they walked through the darkness toward the train. Even carrying his saddle and rifles, he was still impossibly fast for a man his size. "I don't see why you're so cross, Buck."

"That damned mouth of yours is going to get me killed," Trammel said.

"We're free, aren't we? Heading to Laramie, just as I planned?"

"Antagonizing Barnwell like that could've gotten us locked up or shot."

Hagen was taken back by Trammel's anger, especially after what had happened. "You're annoyed about my antagonizing him? You defied the man in your underwear!"

"But I didn't make him feel like an ignorant fool," Trammel said. "You did. From now on, if there's law around, best to let me do the talking."

Hagen had never been one to enjoy rebuke. He hadn't enjoyed it from his father or his superiors at West Point or while in the army, either. But his friends were a different matter entirely and, after all they had endured together, he had come to think of Buck Trammel as a friend.

"Perhaps that would be for the best," Hagen agreed. He decided to change the tenor of their conversation, given that they still had quite a bit of a walk to the train and Hagen abhorred silence. "You know, you really impressed me back there. The way you handled the sheriff, I mean."

"Didn't do it to impress you or anyone. Just didn't want to miss this train."

"Neither do I," Hagen said. "Still, you showed remarkable grace under a different kind of fire. You had him turned from the moment you defied him. That was very quick thinking on your part."

Trammel didn't break his stride. "I didn't live this long in this line of work by being stupid, Hagen. I might not be able to ride or shoot or talk as well as you, but I can handle myself in most circumstances just fine. And I'll go on that way as long as you can keep that tongue of yours in your head still."

In another time and place, Adam Hagen would've bristled at the man's ingratitude. He had saved his life on the trail several times. He had kept him alive by procuring goods and keeping them on the right trail away from Bowman and his men.

But this wasn't another time or place. They were in Ogallala, and they had been through quite a bit together. They had fought side by side and, he remembered, Trammel had saved his life on more than one occasion.

Adam Hagen knew he was a man of many faults, but ingratitude had never been one of them. "I will."

Trammel stopped walking. "That's it? Just 'I will'?"

Hagen was completely confused. "Yes. What do you want me to say?"

Trammel resumed his pace. "That's the shortest answer I've ever heard from you. Maybe you should've bought another bottle back at the hotel after all. Have myself a celebration to mark the occasion."

"Sarcasm is quite unbecoming," Haden said, but left it at that. If anyone had earned the right to be sarcastic to him, it was Buck Trammel.

At the station, Hagen showed the conductor the two tickets he had purchased the day before. The fat man looked at the two men, then at the tickets. "Which one of you is Mitchell?"

Hagen spoke up, as it was he who purchased the tickets and invented the names to write on them. "That would be my large companion here."

The conductor handed Trammel one of the tickets. "You're in private coach 'C.' Step on here and someone will show you to your berth." He looked at the saddle and rifles Trammel was carrying. "I encourage you to check them with the porter. They'll be perfectly safe with the horses."

"That encouragement an order?" Trammel asked.

"Not at all."

Trammel picked up his rig and hoisted it on his shoulder. "Good."

The conductor shook his head at the passenger's stubbornness as he handed the other ticket to Hagen. "Your seat's at the back of the train, but I've got a feeling you'll be in the salon car most of the trip."

Hagen slipped the ticket into his pocket. "Now why would you ever think that?"

The fat man walked away and tended to another group of passengers walking down the platform.

"He has your sense of humor," Hagen said to Trammel.

Trammel didn't laugh. "When do you want to meet up again?"

"We've no set schedule," Hagen said. "Just enjoy the ride and get off when we come to Laramie. We'll collect our horses and ride to Blackstone from there. It's less than half a day's ride north. If all works out, our days of living on the trail are well behind us."

"And if it doesn't work out?" Trammel asked. "If your old man doesn't treat you like the prodigal son."

Hagen couldn't bring himself to entertain such a notion but didn't blame Trammel for doing so. "If that's the case, it's like you said. You're not stupid. Neither am I. We'll figure something out."

He ignored Trammel's grumbling as he watched the big man climb onto the train.

CHAPTER 17

Lefty allowed the telegram to sit on the table a long time before he even looked at it again.

"Well," Skinner prodded. "You going to tell us what it says?"

"It says that the sheriff in Ogallala doesn't think it's Hagen," Lefty finally told them. "Or Trammel. Says the descriptions weren't close enough to confirm it was them. Said he's mailing their sworn statements to Bassett on the next post."

Hooch finished his whiskey and poured himself another. "Well, I guess that's that."

Lefty glared at him with his one good eye. "That's *nothin'*."

"That's right," Parrot repeated. "That's nothing!"

Lefty pulled out the newspaper article he had torn out of yesterday's paper. The headline read "Moses of the Plains." The article detailed how a single man saved a group of Quaker women from an army of bandits who sought to sell the women into slavery.

He slapped the article next to the telegram. "That's why 'that ain't that,' damn you."

Chico looked at the newsprint, though he couldn't

read. "That the article you found on that man who saved them ladies?"

"It is," Lefty told him, "and there's no way in hell a man who looks like Hagen could've rescued all those women by himself. That meant he had help, someone who kept himself hidden on account of him being so memorable. A man like Hagen can't help but play it loud. A man like Trammel doesn't like attention. And I'm wagering he did just that."

Lefty looked at Hooch. "You're the gambler of the group. What are the odds that the sheriff finds two men matching Trammel and Hagen in the same town at exactly the same amount of time it'd take them to get up to Ogallala?"

Hooch shrugged. "Pretty steep, but hell, Lefty, we've made better time than they did, and that was on a cattle drive."

"So they were slower," Lefty said, "but stumbling upon them women slowed them down some. I'm telling you boys that the sheriff found Trammel and Hagen and let them go. I don't know why, but I'm telling you it's them. I can feel it in my bones, and that feeling's never let you boys down before, now has it?"

"Has it?" Parrot repeated.

The men all looked at each other, save for Walt, whose head was on the table. The boy had been in a stupor since they had ridden into town weeks ago.

"Okay," Skinner said. "Maybe it's them. Let's say you're right and it *is* them. What good will it do to keep goin' after them like we've been doin'?"

He looked around and lowered his voice. "Hooch might be the gambler here, but it don't take a gambler to appreciate the odds and to know when it's time to quit while we're ahead. We already got the law believing that they killed Bowman and the others. We've got their money, which is running mighty low right now, so what more do you want?"

Chico said, "Maybe it's time we let things take their course, Lefty. We've had ourselves a hell of a time here, but I miss Texas. I miss cowpunchin' and all the fun we used to have. I say we fall in with an outfit heading back to Wichita and hire on drivin' cattle again."

Hooch added, "Ogallala's a long way from here, Lefty. And who knows where they went from there? They could've gotten on a horse or bought a train ticket to anywhere by now. They could be back east or out west. Hell, we ain't never been to any of them places. I'm of a mind that we ought to go back to doin' what we do best and leave Trammel and Hagen to God or the Devil, whoever gets 'em first."

Lefty might have only had one good eye, but he could see the agreement settling over them. Except for Parrot, of course. They had talked about this behind his back. They had come to a decision, despite his best efforts to keep them from doing so.

He had always known this day would come. The day when he found himself on the opposite side of them. It was bound to happen. It was the curse of leadership. He'd heard old sailors talk about it before down in Texas.

Mutiny.

He fought the urge to draw and gun them all down where they sat. Not because he didn't think he could kill them and not because of all the miles they had ridden together. No, he didn't kill them because he needed them.

And he needed them because they were going to Ogallala. Because that no-good Trammel had taken his eye and there was no way he could go on living with himself as long as that man was alive.

He decided to reach a compromise. "You boys want to punch cattle again? Fine. We can sign on with an outfit heading up to Ogallala."

The three of them looked at each other. Parrot kept looking out the window, waiting for a random bit of conversation to strike him to repeat. Walt Bowman remained slumped forward in his chair and drooled on the table.

As Lefty expected, Hooch spoke first. "I'd say that's a good idea, except that most of the outfits that have driven this far are all full up with hands. Hell, just look around this place. You can't spit in here without hitting a puncher on a drive."

Lefty grinned. "Then I guess we'll have to make some vacancies, now won't we?" He looked over at the table to his right. The five men drinking there were already slurring and hadn't taken the time to slap the dust from their clothes. He launched a stream of tobacco at the closest man's boots, but he hardly noticed.

Lefty decided on another way to get their attention. "Any of you boys riding north to Ogallala?"

Chapter 18

Trammel didn't like the side-eye he was receiving from the assistant conductor. "Something on your mind?"

"No, sir," the skinny man said. "Just wondering why you've decided to bring your saddle and rifle into your cabin. Most of our customers are content with securing their rifles in the livery car."

"I'm not most of your customers," Trammel said, "and there's no law against it."

"Of course, sir. As you wish. Just irregular is all."

Trammel looked down at the man. "Anything about me strike you as normal?"

"No, can't say that it does. Takes all kinds in this world, I suppose." When they reached his cabin, the conductor opened the door. "Here you are, sir. Plenty of room, even for a big man like you. If there's anything I can do to make your trip more comfortable, just ask."

Trammel set his rifle on the bunk. During his time with the Pinkerton Agency, he had spent time on some private cars before, but never a cabin. He was pleasantly surprised by how spacious it was; large enough for not only a bed, but also a cushioned bench and chair.

"As a matter of fact, there is something you can do for me," Trammel said. "You see that little guy I was talking to on the platform just now?"

"I would describe him more as having an average build, sir, but yes, I saw him. What about him?"

"You boys run a card game on this train?"

The conductor cleared his throat. "Well, not an official one, of course, but our customers have been known to begin a game on their own to help pass the time. No real money is exchanged, of course. It's purely for enjoyment, you see."

Trammel admired the conductor's attempt at respectability, either for himself or for the sake of his railroad. "He's got a habit of getting himself into trouble at the card table. If he does, I'll expect you to come fetch me to get him out of it before it gets out of hand. Me and only me, understand? No one else, not even the head conductor."

"I understand clearly, sir." The man cleared his throat again and rocked up on his tiptoes as he smiled at Trammel. The native New Yorker knew what the conductor was waiting for. He was looking for a tip.

Trammel bent to whisper directly into the man's ear. "You'll get money if you live up to your end of the deal. And if you don't, if something happens to him and you forget to tell me, I swear to Christ that I'll throw you off this train while it's moving. Understand?"

"Perfectly, sir. Forgive me."

Trammel slammed the coach door as the conductor scurried away. He laughed to himself as he sat on the bed and pulled off his boots. Being his size wasn't always easy, but every so often, it was fun.

Trammel wasn't laughing when a frantic rapping at the cabin door woke him out of a dead sleep in pitch darkness. He'd meant to put his head down for only a moment before dinner, but given the darkness of his cabin, he realized he must have been asleep for much longer than that. "Who is it?"

"It's Farber, sir," came a harsh whisper. "The assistant conductor. You need to come quickly. I think your friend is in some distress."

"Thanks." Trammel cursed as he felt for his boots in the darkness before finding them. "I'll be along in a minute."

"Sooner, if possible, sir. Your friend is in quite a bit of trouble."

Trammel pulled on his second boot and cursed again as he stumbled to find the door.

He could hear the commotion before he entered the dining car. Through the train doors, he saw Hagen sitting alone at a card table while three other men were standing over him.

As he followed the conductor between the cars, he heard the larger of the three men, "You are a lousy cheat and a damned liar."

Trammel closed his eyes. *Where have I heard that before?*

"Everybody just calm down," Trammel pushed his way past the conductor. "What's going on here?"

The loudmouth glared at him. He was a lanky man who had the look of the gambler about him despite the plain suit he wore. Trammel pegged him for a cattleman or a railroader who'd recently made good. "This is none of your concern."

"This man is my concern," Trammel told him. "What're you accusing him of?"

"Thievery," said a second man. He was in a suit, too, but it didn't fit him quite so well. "It's plain and simple. The sorehead here was losing all night, letting the pot build up before he pulls a full house out of nowhere. Broke every one of us."

The third man nodded in quiet assent. He seemed content to let the other two do his arguing for him.

Trammel looked down at Hagen. He couldn't remember what aliases they were supposed to be using, so he avoided using his name. "This true?"

"Superior strategy isn't cheating," Hagen said. "I lulled them into thinking I was a poorer player than I was, but I didn't cheat. I offered to submit to a full search to prove I am not hiding any cards. They are angry their own gullibility got the better of them."

Trammel looked at the lanky man who had been doing all of the complaining. "That true?"

"Sure, he submits to a search now, after he wins. What about before? He could've been holding on to a paint card all this time without us knowing."

Trammel looked at the two other players. "Anyone notice anything funny in the card play before my friend here broke the bank?"

He looked at each of them in turn, even the loudmouth. None of them said a word.

He hadn't expected them to. "You boys have a dealer or did you change who was dealing the cards?"

The lanky man pointed at the conductor. "He was dealing the cards on account of his impartiality."

"Any of you object to him searching my friend here in front of you? See if he's got an extra deck or maybe a few cards stashed away?"

None of them objected, so Trammel stepped aside and let the conductor get to work. Hagen stood slowly and held his hands up while the conductor patted him down. He turned out every pocket he could find. He took off Hagen's coat and shook it out before laying it on the table and searching the pockets and the lining. "Nothing here," he pronounced, before patting down Hagen's pants and shoes and vest coat once again.

When he was done, the conductor stood up. "I'm sorry, gentlemen, but as you can see, this man wasn't holding back any cards. I couldn't find anything on him and neither could any of you. I have no choice but to give him the money he's won fair and square."

Hagen lifted his jacket from the table and began to put it on. "I'm sorry to have upset you gentlemen, but poker's as much about the cards you're dealt as it is about the men you're playing. I can understand how you might've thought I was cheating, but—"

The lanky man grabbed Hagen's arm before he pulled the jacket on. "Wait just a damned minute. Check them sleeves again."

"I . . . I already checked them," the conductor stammered. "You saw me check them. There's nothing there, sir. Nothing at all. He outplayed you, plain and simple."

The lanky man began to pull Hagen across the table. Trammel fired a straight right hand that broke his grip and sent the big man sprawling backward into the crowd of passengers who had gathered to watch the confrontation. The man was out cold before he hit the carpeted floor of the salon car.

Hagen resumed putting on his coat. "Nothing quite so uncouth as a sore loser."

Trammel stepped past him and moved toward the man he had just knocked out. He took a knee and began going through his pockets. He wanted to know if the man was carrying any weapons he might need to worry about later on. It was still a long ride to Laramie, and an armed man with a grudge could prove to be a problem.

He threw open the man's coat and froze. A .38 Colt hung from beneath his left arm. A shoulder rig, just like the one Trammel wore. A cold feeling began to spread through him as he continued patting the man's pockets until he found what he feared he would find. In the inside pocket of his waistcoat, there was a thin, black leather wallet.

He opened the wallet and saw the identification card saying his name. Jesse Alcott—Pinkerton National Detective Agency.

Trammel closed his eyes and hung his head. Of all the people on the train that Hagen could have played cards with, much less cause Trammel to punch, it had to be an operative from Trammel's old detective agency.

Trammel couldn't remember anyone named Jesse Alcott from his time at the agency, but that was hardly remarkable. The organization had hundreds of operatives all over the country. He hadn't been with the organization long enough to meet them all. He wondered if anyone had.

But once Alcott woke up, he'd remember the fancy gambler he believed had cheated him and the giant of a man who had laid him out cold. Trammel hadn't left the agency on the best or quietest of terms. Reports of Alcott's misfortune were certain to reach the ears of Mr. Allan personally, and that may or may not prove to be a further inconvenience to Buck Trammel.

Trammel stuffed the thin wallet back into Alcott's vest pocket. He stood up and glared at the spectators until they gradually melted away to wherever they had been before the melee broke out. Even the gamblers disappeared, leaving Hagen, Trammel, and the conductor alone near the table piled with money.

Trammel asked the conductor, "What station is he supposed to get off at?"

"T . . . the next stop." The conductor fumbled as he pulled his pocket watch from his vest and opened it. "We'll be there in two hours. More than a day before your stop, sir."

Trammel grabbed several greenbacks from Hagen's pile and stuffed it into the conductor's pocket. "Let's keep that to ourselves. Get this man ready and off this train at his assigned stop. I don't want him hanging around, understand?"

"Yes, sir. I understand. I'll see to it. You can count on me."

Hagen protested when Trammel swiped another bill and stuffed it into the conductor's pocket. "Let's keep it that way."

He came around the table and took Hagen by the arm. "Let's go."

The gambler scooped up the greenbacks in his arms as he stumbled forward. "But I have silver on the table I need to collect."

Trammel blocked his way and shoved him toward his sleeper coach. "Leave it. You've won enough for one night. And probably caused us enough trouble for a lifetime."

Trammel sat in a chair in the doorway of his coach; keeping an eye on the passageway as Hagen whispered, "I don't know why you don't just let me keep watch and you go to bed. It's my fight anyway."

"Because that man who grabbed you was a Pinkerton man." Trammel moved his Colt from one hand to the other to stay alert. "And when he wakes up, he's not going to be happy."

"A Pinkerton man?" Hagen repeated. "Did you know him?"

"No."

"Do you think he recognized you?"

Hagen's questions were beginning to annoy him. "He didn't at first, but he might now. I had a reputation at the agency, and he's bound to put two and two together if he gets wind of our being questioned back in Ogallala. And when word about this reaches the home office in Chicago, the agency may figure out it was me."

Hagen propped up his pillow. "Don't be dramatic. How likely is that?"

"Damned likely." Trammel kept his eyes on the

passageway. "The railroads are the Pinkerton Agency's bread and butter. That loudmouth Alcott was most likely assigned to keep the peace on the train while he was on his way to some destination or another. He might not want anyone knowing about this, but someone in the home office will. And when they do, they'll have a good line on where I am."

"Are they looking for you?"

"I don't know." Trammel kept watching the passageway. "I didn't wait around long enough to find out. We didn't part on the best of terms."

Trammel hoped Hagen let it go at that and was glad he did. "So your plan is to shoot him before he gets the chance?" Hagen asked. "Murder doesn't suit you, Buck. You're not the type."

"I'll only shoot him if he comes down here with a gun before he steps off the train. I damaged his pride and that's not going to sit well with him, especially him being a Pinkerton man."

Hagen continued to explain how paranoid he was when Trammel noticed a shadow at the end of the passageway. He'd never put much stock in shadows, but given the size of this one, he knew it was either the conductor or Alcott.

He shifted the Peacemaker to his right hand and waited.

The shadow flattened as the man who owned it rounded the corner.

It was Jesse Alcott of the Pinkerton National Detective Agency.

He stopped at the end of the passageway when he saw Trammel sitting with the Peacemaker in the doorway of his coach. He was careful not to aim the pistol at Alcott. He didn't want to start any trouble, but he intended on finishing any that came his way.

Beneath the bandage across his face, Trammel could see Alcott's eyes had already begun to blacken from the broken nose. He wondered if whoever had patched him up had been skilled enough to set the cartilage properly. Trammel's nose had been broken several times, and he knew how much it hurt. He knew how much it could blur a man's vision, and he hoped Alcott's vision was too blurry to start any trouble.

Trammel didn't like the way the man just stood at the other end of the train car, so he decided to spur some conversation. "You lost, Alcott?"

"You know my name," the Pinkerton man said. "Guess it's only fair, seeing as how I know yours. Your real name, that is. Not that fiction you wrote on your ticket. Buck Trammel as I live and breathe."

"Can't be breathing too well through all the packing in your nose." He lowered the Peacemaker a hair. "As for living, that's up to you."

Even from that distance, he could see Alcott grin in the dim light of the sleeper car. "I'm alive and well, and I intend on staying that way. I'm not fool enough to go up against a man who's got the drop on me. For now."

"For now and forever," Trammel said. "I don't want to shoot you, Alcott. You strike me as a good man who got a little heated over a game of cards. You got rough with my friend, and I did what I had to do. I'm willing to call it even if you are."

He saw Alcott's fists ball at his side. "And if I'm not?"

"Then the next time I see you, things will have a different ending."

Alcott's booming laugh filled the car. He wondered how many people in the other berths could hear them. He wondered how much they'd heard and if they'd remember his name, too. There wasn't much he could do about that now. He had enough to worry about with the big man at the other end of the car.

Alcott stopped laughing. "Yes, I believe it will end different, Trammel. Much different indeed."

Trammel felt the train begin to slow as it approached the station. He lowered the Winchester enough so that it was pointed in Alcott's general direction. "Looks like your stop, Jesse. Wouldn't want to miss it, would you?"

Alcott touched the brim of his bowler hat. "I'll be seeing you, Trammel. Real soon."

"Give my best to Mr. Pinkerton when you get back to the home office. Make sure you tell him I sent my regards to Joan."

Alcott stepped back around the corner.

Trammel kept the Peacemaker aimed down the passageway until the train pulled out of the station. He didn't think Alcott could've wired ahead for any colleagues to meet him here at the station, but only a fool would take a Pinkerton man lightly.

He was surprised when Hagen spoke from the window. "We're clear, Buck. He walked into the station building and never came out again. Though I must say, you know the most interesting people."

Trammel stood up, pulled the chair back inside and shut the door. "You and that damned mouth of yours. But you're right about one thing." He set the rifle on the bunk and sat beside it. "I didn't get much sleep last night. You can sleep on the bench over there. And try not to get us killed before we reach Laramie."

Chapter 19

Trammel was glad to leave the controlled chaos of Laramie, Wyoming, behind them. When he and Hagen had first collected their horses upon stepping off the train, he feared Hagen would be drawn in by the town's lively nature. He had heard of Laramie before, of course, but wished he had known how nice it was beforehand. He might have come here instead of Wichita and saved himself a lot of problems in the bargain.

Laramie was a hive of all sorts of activity with wagonloads of goods and crops and freighters from all over coming to and from the train station. The streets were packed with bankers and lawyers and businesspeople and ladies of all types on their way to various places.

He thought the cackles and cheers from the dozens of saloons and gambling halls that lined the town's streets would be too much for Hagen to resist, especially after all they had endured on the trail to Ogallala and since.

But Hagen had been uncharacteristically quiet

that last day on board the train. It seemed the closer he got to home, the less he wanted to speak. He simply looked out the window at the scenery rolling by. Trammel wasn't complaining. It was the first time he could remember Hagen keeping quiet since their short association began back in Wichita. It seemed a lifetime ago. Trammel was beginning to enjoy the silence, even though he didn't understand it.

Which was why he quietly followed Hagen out of town once they collected their horses and gear. He didn't even ask if they were heading straight to his family's place up north. Judging by the position of the sun when they rode away from town, Trammel figured that was exactly where they were heading.

The busy distractions of Laramie quickly fell away as the two men rode the trail north. Most towns he had seen in this part of the world ebbed away slowly. A blacksmith or a livery or a rundown whorehouse often stood on the edges between town and wilderness. But Laramie had itself hemmed in well. Even the smell of beer and whiskey and baked bread and fireplaces stopped as soon as they left town. The trail north to Blackstone bore no hint of civilization save for the dead, trampled grass and wheel ruts of a well-traveled road.

Such sights made Trammel feel a bit better about where they were going. He hadn't asked Hagen many details about his hometown as he sensed it was one of the few topics his friend did not wish to discuss. Did Blackstone have a town worth mentioning or just a scattering of buildings at the foot of his father's ranch? He had once asked Hagen what they would do if his father turned him away. He hadn't given Trammel much of an answer.

Trammel knew there wasn't much he could do about the elder Hagen's reception of his son returning home. He just hoped Blackstone was enough of a town to have a decent hotel. He judged they might need it if Adam's homecoming was met with a closed fist instead of open arms.

It was then, as they rode the straight trail northward, that Buck Trammel's thoughts turned to the idea of his own future. He had never planned to venture farther west than Kansas. He'd never really planned on venturing at all. He'd been happy as a policeman back in New York, but the money offered by the Pinkerton Agency had been too great for him to pass up. He joined their ranks in the hopes of seeing the country while saving up enough money to afford a set of rooms along Washington Square or perhaps in one of the newer places they were planning for the swamplands along the Hudson River. Returning to New York had always been in his mind, but a return to a different part of the city that was as far away from the death and squalor of Five Points as possible.

But when the Pinkerton Agency sent him mostly to Chicago and Cleveland and other places along the railroad to break strikers, his dreams of a grand return to New York began to fade. And the moment he struck his supervisor after refusing to beat a starving striker to death in Cleveland, that vision evaporated along with his career at the agency. His plans, vague though they were, had then turned west, where a man could lose himself for a time while he decided what he might do with the rest of his life.

Trammel had decided Wichita was as good a place as any to wait for inspiration to strike him. Maybe a drunk with a gun would make his decision for him one night at The Gilded Lilly. But when a quick death had not come, Trammel had begun to allow himself to think about finally settling down with Lilly if she'd have him.

But in all of his limited planning, Trammel never thought life would lead him to Hagen and to the deeply rutted road to Blackstone, Wyoming, just north of Laramie, with a trail of dead men behind him and a vengeful one-eyed man on his tail.

Yes, Trammel wondered what kind of welcome Adam Hagen would receive at his father's house. His mother's teachings from the Good Book came back to him. Would he be the prodigal son or the Judas goat?

Trammel reined in when Hagen suddenly stopped where the road split. He remained behind the gambler, knowing he must have stopped for reasons of his own. He watched him looking ahead as if deciding which road to take. Trammel saw no reason to speak, so he kept his silence.

Their mounts seemed grateful for the stoppage and were content to nose the grass around them.

After a time, Hagen looked back in Trammel's direction. "Thank you."

"For what?"

"For more than I could repay, but mostly for your silence just now." The gambler nodded to the left trail. "That way leads to the town of Blackstone. It's not Wichita or Laramie, God knows, but it has a quaint charm of its own. It's a midway point for herds coming down from the north and west on their way to Laramie. Some of the smaller outfits pen their cattle in Blackstone while they ride to Laramie to negotiate a price. It's hardly Eden, but it doesn't hold a candle to Dodge City."

Then Hagen looked at the trail to his right. "This way leads to Blackstone Ranch. My home, or at least it used to be. If you stand high in your stirrups, you just might see the outline of the black stone outcropping that gives the town and ranch its name. There are other roads to the ranch, of course, but this was where Father decided the main road would lead. Unfortunately, a ridge of black rock barred his way. Not one to be deterred by Mother Nature or anything else, he used his influence to arrange to have the railroad men blow up enough of the ridge to allow the road to go through. It's even been given its own name, Stone Gate, and is used by Father and other ranchers as a chokepoint where they can get a more accurate count of their cattle. Leave it to Father to put an act of defiance to his benefit."

Trammel had to admit he was interested in meeting this man. "Let's just hope his attitude toward you has softened over the years."

"I've no idea of the welcome we might receive there," Hagen admitted. "Or what you might receive, for that matter. Father is an unpredictable man and may not want either of us under his roof. One of us or both of us might find ourselves in town tonight and for the foreseeable future."

"Anything beats Ogallala," Trammel said. He'd hoped his attempt at humor might make his friend smile.

But Hagen didn't smile. He just kept looking at the two diverging trails. "The proverbial fork in the road. How Shakespearean. Everything in my soul tells me to ride into town, gets us rooms, and ride to see Father tomorrow. But I know the same reasons that drove me from this place will prevent me from doing that. Tomorrow will continue to be an option until chance brings us together. Father would eventually find out I'm there, of course, and in a day or two, the confrontation I dread would be upon us anyway. I wouldn't have to do anything. It would just happen whether I wanted it to or not."

Trammel watched his friend looking at both roads before him. Hagen had grown in his estimation on the road from Wichita. He'd proven to be more than just the gambler who drank himself into oblivion each night in The Gilded Lilly.

He had been content to keep his silence when they had first stopped, but now felt compelled to answer a question his friend had not asked, but didn't have to. "Seems to me that you had no choice the last time you were told to leave, but you've got a choice now. This time, you're returning on your own terms. That makes the difference."

Hagen smiled. "That choice was made for me at gunpoint in Kansas."

"Nope. That might've been what led us here, but it's up to you to decide which road we take. There's a town due west of here where we could put up for a day or two. There's a whole lot of country between that town and the Pacific Ocean. Lots of other towns in between, too. Now, we can ride up to your father's place or we can head into town. The choice is yours, but it is a choice. Your choice."

Hagen turned in the saddle to face him. His eyes were red, and his cheeks were damp. "You're quite a philosopher for a copper."

"Our secret. Now choose."

Hagen turned back in the saddle and pulled his horse right. Toward home.

Trammel followed.

CHAPTER 20

Trammel could hardly believe his eyes when they rode through the rocky outcropping known as Stone Gate and saw the trail break through the tree line. A vast field spilled out before him dotted with fence posts on either side of the trail. On the left, large black dots he pegged for cattle grazed in tall grass for as far as the eye could see. To the right side of the trail, more horses than he had ever seen in one place roamed a pasture of their own.

On a rise in the distance, a huge stone house with eight gables loomed over the valley below it; framed by the snowcapped Laramie Mountains beyond. Gray clouds parted, bathing the scene with shafts of gentle sunlight.

It was the most majestic sight Buck Trammel had ever seen. He had never held out much hope of reaching Heaven and therefore hadn't wasted much time pondering what it might look like. But if he had, he imagined the place would be hard pressed to look any more beautiful than this.

He realized Hagen was looking at him. "I wish I had a photographer on hand to capture the expression on your face. Majestic, isn't it?"

That was the word that had eluded Trammel. *Majestic.* "Yeah. It is."

"Come, let's see what greeting Father has in store for us."

They rode beneath an iron gate that, Trammel imagined, bore the Blackstone Ranch brand, a "B" with two bars on either side of it. He imagined the bars represented two streams or rivers that fed the ranch its water.

The trail became more of a roadway the closer they got to the ranch, becoming completely devoid of grass or weeds in exchange for compacted dirt. The animals on each side ignored the men and horses as they passed by. Trammel saw a brook that wrapped around the pasture, allowing the animals on both sides of the road plenty of water from which to drink. A small stone bridge spanned the brook and led to the main house he judged was half a mile beyond.

Yet, even from there, he saw three riders approaching at a hard clip.

Hagen kept his horse moving at a steady pace, so Trammel did likewise.

"That will be Father," Hagen said, "if he's still alive. One of my brothers is likely to be with him. Perhaps both. They're not exactly pleasant, but I doubt they've matched Father in terms of fortitude. He's likely to be gruff with us, so I must ask your indulgence in advance."

"I've got manners, Hagen."

"Father could test the manners of a saint," Hagen said. "I'd like to avoid shooting him if possible, no matter what insults he may throw at us. I'd appreciate it if you could keep that infamous temper of yours in check during our visit."

Trammel was grateful for the warning. "I'll keep it in mind."

As the three riders drew nearer, Trammel had no problem picking out which one was Mr. Hagen. He was the one in the middle, in front of the other two riders. He reminded Trammel of photographs he had seen of J. Pierpont Morgan in the New York papers over the years. But where Morgan was built thin on the top and fat on the bottom like a bowling pin, Mr. Hagen had a broad, compact build. He rode as straight as a general on horseback and with all the power Trammel assumed would come with such an office. In his short time in the West, Trammel had seen men who took on the appearance of the land they worked. In this case, he knew this land had been changed to reflect the man who lorded over it. King Charles Hagen.

The three riders came to a short halt in front of them as Hagen and Trammel pulled their mounts to a stop. A mist of dirt and dust blew over the two visitors. Trammel resisted the urge to cough.

Charles Hagen looked over the two men who had just ridden onto his land. His lean, clean-shaven face bore deep lines. His dark eyes burned beneath the wide brim of his black hat. The silver hatband and white hair beneath it did nothing to soften his stern appearance.

He looked at Trammel and edged his mount closer to him until they were only a few feet apart. Trammel had to control his sorrel to keep it from moving away.

"Who the hell are you?"

"Buck Trammel, sir."

"He's a good friend of mine, Father," Hagen said. His voice was small.

Mr. Hagen's eyes never left Trammel. "I'm talking to him, not you, boy." His tone told Trammel he was now talking to him. "What are you doing here?"

"I'm here at your son's invitation," Trammel told him. "We've come a long way together."

"Yes," Mr. Hagen sneered. "I'm sure you have. What hellhole did he find you in?"

"Wichita, sir." He didn't know why he kept calling this surly old cuss "sir." It just seemed to fit. "In Kansas."

"I know where Wichita is." The old man kept eyeing him. "And I know what it is, too. Where exactly did you two meet? I know it wasn't at a church meeting."

Hagen said, "It's a long story, Father. One much better told in front of a warm fire."

But Mr. Hagen's eyes still hadn't left Trammel. "All these years and you still haven't learned to keep your mouth shut 'til spoken to, have you, boy?"

Trammel saw no reason to lie. "I met your son while I was working at a place called The Gilded Lilly."

"Whorehouse, I take it," he sneered.

"Gambling hall, mostly. But there were rooms upstairs for the sporting ladies, yes."

"Figured as much." He seemed to sit a little taller in the saddle, as if that was possible, content he had been correct. "What bait did Adam use to bring you here, Mr. Trammel? Promise of a job? Money?"

"His friendship. That's all."

"I sincerely doubt that." Mr. Hagen looked Trammel up and down. "Fella your size working in a whorehouse. Must be some kind of pimp."

Trammel felt his neck begin to redden. "I sat in a lookout chair overseeing the gambling tables. Had a shotgun over my lap most nights. Never was a pimp and never plan on being one." He nudged his sorrel closer to Mr. Hagen's mount. "Never had anyone accuse me of being one, either."

"Well, someone just did, mister. Me."

Trammel gripped the reins a little tighter. "And for the last time."

He sensed the two men behind Mr. Hagen tense. He didn't care. He knew where they were. He figured Hagen could take care of them if the iron came out and the lead started flying.

"You're on my land, boy, and I can talk to anyone on my land any damned way I please."

"Anyone but me."

Mr. Hagen's eyes changed. The fire remained, but shifted somehow. Trammel didn't know if that meant he was about to go for the gun on his hip or backhand him for insolence. Trammel was ready to stop him either way.

Mr. Hagen looked in Adam's direction, but not at him. "How long you been riding, boy?"

"Just from Laramie, Father. We took the train from Ogallala."

The elder Hagen glanced at their horses. Trammel imagined a glance from him was as detailed as a full examination from any veterinarian. "These mounts are in poor shape. Gentry here will see to them while you eat. After that, we'll see."

Adam Hagen looked like a boy as he spoke to his father. "Thank you for your kindness, Father. I wasn't expecting—"

But Mr. Hagen pulled his horse around and began

riding back up toward the house. His two men rode with him.

Buck inched his mount next to Adam's. "Friendly old geezer, isn't he."

"We seem to have caught him on a good day. He didn't shoot us. Come and welcome to my home."

Trammel followed him at a good trot up to the road to the main house. He wasn't sure if Hagen had been joking about his father, but something told him that he wasn't.

Chapter 21

Trammel felt uneasy in the large leather chair near the living room fireplace. The inside of the main house was every bit as grand as he had expected it to be. It put the lobbies of the finest hotels he had seen in New York and Chicago to shame.

Thick wooden beams towered over the main room, and oak paneling adorned every wall save for the massive stone fireplace that dominated the room. The chairs and the settees were all heavy leather, and the brass lamps on the wall cast a soft light in the dark room. He hadn't realized how cold he was until the warmth of the fireplace reached him.

Adam Hagen sat on the sofa, as expectant as a student waiting for his teacher to arrive. Trammel had never seen the flamboyant man so small and it wasn't just because of the size of the furniture. His father's presence dominated every inch of the house even though they hadn't seen the old man since they had arrived.

Both Hagen and Trammel came to their feet when

a pretty blonde woman in a frilly pink dress entered the room. "Remember me, Adam?"

"Elena!" Hagen exclaimed as he jumped to his feet and took her in his arms.

She wrapped her arms around his shoulders as he lifted her. "God, it's good to see you again, my brother. It's been so long."

Trammel found himself rising to his feet before he realized it. Her long golden hair swayed as Hagen rocked her back and forth. Even as tears streamed down the porcelain skin of her face, Trammel was convinced she was the most beautiful woman he had ever seen.

"Let me get a look at you," Hagen said as he held her at arm's length. "Good God, look at how you've grown."

"Fifteen years will have that effect on a woman," she laughed as she wiped away her tears with the back of her hand. "You've changed some, too, Adam. Taller and much more handsome. Have to do something about this, though." She pulled at the Vandyke beard under his mouth. "Is that how they look in the fancy salons back east, brother?"

"It's been so long since I've been there, I wouldn't know." Hagen hugged her again as he looked back at Trammel. "Close your mouth, Buck. You'll let the horseflies in."

Trammel hadn't realized he was gaping and quickly closed his mouth.

Hagen said, "I've been away so long that I've forgotten my manners. Miss Eleanor Hagen, allow me to present my great friend Mr. Buck Trammel of New York City. Mr. Trammel, my sister Eleanor."

"But everyone calls me Elena." She curtsied. "Mother thought it sounded much more sophisticated."

Trammel swallowed; his mouth suddenly dry. "Everyone just calls me Buck."

She surprised him by rushing over and hugging him, too.

Hagen was clearly enjoying his friend's embarrassment. "You must forgive my younger sister. We're a bit informal around here. Life in the wilderness tends to soften one's manners."

She patted him on the chest as she broke off the embrace and took a step back. "It's so good to have you both here. And two dashing men at that. We don't get many visitors up here. Father won't allow it. Oh, we do our fair share of socializing in town of course, but we rarely entertain here in the main house." She looked around the room. "It's a shame, really. Mother always dreamed of holding big parties here for all the other cattlemen and ranchers in the valley."

"You're the spitting image of Mother," Hagen said. "I hope you know that."

She blushed, which made Trammel's heart even lighter. *What the hell is the matter with me?*

"Elena is the 'E' in our familial alphabet," Hagen explained. "I was the first born, so I was named Adam. Then came my brothers Bart and Caleb, then my sister Deborah and our fair Elena here. Deborah's been married for some time, hasn't she?"

"To an old miner in Denver." Elena frowned. "A dreadfully droll man, just like Father, though not nearly as intimidating." She brought her hands up to her mouth as she looked around. "Don't tell him I said that. He doesn't like to be teased in front of other people. Not even me."

"Your secret is safe with us," Hagen said. "Where are Bart and Caleb?"

"Bart's in Denver, too, managing Father's affairs. Oil, I think. Caleb is in Cheyenne, exploring the possibility of opening a bank. He lives in Blackstone most days, but Father wants our bank to have a presence in the capital." She lowered her hands to cover her belly, causing Trammel to notice the curves of her body and he quickly looked away. "How long will you be staying with us, Adam? Please say it'll be forever."

"That's entirely up to Father," Hagen said as they all sat down. Elena sat next to her brother on the couch. "He rode out to meet us, then disappeared."

"You know how he is," Elena said, then turned to Trammel to explain. "I hope he didn't give you too much of a hard time. He's like an old wolfhound. His bark is much worse than his bite. He's a wonderful, sweet man once you get to know him."

Trammel doubted that but smiled anyway for her sake. He had a feeling Miss Elena Hagen could make him believe just about anything.

"He'll probably be back in a minute," she said. "He's just attending to some business, but I can tell he's happy you're here, Adam. He's never been one to allow sentimentality to get in the way of commerce."

"Or anything else," Hagen said.

She took her brother's hands in her own. "Promise me you won't ever go away again, Adam. Please. We've missed you so."

"Even Father?"

"I'm sure he has," she allowed, "in his own way. But

I was so young when you left, I feel as though I barely know you. I lived for your letters, you know? All of those tall tales from all those grand places you visited. And the opera house in Wichita? Imagine so much culture and refinement all the way out here." She looked at Trammel again, her blue eyes wide and questioning. "Did you see many performances at the opera house in Wichita, Mr. Trammel?"

Of all the many kinds of houses in Wichita, Buck Trammel had never heard of an opera house being there and he found himself stuck for an answer.

"The Gilded Lilly," Hagen helped. "Surely you haven't forgotten so soon, old friend."

"Yeah," Trammel caught on. "I mean, yes. Many a fine voice can be heard at The Gilded Lilly most nights." *I never talk like this. What's happening to me?*

"Oh, I'm so jealous," she said to her brother. "You've seen so much more of the world than I have. You must promise you'll take me there one day."

"Of course, my love," Adam said. "Anything for you."

She looked around at the tables and seemed to remember something. "Why, hasn't anyone offered you refreshment? Where have my manners gone? What can I get for you? Whiskey? Father has a lovely bottle brought all the way from Scotland. Buys it by the caseload."

Hagen perked up, but stopped when Mr. Hagen entered the room. He was as tall as Trammel had expected him to be and had a thick head of white hair that made him look as intense as he had on horseback. His black suit only enhanced his bearing. "You're a Hagen, Eleanor. Not some damned servant. They can get their own drinks."

The two Hagen children stood up. Trammel remained seated.

"Now leave us, child. I have business to discuss with these two."

Elena squeezed her brother's hand as she kissed him on the cheek. She went to her father and went on tiptoe to do the same to him. "Be nice, Papa. After all, we have a guest."

She looked over at Trammel and smiled warmly. "Welcome to our home, Mr. Trammel."

Trammel stood and smiled back. "Thank you, ma'am."

The three men sat down when Elena left the room. And again, Mr. Hagen continued to look at Trammel. "You're quite a size, Trammel. How tall are you?"

"Six feet and a half, last I checked," Trammel said.

The old man grunted his approval. "Scottish blood, I take it."

"On my father's side. My mother's from Norway."

"That explains it," Mr. Hagen decided. "Viking stock through and through. I know my husbandry, Trammel, be it animal or human."

Adam cleared his throat. "Speaking of that which hails from Scotland, Eleana mentioned you have some whiskey—"

Mr. Hagen looked at his son for the first time. "You'll have water in this house, by God. Or buttermilk. I know your fondness for spirits, boy, and I'll not have you lose your senses under my roof."

Adam sat back in the couch as if he'd been slapped. "But I've never touched a drop while I was here. I was too young when you sent me away."

"Don't let the lines on my face or the white hair on

my head fool you. I have two good eyes to read and two good ears to hear plenty about what you've been up to back east. I know what you've been up to since you left here and not from those fairy tales you spun to my daughter in those letters of yours." He laughed, but there was no humor in it. "Opera houses in Wichita indeed."

He looked at Trammel. "You look like a man who appreciates a drink, Mr. Trammel. You're welcome to the whiskey if you wish."

"Water's fine for me, too."

Adam got up and motioned to a place in the far corner of the room. "I take it you haven't moved the bar?"

"Of course not. What kind of a damned fool question is that?"

Adam sighed heavily as he went to get the water.

Mr. Hagen looked at Trammel again and Trammel looked back. He knew the old cur was trying to get his measure; trying to see if he'd buckle. He imagined most men did beneath that glare. The rancher seemed to have long grown accustomed to getting his way with most people.

Buck Trammel wasn't most people.

As if he was reading his mind, Mr. Hagen said, "I don't scare you, do I, Mr. Trammel?"

"No. You don't."

"Seen a bit of the world, have you? Like the man you rode in here with?"

"I've seen my share of it," Trammel said. "And the man I rode in here with is your son."

Those dark eyes narrowed. "I'll not have anyone remind me of my family under my own roof, boy."

"And I'll not have anyone call me 'boy' or 'son' anywhere," Trammel answered. "If you're waiting for me to lose my temper or kiss your feet, you'll be waiting a long time. You invited us in here, so we're here. The second you want me to leave, just say the word and I'll go. Just have your man bring my horse around and I'll be on my way. Now I'm grateful for the comfort of your home and the warmth of your fire. But if you're looking for a whipping boy, I'm not the one. I'd wager you pay someone handsomely for that privilege."

Mr. Hagen glanced at his son. "Bring me a whiskey. One glass, not for you."

Trammel could feel Adam tense from across the room. The old man certainly liked to give the spurs to people he thought could take it.

Mr. Hagen looked at Trammel again. "Tell me about that mess that happened in Wichita and tell it to me plain. Your friend over there has a tendency to use flowery words to obfuscate the facts. Got that from his mother."

Trammel heard a glass shatter at the bar.

Adam said, "How the hell did you hear about that?"

Mr. Hagen still wouldn't look at his son. "All that drinking must've softened his brain. I already told him I've got two eyes and ears that are still in working order. Not much happens between here and the Atlantic that fails to reach me. Nothing worth knowing anyway, and matters involving my sons still matter to me."

"How touching," Adam said as he carefully picked up the pieces of the shattered glass.

"Sentimentality plays no role in it," the elder Hagen

said. "It's a matter of business. I can't have any of my children's embarrassments sprung upon me in the course of my business activities. A man of my wealth has considerable enemies, Mr. Trammel, so it's only prudent that I know the worst about my relations before they do. Knowing the inadequacies of one's family can be an advantage at the right time, and I have no intention of being caught out on account of ignorance or sentimentality. Now, tell me of what happened in Wichita and spare no details."

Trammel told him about the deaths in The Gilded Lilly, the ambush on the trail, the attempted frame from Lefty Hanover, and the rescue of the women on the trail to Ogallala. The old man wanted it raw, and that's just how Trammel told it.

And through it all, Mr. Hagen sat stone-faced as he took it all in; holding his whiskey in his left hand while his son was content with water. Adam had refilled his glass several times while the old man held the glass before him like a temptation. It was gold to his son, but sand to his father.

Trammel had seen the ruin whiskey could bring to Adam, but still found himself resenting the old man for it.

After the story had been relayed, Mr. Hagen sat quietly for a time as if he had just ingested a large meal. "That business with the women you rescued happen exactly as you told it?"

Trammel gripped his glass of water tightly. "You calling me a liar?"

"I'd have called you one if I thought that," King Charles said. "I asked if you built up my son's role in the rescue for his benefit. Friends have been known to do that for each other."

"I'm not that creative," Trammel told him, "and there was no reason to add more to it than what happened. Your son was very brave and probably saved my life. He definitely saved the lives of the women in that wagon train."

Trammel didn't think the old man's glare could become any more intense than it already was, but it did as he asked, "And that surprised you, didn't it?"

"Yes," he admitted. "It did. Adam was a cavalry officer, so it shouldn't have, but it did."

Mr. Hagen shifted that glare to his son, his eyes shadowed by his thick brow. "That the way it happened?"

"Yes, Father. Mr. Trammel's telling of the event is accurate."

The old man pounded the arm of his chair. "Damn you! Can't you just say 'yes' and leave it at that?"

Adam drained his water and held the glass on his leg. For the first time since Trammel had met him, Adam Hagen was cowed.

The old man spoke to Trammel again. "He got that habit from his mother, you know? Always filling his head with fancy ideas, which only filled his mouth with fancy talk. This isn't a world made for fancy things, Mr. Trammel. Not out here in Wyoming. Fancy can cost a man his life out here."

Trammel made a show of looking around the ornate room. "I noticed."

Those dark Hagen eyes narrowed again. "I built this, damn you. By the sweat of my brow and the steel in my spine I built every slat of wood and every stone of this home from nothing. I broke this land before it broke me and, by God, I'm not ashamed of it."

The words escaped Trammel's mouth before he could stop them. "And you've got no reason to be ashamed of your son, either. Adam's not a perfect man and he's not a man like you, but he's his own man. One I consider myself damned lucky to know. If you can't see that after all I've just told you, then I guess we don't have much more to say to each other."

Mr. Hagen's hand quivered a bit as he brought the glass to his lips and drained the whiskey in one surprising gulp. Surprising because Adam had filled it four fingers deep.

When he spoke, his voice bore no rasp from the liquor. "Are you a Christian man, Mr. Trammel?"

"In a fashion. I was brought up Catholic."

"Catholic?" Mr. Hagen spat. "Popery, eh? More fancy ideals that have no place out here, or anywhere by my reckoning. But your people do believe in redemption and atonement, don't they?"

"From what I remember."

"And it would be un-Christian of me to withhold forgiveness from someone who has trespassed against me."

Adam moved to the edge of the couch.

Trammel said, "From what I remember."

"And you said my son made no promises to you when he invited you to come here."

"I did."

Mr. Hagen set his glass on the floor next to his chair.

Adam hadn't moved from the edge of the couch.

"When I saw you boys riding here," Mr. Hagen

said, "I expected my boy had run through his money and was looking for a handout. I figured he'd lured you here with promises of wealth and other riches. I see now that isn't the case."

The old man grew silent again. Trammel decided that was probably as close as he could bring himself to admitting he was wrong. He hoped it would be enough for Adam, because it was likely to be all the apology he was going to get.

He was glad when Mr. Hagen finally turned to face his son. "You've been gone a long time, boy, and you've forged a great many chains you're going to have to carry with you for the rest of your life. You've brought dishonor on this family many times over, though I'll admit not as much as I had feared you would. I always thought you had too much of your mother about you, which is charming in a woman, but not in a man." He pointed at Trammel. "But after what this man has told me today, I'd be a fool not to think that you might just be more than I had believed you to be."

Tears streaked down Adam's face. "Father . . . Papa, I've never been anything different."

"Time will tell." He stood up, and Adam stood with him.

Trammel took his time getting to his feet, sensing the end of something had come. Something good or bad, Trammel didn't know, but something.

Mr. Hagen spoke again to his son. "Do you remember the Clifford Hotel in town?"

"I do. We dined there often."

"I own it now. Joe Clifford still runs the place, but I bought him out years ago. He's getting on in years, and the time has probably come for him to step aside. I want you to help him run it with an eye toward taking it over eventually. It's a good, solid business and, with some improvements, could be made even better."

"Yes," Adam nodded quickly. "Yes. I'll be happy to run it for you, Father, if you'd like."

The hard glare returned. "And by improvements, I don't mean whores or excessive gambling, understand? I mean better accommodations. Better food and drink. Beds and bedding. That sort of thing. It'll help us charge more than we currently do."

"I understand, Father. I won't let you down."

"That remains to be seen." King Charles looked at Trammel. "Sheriff Bonner's a good man, but he's getting on in years, too. Drinks and gambles more than he arrests people these days. You mentioned you have experience as a lawman of sorts back east, so you'll be his deputy. Things have been getting out of hand in town as of late, and a man of your size might help discourage some of the criminal element in town from getting too comfortable. That sound fair to you?"

Trammel wasn't sure how it sounded. He hadn't counted on being a lawman again. He hadn't counted on being much of anything again. But for Adam's sake, he didn't dare refuse. "I'll be happy to do it."

"Then it's settled. I send my man Bookman into town with you to make the introductions."

Adam smiled. "Johnny Boy Bookman is still here, eh?"

A withering glare made Hagen's smile evaporate. "He's put that behind him now. He's been simply called John for the better part of twenty years. He's my right hand, and I'm damned lucky to have him."

Adam Hagen looked away. "Yes, Father."

Charles Hagen pulled a gold watch from his vest pocket. "If you head back to Blackstone now, you'll be there in plenty of time before dark. You'll both have rooms at the Clifford. Bookman will see to that, too."

He walked out of the room toward the front door. Trammel patted Adam on the back and urged him forward. Adam wiped away tears as he walked.

At the door, he held out his hand to his father. "Thank you."

Mr. Hagen opened the door instead. "I'll shake your hand when you've earned the right." He bellowed for Bookman and told him to have someone bring around their horses. "I'll see both of you in town in the near future."

He closed the door as soon as they stepped out onto the porch.

Adam Hagen wiped his eyes clear and took in a deep breath of mountain air. "Thank you."

Trammel looked out at the livestock grazing on both sides of the road. He'd never thought he would ever be part of anything like this but now, in a way, he was.

And he wasn't sure he liked it. No one ever worked for a man like Mr. Hagen without paying some kind of price. "I wouldn't be too quick to thank me until we know what he's given us yet."

"Whatever it is," Adam said, "it's because of you. He would've spent days berating me before he showed me the slightest kindness. You held him accountable, and I'll never forget that."

Trammel was glad Bookman had appeared with their horses, including the pack mule they'd brought all the way from Dodge City.

It saved him from the embarrassment of Hagen's gratitude.

Chapter 22

As they followed John Bookman on the road to Blackstone, Buck Trammel saw the town was more or less what he had expected it would be. He wasn't sure if that was good or bad, considering he was supposed to become part of the law in this burg. He had learned long ago to simply accept things as they were, not as he would like them to be. It was a philosophy that tended to make his life easier.

John Bookman had the air of a man who was decent at just about everything he tried, but excelled at nothing. Trammel had seen a lot of men like him in his short time on the frontier; men who could fix a fence or rope a cow or fire a gun adequately enough, but not enough to be considered great at it. Trammel figured as long as Bookman got them settled in town, he'd be happy.

Bookman turned in the saddle and spoke to the two men as he led them into Blackstone. "The town's layout is easy enough to remember. Place looks like an E, and I mean that literally. Main Street is the long line forming the spine. That's where you'll find the Clifford Hotel, the jail, and most of the saloons, gambling halls, and dining rooms in town. Spruce Avenue, Mountain View Avenue, and Bainbridge Avenue are the three lines shooting out from it."

"There were no streets when I was last here," Hagen said. "Was that my father's idea, too? He's always been such a literary man."

Bookman ignored the barb and Trammel wondered when Hagen would learn to shut his damned mouth. He tried to move past it by asking Bookman, "What's the nature of the town? Quiet? Rowdy?"

Hagen's chief ramrod shrugged. "It's got its good and bad elements same as any other place, I suppose. Not much to look at, mind you, but they made the jailhouse of stone so it'll never burn."

Trammel didn't care what it looked like. "Does it get much use?"

"Drunks and brawlers, for the most part," Bookman allowed, "particularly when drive season starts up. Ranchers like to keep their cattle here while they ride down to Laramie to negotiate a price. When they leave their cowboys behind, they can get a bit rowdy. Got the occasional words said over cards at the Clifford and other places. Railroad workers on leave like to come up from Laramie, to raise some hell now and then. Nothing a big man like you can't handle."

Bookman turned completely in the saddle and took a good look at Trammel. "Say, how big are you, anyway?"

"Big enough." He had other questions. "What kind of man is the sheriff? Bonner's his name?"

"Randall Bonner," Bookman told him. "Not the man he was when he came to town a few years ago. Maybe it's boredom or age, but he's definitely lost a step or more since taking the job. Tends to let trouble burn itself out rather than taking it on. Shame, really. He had a hell of a reputation when Mr. Hagen hired him." Bookman shrugged. "Guess old Father Time catches up to us eventually."

Trammel understood how a man could think that way. He'd come to Wichita with similar inclinations. "What about the mayor?"

"Jonah Welch." Bookman grinned. "You'll do just fine by him, so long as you don't do anything that'll take him away from that damned hotel of his. The Oakwood Arms is all he cares about. Runs it with his wife, Nell. She has to run the front desk when he's not around, and she makes him pay for it every second he's gone."

Trammel thought Blackstone sounded like a hell of a town. "I'll keep that in mind, thanks. Any saloons in particular I should watch out for?"

"All of 'em," Bookman said. "There's no call to remember their names on account of them always changing owners. Just walk toward the sound of the glass breaking and the hollering whores and you'll be where the action is. Had ourselves a run of funny names for a while about three years ago. Places like The Green Cactus and The Prickly Pear, but now they're just as forgettable as the next. All of them have gambling. All of them have sporting ladies, too."

"Wonderful," Trammel said. In his experience, liquor and working girls didn't mix.

"The Bull Moose has some Chinamen who run an opium den out of canvas tents out back of the place."

"Opium?" Trammel asked. He'd seen what the sticky tar could do to good men. He'd seen what it could turn them into. "Why does Bonner let it stay open?"

"No town ordinance against any of it," Bookman

explained. "There's not likely to be one any time soon, either. Why, the mayor himself is fond of a whore who hangs her girdle at The Painted Dove. Her best years might be behind her, but Mayor Welch doesn't seem to mind it any. Given he bears a striking resemblance to a foot, he's lucky he can get any affection at any price."

Trammel listened while they crested an incline and the Town of Blackstone came into view.

From this distance, he could see most of the buildings had been erected without the benefit of a plan. Some were narrower than others, and the windows, especially on the upper floors of the taller buildings, weren't quite lined up correctly. Some were too close to each other while others were too far apart.

Trammel didn't know if this was due to poor craftsmanship or the settlement of the buildings. The tallest structure was painted red and three floors high, which he judged to be the Clifford Hotel, given all of the buildup Mr. Hagen had given it.

Every building Trammel could see was made of wood, save for the Clifford, which was brick, and the jail, which was a squat stone structure at the end of Main Street. Trammel normally would've taken so many wooden buildings huddled together against the bleakness of the Laramie plains as a bad omen. One spark either on the prairie or in one of the buildings would set the whole town ablaze. But the town seemed to have weathered many seasons and looked the worse for it. But they hadn't burned yet, which was saying something.

Trammel asked, "Now that we know all about Main Street, what about those side streets you mentioned?"

"They're called 'avenues' in Blackstone, Trammel.

I don't care what you call them personally, but the people of Blackstone do. They'll snap you right back into place if you go calling them streets. I'm still smarting from the time Mrs. Baldwin at the Beacon rebuked me in public."

"Duly noted."

Bookman went on. "Spruce Avenue is where you'll find your hardware and dry goods places. Mountain View is where the outfitters are. Even got ourselves a fancy clothing place for men and women alike, if you can believe that for a town this size. Seem to do a fairly robust business, too. Bainbridge Avenue is a mix of smaller shops, but mostly doctors' and lawyers' offices. All three avenues have houses on them where people live. Bainbridge is a little nicer than the rest, but not by much. We'll pass the church on the way into town and, at the end of Main Street, you'll see the school."

Trammel saw all of that and more as they reached Main Street. Hagen seemed bored by the whole scene, which was understandable since he had grown up there. But Trammel took it all in with a practiced eye.

Bookman turned out to be a fairly decent tour guide as the town was, in fact, set up like an 'E'. Main Street was lined with nameless saloons and eating places where he could hear glasses clink and tinny pianos play over bawdy laughter.

The avenues, on the other hand, were as quiet as Main Street was loud. He saw people ambling about their business and paying no attention to the noise on the thoroughfare. He wondered how the people on the side streets could live so close to such noise, but decided he'd find that out soon enough.

Bookman led them to the hitching rail in front of

the jail as he stepped down from his horse. "You stay here while I smooth things over with Sheriff Bonner. Mr. Hagen, I take it you haven't forgotten where the Clifford is? It's just across the boardwalk here, right next door."

"You take it correct, my good man," Hagen said. "And I won't forget to tell my father how very helpful you've been to us lonely pilgrims. He might give you a shiny new penny for your trouble."

The top hand looked like he wanted to say something else, but settled for, "I'll meet you over there in a bit," before stepping into the jail.

Trammel was more than annoyed with Hagen. "What the hell is the matter with you? Bookman's been nothing but nice to us. He didn't deserve that."

"He works for my father, so he deserves it, believe me." Hagen's scowl softened. "No, I suppose you're right. He didn't really deserve that. I suppose I'm still smarting from having to grovel before my father."

Trammel could see the pain on his friend's face. He knew his first meeting with his father had been hell on him, but it had still gone better than expected. He tried to change the subject. "Think this Sheriff Bonner will take me on?"

Hagen shrugged. "I don't know the man. But if he's been working for my father for five years, I'd wager he'll wear a dress if Bookman tells him that's what my father wants. Strong-willed men don't last very long around King Charles Hagen."

Trammel adjusted himself in the saddle. "Guess I'd better not unpack my bags just yet."

"No, you're different," Hagen said. "I've seen plenty of people stand up to my father over the years, but very few withstood him long enough to tell the tale. You did. He respects you in his own way. Resents you, for certain, but respects you. I think you've got a place here as long as you've a mind to stay. How long do you think that might be?"

Trammel nodded toward the closed jailhouse door. "Depends on what's going on in there. I won't stay where I'm not wanted."

"You're wanted by Father, and that's enough in Blackstone." Hagen tipped his hat and slowly brought his horse around. "I'll be seeing you, Deputy Trammel."

Trammel watched Hagen put his heels to his mount and guide him down the street toward the tall three-story building he'd guessed was the Clifford Hotel. The large sign hanging over the boardwalk proved Trammel had been right.

Trammel looked when the jail door opened and Bookman stepped outside. "How'd it go?"

"You're all set, Trammel." Bookman untied his horse and climbed into the saddle. "He said he's happy to have the company. Just go easy on him. He's a bit timid."

"Timid?" Trammel's eyes narrowed. "Hell, that's not good in a sheriff."

"No, I suppose it's not." Bookman mulled it over. "Maybe that's not the right word, but, hell, you'll figure it out." He inclined his head toward the Clifford. "His lordship head over to the hotel?"

Trammel grinned. "With all the pomp of a royal prince."

"Royal pain is more like it, but don't tell Mr. Hagen I said so. He might not like his son all that much, but he's still kin and I'm not."

Trammel climbed down from the saddle and

wrapped the reins of his horse around the hitching rail. "Your secret's safe with me, Bookman. I promise."

The top hand tipped his hat and rode down toward the Clifford Hotel.

Trammel stepped up to the boardwalk and stomped the blood back into his legs. He didn't want to appear wobbly when he met his new boss for the first time. He ignored the looks he received from the people walking along the boardwalk as he slapped the dust from his coat before walking inside.

Sheriff Randall Bonner's mouth dropped open when Trammel shut the door behind him. "Good God. Look at the size of you."

"Don't have a mirror handy." Trammel was getting awfully tired of people making remarks about how big he was. He hadn't grown since New York or Wichita, but everyone he'd met in Wyoming seemed determined to comment on it. "I guess Bookman told you I'm your new deputy."

"Yes, sir," he said a little too eagerly. "By God, you certainly are."

He watched Bonner just standing there, grinning like an idiot while he pawed at his mouth with the back of his hand. He was maybe fifty years old, though the burst blood vessels in his nose made him look even older. But Trammel had seen enough drunks in his time to know the sheriff was sober now and likely had been for some time, which might've accounted for what Bookman took to be nervousness.

He also noticed Bonner wasn't wearing a star on his chest.

Trammel motioned to it. "Never been in a town

where a lawman didn't wear some kind of star or badge telling people who he was."

Bonner slapped the spot over his heart where the star should've been. "Sorry. Guess I've kinda let standards slide around here, bein' on my own and all."

Trammel ignored the uneasy feeling he felt spreading in his gut. "Well, I'm here now. You going to swear me in or something?"

Bonner went to his desk and pulled out a dusty Bible from the bottom drawer. He held it out to Trammel, who placed his left hand upon it. "Now, raise your right hand and repeat after me."

Trammel did and repeated the words Sheriff Bonner said. "I, Buck Trammel, do solemnly swear to faithfully defend the people of Blackstone, Wyoming, and enforce all laws without prejudice."

Bonner's hand trembled as he took the Bible from Trammel and slowly laid it on the desk, resting his hand on it for a moment before taking it away.

Yes, Trammel was sure something was off about Sheriff Bonner. He broke the awkward silence by asking, "So, where do we start?"

Bonner looked as if he'd been startled from a dream. "Start? Ah, yes. Start. I've got just the thing. Take a seat right here and I'll be right back."

The sheriff patted Trammel's arms as he slid past him and out the door, then breaking to his left. A few people bid him good afternoon, but he kept his head down as he moved.

Trammel wondered if the coward was running out on him. *But why? I'm not taking his job. I don't even know if I want to be a deputy, much less a sheriff. I'd be just as happy following his lead instead of having the wind in my face.*

He'd been a lawman once, albeit mostly in cities back east. He wasn't even sure he wanted to be one again. He'd only agreed to take the job because he had a feeling Mr. Hagen would've thrown Adam to the wolves if Trammel turned him down. At least here, he could keep an eye on his new friend until Adam got settled. Then, Buck Trammel would have to take a long look at his life and decide what he wanted to do next.

He wasn't sure what that next step might be, but he was pretty sure it didn't involve being a lawman again. He'd been a copper in New York City and again with the Pinkerton Agency, but this was different. Out here was nothing like back home. Hell, Wichita had been the closest thing to a frontier town he'd seen and Blackstone, north of Laramie, was a long way from Wichita.

Realizing Sheriff Bonner wasn't coming back any time soon, the new deputy decided to take in his surroundings. The jail didn't look like much on the outside, and his perception of the inside of the place wasn't any better. Just about the only thing the squat building had going for it was that it was made entirely of stone. A rounded arch held up the roof, unlike any construction he'd ever seen in a jail before. The more he looked around, he began to realize this may have been a small chapel at one point. That might explain why it had been built to last, probably by some wealthy landowner back when this part of the world belonged to France. Or maybe it was a church for missionaries looking to bring the word of God to the savages of the plains.

He laughed at that. He was the only savage who needed saving now, and he decided to check the gun cabinet on the wall for the weapons he might need for that salvation.

The cabinet wasn't even locked. He opened it and was surprised to find it empty. Not even an old box of ammunition. Just an aging spider carcass dangling from an ancient web. Not only were there no rifles in the rifle cabinet, but there hadn't been any rifles in there for some time. He figured Blackstone for a sleepy town, but every sheriff needed to show some iron now and then. Had Sheriff Bonner been wearing a sidearm? Trammel had been too taken by the lawman's demeanor to remember if he had.

Trammel went to the lopsided desk and began going through the drawers. Here he found two boxes of .45 ammunition, but no sign of a gun. No sign of a bottle, either, which confirmed his suspicion that Bonner was no longer a drinker.

The rest of the desk drawers were empty, save for the top drawer. A brass, six-pointed sheriff's badge glinted in the dim light of the jailhouse. Trammel picked it up, impressed by the dense weight of such a small hunk of metal.

The letters embossed on the curved brass around the star read: SHERIFF—TOWN OF BLACKSTONE.

Bonner hadn't sworn Trammel in as a deputy. He had sworn him in as sheriff of Blackstone.

Trammel sank back, looking at his warped reflection in the dull brass. The wooden chair cracked beneath his bulk. "No wonder he was in such a hurry to get out of here. But why?" He realized he was speaking aloud to an empty room and stopped himself. Anyone passing by might overhear him and think he was crazy.

Had Bookman run off Bonner? Why would he do

that? Mr. Hagen could've told him he'd be replacing Bonner if that had been the case. Trammel would've taken a sheriff's job just as reluctantly as he'd taken the deputy's job. Or had Bonner run off on his own? Had he seen Trammel's arrival as a chance to finally get the hell out of town? But get away from what? He hadn't been in town for more than thirty minutes, but he could already tell there wasn't much to run from around here.

He fogged up the star and rubbed it quickly on his pants leg. He saw some of the luster had returned to it and pinned it on his shirt. He supposed that made it official. He was now the law in Blackstone.

He looked around his center of authority, with its empty rifle cabinet and crooked old desk. All he had were the guns he'd brought with him, a dusty old Bible, and an old brass star pinned to his shirt. He'd come a long way from Five Points back in New York. Whether it was higher or lower was a matter of interpretation.

He drew in a deep breath and let it out slowly. "Damn it."

"Who's out there?" boomed a voice from the back. "I said who the hell is out there? Sure as hell ain't Bonner, that's for sure.

Trammel shut his eyes. He'd forgotten to check the jail cells in the back to see if there were any customers.

He pushed himself out of the creaky chair and walked toward the cells. An old wooden door with a window in the shape of a cross had been kept open by a piece of wood at its base. The back room was comprised of three small cells comprised of iron bars.

Only one of the cells was occupied by a scrawny

red-haired kid of about seventeen who looked like he hadn't bathed in days. He sat on his bunk, glowering up at Trammel. "Who the hell are you?"

"Name's Trammel. I think I'm the new sheriff." He grabbed hold of one of the bars and gave it a good pull. The old iron didn't give an inch. A good sign. "Now tell me who you are and why you're here."

The young man stood up and smoothed down his matted hair. "People call me the Blackstone Kid on account—"

Trammel hit the bars with the side of his hand, making the young man jump. "I didn't ask for a story. I asked you for your name. Your right name and why you're in here. Keep running your mouth, and I'll leave you in here without food for a week."

The kid snapped out of his act. "Name's March. Sam March. And Sheriff Bonner locked me up solely on account of me delivering a message to him last night. That's all I've done and that's the God's honest truth. I'll swear to it on a stack of Bibles."

Trammel looked at the condition of the cell. His water bucket was full and threatening to overflow. And he didn't see the remnants of any meals, either. "Looks like he didn't like your message. What was it and who was it from?"

"It was innocent enough," March said. "Just reminding him that he owes Madam Peachtree five hundred dollars, and she's getting tired of waiting on her money. Said she was tired of extending credit to him on account it was making her look bad. Even sheriffs got to pay their debts, especially to Madam Peachtree. I told him that and he locked me up without nary a word of warning or reason. Been here since just before nightfall yesterday."

"Madam Peachtree?" Trammel repeated. "Sounds like someone out of a children's story."

"The madam ain't out of any kid's book I've ever read, I can tell you that much for certain." March laughed.

"You said you work for this Madam Peachtree?"

"Yes, sir." Some of March's pride seemed to return. "I do whatever her m'lady asks of me. Run errands. Fetch people. Deliver messages. Tasks of that nature."

Trammel had never heard of—much less seen—Madam Peachtree, but he could only imagine the other tasks she gave this dopey kid to do.

Trammel decided that playing to his pride might give him a better picture of what he was up against in his new town. "Guess you're her right-hand man."

March tucked his filthy shirttails into his pants. "Well, I reckon you could say I'm right up there. Though Hastings is usually the man who takes care of the more brutal work, purely on account of him being bigger and a mite older than me. Not on account of any weakness or inability on my part."

"Of course not," Trammel said, playing along. "I can tell you're a man to be reckoned with. But why didn't this Madam Peachtree send Hastings to talk to the sheriff?"

Trammel enjoyed the look on the kid's face. He really hadn't thought of that until that moment.

The kid recovered quickly. "On account of this being a warning, I suppose. Her ladyship likes to give people a fair chance to make good on their debts. And, seeing as how Bonner was the law in town, she obviously decided on a more gentle approach."

Or set you up to take a beating, you damned fool. He looked around for the keys and found them on a peg behind the propped-open door. He took them down and jangled them in front of the prisoner. The kid's eyes widened like a dog gazing at a bone. "Now, you're sure that's all you're in here for? Because if I find out you're lying, I won't be happy. And neither will you when I find you."

March raised his right hand. "I swear it on my honor as a gentleman, sir."

Trammel grinned as he found the right key and opened the iron door. The kid had some set of words at his disposal, a result, no doubt, of Madam Peachtree's influence. He wondered if he'd fall in with Hagen as some kind of protégée. He certainly had the vocabulary for it.

March stepped out as the door swung open, but Trammel stopped him. "Pick up that bucket and empty it out back before you go, then bring it back here."

The kid did as he was told, needing two hands to lug the heavy bucket. The kid turned right and walked down the hall toward a back door Trammel hadn't noticed before. "You'll have to use one of them keys to open it. I can dump it right outside where it'll run downhill."

Trammel found the right key and opened the back door. "Looks like you're familiar with the jail."

"Been here for more justifiable infractions," March said as he heaved the contents of the bucket down a steep hill. "But this time was wrong. You've got my word on it, Sheriff." He held out his hand. "It's a pleasure to meet your acquaintance."

Trammel looked down at the filthy hand. "We'll shake after you've taken a bath."

"Agreed." He went inside, placed the bucket back in the cell, and strode toward the front door.

Trammel called after him, "And don't forget to tell Madam Peachtree the sheriff's gone and she'll have to find another way to settle her debt."

March stopped in mid-stride and almost fell over. "Her ladyship won't like that. She insists upon payment and in full."

Trammel locked the back door. "I don't give a damn what she likes. Tell her that's the way it is. She's not the first whore who had a client skip out on her and she sure won't be the last."

"Madam Peachtree is no whore, I assure you."

The kid was beginning to get on his nerves. He tossed the iron keys on the desk and strode toward him. "Leave. Now."

Young March scampered out the door like a deer and broke left as soon as he hit the boardwalk, scattering a couple of drunks in the process.

Trammel grinned. Young Sam March was the first person he'd met in Wyoming who hadn't remarked on how big he was. Maybe that was a sign of something. Of what, he wasn't certain.

Chapter 23

After stowing his coach gun and his Winchester Centennial in the rifle cabinet, Trammel locked up the jailhouse and climbed back atop his sorrel. He rode over to the livery he had noticed on the north end of town. It was in the same direction Sheriff Bonner had headed toward when he left the jail.

He ignored the strange looks he received from the townspeople as he rode by. Some of them tipped their hat to him, but he didn't return the gesture. He figured there'd be time for proper introductions once he had his situation sorted out. He needed to know Sheriff Bonner was gone for certain before he felt comfortable assuming any office, even if he had sworn an oath.

He glanced at the Clifford Hotel as he rode by. He couldn't see inside on account of the front door being closed, but he could see why Mr. Hagen favored the place. It was the one solid building in town beside the jail. At three stories high, the redbrick building towered over Blackstone. Each floor had a balcony that wrapped around it, giving it more of a New Orleans feel than a western one. Its structure easily lent itself to an elegance he believed Mr. Hagen wanted his son to bring to the building. Buck Trammel had never acquired an eye for fancy things, but knew quality when he saw it. And he had no doubt that Adam Hagen could turn the stately hotel into a regal palace for the enjoyment of cattleman and cowboy alike.

He only hoped Adam wouldn't allow his past as a drunk get in the way of his future as a hotel man.

When he got close to the livery, Trammel dismounted and walked his horse the rest of the way into the livery. A black man clanging away at an anvil set his tools aside and greeted him. "Can I do something for you, mister?"

"If you run this livery, you can. I'd like to put my horse up here for a while."

"Name's Josiah Smith, and I'm the liveryman and blacksmith in Blackstone. I'm not the only one of either, but I'm the best you'll find between here and California."

"And I'm Buck Trammel." He admired the man's confidence. "How much would you charge to take care of my animal here?"

Smith's face brightened with recognition. "You're the one whose animals Mr. Bookman brought in here a little while ago. You're the new deputy."

"Something like that," was all Trammel was comfortable with saying at the moment.

"We charge by the day, the week, or the month." Smith told him his rate, which Trammel found fair and agreed to. "Town pays for it all, even your personal animal, so it's no cost to you."

Then the blacksmith noticed the star on his chest. "That's Sheriff Bonner's star, ain't it?"

"I suppose it was," Trammel said. "Seems to have

taken it off. Kind of left me the job when he let out of here a while back. You see him around that time? Maybe half an hour ago?"

"Sure did. Never saw him in a hurry like I did just then. Climbed on top of his horse and just rode out of town that way." He threw a thumb over his shoulder, indicating south. "Don't know if he was riding for Laramie or Mexico, but wherever it was, he sure wanted to get there in a hurry. Put the heels to that mount something awful. Poor thing was played out as it was. He'll be lucky if she lasts until Laramie at that rate."

So that settled it. Bonner was gone and he probably wasn't coming back, especially since he was into Madam Peachtree for more than he could likely repay. That left Trammel holding the bag, or the badge, as it were.

Trammel handed the reins of the sorrel to Smith. "Take care of her for me if you can. She's been a better horse to me than I deserve, considering I don't know much about them."

Smith stroked the sorrel's neck and patted her gently on the side. "Been tending to horses my whole life, Sheriff Trammel, and it's my experience that they know more about us than we know about them."

Trammel thanked him and was about to be on his way, when another thought came to him. "Any idea where Sheriff Bonner lived? I didn't see a bed in the jail."

"That's because he stayed at Mayor Welch's hotel. The Oakwood Arms over on Bainbridge Avenue," Smith told him. "I know what you're thinking. The byways in this town barely qualify as streets, much less avenues, but the town elders have big dreams for this place. Maybe they'll wake up one day and realize all they've got are streets, but until then, they're avenues. Mighty prickly about them being called anything else, too."

"So I've been told," Trammel said. "Got a feeling you and I will be talking quite often. And soon."

"Always love the company," Smith said as he led the horse into the livery. "Stop by any time."

Trammel stood outside the livery and got his bearings. To the right was the jailhouse. God knew that place needed tending to. But to his left was Bainbridge Avenue, and a battered hand-painted sign reading THE OAKWOOD ARMS swung in the wind. If what Bookman had told him was true, he'd be more likely to find the mayor there than at town hall. It might be a good idea to meet his new employer.

Or at least the man who thought he was his employer. Trammel imagined everyone in Blackstone ultimately worked for Mr. Hagen.

It took Trammel a bit of effort to push in the large door to the Oakwood Arms. He coughed as a thin cloud of dust rose up and choked him.

A tall, hatchet-faced man with a high, stiff collar and brown hair stood behind the check-in desk. He looked at Trammel over round wire glasses perched on the bridge of his nose. "I'm sorry, but we've no vacancies at the moment. We're all booked up."

Trammel had to put a shoulder into the door to get it to close. "Not looking for a room."

One of the hotel man's eyebrows rose. "Ah. I see. One of those, eh? Well, we're not hiring at the moment, thank you."

"Not looking for a job, either." Trammel stepped

closer to the desk. "Already have one. In fact, that's why I'm here. You're Mayor Welch, I take it?"

Welch readjusted his glasses and saw the brass star pinned on Trammel's shirt. "What's that doing there? Who are you? What have you done to Sheriff Bonner?"

He gave the mayor a quick rundown of how he'd come to Blackstone and the job offer Mr. Hagen had made him and how he'd agreed to be a deputy, not the sheriff.

When he'd first begun telling it, Trammel doubted the mayor would believe a word of it. He was prepared for him to fly around the place, demanding proof. He hoped to God that Bookman was still over at the Clifford Hotel to back his story.

That's why he was surprised when the mayor simply said, "Adam's back?"

"Rode in with me and Mr. Bookman. They're over at the Clifford Hotel right now."

"The Clifford!" Welch exclaimed. "Why, this is absurd. I practically grew up with Adam. Why didn't he come stay here?"

He couldn't believe the mayor cared more about Adam Hagen than he did the loss of his own sheriff. "Maybe on account of his father owning the Clifford. But you heard what I said about Sheriff Bonner leaving."

Mayor Welch waved it off. "He's no loss. His gambling habits were becoming too great a distraction anyway. Mr. Hagen and I spoke of his replacement several times over the past year. We believed his debts had put him under the thumb of that damnable Madam Peachtree." His beady eyes narrowed. "Have you met her yet?"

"Can't say as I've had the pleasure."

"I'd call it more of a chore than a pleasure," Welch spat. "A tedious woman of cheap sophistication, I assure you. All that paint and perfume serve to do is cover a rotten interior. I imagine his debt to her is a reason why he ran off." The mayor smiled at him. "Which leaves her that much weaker and that much easier to get rid of."

Trammel watched the nasty smile disappear. "Who are you anyway, Trammel? I mean, where are you from? What's your background? You'll need to be pretty rough if you're going up against the likes of that woman and her man Hastings or that puppet March."

Before Trammel could speak, Mayor Welch motioned for him to be quiet. "Enough talking, man. I have to see Adam Hagen and get to the bottom of what's really going on here. This is all quite disturbing."

He took a key from the rack behind him and tossed it to Trammel, who caught it in midair. "Room 210 in the back. Comes with the job. If it was good enough for your predecessor, I imagine it'll be good enough for you."

Trammel didn't even have a chance to ask where the room was before Welch threw up the flap at the side of the desk and shrugged on his coat. "You have the desk, Mother. I have town business to attend to."

The new sheriff watched Welch open the front door and shut it behind him as easily as if it were a broom closet. The same door that had given Trammel so much trouble. "Now how the hell did he do that so easy?"

"Language, young man," said a female voice. He spotted a round woman pattering her way toward the front desk from a back room. He imagined this must be the dreaded Mrs. Welch he'd heard so much about. He wondered if her reputation rivaled that of Madam Peachtree.

He was getting dizzy just trying to keep the names straight.

"I don't care how big you are," Mrs. Welch went on, "but we're all insignificant in the eyes of the Lord, and I'll not have cursing under my roof." She flipped through the ledger with great importance. "And I'll have you know you're under my roof at this very moment. We have neither rooms to let nor jobs to offer, so state your business or be gone with you. This isn't a public house. Heaven knows our poor township has plenty of those from which to choose."

Trammel held up the key the mayor had tossed him. "Mind telling me where room two-ten is, ma'am?"

Room two-ten was about as sparse as Mr. Welch had said it would be. It was more of an addition to the side of the hotel than inside the building itself. Trammel decided the carpenter who'd built it must've been on the third day of a five-day drunk when he built the place. The wallpaper had been hung crooked, and the water stains behind it made it difficult to make out the pattern on the paper. A cold draft constantly blew through the room despite that it was almost springlike outside. The wooden bed was creaky, and the mattress bowed in the middle. If it had buckled under Bonner's weight, it would be reduced to toothpicks under Trammel's.

The furniture was all fly-specked and scarred and, just like the front door, warped to the point where they were impossible to open.

"This town sure is hard on furniture," he murmured to himself as he tried in vain to work one of the dresser drawers open.

Giving up, he stepped back and wiped the sweat from his brow. Trammel couldn't blame Bonner for taking off, considering the mountain of debt hanging over his head and a hovel like this being the only place he could hang his hat. Hell, he might be on the trail behind Bonner if he was forced to stay in a room like this.

That's when he noticed one of the floorboards beneath the dresser had risen up. Trammel figured it might've happened while he'd been trying to get one of the drawers open. The board hadn't split, but popped aside cleanly. Like it had been loosened before at some point and put back into place.

Trammel shoved the dresser aside and took a knee beside the loose plank. He lifted it up and saw a thin cloth bag had been placed in the floor beneath it. He reached in and pulled it out, realizing the book was actually a ledger of some kind. He opened the ledger and saw a series of names and amounts and dates, none of which made sense to him. The letters were English, but the words were not. He had run into this sort of thing on a couple of cases he had worked on as a Pinkerton. He wondered if they were written in some kind of code.

But it had made sense to someone. And he had no doubt the contents of this ledger were probably the reason why Bonner had been so eager to get out of town. Not only did he have debt. He had knowledge. And knowledge could be a dangerous thing.

"What were you into, Bonner?"

Trammel flipped through the pages some more,

hoping some explanation of what they contained might become clear to him. But they didn't. He shut the book and slipped it back into the bag. He replaced the floorboard, but took the ledger with him when he left.

Although he wanted to see more of the town that was now under his protection, Trammel also wanted to get the ledger somewhere safe. Unfortunately, he didn't know too many safe places in town, but he knew someone who might. Adam Hagen.

Trammel had turned the corner on Main Street, intent on visiting Hagen at the Clifford Hotel when he saw a crowd of men moving in and out of the jail. He saw men lift the old desk onto a wagon and the chair right along with it.

He dodged past an oncoming wagon and a cluster of riders heading his way as he ran across Main Street toward the jail.

"What the hell is going on here?"

The men cleared a path for him as Trammel shoved his way into the jail. He was surprised to find Adam Hagen sitting in a leather chair with his feet up on a dark wood desk.

Town life appeared to agree with Hagen. Even though he had only been in town for a short amount of time, his hair had been cut, his beard neatly trimmed into a fashionable goatee and he sported new clothes. A black suit, a white shirt, a black brocade vest, and shiny black boots. "Forgive me, Buck, but I took it upon myself to freshen things up a bit. After all, if Blackstone is going to change its image, it has to do so from top to bottom. The jail, I'm afraid, is the bottom."

Trammel noticed that, in addition to the new desk and chair, a proper rifle cabinet had been hung on the wall. It was also made of dark wood, matching the desk. "How'd you get in here?"

Hagen pointed to a set of keys on the desk. "Father always insists on having a key to every lock in town, and the jail is no exception. But I intend on leaving those keys with you as you're now the new sheriff."

The ledger under his coat felt a bit heavier now. First Bonner leaves suddenly and without the ledger he'd gone to great lengths to hide. Why? And how did he get hold of it? Now, the jail gets redone while he wasn't there. It was all too neat for Trammel's taste. In Trammel's world, nothing was ever neat by accident.

He looked at the workman around the jail. "Everyone out. Now."

The workers cleared out as they were ordered. The last one left the door open and Trammel shut it. "You're going to tell me what's really going on here, and you're going to tell me right now."

"There's no reason to be cross, Buck," Hagen said. "New sheriff means a new office. It's just some stuff I found in the Clifford Hotel basement anyway. And you needed a real rifle rack anyway. That other one was barely a broom closet."

"I'm not talking about the damned furniture," Trammel said. "I'm talking about all the odd crap that's been happening since the moment we got to town. Why'd Bonner just up and leave like that? Did Bookman tell him to do that?"

"Ah, that?" the gambler said. "Well, I'll admit I was

as taken aback by that as you were, but as you know, I had nothing to do with it. That was all Bookman's doing. On orders from my father, of course. I knew something must be up when he sent Bookman along with us. He relishes playing the heavy and does all of Father's dirty work for him. I think he told Bonner to get out of town before he fed him to this Madam Peachtree."

Hagen threw his head back and laughed. "I've already heard of her. The real name is Pinochet. The local idiots around here simply can't pronounce her real name and 'Peachtree' is as close as they could come. I look forward to meeting her, though. Sounds like my kind of woman."

Trammel didn't care about that just then. "Why'd your old man sour on Bonner?"

Hagen shrugged. "Father's a fitful man. His gambling probably had something to do with it. It could also be because his boots weren't as shiny as he thought they should be. Or because he just felt like making a change." An idea seemed to dawn on him. "Ah, I get it. You're angry he didn't tell you first, aren't you? Well, you shouldn't take it personally, and you'd better get used to it. Father's not in the habit of speaking his mind until he's ready. He always has his reasons, whether or not we agree with them. And more often than not, he's usually right."

Everything Hagen had said made sense to Trammel. The elder Hagen didn't seem the type who took many people into his confidence. He moved slow and steady and, when Trammel came along, he saw his chance to move Bonner out. Trammel only wished Mr. Hagen had told him about it first, but that obviously wasn't his way.

Trammel remembered the ledger under his coat. He thought about showing it to Hagen to see if he could make sense of it. But he decided to have another look at it first before sharing it with anyone. He knew he wasn't a smart man, but he wasn't a dumb man, either.

"I appreciate the new stuff, Adam. I really do. I'm just trying to get used to all of this." He pointed at the star on his chest. "And this, too. Kind of got out of the habit of thinking of myself as a lawman anymore."

Hagen uncrossed his legs and stood up. "That's understandable, but here's something else to remember. Father's an excellent judge of character."

Trammel wished that made him feel better. "You know, we've still got Lefty and his men on our trail."

"I doubt it." Hagen patted him on his arm as he made his way to the door. "They've probably drunk themselves half to death in Dodge City by now. If they aren't dead, they're probably dead broke and on their way back to Wichita with powerful hangovers. I don't think we've much to fear from them."

Trammel ran a hand along the new desk. It sure was nice. "That makes one of us."

"You'll see things in a better light after a good meal and a good night's sleep. I've secured you a room on the ground floor of the Clifford. It's a hell of a lot nicer than the hovel over at the Oakwood Arms. Stop by the front desk and they'll give you the key to your room. And you'll find plenty of ammunition in the rifle cabinet, too, just in case your one-eyed friend is foolish enough to pay us a visit."

Hagen shut the door behind him when he left. Trammel threw the bolt across the door and dumped the ledger on his desk and dropped into the chair.

Hagen had been right. The new furniture was a big improvement over the ratty old stuff that had been there before. He pulled open the bottom drawer and found it was deeper than the others. It also had a lock with a key in it. A perfectly good place to store the ledger from Bonner's place.

He pulled the ledger from the satchel and began reading it, hoping it would make more sense in more refined surroundings.

Chapter 24

Lefty Hanover pocketed the money as soon as the Boss Lomax handed it to him.

"Ain't you going to count it?" Lomax asked him.

Lefty played it humble. "No, sir. I trust you. You've got an honest face, and you was real good to take on me and the boys back in Dodge City like you done."

"It's me who should be thanking you," Lomax said. "Never could've finished the drive without you. Still can't figure why them boys disappeared the way they did. They was always reliable fellas. Guess the drink must've gotten the better of them."

Lefty knew why Lomax's men had disappeared. He even knew where they were buried. But he decided to keep that part to himself. "I've been drivin' cattle for as long as I could walk, Mr. Lomax, and if there's one thing I learned in all those years, it's that there's just no way to figure folks. Even the most seasoned hand can go wild when they get a taste of women and whiskey after a long time on the trail."

"Well you saved our hides for certain." Lomax looked around Lefty at the four men behind him.

"That goes for all of you boys. That's why I gave you the wages coming to those who left us. You can ride with this outfit any time."

The men grumbled their thanks, but Lefty spoke the loudest. "Thank you, sir, but we've got other business to tend to in Ogallala. I've no doubt we'll be seein' you again somewhere on the trail."

Parrot, Chico, Skinner, and Hooch collected their wages and bid their good-byes to Boss Lomax as they ambled into Ogallala proper.

Skinner nudged Lefty. "Listen to you, shining on that old fool like that."

Lefty grinned. "A con ain't done until it's all the way done, right up to and includin' the payout. There's liable to be talk about them missin' men when Lomax gets back to Dodge, and I don't want him thinkin' unkindly of us."

Chico spat into the street. "Hell, we buried those boys so deep, the worms probably haven't reached them yet."

"We fell under Bassett's gaze, boys. There's no harm in playin' it humble and leavin' a good impression in Lomax's mind."

"Humble," Parrot agreed.

"Where to now?" Hooch asked. "I take it you haven't changed your mind about Trammel."

Lefty ran his fingers over the coins in his pocket. No, he hadn't changed his mind about Trammel. In fact, every hardship and miserable night they'd endured on the long trail from Dodge City to Ogallala had made his hatred for the big man grow even more from each day to the next. His empty eye socket ached mightily on cold nights, and there were plenty of cold nights out on the prairie. There were times when he thought the agony would rob him of all his remaining sense entirely.

But the fierce pain only deepened his resolve to find the man who had done this to him. To find him and make him hurt a long time before he let him die.

"No," Lefty answered the question. "I haven't changed my mind. Ain't goin' to change it, either."

"So what're we going to do now?" asked Chico. "Want us to fan out and see if him or that Hagen fella are still here?"

But Lefty already knew what he wanted them to do. "You boys stay together. Take a walk around town and try to spot them. Men of Trammel's size and of Hagen's appetites are bound to stick out. You can settle on one place if you want, but don't spend all that money in your pocket, you hear? We're gonna be needin' it before long."

Skinner asked, "What'll you be doing while we're doing all this walking around?"

Lefty removed a faded piece of paper from his pocket. The original newspaper article about the rescued women from the Dodge City paper. "Goin' to see a man about some answers."

Lefty pulled the reporter's head out of the rain bucket and threw the man against the building. He looked around the alley to see if anyone had heard the struggle, but everyone seemed to be going about their business.

He loomed over him, watching him gasp for breath.

"Damn it, boy. I told you I want the truth and I aim to get it or drown you tryin'."

When Richard Rhoades, reporter for the *Ogallala Bugle,* finally caught his wind, he said, "I swear to the Almighty God I don't know about the sheriff asking about any dead men in Kansas. Do you want me to lie and make something up?"

Lefty stuck the faded newsprint in the man's face. "You wrote that story, didn't you? About some fancy man who rescued them ladies a few weeks back? Where's that fancy man now?"

"I don't know, damn you. I only spoke to him for a few minutes and he refused to give me his name. All I know is that he drank at a couple of saloons because everyone wanted to buy him drinks. He kept giving people different names, and I swear I can't remember any of them now. All I know is he disappeared a day or so after he brought those women to town. No one has seen him since. That's the God's honest truth. Why would I lie?"

"Because he paid you." Lefty grabbed Rhoades by the collar and pulled him to his feet. "Just like he paid off your sheriff to let him go. Probably paid you to keep his right name out of the paper, too."

"No one paid me anything," the reporter moaned. "I'd tell you if I knew anything. Why would I hold it back?"

Lefty ignored the cold feeling spreading in his belly. He was beginning to believe the scribbler was telling the truth. That was a bad sign. The reporter was the best chance he had at getting the unvarnished truth about where Trammel and Hagen had gone. He and the boys could work the saloons, of course, but Lefty knew a drunk would say just about anything for a drink. He didn't need stories. He needed facts.

"Where'd they go when they left?" He shook Rhoades hard when the reporter began to tell him he didn't know. "I'm talkin' about rumors, boy. Whispers, maybe. A town this size, people are bound to talk about something like that."

Rhoades shook some water from his head like a wet dog. "I heard a couple of rumors that people saw him and some big fella getting on the westbound train, but I don't know that for certain. The station-master said they had tickets to Laramie, but don't hold me to it. Please! It's just a rumor!"

Lefty relaxed his grip on the man's collar and let the man breathe. Laramie. It was too specific a place to just be a rumor, so he had to put some stock in its accuracy. But he had to be sure.

He shook Rhoades again. "And that's it? No other rumors about where they went?"

"Some said he just rode off one day, but I never saw him again, so the train makes the most sense. But again, please don't—"

Lefty released him with a shove and watched him fall to the ground. "Don't say you can't be certain again or I'll kick your teeth in. And don't go reportin' this to the sheriff, neither. This here was a peaceful discussion between the two of us, understand?"

"Peaceful?" Rhoades wrung out the lapel of his soaking jacket. "You call this peaceful?"

Lefty produced the bowie knife he kept tucked on his belt. "I can make them your final words if you want."

The reporter's eyes widened as he looked at the blade glinting in the sunlight. "Peaceful. Sure. Peaceful."

Lefty tucked the blade back into his belt and left the alley. He had to find the others.

They had a train to catch.

CHAPTER 25

Trammel woke with a start the next morning. It took him a few seconds to realize he had fallen asleep at his desk in the jail, facedown in the ledger.

He had no idea what time it was, but judging by the light filtering in through the windows, it wasn't much past dawn.

His back and neck ached when he tried to sit up. His bones cracked as he stood and tried to stretch some life into his tired body. Get the blood flowing again.

If he hadn't known better, Trammel would've thought he was suffering a hangover from too much whiskey. But he hadn't touched a drop since coming to Blackstone. His stomach reminded him that he hadn't eaten anything, either.

No, he felt this way from too much reading. He remembered spending the better part of the afternoon and previous evening trying to make sense of the ledger he had found in Bonner's room.

No one had ever accused Buck Trammel of being good at math, but he knew his troubles with deciphering the ledger had nothing to do with numbers.

It was because most of the entries were written in some kind of code. The letters were English, but the words weren't. They were spelled differently and had funny markings on them. The numbers in the right-hand column were clear enough, but he couldn't tell what they were for.

Whatever they were, they were important enough for Bonner to hide. And it might've been part of the reason why he was so damned anxious to leave town so fast. *Figure out the words and the numbers will make sense.*

But he knew he wouldn't be making sense of anything until he had some food and coffee in his belly. He went over to the old stove next to the desk and found the coffeepot empty. He checked around for coffee grinds, but found nothing. "Sidewinder didn't leave me much, did he?" Trammel said to the empty room.

He remembered Hagen had told him he had a room waiting for him at the Clifford Hotel. He decided now might be a good time to get acquainted with his new place and find himself something to eat.

He locked the ledger in the bottom drawer of his desk and pulled his coat off the back of his chair. He rolled his left shoulder to try to get some feeling in it. Sleeping on a desk with a gun strapped under his arm didn't make for the best circulation.

He looked up when he heard pounding on the jailhouse door. When he opened it, he found Smith the liveryman standing on the other side in a frantic state. Trammel got a bad feeling when he saw his horse was already tied to the hitching rail.

"You'd better come quick, Sheriff. A fella says he found a dead body on the road to town."

Trammel shut the door behind him. It looked like breakfast was going to have to wait.

"It's right up here, Sheriff," the toothless man told him. "You can see the buzzards already hoverin'."

Trammel made sure to ride several paces behind the stranger who was leading him to the spot of the dead body. He didn't know this man and, from what he saw of him, he didn't like him. His guide was a toothless old codger with one foot in the grave. His ratty clothes hung off him like a skeleton, and he reeked of tobacco juice and stale rotgut. His gray beard was as bushy as it was matted, and his moth-eaten hat looked as old as the man wearing it.

Trammel didn't know how much of the man's word he could trust, but he saw the buzzards circling overhead.

"You said you spotted the body after first light?" Trammel asked.

"No sir," the man said. "I spotted them buzzards. Heard 'em is more like it. They was squawking and fightin' somethin' fierce when I rode along. I saw them pulling at somethin' I figured might be good for a pelt. But when I got close enough, my horse here reared up on me. That's when I realized it was no dead wolf or coyote but a man." He patted the horse's neck. "Old Sunshine here's always been a bit skittish around blood."

Trammel wasn't all that familiar with the life and death of wildlife on the prairie, but he knew plenty about death in general. And as he rode closer to where the buzzards had settled, his own horse tried to pull away.

Now that he was close enough to see the body for himself, there was no questioning that the dead body was definitely human. He climbed down from the saddle and handed the reins to the man. "What do they call you, anyway?"

"Elmer, when they ain't callin' me other things."

"Well, don't go riding off without me, Elmer, and we'll get along just fine."

"Got nowhere to be so I've got no call to go ridin' off anywhere. Take as much time as you need, and me and Old Sunshine'll be right here waitin' for you."

The buzzards squawked at Trammel as he got closer. They had already begun feeding on the body and weren't eager to give up their meal. Trammel drew his Colt and fired over their heads, scattering the scavengers.

Trammel slid the Colt back into his holster as he approached the corpse. Judging from what the buzzards had left behind, he recognized the body even though he had only seen it briefly in life.

It was the former Sheriff Bonner. And although it was difficult to be sure after the birds had been picking at him, Trammel was pretty certain he'd been shot twice in the back.

Elmer sat proudly on his old dairy horse. "I was right, weren't I? It was a human, weren't it?"

He decided the less the old drunk knew, the better. "You were right. Say, I'm new to town. You got a doctor or an undertaker or someone like that?"

"Our doctor is our undertaker, Sheriff. And a right pretty one at that."

A woman doctor? Blackstone, Wyoming, just got more peculiar with each passing minute. "I'm going to need you to ride back into town and get her. Or at least get a wagon of some kind so I can bring him back to town for examination."

Elmer handed Trammel the reins of his own horse back to him. "And if I can't find one, I'll get Smith to lend me one of them livery horses. We can just throw him over the saddle and bring him into town."

Trammel looked back at the decomposed body. "He'd never make it that way. Just get the wagon like I told you."

Elmer grumbled as he brought his horse about and headed back to town at a good trot. Trammel watched the old man until he dipped out of sight below a slight rise. He hoped the damned fool was good at following directions. Otherwise, he might be out here with his predecessor for quite a while.

"Damn it, Bonner," he said to the prairie wind. "What did you get yourself into?"

A buzzard dropped next to the carcass and craned its neck as it cawed at Trammel. The sheriff drew his Colt and shot the scavenger dead.

He was glad he hadn't lost his skill with a pistol. He was pretty sure he'd be needing it before long.

CHAPTER 26

"Well, this is a first." Emily Downs looked at the corpse Elmer and Trammel had brought to her barn. "Two Blackstone sheriffs in the same place at the same time and one of them dead."

Trammel heard the words, but was too distracted to pay much attention. Elmer had warned him the town doctor was pretty, but he hadn't taken him seriously.

She had thick, sandy-brown hair that she wore in a bun and that framed a face of delicate features. She was taller than he had expected, though luckily enough, not as tall as him. She wasn't heavy, though she wasn't skinny, either. She moved with a purposeful grace that Trammel found appealing. Her hazel eyes were active, curious as she looked over Bonner's corpse. Her right eyebrow rose as she took a closer look at the wounds in his chest and didn't seem to mind the gore. Trammel judged her to be around thirty, but given how life in the West could age a woman early, imagined she might be a good deal younger.

She wasn't as fancy or as pretty as Miss Lilly back in

Wichita. Emily Downs was certainly a much plainer woman, but she also had a certain alertness about her that Lilly didn't have. An alertness Trammel found strangely appealing.

Still bent over the corpse, she looked at Trammel. "He's dead, you know?"

"I figured that part out myself."

"So have the buzzards, as you can see." She took a bedsheet from a shelf in the barn and threw it over Bonner's corpse. "Surprised the coyotes didn't get at him, though. That's strange. They usually tear into anything as soon as it dies."

Trammel hadn't thought of that. "That tell you anything about when he died?"

Miss Downs shook her head. "Nope. Just means they didn't get to him is all. I'd say he died as soon as he left town, though. And that's just based on where you found him and when. But judging by those holes in his chest, I'd say he was already dead by the time the vermin got to him, which is something of a blessing. Sheriff Bonner wasn't good for much, but he didn't deserve to die like this. I don't know what you want me to tell you, Sheriff. We don't get much call for inquests out here, and I'm not one for doing them. I dress them up and make it so their bodies don't rot for a couple of days, but that's about the extent of my skills."

Trammel followed her out to the well outside the barn and watched her wash her hands. "Any idea who might've killed him? As a woman who lives in town, I mean, not as a doctor."

She shook the water from her hands and dried them on the apron around her waist. "You're the one with the star on his chest, Sheriff. That's your job, not mine."

Trammel felt himself begin to blush. "I'm new to the job. Guess I didn't ask it right. I meant if you knew if Bonner had any enemies."

She continued to dry her hands as she thought it over. "Not that I know of, but I'm not one for socializing. People tend to like to stay away from undertakers and doctors until they need them. I know he'd been good when he started, but had already begun to slack off when my husband and I got here three years ago."

Trammel felt his heart sink a little. She didn't have a ring on her finger, but he imagined one would get ruined if she did. It served him right for thinking such a woman wouldn't have a husband somewhere. He decided to focus on Bonner instead. "Anybody ever say why he slacked off?"

"Nope, but I noticed he got a little lazier each year based on what little I saw. Started to let things slide, especially over at The Lion's Den. I heard he was well paid to look the other way when trouble broke out in that place."

Trammel hadn't seen a saloon named The Lion's Den when he'd ridden into town, but that didn't matter. Bookman had said saloons and eating rooms changed names all the time in Blackstone.

"The Lion's Den?" He played a hunch. "That Madam Peachtree's place?"

She put her hands on her hips and smiled. "So you've already heard about her."

Trammel shrugged. "Small town. New sheriff. People talk."

"Well, her name's not Peachtree, for one thing.

She's from France and her name is Pinochet. Amanda Pinochet. But the ignorant bunch who go into her place couldn't say her name right and changed it to Peachtree." She laughed as she shook her head. "Got to hand it to people out here, Sheriff. We aren't much on culture, but we always find a way to make it work. By the way, she's not a madam, either. Not in the way you're probably used to the term in Wichita and New York. The Lion's Den is strictly a gambling den and saloon. She's also got an opium den in the back, but no one's supposed to know about that except her special customers who pay extra for the privilege. Got herself a couple of Chinamen who run that part of the operation separate for her. Makes some good money off it, too."

Trammel was beginning to like the young doctor, and not just because she was pretty. "For someone who says she's not sociable, you know a lot. Especially about me. Who told you I was from New York and Wichita?"

"Small town, like you said." She beckoned him to follow her into the house. "I'll bet you haven't had breakfast yet. My mother-in-law should have something ready by now. You should join us."

Trammel didn't move. "I wouldn't want to intrude, ma'am. Your husband might not—"

"My husband's dead, Sheriff." She nodded toward an old elm tree to the left of the barn. "Been dead two years now. The flu took him."

Trammel looked over and saw a small gravestone beside the elm. "I'm sorry to hear that."

"Don't be. He wasn't much of a husband. And you're a lousy liar, Sheriff."

Trammel was taken aback. "Lie? When did I lie?"

"When you said you were sorry to hear he was dead." She began walking toward the house again. "Come on if you want to eat. Whatever she cooked is likely getting cold, and Mrs. Downs isn't a woman who enjoys serving cold breakfast, especially with a guest come to call."

Trammel willed himself to stop blushing as he followed the undertaker into her house.

Mrs. Downs glaring at him throughout his breakfast didn't diminish Trammel's enjoyment of the eggs and buttermilk biscuits she had prepared. And, although he knew he was hungry, the coffee was the best he could ever remember having.

He made it a point to not look at Emily's mother-in-law while he ate. The old woman was dressed entirely in black and never took her eyes off him.

Emily Downs seemed to be enjoying the scene even though she never acknowledged it. "Mother," she finally said, "I'll clean up here. Why don't you go inside and rest now?"

Trammel was relieved when the old woman rose from her stool and moved into the other room.

He snagged another biscuit and ate it. "I get the feeling she doesn't like me much."

"You're in good company," Emily said. "She doesn't like me much, either. Or at least she didn't when she could still speak. She had an episode the day my husband died. A stroke, I think. She's been in mourning ever since. Hasn't spoken a word since that day, either. Two years since her son passed and she won't wear anything but black."

"Forgive me for saying so," Trammel said, "but I couldn't help but notice you're not wearing black."

"Never have," she told him. "Brian was a good man in some respects. He had a way with animals I'll never have. He taught me just about everything he knew about taking care of animals, and later, people. But there was already a doctor in Blackstone when we moved here, so he took up undertaking and I learned that trade, too. The same flu that took Brian took the doctor, too." She looked out the window. "With both of them gone, I went from helping my husband every now and then to being the only doctor and undertaker in town."

Trammel had liked the way the morning light fell across her face. He liked her before learning all of this, but now found himself admiring her. "That's a lot of responsibility for anyone to take on."

"Not really. The ranch hands know horses and cattle better than I ever will, so they never call me. The sick are grateful I don't make them any worse, and the dead don't need much tending to. I just fix them up long enough so they don't rot while the family grieves. There's always a couple of castoffs who need drinking money, so there's never a shortage of grave diggers around."

Trammel laughed. "Sounds like you've got it all figured out, don't you."

"Never had much of a choice." She cast a hand in her mother-in-law's direction. "She can't take care of herself, and no one around here is lining up to take care of us, so I did what I have to do to survive."

"I've got a hard time believing that." He caught her looking at him and he immediately regretted it.

He wiped his face with a napkin to hide his shame. "About nobody lining up to take care of you, that is."

"Anyone worthwhile is either married or a drunk," she told him. "The ranch hands only have one thing on their minds when they come to town and they're not exactly the courting type anyway." She placed her chin on her hands. "I'm curious about you, Sheriff Trammel. What brought you to Blackstone, anyway?"

"I'll tell you if you promise to call me Buck."

"I'll listen if you promise to call me Emily."

"Fair deal," Trammel smiled. "I'm here because I've run out of other places to be and figured here was as good a place as any, especially because my friend's father seems to draw a lot of water in this town."

"Mr. Charles Hagen," Emily said. "King Charles the Great they call him around here. Thinks he owns this valley and everything in it. He practically does. But he's not content with just being the biggest rancher in this part of the state. I have a feeling he's got other plans. Plans that involve Blackstone somehow."

"What makes you say that?"

"You're here, aren't you?"

Chapter 27

As he rode back to the jail, Buck Trammel found himself feeling better than he had in a long time. Maybe in as long as he could remember. His belly was full, and his mind was still buzzing from a nice conversation with a pretty lady. A doctor, no less. She wasn't as fancy as Miss Lilly was, but few women were. This wasn't Wichita. This was Blackstone, Wyoming, and things weren't supposed to be the same. He hoped they'd be calmer, for his sake and Hagen's.

He reached Main Street and decided it was probably a good idea for him to go to the Clifford Hotel. Check in on Adam and see the room he had spoken of. Maybe change his clothes and take a bath.

But when he saw a knife sticking out of the jailhouse door, he knew that bath would have to wait.

He tied off his horse at the jail's hitching rail and climbed up on the boardwalk. The knife blade had been used to pin a handwritten note to the door. He knew it wasn't there when Smith had told him about Elmer finding Bonner's body. It must've been stuck there after he'd ridden off.

The note flapped in the morning breeze as he read it:

Bonner had debts. Bonner was the sheriff. Now you're the sheriff. His debts are now yours. Come down to the Den to arrange payment. M.

The Den. The Lion's Den. Madam Peachtree's place.

Trammel yanked the note free and balled it up. He looked behind him and saw the clock above the Blackstone Bank said it was already eight in the morning. All of the stores in town looked open. The boardwalks had a fair amount of people milling around in front of the stores. All of the townspeople were trying hard not to look in his direction, but he knew they were.

He may have been a newcomer to this part of the world, and to Blackstone in particular, but Buck Trammel knew people. They were the same here as they were back in Wichita or New York City or any of the other towns and cities he had worked as a Pinkerton. Maybe anywhere in the world. People everywhere loved to gather in groups, and when they gathered, they gossiped.

He imagined there was only one item that might be higher on their list of topics than finding Bonner's body on the outskirts of town.

The note that had been stuck to the jailhouse door with a knife.

His authority had been challenged before he'd even had a full day on the job. He looked like a fool to people he hadn't even met yet. Buck Trammel knew he might not have much going for him, but he had never allowed anyone to make him look foolish.

He wasn't about to start now.

He felt his neck begin to redden and his breathing grow shallow as the old warmth of rage began to envelop him. He fought to control it and fought hard.

You're new to this town. You're new to this office. They don't know you. They have to learn. Go easy. They have to learn.

His right hand balled into a fist until he heard his knuckles crack. Yes, they'd have to learn the hard way. And soon.

He turned when he heard Adam Hagen clear his throat. "I see you've found the love note Madam Peachtree left for you."

Trammel showed him the balled-up note. "You read it?"

The gambler nodded. "I'm afraid half the town has seen it. The other half surely knows about it by now, or at least they will before we get halfway to luncheon. Small towns love gossip."

"Big towns do, too. Even cities." He thought of what he had seen of drawing-room society back in Manhattan. All those clean people dishing dirt about people they considered friends. "Same everywhere, I guess. You heard about Bonner?"

"Heard but wasn't surprised." Hagen nodded at the knife in the door. "I know you understand there's a correlation between his body being found and that note."

Trammel wasn't exactly sure what a correlation

was, but if it meant the note and Bonner's death were related, then he understood it. "Yeah, you could say that."

"I thought about removing the note and slipping it under the door," Hagen said, "but by the time I saw it, there was already a crowd around it. I even tried to pull the knife out, but it's stuck too deep. I looked like a damned fool trying, too. I'm sorry about that."

"You didn't put it there. You've got nothing to apologize for." Trammel wrapped his big hand around the knife handle and pulled it free in one tug. It wasn't as difficult as Hagen had made it out to be. "The one who put it there does."

He tucked the knife in the back of his britches. "Any idea where this Lion's Den is?"

"The people I saw reading the note this morning tell me it's right here on Main Street toward the other end of town. But don't worry. We'll find it together."

Trammel noticed the gambler had changed clothes again. He was dressed in all black and sported a new Colt on his hip.

"Not we, Adam. Me. You're not the sheriff around here. I am. This is my fight, not yours." He pointed at the Clifford Hotel. "Now, get back in there and set aside a nice room for me. Tell them to draw me a bath, good and hot. I'm looking forward to a good soak when I get back from the Den."

Trammel began walking toward the saloon and heard Hagen call after him. "What if there's trouble?"

The new sheriff of Blackstone kept walking. "Then I'll handle it."

* * *

He ignored the looks he drew from the drunks loitering on the boardwalk between the saloons. They either ducked back inside whatever watering hole they'd crawled out of or stepped aside. He didn't pay much attention to what they said to each other as he passed, either, since he knew it was pretty much the same as everywhere else. "He's a big one, ain't he?" was the general theme of what little the sheriff overheard.

Trammel drew his Colt when he saw the faded sign with THE LION'S DEN painted across it. The doors were of thick ornate wood, save for the stained glass in the middle of each door.

Trammel tried the door, but it was locked. A male voice called out from inside. "Can't you see we're closed? Come back later."

Trammel reared back and kicked the door in, sending it crashing open. He raised his Colt as he stepped inside.

At the periphery of his vision, Trammel saw gamblers look up at him from their cards. A faro dealer ducked beneath his table while players fought each other for the unattended money. Some sporting ladies screamed and moved away from the big man as he entered the saloon.

But it was the man in the lookout chair who had commanded all of Trammel's attention. The same man who was pointing a double-barreled shotgun at him.

"I told you we was closed, mister," the shotgun man yelled. "Now set the iron on the floor and back up out of here so we don't have any more trouble. We'll talk about your payin' for the door at another time."

Trammel didn't move and he didn't lower his Colt, either. "Either you put down that shotgun or I blast you out of that chair."

The sheriff began to notice the barrels of the shotgun begin to waver. "O-o-only guests of Madam Peachtree are allowed to be in here right now."

Trammel held up the balled note in his left hand. "Got my invitation right here."

The barman spoke up. "Put down the shotgun, Conroy. This here's the sheriff her ladyship sent for. Sheriff Tanner, isn't it?"

He kept his Colt on the lookout man. "Name's Trammel."

"I stand corrected. Damn it, Conroy. I told you to lower that damned thing. This ain't Texas, you know. You can't go pointing guns at officers of the law. Ease down them hammers and put it away. Hell, I've got ten bucks it ain't loaded anyway."

Conroy lowered the shotgun as he turned to argue his point. "Well, it would be loaded if you cheap mothers would buy—"

While Conroy was distracted, Trammel reached up and knocked the shotgun away from him with his free hand, then pulled him out of the lookout chair. Conroy landed on an empty card table, breaking it easily.

Trammel stepped on the back of the man's neck as he tried to get to his feet. He aimed the Colt down at his head. "The next time you aim a gun at me, you'd better squeeze the trigger."

"Enough!" cried out a female voice from the darkness. "You've made your point, Sheriff. No sense in killing a man over nothing. Might as well come over here so we can talk civil like."

Trammel tucked the Colt back in the holster under his arm and slowly approached the bar. It was dark in that part of the gambling hall, probably by design. In his experience, people often preferred to tend to their vices under the cover of darkness.

The bearded man behind the bar greeted him with a big smile. "I can see you're going to fit right in here, Sheriff." He was much bigger than Trammel had thought at first. In fact, he was almost the same size as Trammel.

Almost.

The barman held out his hand. "Name's Hastings. Johnny Hastings. Pleased to make your acquaintance, Sheriff Trammel."

Trammel pulled the knife from the back of his britches and brought it within half an inch of Elwood's throat. The barman didn't flinch.

"You stick this in my door this morning?"

"He did," said the lady in the shadows. "On my orders. I wrote the note and I sent it. Looks like it worked. It got you here, didn't it?"

"Yeah, it did."

Trammel withdrew the blade, flipped the knife, and drove it deep into the bar.

Hastings grinned. "Pretty strong for a lawman."

"I'm new to it. Maybe in a little while, I'll be just as soft as Bonner was. Might even get so bad, I'll be worse off than you."

For a split second, Trammel thought Hastings might try to hit him. He hoped he would. He judged the big man to be about five years older and just a bit heavier. All of it had been muscle at one point, but not anymore. Life in a saloon tended to ruin a man, no matter what side of the bar he stood on.

"I sent the invitation," the lady said, "so you should be talking to me, not my men."

"Fine." Trammel began walking toward the sound of her voice, but stopped when he heard a metallic sound. It could've been the closing of a coal-oven door or a metal latch on a jewelry box. It also could've been the click of a derringer being cocked and ready to fire.

He'd been shot by derringers before and, other than leaving scars the ladies found interesting, he hadn't suffered much for it. But the other times he'd been shot had always been in the middle of some kind of fight where chaos made the shots go wide. This time, the lady in the darkness had the drop on him. And even a derringer could be fatal if he took a bullet to the belly.

"Now that I've got the man's attention," the lady said, "give the man a whiskey, Hastings."

"I came here for answers," Trammel said, "not your whiskey. I take it you're Madam Peachtree."

The voice laughed a sharp laugh. She had an accent, too, though he couldn't quite place it. He remembered the doctor had mentioned she was from France, and he imagined that was the accent he heard.

"The name is Pinochet, Sheriff Trammel," she told him from the darkness, "but my customers have come to call me Madam Peachtree. It's quaint, so I've allowed them such familiarity. It's good for business."

"You'll find sticking notes to my door at knifepoint is bad for business," Trammel said. "Don't do that again. And don't go handing me bills that Bonner ran up." He decided to try something to see if it worked. "If Bonner owes you money, go collect it from him, not me. The debt's not mine, and I'm not paying it."

That laugh again. "Oh, Sheriff Trammel. I know you're new around here, but even you must see the futility in trying to get money from a dead man."

Trammel grinned into the darkness. "How did you know he was dead?"

"Elmer told us," came the response too quickly. "Right after he brought you to the doctor, he came galloping over here telling us all about it. He's still here, you know. In the back parlor. You can go back and see him if you wish, though I doubt he'll be able to tell you much now. He's had a taste of the dragon's breath, courtesy of my exotic friends from the Orient. I can send someone to come get you later when he's more himself."

"And what if I said I think you knew Bonner was dead long before Elmer ever came in here."

He could hear the shrug in her voice even though he couldn't see her. "Then I supposed I'd have to ask you to prove it, which we both know you couldn't. You'd be left with a lot of foolish supposition, Sheriff, and a man in your position can't afford to look foolish. Well, any more foolish than you already do, anyway. I'm afraid my invitation has already caused quite a stir among the locals. The people of Blackstone are already questioning how you got the job and where you came from."

"That's funny. The doc already knew all about me thanks to Hagen. I'd wager the people know, too. That means they're talking about your note and how I'm going to respond."

"A smart man would respond the way Bonner did," the lady told him. "Take his cut and look the other way. You can be as upstanding and righteous as you want in any other place in town, but you'll turn a blind eye toward the doings of The Lion's Den and whatever happens in it."

Trammel didn't like people thinking he could be bought, but he kept his temper at bay. "I don't like negotiating with someone I can't see."

He almost flinched when the woman leaned forward just enough to show half her face. She was older than she sounded, and her face was covered by a thin black veil. But he saw enough to understand why she wore it. The left side was horribly scarred, probably from a fire.

"Darkness can be a lady's best asset, Sheriff Trammel. For a lawman like yourself, common sense is the answer. Learning who to buck and who to work with. Who to run in to jail and who to let go. Pick your battles, Trammel, as long as they're not with me."

"What do I get?"

"Five percent of the house take each month. Books are open to you whenever you want to see them so you know we're on the level. You stay away until you're sent for and do as you're told, you might get a little extra come the Lord's birthday. Five percent, Trammel, for doing absolutely nothing."

Trammel played along. "Sounds like a nice deal. How'd Bonner screw it up?"

"Got stupid," she told him. "Got lazy, which made him greedy, which got him dead. But you're different. You're much smarter than that." She looked him up and down and smiled. "I can tell that just by looking at you."

Trammel folded his arms across his chest. "And if I say no?"

He noticed the glint of a derringer at the edge of the shadow. "A bullet in the belly's a hell of a lot cheaper for me. And a hell of a price for you to pay."

Trammel could sense Hastings tense behind him, though he knew the barman hadn't moved.

The sheriff looked around The Lion's Den while he made a show of considering her offer. It may have been a nice place once, but hadn't been for a long time. Cracks spiderwebbed along the plaster ceiling, chipping in many places. The paintings that hung on the walls were old and stained by years of heavy cigar and cigarette smoke. The felt on the gambling tables was worn from use and bore generations of stains from countless spilled drinks. The mirror behind the bar looked like it hadn't been cleaned since the place was new. Near the door, Conroy had managed to crawl away from the ruined table, but still hadn't figured out how to get to his feet. And none of the gamblers saw fit to break from their respective games long enough to help him.

Madam Peachtree seemed tired of waiting. "It shouldn't be this hard of a decision, Sheriff. A man like you should know a good thing when he sees it. God knows you've been given worse choices. What's to think over?"

"I'm thinking of a lot of things," Trammel said. "I'm thinking of why Charles Hagen asked me to become a deputy to a man with one foot out the door. He's not the type who misses things, so I think he knew Bonner was in trouble. I think he knew he'd run the second he had the chance, and I think he knew you'd kill him. I think he knew I'd wind up as sheriff, which would put me against you."

"Saint Charles Hagen," she laughed. "The Savior of Blackstone. Is that it?"

"Never met a wealthy man who was a saint. Never met a wealthy man who was stupid, either. At least, not when they made their fortune themselves. I think he wanted this confrontation to happen just the way it's happening now. And I think I'm going to walk out that door before we both do something we're all going to regret."

She stood up and disappeared back into the shadows. Only the derringer remained visible, and that was aimed at his belly. "You're not going anywhere until we have a deal."

"Sure I am, and you're going to let me because it's only you against me and, the gambling woman you are, you know those are lousy odds."

Hastings laughed from the other side of the bar. "You're forgetting about me, Trammel."

But Hastings wasn't laughing when he heard Trammel thumb back the hammer of the Peacemaker in his shoulder holster. "You're covered, stupid. One move and I shoot you through my holster."

Hastings spread out his hands on the bar.

The derringer in the madam's hand seemed to float higher in the darkness, though he knew it was her gloved hand that held it. "You're covered, too, Sheriff."

"By a toy gun," Trammel said. "Unless you're handy with that thing, you won't kill me. Not before I take down Hastings back there. And you're going to have to kill me, lady, because if you shoot, I'm shooting back."

Things grew very still in that part of The Lion's Den saloon. Time felt like it slowed down for Trammel as he became aware of every sound and everyone around him.

The scrape of cards across old felt seemed louder. The setting of a glass of whiskey on a table sounded like a judge's gavel. The scrape of a chair leg on wood sounded like a great tree being felled.

The snap of a floorboard meant Hastings was moving.

Trammel squeezed the trigger and bucked forward as the bullet blew through the bottom of his holster. Another gunshot rang out as he pulled the Peacemaker free. He moved to the side as he saw the smoking derringer move with him and fire again.

Two shots. Empty.

Trammel lashed out at the gun with the barrel of his Peacemaker. Madam Pinochet cried out as the tiny weapon skittered to the floor. The sheriff reached into the darkness, grabbed the first hint of cloth he felt, and pulled her toward him. He'd grabbed her by the arm, but she was too crazed with anger to notice. "Jim!" she cried out. "Oh, no. Jim!"

Trammel looked and saw Jim Hastings had fallen dead behind the bar, a neat hole just above his left eye. The mirror behind him was now cracked and splattered with gore.

Trammel realized he had her by the arm and steered her toward the front door as the gamblers backed away from him, hands up and away from whatever weapons they might have.

Trammel swept the room with his smoking Peacemaker. "Anybody else feeling stupid today?"

Conroy screamed as he got to his feet. This time, he wasn't holding an empty double-barreled shotgun. He was holding a Winchester.

Trammel pushed Madam Pinochet out of the way as he fired twice at Conroy. Both bullets caught him in the chest; bouncing him off the wall before he fell face-first to the floor. As dead now as he'd ever been alive.

Trammel swept the gambling hall again. "Anyone else? That it?"

As none of the men sought to challenge him, they cleared a wide path for the large sheriff and his weeping prisoner as he pulled her out of the saloon and took her to jail.

CHAPTER 28

Trammel didn't expect such a meek-looking man like Mayor Welch to have such a loud voice. "You've been in your position for less than a day and we already have three dead bodies on our hands and one of the town's most prosperous business leaders in prison. A harmless woman, no less."

Trammel decided to allow the mayor to yell at him. He had been elected to office and Trammel had not. He had a right to holler if he was of a mind to. But he wasn't entitled to make accusations.

He opened the top drawer of his new desk and pointed down at the derringer he'd taken from the lady. "She had that aimed at my belly the whole time. Took two shots at me, too." He slammed the drawer shut. "I'm charging her with attempted murder of a peace officer. I'm also going to charge her with obstructing justice, threatening the life of a town official, and disturbing the peace. If I can, I plan on charging her with Sheriff Bonner's murder, too, but that's up to a judge to decide."

"Bonner's murder?" Welch ran a hand through his

thinning brown hair. "How in the world do you expect to prove that?"

"She had it done," Trammel said, "probably Hastings or Conroy did it. I don't think that kid who works for her, March, I think his name is, could've done it without fouling it up. But the other two could've done it. My money's on Hastings. He seemed a capable man."

"Until you shot him," Welch said. "Through the head."

Trammel nodded toward the sawed-off shotgun he had placed in the corner of his office. "On account of him reaching for that under the bar."

"You saw him do it? Because the people I've talked to in the saloon claim you shot him blind."

Trammel grinned. "You running investigations now, Mr. Mayor? I thought that was my job."

"I can't help if the people decide to speak to me about a traumatic event they witnessed," Welch countered. "I'm their mayor after all. You're just a . . . a—"

Trammel held up a finger. "Careful."

"An accidental officeholder," Welch said, finally finding the words. "The people elected Bonner as sheriff. Overwhelmingly, too."

"So have another election and see who runs against me. Until then, I'm the law in Blackstone since Bonner ran out and consequently died in the process."

Mayor Welch straightened his collar at the mention of the town's patron, Mr. Charles Hagen. "Normally, I can follow Mr. Hagen's thinking on such matters. His reasoning in this instance fails me. Mr. Charles Hagen, that is."

Trammel wasn't sure about it himself, but the mayor wasn't a man you showed doubt to. He was the kind who used a man's indecision as a wedge. Trammel already had enough to worry about without giving a parasite like Welch any more leverage than he already had. "As mayor, I'm sure you know if Blackstone's got a law on the books about legal businesses having to be open during certain hours of the day."

"I certainly do. Helped draft it myself."

"Good, because I can add another charge to Madam Pinochet's sheet. She had the door of her saloon locked and allowed gambling to go on during off-hours."

Mayor Welch rolled his eyes. "God help us. Aren't you leveling enough serious charges at her than to pile on with minute indiscretions?"

"The law is the law," Trammel said. "I won't bend it for you or anyone else."

Mayor Welch checked to make absolutely sure no one else was in the jailhouse and that the door was locked before saying, "You're new to town, so I can't expect you to know how we do things around here, but arresting that woman is a mistake. She kept a lid on this town, Trammel. She controlled the saloons and the gambling to make it so that decent folks could walk down the street. She helped make this town fit to live in."

"That's the sheriff's job," Trammel said. "Besides, those men I killed were trying to kill me. Maybe that would've been pretty good for you, come to think of it. With me out of the way, you and the madam would have free rein over this town."

"Maybe we should have a new election for sheriff

as soon as possible," Welch countered. "And maybe I'll get working on that this very day." He opened the front door and spoke loudly enough for anyone outside to hear. "And I demand Madam Peachtree be treated with the respect deserving of a woman of her standing, sir!"

He stormed out of the jailhouse and didn't bother to close the door after him.

"Quite a speech," Trammel muttered. He saw the gash in the door from Hastings's knife and decided to add destruction of public property to Madam Pinochet's list of charges. The mayor would enjoy that.

Someone waved a white handkerchief from the left side of the doorway before Adam Hagen poked his head out, hands raised. "It's just me, Sheriff. Don't shoot."

Trammel remembered that he had to reload the Peacemaker. "I shoot you, I lose the only friend I've got around here."

Hagen shut the door behind him and leaned against it. "You look mighty good behind that desk, Sheriff Trammel, if I do say so myself."

Trammel eased his Peacemaker out of his shoulder holster and laid it on the desk. "Won't be sheriff for long if Mayor Welch has anything to say about it."

"He doesn't have anything to say about it at all," Hagen said. "Father does, and he wants you to have the job. In fact, I've got a feeling he set this whole thing up knowing exactly what was going to happen."

Trammel was glad he said it first. "That thought crossed my mind, too." He cracked open the cylinder and took out the spent rounds. He took a box of ammunition from the top right drawer and reloaded. "Think Bookman told Bonner to clear out?"

"He said he didn't," Hagen said, "and I tend to believe him. Bookman is a deliberate man and not given to lying. He's been with Father for years, and Father never gives him much room for independent thinking. No, he didn't tell Bonner to clear out, but I'd wager a thousand dollars that Father knew Bonner would take the opportunity to run out. I take it you're not much of a chess player, are you, Buck?"

Trammel was glad to be able to surprise him. "I know the game a little. An old partner of mine liked to play it as a way to pass the time. Picked a bit of it up myself. Why?"

"Father views himself as the king on the board, while the rest of us are pawns to be sacrificed so he can have freedom of movement. And, like a chess king, he only moves north and south, east and west. He'll wait for a clear shot at a piece, then buffalo it off the board." He pointed back toward the cells. "I take it the queen of our game is back there?"

Trammel shut the cylinder and put the Peacemaker back into the ruined holster under his arm. "Yeah. She claims I broke her arm. I've sent for Emily, but she's not here yet."

Hagen cocked an eyebrow. "Emily is it? On a first-name basis with the comely young doctor already. And you said I'm the only friend you had in town."

Trammel willed himself not to blush, but wasn't sure it was working. "Met her when I brought Bonner's body in from the outskirts. She seems capable enough."

"Available enough, too, from what I hear." Hagen

looked back at the cells. "I've never seen a criminal mastermind before. Think I could steal a peek?"

"This is a jail," Trammel said, "not a zoo. But take a look if you want."

As Hagen looked at the lady, Trammel remembered Bonner's ledger was in the bottom drawer of his desk. He knew he'd never make heads or tails of it if he looked at it for a year. He wondered if Hagen might be able to understand it. "After you're done there, I need you to take a look at something else."

He pulled out the ledger and tossed it on his desk. "I found it in Bonner's room over at Welch's place. Had it stashed under a floorboard under his dresser."

Intrigued, Hagen walked over and opened the ledger. Trammel watched his pale eyes as they moved over the pages. "It's written in an elegant hand. Too elegant for a man of Bonner's disposition, I'd wager." He looked at the sheriff. "Think your guest in the back wrote this?"

"I didn't think so until they stuck that note to my door this morning. Now, I don't know what to believe. She never even told me how much Bonner owed before we started shooting at each other."

Hagen flipped through a few more pages. "Maybe this ledger was part of the debt. I wonder how he managed to get his hands on it. From what I hear, he wasn't a very clever man, and it would take a clever man to get something like this away from Madam Pinochet."

"I'm not sure of what it is," Trammel admitted. "I can't make sense of the damned thing. Figured you might."

Hagen kept turning pages. "Perhaps. It seems to be

written in some kind of code, but I may be able to crack it upon closer examination. May I take it with me?"

Trammel wondered if that was wise. He trusted Hagen to a point, but wasn't sure if he could trust his friend's instincts. He had learned a lot about the man on the trail between Wichita and Blackstone, but Adam Hagen was still a gambler in more ways than at the gaming tables. He wondered if he should show it to Charles Hagen first. After all, he ultimately worked for him.

But Trammel had worked for men like Charles Hagen before. They often didn't like their inferiors asking them what to do. They liked giving orders and reprimands, but they weren't great on direction. Sometimes, they preferred their people to take the initiative, which is exactly what Trammel decided to do. "I'll have to make you sign a receipt for it."

Hagen took a step back. "My, how official. Pin a star on a man's chest and watch him change."

Trammel pulled out a piece of paper from his desk and began writing out a receipt. "I was a copper for a long time before I was a bouncer, remember? Records keep things easy to track."

"I stand corrected once again." Hagen watched him write up the receipt. "I think Father got more than he bargained for when he asked you to become a deputy."

Trammel looked up when he heard a knock at the door. A slightly flustered Emily Downs stood in the doorway, her medical bag in hand. "Sorry I couldn't come sooner, but I had to talk a teamster out of shooting one of his horses. He thought it had a broken leg. I convinced him it was just a cramp. A little liniment on the muscle and some rest should do the trick."

Trammel forgot all about the receipt for a moment. "Come on in, Doc. The patient's in the back. I'll let you into her cell in a minute. Just writing up a receipt for my friend here. You know Adam Hagen, don't you?"

"Only by reputation."

Hagen took her hand when she entered the jail and kissed it. "My, a female crime boss and a female doctor all in one tiny jailhouse out here in the wilderness. Blackstone has become quite a cosmopolitan place since I left."

"You're a live one, aren't you?" she said.

"You have no idea," Hagen said.

She glanced at the open ledger, then at Trammel's handwriting. "Nice penmanship, Sheriff."

"One of my few good qualities, for all the good it does me." The receipt completed, he handed the pen and paper to Hagen. "Sign there."

"It's a pleasure to be able to sign an official document rather than a marker for a change." He signed the receipt and promptly closed the ledger before tucking it under his arm. "Now, I'm afraid you must excuse me while I return to the Clifford to resume my duties. Much to be done. But I'd be honored if both of you would join me for dinner this evening. I'm arranging something of a welcoming for myself and our new sheriff here. I've invited all of the town's leading citizens. Would be a good way for you to meet all of the important people in town, Buck. I even bent the rules a bit and invited Mayor Welch."

Emily giggled.

Trammel said, "I don't think he'll have much of an appetite seeing me there."

"All the better, then. We'll dine at six. I hope to see you both there." He touched the brim of his hat to the doctor, then to Trammel. "Good day."

Trammel and Emily watched him stride out of the jail, a man of purpose.

"I'm glad he lived up to the billing," Emily said. "I heard he's quite a character."

"That's one way to put it." Trammel gathered up the ring of keys as he stood. "Let's take a look at your patient."

She stopped him cold by placing a hand on his arm. "I'm more concerned about you at the moment. Three dead men on one day and two of them by your own hand. How are you holding up?"

Trammel wasn't accustomed to talking about himself. He was accustomed to people caring about him even less. "I'm alive and they're dead. I'd say I'm doing just fine." He motioned toward the cells. "Shall we?"

Emily shook her head as she followed Trammel into the back.

Madame Pinochet glowered at him from her cot as Emily examined her arm. "Murderer. Fiend. Assassin."

Now that she was no longer in shadow, Trammel could see why she preferred veils and darkness. The entire left side of her face was a mass of ruined skin that he judged was from a burn of some kind. Not from a fire, but more like an iron. Whoever did it to her must've loved her very much at one time, an emotion that had evolved into hate. Only hate could force someone to do that and let the woman live afterward.

"Coward," she spat as she cringed from Emily's examination. "Assassin."

"You're repeating yourself," Trammel said. "Now sit still while the doctor looks you over."

"I have no intention of sitting still. I have no intention of allowing any of this charade to continue a moment longer than it has to."

"You're not in any position to allow anything," Trammel told her. "You're looking at a lot of serious charges. A judge might spare your life, but you won't be breathing free air anytime soon."

"Which judge?" she sneered. "Where will the trial be held? You don't even know, do you? I'd wager you don't even know where to take me. It doesn't matter. I already own any judge you can name. I'll get a slap on the wrist and you'll get egg on your face. I'll be back at The Lion's Den within a week, and you'll be a dead man."

Trammel admired the woman's spirit, even though he didn't like her. He didn't know where to take her and doubted anyone in town would help him. He imagined Laramie would make the most sense, given it was less than a day's ride from Blackstone, but he'd find that out in due course. He could always ride up to Mr. Hagen's place and ask him if he had to.

But she was right that he didn't have any help and wasn't likely to get any help anytime soon. None that he could trust anyway.

"Enfant terrible," she went on. "You have no idea what's happening in this town, do you? This territory? Shame for one so strong to die so ignorant so soon.

You haven't the slightest grasp of what's happening here, do you?"

"Threatening the life of a peace officer," Trammel said. "This time in front of a witness. Another count for your sheet."

Madame Pinochet cried out when Emily touched her arm and cursed her in what Trammel considered her native tongue.

Her examination finished, Emily shut her bag and stood up from the cot. "Her arm's just bruised, not broken. I'm sorry to report she's in otherwise excellent health, much to your dismay, Sheriff Trammel."

Trammel locked the cell door when Emily stepped out.

The lady sprang off the cot and grabbed the bars. "My attorney will be here soon, and when he comes, I'll be back at the Den where I belong, and you'll be powerless to touch me ever again."

Trammel ignored her threats as he escorted Emily into the outer office and closed the door to the cells behind him.

"She's not the most pleasant person in the world even at the best of times," Emily said. "I'm afraid her situation will only make her worse. I'm sorry about that."

Trammel shrugged. "It's just words. I can handle it."

"Not with her, it's not. She's a dangerous woman, Buck, even in jail. She's got a lot of friends in Blackstone who won't like her cooped up like this, especially that you've got her ledger."

Trammel stopped before they got to the jailhouse door. "Her ledger? How do you know I have her ledger?"

"Why, I saw you giving it to Mr. Hagen when I came

in. You wrote a receipt for it and everything. Don't you remember?" She went on tiptoe to hold the back of her hand against his forehead. "Are you okay? Did you hurt your head in the fight?"

Trammel gently eased her hand away. "I'm fine. You've seen that ledger before? I know you said you'd treated her a couple of times."

"I haven't," she admitted, "but I recognized her handwriting, even though it was in French."

That's why he couldn't understand it. It wasn't in code. It was written in French. "How do you know that?"

"My maiden name is Deveraux. I grew up speaking French at home. I don't even want to tell you what she called you back there. They weren't pet names, I can promise you that."

But Trammel didn't care about that. "You saw what was written in the ledger just now? You recognized it as French?"

"I only saw a few words, but yes, I did."

A cold sweat began to break out across his back. "What words did you recognize?"

"I only saw a few in passing, but one leapt out at me in particular. *Maire.* It's the French word for 'mayor.'"

Trammel leaned against the doorway. That's why Mayor Welch had taken such an interest in her arrest. He was in her ledger. He was on her payroll.

Emily took him by the arms and attempted to steer him toward his chair. "Now I'm really worried, Buck. Let me examine you."

Trammel stood upright and, once again, eased her hands away. "There's nothing wrong with me that you can fix, unless you know how to fix stupidity."

Her brow furrowed, and Trammel smiled. She looked so pretty, even when she was confused. "Don't worry about it. I hope you'll be able to go to Adam's dinner this evening."

"I'll only go if you're going."

He managed a smile as he opened the door for her. "Then I'll be by to pick you up at a quarter to six."

"I'll be waiting," she said. "And Buck, please be careful between now and then. Her arrest has stirred up quite a hornet's nest in town. Someone may try to do something stupid, maybe even you."

He assured her he would and watched her climb aboard her wagon. She waved as she released the brake and snapped the reins to make the horse move. Trammel waved back.

He leaned against the doorway and took his first good look at Blackstone since he'd ridden into town. He could hear the drinking sounds from the saloons on either side of the jail. He heard tinny pianos banging out familiar songs and drunks trying to carry a tune.

Across Main Street, the avenues were filled with people going in and out of stores like bees approaching a hive. Men and women stopped and spoke to each other, casting furtive glances back toward the jail, doing double takes when they saw him standing there. Ladies nodded and men tipped their hats to him. Trammel faked a smile as he responded in kind.

How many of them are for me? How many of them are against me? How many of them are working with Madam Pinochet? How many of them will try to save her? Any of them? How many of them will try to kill me? All of them?

It was the final question that burned him the most.

How stupid of me to let Hagen walk out of the jail with the best evidence he had against Pinochet?

Especially because he was fairly certain Hagen knew at least a little French. He had the same familiar expression on his face as Emily had when she saw the ledger. *He knew.*

That ledger might just be the most powerful item in the territory and he had just let Hagen walk out with it in broad daylight.

Trammel thought about going over to the Clifford Hotel and taking the ledger back from Hagen. Adam was a dangerous man, but not dangerous enough to keep Trammel from getting it if he wanted it.

That's when something Hagen had said that morning came back to him.

This is a game of chess. Pawns and kings and such.

Was Adam Hagen trying to be king of the town the way Charles Hagen was king of this part of the territory?

Maybe it would be better if Trammel let the gambler play his hand and see what happened? Maybe Adam Hagen wasn't as smart as he thought he was.

And maybe, Trammel thought, *I'm not as dumb as I'm supposed to be.*

And maybe it was time for him to prove it. He went to the desk and put the receipt for the ledger in his pocket. He had a feeling that would come in handy before long.

CHAPTER 29

After a long bath and a shave, Buck Trammel felt like a new man. He toweled off and began to put on some of the new clothes he had purchased at Robertson's General Store before he'd come up to his room.

"No charge, Sheriff," Tom Robertson had told him. "Think of it as a welcoming gift for agreeing to be our sheriff. We're all confident you'll be a marked improvement over the worthless, lazy lout who preceded you in that office."

Trammel was usually suspicious of gifts, but as he was new in town, decided to play along. "I thought Bonner was pretty popular around here."

"Popular with all the wrong people if you ask me and plenty of others," the shopkeeper said. "He met a fair and equitable end, dying the way he did as he ran out of town. Should've been ridden out on a rail years ago if you ask me."

"But no one asked you," his wife had shouted from the candy counter on the other side of the store. "And best not to speak ill of the dead lest they speak ill of us."

Robertson beckoned Trammel closer. "That letter

being tacked to the jailhouse door was mighty fishy. I think it was the work of the Lutherans, if you ask me. A mighty angry bunch, that lot. Mrs. Robertson's a Lutheran, you know."

"I heard that, you godless heathen!" his wife yelled back.

Trammel had been glad to take his bundle of clothes and escape the store as a full-on family squabble broke out. He'd been in enough scrapes for one day.

Now in his room at the Clifford Hotel, he buckled his new gun belt and secured the strap to his leg. He preferred the comfort of his shoulder rig, but after shooting Elwood through it, the bottom was ruined. The Peacemaker no long fit as snugly as it once had. Robertson took it and said he'd have a tanner either fix it up or give him a new one also free of charge.

The new rig sat against his right leg. The leather was soft, but Trammel knew it would take some getting used to. This was the wrong time to get used to a new rig, but he didn't have a choice. Still, he enjoyed the sound the Peacemaker made when it slid home in the holster. Maybe he could get used to it after all.

He slid on his new coat and took a moment to admire himself in the mirror. Still ugly, he decided, but at least his clothes matched. Everything was the same relative shade of dark brown, but he liked the look. Should be good enough for whatever dinner party Hagen was throwing in his and Emily's honor.

Instinct made him draw his pistol when he heard a sharp rap at his door. "Sheriff Trammel? You in there?"

Trammel stepped away from the door. "Who's asking?"

"I'm Jimmy Hauk, sir," a young voice said. "I work

down at the Moose. You'd better get down here and quick. Sam March from the Den is out on Main Street, sayin' he's gonna gun you down the second he sees you."

Trammel holstered his Peacemaker. If Hauk was a threat, he would've shot by now. "Where is he now?"

"On the other end of town in front of the Moose. They're tryin' like hell to keep him there, but he's got a pistol with him and he's awful drunk. My boss, Mr. Springfield, didn't want you getting shot on account of him not telling you, so he sent me to do just that."

Trammel wondered if he had a few more friends in town than he thought. "Step away from the door about ten paces, but don't leave. Understand?"

"Yes, sir," came the response through the door. Then, "I done what you told me to, but hurry."

Trammel threw open the door, but stepped to the side, waiting. When nothing happened, he looked out and saw a young man of about twenty at the end of the hall. Alone.

"Mercy," Hauk said. "You're even bigger than they say."

"So everyone keeps telling me."

"Please, Sheriff. Come quick. The boys have an eye on him, but he's liable to hurt someone or get himself shot if he keeps up the way he is. The men of the Moose hate loud talk. Cuts into their drinking."

Trammel shut the door behind him and let the young man lead the way.

Dusk had already fallen over Blackstone as they walked along the boardwalk to the Moose. The sky bore dark purple and pinkish lines; a sight Trammel normally would have taken in and enjoyed watching had circumstances been different. He hated wasting a good sunset.

He noticed Hauk may be about twenty, but carried himself with the assurance of someone much older. "You ever in the army, son?"

"No, sir. Rancher. Or at least my daddy was until he gave up the family spread to Mr. Hagen a couple of years ago. Daddy drank the profits, but I'm still here. Sort of work out of the Moose these days doin' whatever Mr. Springfield needs me to do."

"You like that kind of work, Hauk?"

"Keeps me out of the gutter if that's what you're askin'," he said. "And call me Hawkeye. Everyone does. Kinda sounds like my name, so I let 'em use it. Kinda like it. A little Injun soundin' for my taste, but I do like it."

"Hawkeye," Trammel said, trying it on for size. "I like it, too. You know this town better than I do. How you think I ought to go about stopping March from running his mouth?"

"I'd go at him through the back door of the Moose. Come out the front and get him that way. He's liable to start blasting away if he sees you straight on. He's too drunk to hit anythin', but he'd likely miss you and hit someone else."

Trammel liked the way Hawkeye thought. "This back door open?"

"It will be once I open it for you." The boy pointed toward an alley between a saloon and a feed store. "Head down that way and keep walking in this direction. I'll be standing out back waiting for you."

Trammel, sensing a trap, stopped.

Hawkeye looked surprised. "I'll go with you if you want, but it'll take that much longer for me to go around and open the door. I've got no trouble with you, Sheriff, and I sure don't want any, either."

Trammel didn't like it, but he had no choice except to trust the young man. "I'll see you around back, then."

He watched Hawkeye run down the boardwalk. Trammel drew his Peacemaker and held it in front of him as he slowly moved down the alley, mindful of any sound that might be a gun.

He reached the mouth of the alley without incident. He looked to his left and found Hawkeye beckoning him from the back door of a saloon he took to be the Moose.

Trammel moved, but not as quickly as one might expect, careful of anyone who might be waiting for him in the growing shadows. He reached the doorway without incident.

"Thanks," Trammel said to Hawkeye. "March still out front?"

"And drunker than ever. Want me to go around and distract him?"

"Best you stay here until it's over. This won't take long." He paused before heading into the saloon. "And Hawkeye, thanks."

"Thank Mr. Springfield," the young man said. "He's the one who sent me, remember?"

Trammel was in no mood to argue.

He moved into the saloon, ignoring the looks he got from the men who separated as he walked in. The murmurs about his size spread through the room as he caught sight of March through the open door. He was swaying and shouting just as Hawkeye had described. The kid aimed his pistol at anyone he felt was looking at him too long, laughing at their reaction when they backed away.

Trammel decided shooting a drunkard, especially one who worked for Madam Pinochet, would only cement his reputation as a ruthless bully. He'd already killed two men from The Lion's Den. He didn't want to kill another if he could avoid it.

He holstered the Peacemaker as he cut through the bar crowd. He reminded himself not to hit March too hard, lest he meet the same result as his companions from the Den.

Trammel broke into a trot as he neared the saloon door. March faced the opposite direction and was still too drunk to hear him. He'd swayed to face the other side of Main Street and shouted, "Trammel! Come out and fight me, you yellow son of a—!"

Trammel burst from the saloon and tore the pistol from March's hand. The young man turned and Trammel decked him with a short right hand to the temple. March was out cold before he dropped to the thick mud of the thoroughfare.

One of the bystanders said, "Sweet Jesus! Man hits like a mule I had once!"

Trammel looked at the pistol he'd taken off March. Even in the dying light of day, he could see that it was brand new and probably hadn't even been fired yet. Too nice of a firearm for a barman like March to—

From inside the saloon, Hawkeye cried out, "Look out behind you!"

Trammel jumped back as he turned, narrowly missing a knife thrust. This attacker was no boy, but a man of about forty who clearly knew how to handle a knife. His instincts had been right after all. He'd been set up, only this time, it was by March.

The crowd scrambled off the boardwalk as Trammel jumped back from another swipe of the bowie knife.

Trammel hated knives.

He jumped back again as the man slashed the blade from right to left. "I've got you now, you big blunderbuss!"

When his assailant lunged again, Trammel smacked him in the side of the head with the handle of March's gun. The blow stunned the man, dropping him to a knee, but not totally out.

Trammel followed up with a kick that caught him under the chin and sent him sprawling onto his back.

The man's arms splayed on the boardwalk, Trammel brought his boot down on the knife hand with a sickening crunch that made the spectators groan and his attacker scream.

Trammel plucked the knife from the ruined hand and slammed the butt of the knife handle across the man's jaw, rendering him unconscious.

Trammel stood up and looked at the townspeople. None of them would meet his glare. "Anyone else want a turn? Might as well get it over with now that I'm here."

The crowd backed away even farther.

Hawkeye pushed through the crowd and gaped down at the two unconscious men. "I thought you were a goner for sure."

"So did they," Trammel said. "And I might've been if you hadn't called out to me like that. Thanks."

Hawkeye nodded. "Lucky I saw him when I did."

"Luck's not the half of it." An idea came to him. "You got a knife?"

Hawkeye said he didn't, so Trammel handed the attacker's knife to him, which he quickly tucked into his belt. "What about a gun?"

Again, Hawkeye said he didn't, so he gave him March's gun. "Check to make sure it's loaded, then keep it on you. You might be needing it before long. You're my new deputy."

"Really?" Hawkeye brightened. "No foolin'?"

"I'm not in a fooling kind of mood, boy." He looked at the townspeople. "Any of you fine upstanding folk got a rope I could borrow?"

Trammel ignored his attacker's screams as he shut the cell door. Hawkeye did the same with March in the next cell over. Both men were still bound at the wrists and Trammel had no intention of untying them any time soon.

From her cell at the far end, Madam Pinochet yelled, "You're not going to lock me up in here. Alone. With two men."

"Why not?" Trammel said. "After all, they work for you, don't they?" He pointed at March. "My first day in town, this idiot proclaimed his devotion to you."

"But I'm a woman," she hissed.

"That's debatable," Trammel said. "Besides, they're tied up and will be for most of the night. They'll be no harm to you, but I'll see about getting you a blanket you can hang in your cell for privacy."

She rattled the cell door, making poor Hawkeye jump back. "These two may have missed you, but your luck is running out, Sheriff. Do you hear me? Not all of my friends are as inept as these two!"

Trammel tugged Hawkeye's shoulder and beckoned him to follow him out to the office.

He locked the door to the cells and tossed the keys on the desk.

"That Madam Peachtree's a handful," Hawkeye said. "She scares the hell out of me."

Trammel couldn't blame him. He checked the old Regulator clock on the wall and saw he was already running late to pick up Emily and escort her to Hagen's dinner. "I've got somewhere I've got to be, so I have to ask you to stay here and mind the prisoners while I'm gone. I'll be back as soon as I can."

"Ain't you gonna swear me in or something if I'm your deputy?"

"Hell, I don't even know if I'm legally the sheriff," Trammel admitted. "But consider yourself sworn in if it'll make you feel any better." The expectant look on the boy's face told him a tin star would go a long way toward improving his disposition. He went to his new desk to see if maybe an old star had been dumped in there with the rest of the contents of the previous desk.

That's when he noticed several of the drawers weren't quite closed.

Trammel always made it a point to make sure the drawers were completely closed. He had a habit of banging his legs on open drawers and cursed himself for his stupidity. He knew he wouldn't have left them open like that.

Someone else had been there. And he had a good idea of who and why.

"Looks like I don't have a star for you," Trammel

said, "but you're on the payroll as of now. That counts more than tin in my book."

Hawkeye looked happy enough to float away. "Could you give me a few minutes to tell Mr. Springfield the good news?"

Trammel admired the boy's enthusiasm. He wasn't a fool, just young. "Just be quick about it as I have something I've got to do."

The kid stopped halfway out the door. "Mind if I ask what it is? Might be good to know, being that I'm your deputy now and all."

Trammel saw no reason not to tell him. "I guess you could say I'm going hunting, Hawkeye."

"Huntin'?" Hawkeye said. "At this time of night? And in them fancy clothes?"

Trammel remembered the half-closed drawers of his desk. "For the kind of game I'm hunting, these clothes are the best kind."

CHAPTER 30

"A punctual man," Emily Downs observed as she watched Trammel climb down from the saddle. "That's a rarity in this part of the world."

"I was hoping to be earlier but it didn't work out that way," he said. He told her what had happened with March and the knifeman.

"As long as you're not hurt," she said. "Do you think you broke the man's arm? Maybe I should see to him before dinner."

Trammel wasn't in as generous a mood. "He can wait until after dinner."

"Trouble's got a really nasty habit of finding you, doesn't it, Buck?"

"Sure seems that way. New York. Wichita. Hell, even way out here in Wyoming. Don't know why I can't seem to shake it, but I can't."

"Well, as long as you're okay," she said again. "You're sure the knife blade didn't nick you?"

"Never gave him the chance. I'm a big guy, remember? Or so people keep telling me."

"How could I forget? Though, you are like most men out here after all."

"How so?"

"You never complimented me on my outfit, silly."

He made a show of looking her over. It was a lavender dress with dark ruffles and pretty bows. He had never had much of an eye for fashion, but he knew she looked pretty. "It's beautiful. Too good for this crowd."

"I didn't wear it for them." She slid her arm through his. "Come, kind sir. We have a dinner to attend."

Trammel smiled for the first time all day.

Adam Hagen didn't much care for the main dining room of the Clifford Hotel. The room was populated by dark, heavy furniture and gleaming silverware. The dishes were gilt-edged and the glasses were cut crystal. The fireplace gave the crowded room an even warmer feeling.

The oak-paneled walls and dark wooden furniture was too close to Father's drawing room for his taste, but it served his purpose for now. Once he ingratiated himself with Blackstone's leading citizens, he'd begin to quietly make changes on his own; changes so subtle even his father and his minions wouldn't notice until it was too late to stop him.

Judging by the number of people who had accepted his invitation to dinner, Hagen knew his plan was off to a spectacular start. From behind the half-closed door of his room, he sipped his whiskey as he counted the number of people who had already arrived.

Mayor Welch and his wife had been the first to arrive. He had been a lowly teller in his father's bank when Hagen had left home years ago. He had been under Charles Hagen's thumb then and, as mayor of Blackstone, even more so now. Owning his own hotel gave him some semblance of independence, but not enough to buck King Charles on his throne. Father only allowed his people to grow so far.

Fredrick Montague, president of the Blackstone Bank, had arrived with his niece, Clara. At least he had told everyone the young woman was his niece from Missouri come west to visit her old bachelor uncle. Hagen thought the young woman may be from Missouri, but he doubted any familial relation. His inability to remember whether or not she was his brother or his sister's daughter had led credibility to the rumor that she had come west via mail order as much as stagecoach.

Hagen remembered the bank president had always enjoyed a reputation as something of a scoundrel. He was glad to see some things remained the same even after all of these years. He planned on putting that reputation to work for him as he laid his plans to take over the town.

Mr. and Mrs. Robertson of The Blackstone General Store had also come, no doubt to politely mention how happy they had been to refuse the new sheriff's money when the poor man came into their store with only the clothes on his back. They wouldn't miss the opportunity to tell everyone within earshot how they couldn't take his money after what had happened to Sheriff Bonner, God rest his soul.

Hagen made a mental note to make sure to pay them twice over whatever Trammel had bought. He had no intention of allowing Buck to be indebted to a damnable general store owner and his chatty wife.

Hagen had other uses for the storekeeper, the mayor, the banker, and their better halves.

He hadn't decided to throw this party as a homecoming for himself or a welcoming party for Trammel or as some kind of jumped-up memorial service for Sheriff Bonner.

No, the purpose of this party was business. The business of the future. Adam Hagen's future here in Blackstone. And, if he played his cards just right, that future just might include his father's ranch.

He had invited Father and his sister, knowing full well they would decline the invitation. He knew his sister would have wanted to attend, but Father's pride wouldn't allow it. He hadn't earned his respect yet. Montague had been president of his father's bank for almost forty years and he still hadn't earned the trust of King Charles, so Hagen knew the odds of his wayward son doing so were against him. Blood didn't count for much where Father was concerned, a notion Adam Hagen had grown to share.

But when he received the polite rejection note from his father, he was surprised he had assigned John Bookman to represent the ranch. Bookman had earned Father's trust after so many years of servitude. He had only been with the ranch for half as long as Montague, but had helped grow the Hagen empire in other, less-official ways. When he saw the tall, flat-faced ramrod of the Blackstone Ranch enter the hotel, he knew it was finally time to begin.

He regretted that Emily and Trammel weren't there yet, but their presence wasn't important to his plan. The people who could help him pull King

Charles off his throne were here, and that was all that mattered.

Hagen set his glass on the dresser and shrugged into his coat. He checked himself in the mirror and admired his new clothes. He had no idea how a small town like Blackstone had managed to attract such a talented tailor, but it had. If Madam Pinochet's ledger continued to be the treasure trove of secrets it already was, then Adam Hagen would give that tailor quite a bit of business in the years to come.

He saw his gun belt on the table by the window and thought about whether he should wear his guns. He decided against it. There may come a time when brandishing iron was necessary with this group, but now was not that time.

He entered the party and received the forced welcome he had expected. He knew they must have heard about his exploits throughout the years. Montague had never been one to keep a secret, and the Robertsons, no doubt, only added to whatever tales they had heard. He could see the judgment in their eyes as they smiled at him and thanked him for his hospitality.

Mrs. Robertson was the first to tell him about the attack on Trammel at the Bull Moose Saloon.

Hagen forgot all about the true nature of the party. "Was Buck hurt?"

"Him?" the mayor laughed. "No. Our new sheriff has proven himself quite indestructible. He crippled both bandits single-handedly. Though March wasn't much of a challenge. He barely weighs a hundred pounds soaking wet."

So says the man who has never been in a fight in his life, Hagen thought. "I suppose that's why he's late. I hope he'll be here soon."

He turned his attention to Bookman. "Thank you for representing the family, John. It means a lot."

"I'm only here because your father sent me," Bookman said. "I wouldn't be here otherwise."

Hagen hadn't expected anything else from his father's right hand. "Glad to see the years haven't softened you any."

"The years gnaw at everyone, boy." Bookman glanced at Hagen's outfit. "Those fancy threads don't impress me or your father, either."

"The only thing that impresses my father is money and power," Hagen said. "And I plan on having plenty of both very soon whether or not he likes it."

Bookman set his glass of whiskey on the table hard enough to make some of it slosh over the sides. Hagen half-thought the cattleman might hit him. "You threatening me or your daddy, boy?"

Hagen regretted allowing his emotions to get away from him. Contrary to popular opinion, honesty was not always the best policy. "Just a momentary declaration of honesty. No offense meant."

Bookman's eyes narrowed. "I'm offended by you just being back here. Anything you say just makes it worse."

Hagen smiled. "Then ready yourself for an epic disappointment, John, because I've come to town with plenty to say."

"Maybe, but you won't stick around long enough

to say it." Bookman finished his whiskey. "You'll get tired of being here before long and wander off somewhere else. California's my bet."

"For a man who has never left Wyoming, you seem to know a lot about the world."

"I might not be as well-traveled as you," Bookman admitted, "but I know this town and your father's ranch better than anyone alive. And I owe your father more than I can ever repay. One word from him is all it'll take for me to put you down."

Hagen felt sorry for the man, even as he glared at him now. This part of the world was filled with men like Bookman, strong, capable men who might very well have made their own way in the world if they hadn't somehow found themselves working for someone like King Charles Hagen. The tragedy of it all was that men like Bookman didn't know how much working for someone else had cost them. He was happy living off the scraps his father fed him from the table and counted himself lucky. He had no idea how much Charles Hagen had kept him from reaching his full potential. Probably for the best, the younger Hagen decided. If Bookman ever figured it out, he'd probably shoot his father, then turn the gun on himself out of sheer desperation.

He was nothing but a hired hand who thought he was more than that. Hagen had no desire to tell him differently. He had read somewhere that it was dangerous to wake people who walked in their sleep.

"Then let's hope it doesn't come to that, Bookman," Hagen assured him. "Father is lucky to have someone so dedicated to his well-being and his fortune."

Hagen looked at the commotion by the front hall

of the hotel. Emily Downs had just walked through the front door with Buck Trammel in tow. "Speak of the devil and he shall appear," Hagen said. "You must excuse me, John, while I great my guests."

Hagen greeted the new sheriff and the doctor by kissing Emily's hand with a flourish as he bowed. "Good evening, m'lady. You do us a great honor by gracing us with your presence this evening."

She laughed at the gambler's air of formality. "You like to lay it on kind of thick, don't you, Mr. Hagen?"

"A mere statement of the obvious on my part."

He released her hand and shook Trammel's. "Evening, Buck. Glad to see you're still in good health, considering what you've been through today."

"You heard about that already?" Trammel asked. "Guess it's true what they say about small towns."

Hagen patted his friend's shoulder. "Give me time and I'll have the scribes writing novels about your exploits. Daniel Boone will look like a two-bit piker compared to you."

"No thanks," Trammel said. "I'm popular enough as it is and for all the wrong reasons." He lowered his voice. "You and I have to talk and soon."

Hagen figured he'd want to talk about the ledger but did his best to sidestep the issue. "And talk we shall, but pleasure must come before business tonight for this is your formal introduction to the elders of the town."

He led them from the lobby into the dining room and spoke over the din of conversation. "Ladies and gentlemen, just a moment of your time, please. Our guests of honor have arrived, and it is my pleasure to formally introduce to you our new sheriff Buck Trammel and a familiar face, Doctor Emily Downs. I hope you will give them as warm a welcome as you've given me upon my homecoming. Don't let the sheriff's impressive size put you off. You'll find he's as approachable as he is formidable, as long as you don't have a gun in your hand."

Polite laughter rose up amid the applause of those who had come to dinner at Hagen's invitation. A part of him enjoyed seeing Trammel's uneasiness at being the center of attention. He had never seen the big man in a social setting before, his perch in the lookout chair at The Gilded Lilly notwithstanding.

As Hagen expected, the mayor made a point of being the first to greet Trammel. "I think I speak for the rest of the town when I say we mourn the loss of Sheriff Bonner, but we are truly blessed to have found such an adequate replacement so quickly. Welcome to Blackstone, Sheriff Trammel."

Trammel removed his hat and shook the mayor's hand. "I'm not sure everyone in town agrees with you, mayor, but I appreciate the sentiment just the same."

Mr. Robertson, already feeling the effects of the spiked punch Hagen had provided, called out, "Is it true what they're saying, Sheriff? That you buffaloed two men down at the Moose just now and one of them had a knife?"

Hagen watched Trammel blush. "It wasn't that exciting. Just a couple of drunks who couldn't hold their liquor. They're sleeping it off in a couple of cells as we speak."

Mrs. Welch gasped. "Why, you mean you put two ruffians in the same jail as poor Mrs. Peachtree? She may not be much of a lady, of course, but she should be locked in a cage with animals like them."

"I've already taken that into account," Trammel

said. "She's as safe as she can be. I plan on formally charging all three of them in the morning, once I figure out who the local judge is and where I can take them."

"Judge Andrew Burlington is the law in these parts," Mayor Welch said. "Only judge between here and Laramie. He couldn't make it tonight, but I think you'll find him a fair jurist."

"On the off chance you can find him sober," Mrs. Robertson said. "He holds court more at the corner table in the Clover Leaf than he does in Town Hall."

The mayor shot her a glare before saying, "His Honor's shortcomings aside, you'll find Judge Burlington a fair jurist like I said. Purest legal mind there is in these parts."

"Pure on account that it's pickled in rotgut," Mrs. Robertson muttered to Mrs. Welch, causing the gathering to descend into a debate over Burlington's fitness as a judge.

Hagen thoroughly enjoyed watching the townspeople engage in their tribal bickering. He was beginning to see where the fault lines were in this town, which would come in handy when he decided to begin to shake things up. Only Bookman stayed out of the fray, seemingly content to stand behind Hagen while the others argued.

"You remember Mr. Bookman," Hagen said to Trammel. "You and Emily talk while I get you both some punch from my private stash. It's much better than the stuff I had prepared on the other side of the room. Easier to get to as well." Hagen turned to the bowl on the sideboard at his elbow and used the ladle to fill the glasses.

"Evening, Miss Emily," Bookman said. "You too, Sheriff. Mr. Hagen offers his congratulations on your unexpected promotion to sheriff. The real Mr. Hagen, I mean, not Adam over here. Mr. Hagen wishes he could be here tonight, but sent me instead."

"Promotion?" Emily asked as she accepted a glass from Hagen. "You mean you didn't hire Buck outright?"

"Only as a deputy, ma'am," Bookman said. "I guess Sheriff Bonner took it upon himself to leave once Mr. Trammel here signed on. Can't say as I know why, but that's how it played out."

"Poor Sheriff Bonner," Emily pondered. "He wasn't much of a sheriff, but he certainly didn't deserve to be gunned down as he rode out of town."

Bookman seemed intrigued. "How did he die, ma'am?

She looked at Trammel, who motioned for her to go ahead. "Well, the formal report hasn't been submitted to the sheriff yet."

"Your secret is safe with me," Bookman assured her. "Mr. Hagen will ask me and I'd like to have an answer for him."

Hagen handed Trammel a glass of punch. "That's the *real* Mr. Hagen, not to be confused with this cheap imitation."

"Hell, it's probably all over town by now thanks to Elmer running his mouth all over town all day," Trammel said. "Looks like he was shot twice in the back, probably while he was riding out of town. Like the doctor just said, it'll all be in the official report filed tomorrow in the town hall, or wherever these things are filed around here."

"Reports?" Bookman said. "Files? Been a long time since we've had that kind of efficiency around here, Sheriff. Mr. Hagen will be happy to hear that. Bonner had been a good man once, but he'd given to let things slide as of late. A little law and a little order would do this town some good."

"That why he picked me for the job?" Trammel asked.

Adam Hagen was surprised by the big man's attitude.

And Bookman was his normal affable self. "As I recall, Mr. Hagen asked you to become a deputy, not sheriff."

"I don't think Mr. Hagen gets out of bed in the morning without having every step he'll take that day planned out a week in advance. So if Bonner was on the slide as badly as you claim he was, then it stands to reason why Mr. Hagen figured Bonner would quit on the spot. I'd like to know what you said to the man before I walked into his office and I'd appreciate it if you told me right now."

Hagen enjoyed Bookman's consternation. He obviously wasn't accustomed to being questioned. Being his father's mouthpiece tended to tamp down questions. When King Charles wanted something to happen in Blackstone—in Wyoming, for that matter—it happened. No, Bookman may not have liked standing for questioning, but Sheriff Trammel hadn't given him much of a choice. It was obvious that Bookman was still trying to figure out how he felt about that when he said, "I told him what Mr. Hagen wanted me to tell him. That he wanted you hired as the deputy. He hadn't had a deputy in years, and Mr. Hagen thought it would be good to have another man around to help keep an eye on things. He told me he'd see to it right away and I left. That was the last time I ever laid eyes on the man. Next thing I knew, he was dead."

"Were you surprised?" Trammel asked.

"That he lit out or that he was dead?"

"Take your pick."

Hagen smiled as he looked away. Trammel was turning out to be much more than either Father or Bookman had bargained for.

Bookman drew a deep breath before he answered. "Plenty of people around town thought Bonner had lost a step or two over the years. Some even say he'd fallen under Madam Peachtree's influence and that he was even paid to look the other way."

"And what do you say?"

Bookman grinned. "I say Mr. Hagen wanted you hired on as deputy. You became sheriff instead. It was probably going to happen sooner or later anyway, and I'm glad it happened sooner. Mr. Hagen tends to get ornery when he doesn't get what he wants."

"And how do you feel about Bonner getting killed on his way out of town? Mr. Hagen want that, too?"

Bookman set his empty glass on the table. "That sounds an awful lot like an accusation, Sheriff."

"If I accuse you of something," Trammel said, "there won't be any doubt about it. I asked you what you thought about Bonner getting shot. The question still stands."

Bookman shrugged. "Didn't affect me one way or the other. He'd fallen in with a bad crowd. I supposed it ended the only way it could have."

Trammel looked at Emily. "You told me pretty much the same thing."

"Bonner wasn't a complicated man," the doctor said. "He died as he lived."

"Sounds like it," Trammel looked at Bookman. "Mr. Hagen got any plans as far as I'm concerned? Like you said, he wanted me to be a deputy, not a sheriff."

Bookman held out his glass to Adam until the gambler took it and began to refill it. "Mr. Hagen usually gets what he wants. If he didn't want you to be sheriff, he would've told me. So far, he seems pleased. Like you, if he's displeased, you'll know that, too." He accepted the full glass of punch from Adam. "Just keep doing what you're doing, and you'll continue to enjoy Mr. Hagen's support."

"And, if not, I'll end up like Bonner," Trammel concluded.

"No, Sheriff. I've got a feeling you won't end up anything like Bonner." He nodded toward Emily. "Especially if you continue to keep good company with people like Miss Emily here." He inclined his head toward Adam. "And as far away from this one as possible. Now, if you'll excuse me, Mr. Hagen asked me to have a word with the mayor."

"That's the real Mr. Hagen," Adam said as Bookman walked away.

Emily laughed.

Trammel didn't. "You never know when to stop, do you, Adam?"

"Forgive me if I don't bend at the knee for my father's lapdog," Hagen said. "He's nothing more than an errand boy, just like that poor fool you have watching Madam Pinochet right now. What's his name? Hauk? Hawkeye."

"Yeah." Trammel set his glass on the sideboard.

"We need to talk about that. Right now. Will you excuse us, Emily?"

"Of course, but something tells me your conversation will be a lot more interesting than the usual small talk out here."

Trammel nodded back toward Hagen's room. "In private. Now."

Hagen saw no other choice but to do what his large friend said and led him back to his room.

CHAPTER 31

Hagen shut the door behind them. "I take it by your tone that I've done something to displease you, Buck."

"Were you in the jail tonight while I wasn't there?"

Hagen crossed his arms. "Why would I be?"

"I'm beginning to understand the way you talk." Trammel began pacing around the room. "You don't outright deny something, but you won't admit to it, either. Fine. I'll ask it a different way. Why were you in the jail after I left?"

"What makes you think I was?"

"Because the desk drawers were opened more than I'd left them," Trammel said. "Like someone had opened and closed them quietly so no one outside might hear it. That and the fact that I know you've got keys to the place thanks to your old man."

Hagen was fully aware he still hadn't answered the question. He intended on stringing it out for as long as he could, just to see where Trammel was going with this. If his dinner had served no other purpose, it had helped him realize that Buck Trammel was far more competent than first believed. Maybe even more than Father had thought. "What could I possibly want there?"

Trammel reached into the inside pocket of his jacket and produced a slip of paper. The receipt Hagen had signed for Madam Pinochet's ledger. "This."

So he'd kept it on him the whole time. Hagen swallowed. "Why would I want that?"

Trammel put the receipt back in his pocket. "You tell me. And make it quick, because you're not leaving this room until you do."

Hagen saw there was no point in denying it. "I did go into the jail looking for the receipt because I want to erase any proof that the ledger exists."

"Why?"

"Because I want to use the ledger to help me."

"Help you?" Trammel's eyes narrowed. "To help you do what?"

"To make something of myself in this town," Hagen said. "To make an Eden of this Hell created of my father's own devising. He can have his ranch and his cattle and his men, but if I play the hand he's dealt me the right way, I can have an empire of my own that starts right here in town and spreads out like railroad tracks all across this territory. Maybe even beyond. The information in that ledger you took from Peachtree or Pinochet or whatever the hell her name is can help me do that."

"I knew there was something different about you when you took it. It's in French, isn't it? You read French."

"I've picked up enough to get by," Hagen said. "I

didn't know Doctor Downs speaks the language herself."

"It doesn't matter who speaks what," Trammel said. "It's evidence against the madam, and I want it back."

Hagen felt a moment of panic. He couldn't lose such a valuable document over something as tawdry as a doomed woman's trial. "You've already got enough on her to make her spend the rest of her life in prison. You don't need the ledger, Buck."

He watched Trammel grow very still. "I'm asking for that ledger for the last time."

"And I'm asking you to give me time to show you the many treasures it contains," Hagen countered. "This is far too important than to be used as an exhibit at her trial. And, once you find out what it contains, you'll most likely agree that there's every likelihood that it'll conveniently be lost before the trial."

Trammel thought it over, before saying, "You've got one minute to make your case."

Hagen went to the wardrobe and placed his hand on the knob when Trammel's words froze him. "Careful, Adam."

Hagen looked in the mirror and saw the big sheriff's hand had moved closer to the Peacemaker on his hip.

Hagen didn't turn around. "You're not going to shoot me, are you Buck? After all we've been through?"

"Not unless you do something stupid. As long as the only thing you pull out of that wardrobe is the ledger, we'll be fine."

Hagen breathed again as he threw open the wardrobe and pulled the ledger out from the bottom shelf. He flipped open the pages and held the ledger out for Trammel to see. "It lists all of the payments Madam Pinochet has been making to all the right people, not just here in Blackstone, but in the territory. Laramie, too. It's as clear as day if you can read her handwriting and are passable in French, which I am."

Trammel looked at the pages, but it was clear they made no more sense to him than they had when he asked Hagen to look at it. "What were the payments for?"

"Everything, really." Hagen pointed to one line. "This one is the amount of opium Pinochet's Celestials sold to Montague's niece." He flipped to a random page. "Here. This shows how much Judge Milton down in Laramie charged for a dismissal on a murder case last winter. There are also the usual mentions of payoffs to sheriffs and territory officials who allow her to keep her opium trade going. If you give me a few more days with that, I'll figure it out."

Trammel flipped through the ledger himself. Even though the words still meant nothing to him, they meant something to a lot of people. Some in the ledger, some who had written in it, too.

"How the hell did a fool like Bonner get his hands on this?"

"Maybe he wasn't as foolish as everyone thought," Hagen offered. "But he obviously got it from her somehow, but didn't have the sand or the wherewithal to use it. I don't know why the good madam didn't have one of her people toss his place. They surely would've found it." Hagen nudged Trammel. "Their loss is our gain."

Trammel closed the ledger. "And what happens when you figure out all the names in this book?"

Hagen offered a nervous laugh. "Guess I hadn't thought that far ahead, Buck."

"I doubt that. I bet you thought about it plenty. In fact, I bet you've already got designs on taking over the madam's operation all on your own."

Hagen tried charm. It had worked before. "Well, the thought had crossed my mind. Don't you see what you're holding there, Buck? The keys to the kingdom! Don't ask me how that damned fool Bonner got his hands on it or how he could've forgotten to take it with him, but none of that matters now. What matters is that we have it and Madam Pinochet's in jail. And I'm free. And you're the sheriff."

"Meaning?"

"Meaning we can step in where she left off," Hagen said. "Run things like she did, only better."

"You think I'll let you or anyone else run opium in my town?"

"It's not illegal," Hagen said, "and I bet Pinochet's payoffs to Mayor Welch were to keep it that way. Same goes for her tribute to the county elders in Laramie. If the numbers in that book are even halfway accurate, she was pulling in quite a penny on dragon smoke, even after the Chinese got their cut. And that was with two nitwits working for her and an addled sheriff too afraid of his own shadow. Now, if you and I were in charge, I'd wager things would be a whole lot better for everyone all the way around."

Trammel rapped his knuckles on the ledger as he thought over what Hagen had said. "You know, if your old man found out you'd become an opium runner not twenty-four hours after you'd come back to town, he'd have your hide."

"To hell with him," Hagen spat. "I've taken his

scraps long enough. I've done my time wandering the wilderness on his say-so and what do I have to show for it? A mediocre career in the army, two medals I don't deserve, and a stipend I get for staying out of his way. Damn it, Buck. I'm thirty-five years old. How long can a man live with himself like that? Without having something of his own?" Hagen tapped the ledger. "That's my future in your hands."

Trammel kept his hand on the ledger. "If Madam Pinochet was paying off officials, and this book can prove it, then I can use this to bring them down, too."

That was exactly what Hagen could not afford to happen. The politicians were no good to him in jail. But he had to frame his argument in a way that would appeal to Trammel. "Do you think that ledger will ever see the light of day? The names on those pages aren't just locals, Buck. There are bankers, senators, lawmen, and even the territorial governor himself. It doesn't take that many people to run dope, but it takes a hell of a lot of people to make sure you're the only one supplying the territory, and the woman you've got locked away in your jail cell right now has cornered the opium market in the Wyoming Territory. I don't think she and her friends will take too kindly to an easterner, much less a newly minted sheriff, stepping on those toes."

Trammel looked down at the ledger. "Your father's name isn't in this book, is it?"

"That's none of your damned business."

Trammel picked up the ledger and slipped it under his arm. "I know it's not in that ledger, because if it was, you'd be up there right now lording it over your old man to get a bigger piece of his hide instead of down here begging me for a fair shake."

Hagen felt himself growing desperate; more than when he first realized what was in the ledger and entered the jail looking to tear up the receipt that proved its existence. He had figured Trammel would be angry that he'd entered the jail without permission, but would see his way clear to allowing him to keep the book.

Now he wasn't so sure, and his angry fear got the better of him.

"This is rich. You talk to me about the law? You call me a beggar? Who the hell are you anyway, Trammel? A broken-down ex-copper, ex–Pinkerton man come west to hide from his past. A few weeks ago, you were watching drunks and drovers from the lookout chair in The Gilded Lilly, and now you're lecturing me about morality? Who the hell do you think you are?" He looked down at the star on Trammel's coat. "And who the hell do you think is responsible for giving you that?"

A left hook from Trammel sent Hagen back against the wardrobe before sliding to the floor. It took a couple of seconds for the pain to register, but when it did, it registered hard. Hagen couldn't remember when he'd ever been hit harder, but he knew it wasn't the hardest Trammel could hit.

As his ears began to clear, he heard the sheriff say, "I know what I am and what I was, Adam. You'd do well to remember the same. I may have saved your life, and you may have led us here, but we're even on that score. I didn't get this badge from you. I got it from your father. Any debt I owe, I owe to him if I decide to keep wearing it. Right now, I'm not sure it's worth the trouble."

Hagen fought the nausea from the double vision

and the pain webbing from his jaw. "But the Bowman clan is worth the trouble. Or at least you are to them. Lefty isn't going to quit coming after us just because his meal ticket is dead or because we got cleared of killing those folks. He's got a score to settle with you, and he's not going to stop until he finds you. We both know how poorly you fare on the prairie on your own, much less with cattlemen stalking you. You've got a better chance here in town with people who can help or at least a solid jail from where you can fight. Because when they run you down, and they will, you're going to need all the friends you can get."

Hagen ran a tongue along his teeth and felt a molar on the right side of his jaw wiggle. "And since I'm known to be riding with you, I'm in the same boat as you."

Trammel placed his hand on the doorknob, but stopped. "What does any of that have to do with the ledger?"

Hagen looked up at the sheriff from the floor. God, the man looked even bigger from down here. "No one knows you have that ledger except you and me."

"And Emily," Trammel said.

"You *told* her?"

"She was there when I gave it to you, remember?" Trammel took one step forward. "And if any of this crap splashes on her, I swear—"

"Don't be absurd," Hagen said. "In fact, there'll be no violence at all if we play the cards we've been dealt properly." He nodded to the ledger under Trammel's massive arm. "That's the best ace we could ever hope for, Buck. If you hand it in when you bring Pinochet to Laramie, we lose it, and the people in it find someone else to run their poison. If we keep that ledger a secret, we might be able to control who is in it, which is better for us, especially with the likes of Lefty after us."

"He's a one-eyed drunk," Trammel said. "I'm not worried about him."

"Then worry about the people in the ledger," Hagen said. "Look, someone's going to run the criminal element in this territory, Buck. Maybe from here. Maybe from Laramie or Cheyenne, but run it they will no matter what you do. Maybe we can get along with them and maybe we can't. Opium is already here in Blackstone. The tiger's already in the house, and there's no way of getting rid of it without a great deal of danger and difficulty. Now, do you want it purring at our feet or lunging for our throats?" Hagen held out a shaking hand to point at the ledger. "What you're holding there can help us make that tiger do whatever we want. If you hand that in as evidence, it'll disappear. And if you let me translate it, we'll have enough dirt on the right people to protect ourselves."

Hagen stayed perfectly still while he let Trammel soak in his words. The big man was a tough one to figure out, and, even weeks into their association, the new sheriff of Blackstone continued to surprise him. He was far more intelligent that Hagen had initially thought. He only hoped Trammel was smart enough to recognize common sense when he saw it.

He got his answer when Trammel threw the ledger on the bed. "I don't know how deep this crap goes, and I'm not sure I want to know. But I don't want it getting any bigger than it already is. What you do elsewhere in the territory isn't my problem. I only care about Blackstone, and I want the opium den here shut down. Understand?"

Hagen began to breathe again. "Of course."

"This war that's pending between you and your father is your business, not mine. Either of you step out of line, you go to jail. If it comes down between you and him, don't expect me to be on your side."

Hagen was beginning to feel encouraged. "Anything I do against him won't be that direct, so you have nothing to fear on that score. Anything else?"

"Just one more thing." He pointed at the ledger on the bed. "You, me, and Emily are the only three who know you have that. It better stay that way. Anyone else finds out, I'm going to blame you, and you won't be happy."

"I've no desire for anything except profit and revenge at my father's expense. I don't want to hurt anyone else, especially you, Buck. You saved my life, and I won't forget it. You're my friend, and I hope you won't forget that, either." He decided to risk pushing his luck a little further. "And that receipt in your pocket?"

"Stays where it is," Trammel said. "I know how these things can get out of hand. People get greedy. They forget who their friends are." He tapped his jacket pocket. "This receipt will help you remember there's a record that you have evidence against some important people. It might not mean much in a courtroom, but the people in that ledger might like to know who has it. You live up to your end of the bargain, it never sees the light of day."

Hagen slumped over. Short of getting back the receipt, Trammel had given him everything he had wanted. "Thank you, Buck. Your cut will be—"

"Keep it," Trammel said. "None of this has anything to do with me. Keep it that way." As he opened the door, he said, "Make sure you wipe your face before you come outside."

He watched the sheriff close the door as he patted the right side of his face. His hand came away bloody. Hagen smiled. It wasn't the first time he'd had blood on his hands. And he doubted it would be the last.

He was just getting to his feet when he heard a sharp rap on his door. He knew it couldn't be Trammel again because he wouldn't knock. He drew his Colt and aimed it at the door. "Who is it?"

"It's Springfield down from the Moose. Got word you wanted to see me."

With all that had happened, Hagen had forgotten that he had sent word for the man who owned the saloon next to The Lion's Den to come see him. He had told the messenger he wanted to see him after midnight, but the drunk he'd sent might've gotten the time wrong.

"Just a minute," Hagen said as he holstered the pistol and went to the mirror. The right side of his mouth was bleeding, but just a trickle. He knew he'd gotten off lucky. He had seen what that man could do with his fists.

He held a towel to his mouth as he grabbed the ledger and tucked it behind the pillows on his bed. He'd find a safer place for it later.

He opened the door and saw a bald, barrel-shaped man with a filthy gray apron standing in the hall. "I know you said midnight, Mr. Hagen, but that's our busy time, and I figured I'd try to see you now. I used the back door, just like you said."

Mr. Hagen, Adam thought. "No trouble at all. Please, come in."

The saloonkeeper looked at the towel at Hagen's mouth as he entered the room. "What the hell happened to you?"

"Cut myself shaving." Hagen shut the door behind him. "Now, take a seat, and let me explain how we're all about to become very rich indeed."

Chapter 32

In the hotel lobby away from the party, Emily looked concerned. "But you can't leave. This party's in our honor."

Trammel tried his best not to laugh. "This is for Adam more than for us. It was just an excuse for him to get to introduce himself to the important people in town. Maybe tweak his father's nose in the bargain. Besides, I've got a couple of prisoners I need to tend to and a rawboned kid watching them all. I've got to get back."

Emily wasn't convinced. "You and Adam had a fight, didn't you?"

He'd never been good at lying, and he didn't intend on starting now, especially to her. "It was just a little shoving, that's all."

She took his hands in hers and saw blood on his left knuckles. "Thank heavens I have my bag in the wagon," she said. "I'll go fetch it and tend to his wounds."

"He's fine," Trammel assured her. "It was just a bloody lip. I promise."

Emily didn't look convinced. "I don't know if you've looked in a mirror lately, but you're almost six and a half feet tall and more than two hundred pounds. Adam's about one-forty if he's lucky and most of that is in whiskey. I'll get my bag."

This time, Trammel did laugh as he held on to her hands. "He'll be out in a while, I promise. We just had to get a few things straight and everything's fine. There's no bad blood between us."

Emily frowned. "I'm going to take your word for it, Sheriff. But if you're downplaying this for my benefit, there'll be consequences."

He enjoyed the way she spoke to him. Most people deferred to him, given his size. But Emily Downs wasn't the least bit afraid of him, and he wouldn't have wanted it any other way. "Yes, ma'am. Do you want me to come back to take you home?"

"Of course," she said. "But I intend on stopping by the jail to tend to that prisoner's arm you broke. After I do that, then you can take me home."

Realizing they were still holding hands, Trammel raised hers to his lips and kissed them. "I saw Hagen do that when you came in and figured I'd give it a try. How'd I look? Sophisticated?"

"Like a horse drinking from a trough," she giggled, "but I appreciate the gesture. Now go. And be safe."

He squeezed her hands lightly before reluctantly letting them go and taking his hat down from the peg by the door. "Yes, ma'am." He touched the brim of his hat as he went to the door. "How'd that look? Better?"

She waved him off and rejoined the party. Trammel grinned as he stepped outside and into the chilly Wyoming night.

* * *

As he walked back to the jail, he realized this was the first time he was seeing the town of Blackstone at night. The previous night had been spent in the jail, trying to make sense of the ledger he'd found in Bonner's place.

Many of the buildings along Main Street had lit torches that cast a flickering light onto the boardwalk. The side streets had lampposts where oil lamps burned, giving a steadier glow. Those streets were as quiet as Main Street was noisy. The saloon sounds were louder now; the tinny pianos more raucous, the bawdy songs they played drowned out by the drunks who sang along with them. The cackles of painted doves pierced the night air, carried on the wind by the gentle breeze drifting along the thoroughfare. Anxious horses tethered to hitching rails in front of the saloons shifted their weight in the deep mud of Main Street, snouts together as if sharing secrets about the men who rode them.

Trammel realized he didn't know much about horses. He didn't know much about anything in this part of the world. About how people lived. About what they wanted and how they went about getting it.

But he'd seen enough in his time as a cop in New York and as a Pinkerton to know people were pretty much the same everywhere. They always wanted more, be it for themselves or their family. They wanted better, even when what they had was good enough. The drunk wanted another bottle. The storekeeper wanted more business. The saloon owner wanted more customers. The rich wanted to get even richer. It had been the same among the wealthy bankers in Manhattan, the railroaders in Chicago, and the people he'd seen in Wichita. He imagined the town of Blackstone was no different. The only difference was him, because he didn't know this place or how it worked. But the people here didn't know him, either. He hoped that would make all the difference. He hoped he learned about them fast enough before his ignorance got him killed.

He knocked five times on the jailhouse door and called out, "It's me, Hawkeye. Open the door."

He feared the boy may have fallen asleep out of boredom and was relieved when he opened the door immediately. He'd found the coach gun in the cabinet and had the sense to hold it as he opened the door. "Didn't expect to have you back so soon, Sheriff."

Trammel shut the door behind him. "Wanted to check on how you're doing. How are the prisoners?"

"Madam Peachtree is as pleasant as ever," Hawkeye told him. "She cursed at me in several languages when I gave her the food they sent over from the Clifford. Thought she might throw it at me, but she didn't. Guess I'd call that a victory."

Trammel quietly cursed himself for not thinking of feeding the prisoners. He'd never been a jailer before and hadn't thought about providing meals for his captives. He figured Hagen must've done that. Or maybe the Clifford just automatically sent over meals when they heard someone was locked up. He saw a wicker basket on the floor next to the desk. "You get something to eat, too?"

"Yes, sir. Hope you don't mind, seein' as how there was an extra plate and all. March ate up his food fast, but the fella with the busted arm's been asleep since you locked him in there. Must've passed out from the pain."

Trammel would check on them in a minute. "You're going to make a fine deputy yet, Hawkeye. I'll go back and see her now. You go take a walk. See how things are in town."

His eyes lit up. "You mean a patrol?"

The kid's enthusiasm was contagious. "Of course." He noticed the tin badge on his vest. He must've found it in the desk. "You're the deputy, aren't you? Deputies go on patrol." He pointed at the double-barreled shotgun he was holding. "Take the Grainger with you. Make sure they see who's boss around here. But no drinking, understand? You're working."

The kid pulled his misshapen hat down from the peg and set it on his head at as sharp an angle as the hat would allow. "I'll report back in half an hour. You can count on me, Sheriff."

Hawkeye was almost out the door before he doubled back and took the pistol Trammel had given him from the top drawer of the desk. He tucked it in his belt behind his buckle and stood so Trammel could inspect him. "How do I look?"

Trammel thought he looked like a boy playing sheriff, but his confidence made up for it. He took the pistol from the buckle and moved it to his right side. "Like a man Wild Bill Hickok himself would cross the street to avoid. See you in half an hour."

Trammel allowed himself a smile after Hawkeye strode out and shut the door behind him. The kid would need some work, which would take time, but his enthusiasm would make up for his lack of experience for now. He wasn't all that different from other men he'd known; men who would surprise you if you just gave them half a chance. He intended on giving the young Mr. Hauk all the chances he could handle.

Trammel opened the door to the cells and took stock of his prisoners. The man with the busted arm was still asleep, just as Hawkeye had reported. Hawkeye must've found another blanket somewhere.

March was on the floor, whispering at the blanket like a man in a confessional. He barely looked up when Trammel's shadow fell across him.

The sheriff found Madam Pinochet on the corner of her cot, curled up and glaring at him like a rattler. The plate of food was on the floor and empty, save for the chicken bones.

"Evening," Trammel said. "I take it you're comfortable."

"I had to eat chicken," she spat. "With my hands, like one of those damnable savages on the plains. Not to mention that I've had to defile myself by using that bucket over there." She aimed a bony thumb at the blanket. "And having to listen to this imbecile babble all night hasn't made me feel any better."

Trammel glanced at the bucket and saw it was half full. "March being your bunkmate is your doing. As for the bucket, you'll have the chance to empty it out tomorrow morning."

Her eyes narrowed. "You know there's a privy in the back."

"Which you won't be allowed to use," Trammel said. "I don't cotton to people trying to kill me."

"That wasn't me." She hugged herself tighter. "They were allies, but when I have it done, it'll be done proper. There'll be a jingling of keys and the creak of a cell door and the sound of me spitting on your corpse left to rot in the mud out on Main Street."

"You've got a way with words," Trammel said. "Should've been a writer or something with a gift like that. Maybe you'll have enough time to jot down your memoirs before you swing in Laramie."

"I won't make it to Laramie except in a coach," she said. "And you'll never see Laramie again."

Trammel was in no mood to debate her. "I hope you ate well, because that's the last bit of food you'll get while you're here. And I'll expect that spoon you're sharpening to be on the plate the next time I come in here. If not, things start getting worse for you."

Trammel turned to leave the cells. "They couldn't get any worse."

"Don't bet on it." He shut the door and locked it.

Chapter 33

The next morning, Judge Andrew Burlington deftly produced a flask and poured its brown contents into the coffee Hawkeye had given him.

"Having a public hearing in a jailhouse is most irregular, sir," Judge Burlington said. "Most irregular indeed. But given that you are new to these parts, and have had this position foisted upon you due in part to the same tragic circumstances that have brought us here today, I'll overlook it."

Trammel hoped whatever the judge had poured into his coffee would steady him down. He was shaking like a man riding in a buggy over cobblestoned streets. "Sorry about breaking with tradition, your honor, but given the attempts on my life by Madam Peach—, I mean, Mrs. Pinochet and her allies, I didn't want to risk taking her to the court in Town Hall."

"Yes, of course," Burlington said as he brought the cup to his lips. How he avoided spilling the coffee on his lap amazed Trammel. "The public has been notified as to the location and nature of these proceedings?"

"Deputy Hauk posted notices all around town." Trammel noticed how Hawkeye stood a little straighter at the use of his title. "Anyone who wants to stop by can do so, as long as they check their guns outside." He nodded at Hawkeye, who moved outside. The Grainger was at his side. "The deputy will see to it."

"Most irregular indeed," Burlington grunted as he took a pen from his bag and began writing. His hand was steadier by then, and he wrote in a surprisingly elegant hand for a man suffering the effects of alcohol. He was just as Mrs. Robertson had described, a round man whose once-imposing stature had been eroded by years looking at world through the bottom of a glass of whiskey. He had a thick shock of white hair worthy of a governor, but the florid nose of a town drunk, burst blood vessels and all.

As long as he's sober enough to write a legal order for the court in Laramie, Trammel thought, *I'll take what I can get.*

Without looking up from his paper, Judge Burlington asked, "What are the charges made against the prisoners?"

"For Madam Pinochet," Trammel began, "attempted murder against a peace officer and conspiracy to commit murder of a peace officer, one Sheriff William Bonner. The other two, one Mr. March and another assailant who won't give me his name, both threatened my life and assaulted me while on duty."

"And I take it you're the peace officer this nest of scoundrels has been trying to kill?" the judge asked.

"That is correct, your honor."

"And were there any fatalities incurred during the arrest of Madam Pinochet or any of her cohorts in the back?"

"Two of them are currently in Dr. Downs's barn awaiting burial," Trammel said. "Since no one claimed them, they'll be buried at the town's expense as soon as we're done here."

"Money well spent, if you ask me." Burlington stopped writing and looked at the sheriff for the first time since entering the jail. "Am I correct in assuming you're responsible for their demise?"

"You are, your honor."

The judge stopped writing and looked at Trammel. "How long have you been in town, boy?"

"The name's Trammel, your honor. You can call me Trammel or Buck or Sheriff or anything else you'd like, but I haven't been anyone's boy for a hell of a long time."

Burlington sat back in Trammel's chair. "No, I suppose you haven't. You're a big man, aren't you?"

Another one. "Glad you noticed, sir."

"Impudence," the judge noted. "I like that. A healthy amount of it is good in a lawman. Can help keep him alive. Too much of it can have the opposite effect. I suppose that's why Bonner is dead. Are you a man of the law, Sheriff Trammel, or just a roughneck passing through?"

"I took on the duty and I intend on keeping it for as long as the town wants me." He realized then that he wasn't sure if he had to stand for election or if Mr. Hagen's desire was enough to keep him in office. "I admit I don't know how that part works."

Burlington smiled and resumed writing. "If King Charles wants you to stay, you'll stay. Blackstone isn't mature enough to run without his say-so, and that goes for the judges, too. But I know the man's mind, which is an honor few people enjoy. I've been the man's lawyer for forty years. Do what he wants most of the time and you'll do fine. He doesn't ask much and he doesn't ask often, so you'll find it an easy burden."

He found Burlington quite lucid for a man who was supposed to be a drunk. "I'll keep that in mind. I take it you're the only judge around here?"

"I'm all the judge this town needs," Burlington said, "though there are two the next county over should conflicts arise." He tapped the flask in the left side of his jacket. "Don't let that fool you. I know what I'm doing where the law's concerned. My order will stand in Laramie or any other court anywhere, I promise you. Now, given the dangerous nature of the prisoners in your care, I'll take your testimony against her now and read it to her when the proceedings begin. I'd advise you have your deputy guard her while you keep an eye on the door. Madam Peachtree has a great many friends in town and I wouldn't put it past them to try to free her while she's out of her cell."

Trammel took the oath and swore out the complaint against her, detailing everything that had happened at The Lion's Den as far as the madam and the two other assailants were concerned. When he was done, the judge turned the paper toward Trammel and held the pen out to him. "Sign or make your mark after you've read it."

Trammel saw all the details were there and signed it. "What happens now?"

"Now the formal inquest begins. You can bring the prisoners out here one at a time, starting with Madam Pinochet. I suggest you keep good hold of her, son. She's a feisty one and, I'm ashamed to say, has first-hand knowledge of some of my more lurid vices. I'd like anything that old witch says kept off the record and between us."

Trammel laughed. He'd never met a judge like this. "Duly noted, sir."

"Good. After she hears your testimony, I record her response and her testimony. Unless she makes some kind of great revelation, I'll issue a writ authorizing you to transport her down to Laramie within the next forty-eight hours. It's less than a day's ride from here, but I'd advise you to be careful on the trail. She's got a lot of friends in the area who'd like to free her. You're obviously a man who can take care of himself, but a cautious man is a wise man. Once she's in the county jail, the judge will notify you when to come back for the trial. Now, bring out the prisoner and we'll start the public portion of the proceedings."

Trammel went back to the cells and found the prisoner with the busted arm curled up in the corner of his bunk, cradling his arm. Emily had stopped by the night before and judged it to be sprained, but certainly not broken.

March was lying on the floor next to the blanket between his cell and the madam's.

Pinochet was in the same position she had been in the night before. Balled up and glaring.

"Get up. Your arraignment is about to start."

"I refuse to attend."

"It's got to be public and you've got to be there for it. Get up and come out quietly or I'm going to come in and get you. And you'll drop that spoon before you do."

She sprang off the cot with surprising quickness. Her right hand shot through the bars. The metal spoon had been sharpened to a dagger aimed straight for his gut.

Trammel easily sidestepped it and grabbed her

wrist, squeezing it until the spoon fell to the floor. "Help!" she screamed. "Help, judge! He's beating me."

Keeping hold of her arm with his left hand, Trammel unlocked the cell door and pulled her along as he opened it. She brought her left hand up to claw his face, but he blocked that, too. She fought him as he pulled her arms behind her and secured the shackles to her hands. He picked up the sharpened spoon and pulled her out of the cell backward by the chain between her hands.

March banged on the cell bars as he dragged his boss outside to face the judge. The injured man just watched them pass with hollow eyes.

Trammel sat her in the chair opposite the judge and tossed the spoon on his desk. "You can add another account of assault to the sheet."

"We've got quite enough already."

Madam Pinochet wasted no time pleading her case. "He's been beating me, your honor. Ever since he attacked me and my friends in the saloon, it has been one vile attack after another. He—"

"Ah, so now it's 'your honor', is it?" Burlington said. "Not 'that old rummy' or 'that useless old drunk' or any of the other things you've called me over the years?"

The prisoner demurred. "Your honor, I'm a businesswoman and a hardworking one at that. Surely you won't hold things said to you in the past against me now, especially when I'm the one who is the victim here."

Burlington picked up the sharpened spoon Trammel had tossed on the desk. "Yes. Quite a victim." He looked at Trammel. "Might as well open it up to the public, Sheriff. And when you do, bring your rifle with you while you keep a sharp eye on the street. I've got your written testimony here, but if something happens to you before her court date, it'll be tougher to get a conviction."

Trammel took his Winchester '76 from the rifle rack and went outside. Hawkeye was standing to the side of the door, the Grainger on his hip. "Keep an eye on her. Make sure she doesn't pull anything on the judge. She just tried to stab me with that spoon you gave her last night with her dinner."

"With a spoon?" Hawkeye repeated. "Damn, Sheriff. I'm sorry about that."

"Don't apologize. Just get inside and keep an eye on her. I'll keep watch from out here."

Hawkeye went inside and Trammel eyed the street. It was Monday morning, but the streets were Sunday quiet. All the shops were open, but foot traffic on the boardwalks was light. The air was cool and quiet, but heavy with something the easterner couldn't quite describe. Tension, maybe, or something worse.

Judge Burlington called the proceedings to order and hollered out to Trammel, "Are there any witnesses who wish to come forth, Sheriff Trammel?"

"No, your honor. No one showed up."

"More's the pity for you, Mrs. Pinochet, as there is no one to testify to whatever claims you make today."

Her icy laughter sent a shiver down Trammel's spine. "My witnesses will speak for me when and where it counts most, you drunken sot."

Burlington began the formal reading of the charges against her, allowing Trammel to focus on Main Street. He heard a few birds chirping. A horse tethered to a hitching rail across the street fussed. Its ears perked up as it pulled against its reins before settling down again. Trammel didn't know much about horses, but knew they could sense things people didn't.

It was also one of the few horses in town. Most of the rails were empty along the thoroughfare. Even the saloons were quiet. He'd only been in Blackstone a few days, but even he knew this wasn't normal.

Something was off.

He glanced inside and beckoned Hawkeye to come to the door. "Lock it and don't let anyone else in unless you hear me tell you to open it."

The new deputy did what he was told. Trammel moved away from the door and began walking to his right.

Trammel heard the riders before he saw them. He braced himself just as a line of five riders, kerchiefs over their faces, came barreling around the corner from Cedar Avenue heading straight for him.

The lead rider aimed a pistol as Trammel brought the Winchester to his shoulder and fired. The shot caught the leader high in the chest, causing him to jerk back on the reins as he fell and making his horse rear up.

The four riders behind him were temporarily blocked on Cedar Avenue by the panicked horse and had to move around it. A second rider struggled to bring his own horse under control as Trammel racked another round, aimed, and fired, striking the man in the side. The impact sent horse and rider into a spin as the remaining three struggled to get clear of the snarl of man and beast.

Trammel racked and fired again into the crowd of attackers, but wasn't sure he'd hit. Another shot rang out from the group, followed by a bullet slamming into the jailhouse wall well to the left of Trammel.

The sheriff rushed his next shot as two mounts charged toward him. His first shot hit the horse instead of the rider, sending both crashing to the thoroughfare.

Another shot rang out and splintered the post next to Trammel's head. The sheriff levered in another round as he took a knee and drew a bead on a fourth gunman who had held his mount steady enough to aim a rifle at him.

Trammel steadied his aim and shot the man in the belly. The impact caused him to lurch forward and drop his rifle, but stay mounted.

The final rider broke free from the chaos and cut loose with a rebel yell as he charged him full on with two pistols blazing. Round after round peppered the boardwalk and the wall around Trammel, but none came close to the mark.

Trammel dropped to a knee as he levered another round and took aim as a bullet smacked into the wall just above his head. The sheriff fired, his shot creasing the charging horse's mane before striking the rider in the head.

Trammel dove out of the way as the dead man fell from the saddle and the terrified horse crashed into the boardwalk, taking out the post and bringing the roof down upon it.

Though he was clear of the wreckage, Trammel knew he still wasn't out of danger. He had lost track of the men he had killed or wounded in the chaos and knew one might still be alive. He kept his Winchester ready as he belly-crawled to the cover of a horse trough in front of the building next door.

Over the sounds of the dying animal's screams from beneath the wreckage, Trammel heard a pistol shot ring out from across the street. He stole a quick glance around the trough.

Two men were dead in the street.

One rider was pinned beneath the dead horse that had rolled on him as it fell. The amount of blood on his face told Trammel he was busted up inside and already done for.

The gut-shot rider was already past the livery and on his way out of town. He was already dead from the belly wound. He just didn't know it yet.

But the lead rider—the man Trammel had shot first—was nowhere in sight.

Another pistol shot punched through the water trough, sending a steady stream of water against Trammel's pants leg. There was no natural cover on that side of Main Street, so he knew there was only one place the wounded man could be firing from.

Behind the dead horse.

Trammel levered another round into the chamber as he crawled around the other end of the trough. The fallen horse and pinned rider were in the middle of the thoroughfare; the rider's screams matching those of the dying horse beneath the collapsed roof. "Damn it, Buck. Help me! I'm all busted up!"

"Shut your fool mouth!" the last gunman yelled.

Trammel aimed at the sound of the voice and waited.

The man's head popped up from behind the horse for a split second before disappearing again.

When he saw the man toss away his hat, he knew the shooting was about to begin again.

The man rolled to his right, just past the rump of the horse, and fired at Trammel left-handed.

Exactly where Trammel was aiming.

Trammel fired at the same time. His round slammed into the horse, sending up a cloud of blood and bone into the man's eyes. The blinded gunman cried out as he dropped back.

Trammel scrambled to his feet as he closed the distance between himself and his assailant. He found the wounded man trying to rub the gore from his face with his sleeve.

By the time he cleared his eyes, he found Sheriff Trammel standing over him, the Winchester pointed straight at his head.

The man blinked hard. The pistol in his left hand twitched.

Trammel took a step closer. "Don't."

But the man jerked up the pistol and Trammel fired.

When the last echo of the shot died away, the sheriff kicked the gun loose from the dead man's hand.

"Please," called out the rider pinned beneath the dead horse. "Please help me."

Trammel spun around, ready to fire, when he saw movement at the corner. He lowered his rifle when he saw it was Emily at the corner, a shotgun at her side. "Buck!"

"Get back inside!" he yelled at her. "It might not be over yet."

He watched her turn and rush back toward her place.

He ignored the dead man as he walked back across

the street to the screaming horse. The animal was trapped beneath a mess of split planks and roofing on all sides. It had been bucking since it had fallen, only pinning itself deeper in the wreckage.

The sheriff switched the Winchester to his left hand, drew his Peacemaker, and put the poor animal out of its misery with a single shot.

With the shooting over, the streets of Blackstone quickly filled with people; many of them were armed with rifles or pistols, brave now that everything was over.

Trammel walked back to the pinned man, who held out both hands to him. "Please, mister. I'm out of it. Don't kill me." He coughed a red mist of blood. The man was already dead. His body just didn't know it yet. "Please help me. I'm all busted up inside."

Trammel kept the Peacemaker against his leg. "Who sent you?"

"I'll tell you as soon as you help me. Please. I need a doctor."

The man screamed when Trammel put a boot on the dead horse atop the man. "One more time. Who sent you?"

"L-Lucien," the man sputtered as a trickle of blood spilled from the side of his mouth. "Lucien Clay out of Laramie, damn you."

The name meant nothing to Trammel. "Why?"

"To try to b-bust out Mrs. Peachtree. Now, damn it, you've got to help me!"

Trammel cocked the Peacemaker and aimed it down at the dying man. Every fiber in his being wanted him to squeeze the trigger. For trying to kill him. For this man and his friends thinking they could ride into town and do whatever they damned well pleased. For putting the lives of people at risk. His people. His town. God knew he'd killed men for far less.

But when he felt the dozens of eyes upon him, he looked around and saw all of the townspeople looking at him. His people, or as close to his as any people had ever been. He had come west to start a new life, to lose himself in the chaos of the frontier, but had found himself here instead. With a gun on his hip and a star once more on his chest. A star that didn't just mean order, but law. He'd had the luxury of vengeance before, but things were different now.

He thumbed the hammer of his Colt down and slid the pistol back into its holster and walked back toward the jail. "Somebody hitch up a team and clear this mess off the road. Bring the bodies over to Doc Downs's office." He nodded down to the man at his feet. "This one'll die as soon as you move the horse off him, so throw him on the pile, too."

The townspeople began to go about doing the task Trammel had given them. With the front of the jail blocked by the collapsed roof, he knew he'd have to go around the back way to get inside. He hoped Hawkeye hadn't panicked and blown Mrs. Pinochet's head off, though he wouldn't shed a tear if he had.

He was surprised to see Adam Hagen leaning against the post of the Clifford Hotel as he passed. His pants had been hastily pulled over a nightshirt, and his Colt was in his hand. "You are a man to be reckoned with, Sheriff Trammel."

He was in no mood to spar with the gambler and kept moving. "Thanks for the help. I appreciate it."

Hagen hopped off the boardwalk and joined him as he walked behind the jail. "I was asleep when it happened. By the time I got out here, you'd just finished off the last one. I'm glad you didn't kill the man under the horse. It showed great restraint and increased your popularity among the townsfolk."

Trammel wished that made him feel better, but it didn't.

CHAPTER 34

Young Deputy Hauk had not shot Madam Pinochet when the gunfire started. He'd placed the prisoner back in her cell, while he and Judge Burlington had taken shelter in the cell block.

"Kept that Granger pointed at that sour bitch the entire time," Judge Burlington told Trammel after it was all over. "If a sparrow so much as pecked at the door before you called out, he would've given her both barrels at point-blank range." The judge toasted them before taking a sip of his spiked coffee. "Got to admit I was wrong about that young man. Always had him pegged for an idiot. Guess you never know about some people."

His reddened eyes fell on Trammel. "Like you, for instance. I never would've thought a city man like yourself could handle yourself so well up against such men. You're building up quite the reputation for yourself, Sheriff Trammel."

"I don't get paid to have a reputation, your honor. I get paid to keep the peace, and I'm doing a damned lousy job of it."

The judge poured some of the contents of his flask

into Trammel's mug before pouring the rest into his own. Hagen looked forlorn when the judge slid the flask back into his pocket without offering him any.

"You haven't had much chance at peace since you signed on," Burlington said. "That's more Bonner's doing than yours. If that greedy slob had done his job instead of taking money from The Lion's Den to look the other way all these years, things'd be more manageable. You've poked a hornet's nest, young man, and you're not responsible for what's happened since you've been here. But I'm glad things have turned out in your favor."

Then Burlington looked at Hagen. "Though the company you've kept before coming here is questionable at best."

"Good old Honest Andy Burlington," Hagen sneered. "Still cleaning up Father's messes after all of these years."

"You being one of them," Burlington shot back. "Your father didn't pay your bills all of these years. That pleasure fell to me and Montague. If you'd been my flesh and blood, I would've cut you loose years ago. You can hate your father all you want, boy, but that man supported you against my advice."

"Honest Andy indeed," was all Hagen managed to say.

"Hello in the jail," a booming voice came from outside. Trammel brought up the Winchester, and Hagen aimed his Colt at the door. "It's John Bookman and some others. We're here to help."

Hagen holstered his pistol. "That'll be Father, I'm sure. Probably with twenty riders, too. King Charles must make an entrance."

Trammel set the Winchester against the desk and

opened the front door. John Bookman stepped in first, followed by Charles Hagen. He looked out the window and, through the wreckage of the roof, saw no fewer than twenty Blackstone Ranch men on Main Street. Sometimes he hated it when Adam was right.

Mr. Hagen wasted no time speaking his mind. "I just heard what happened. You hurt, Trammel?"

Trammel gave him the abbreviated version and punctuated it with, "My deputy cleared the dead and debris from in front of the jail. The dead men are all over at Doc Downs's office waiting to be buried in the morning. I'll try to fill out the paperwork before I leave."

"Leave?" Mr. Hagen repeated. "Where are you going?"

"Transporting the prisoners to Laramie, sir." He pointed to the paper on his desk. "Judge Burlington here signed the writ this afternoon. The sooner Pinochet and the others are out of our hair, the better. They'll be Laramie's problem this time tomorrow."

Mr. Hagen frowned. "Can't we just save a lot of time and effort and string them up right now and be done with it?"

They all looked at Judge Burlington, who slowly shook his head. "I'm afraid that horse has left the barn, Charles. She's going to end up dancing at the end of a rope, but news of her arrest has obviously reached as far as Laramie, as evidenced by the attack on the town here today. Any premature death at this point would be met with considerable scrutiny by our friends in the county seat. Lynching is frowned upon, even here in the wilds of Wyoming."

"Heavens," Adam said. "You mean there are limits even to the power of King Charles Hagen?"

His father fixed him with a withering look. "And just where the hell were you when all of this was happening? Cooped up with a painted dove, no doubt."

"No," Adam said. "She'd already left by that time. I was asleep, but when I came to assist, the good sheriff here had already ably dispatched the assassins."

Trammel saw Adam flinch when his father turned to face him. "How convenient. Convenient, too, that all of this happened less than a week after you came to town. Trouble's got a bad way of following you, boy."

"Some would call it a gift."

"I call it suspicious." He pointed a gloved hand at his son. "I swear before God and everyone in this room that if I find out you had a hand in any of this, I'll drag you to death."

"You mean have me dragged to death, don't you, Father? Heaven forbid you do the dirty work yourself."

Mr. Hagen went for his son, but Bookman moved between him. "He's just trying to goad you, sir. Don't let him."

Trammel tried to take some of the fire out of the situation. "One of the men told me who was behind this before he died. A man by the name of Lucien Clay out of Laramie. I hope one of you have heard of him, because none of us have."

Mr. Hagen turned away from his son and faced the sheriff. "Lucien Clay? The name means nothing to me. Who is he?"

"No idea," Trammel admitted, "but whoever he is, he went through a hell of a lot of trouble to get Madam Pinochet sprung."

"And that's as close as he's going to get to her," Charles Hagen said. "My boys'll run her and the others down to Laramie tomorrow."

"No, they won't," Trammel said. "Transporting prisoners is a sheriff's job. I plan on running her down to Laramie on my own at first light."

Judge Burlington cleared his throat. "Do you think that's wise, Sheriff? After what happened here today? Fending off five men alone in a town is admirable, but there's a lot of open space between here and Laramie. The road is fraught with danger."

"That's why I don't plan on taking the main road, your honor. I plan on taking the least direct route possible."

Mr. Hagen began to say something, but stopped himself before saying, "I don't mean any disrespect, Sheriff, especially after what you did here today. But the back road to Laramie's no place for a tenderfoot with a wagonload of prisoners in tow. If this Clay fellow still means to take her, then ambushing you on the way to Laramie, no matter how you get there, is the easiest way."

"That's the way I'd do it," Bookman added. "I'd wager there's probably at least ten more men out there just waiting for you. Maybe more. They'll be out for blood when they realize their friends don't come back."

"Then it's a good thing I won't be alone." Trammel looked at Hagen. "Your son has bravely volunteered to go with me."

Adam quickly swallowed his surprise before the three men looked at him.

Bookman didn't look convinced.

Mr. Hagen's head inclined back toward his son without looking at him. "That true?" he asked from over his shoulder.

"Of course," Adam said. "I may have been late to

the party, but I wouldn't miss the final dance for all the tea in China."

"All the bourbon in Kentucky's more like it where you're concerned," Mr. Hagen said, then looked at Trammel. "Normally, I'd try to change your mind, but you don't strike me as the kind of man who changes his mind lightly."

"You're paying me to be the sheriff of Blackstone, Mr. Hagen. That means transporting prisoners to Laramie when it's called for. And it's called for now."

"Fine. I'll leave ten of my men here to keep an eye on things while you're gone."

"No need, sir. I've hired a deputy who'll tend to things while I'm out of town."

"Already? Who?"

"Jacob Hauk."

"Hauk?" Mr. Hagen looked at Bookman. "Why do I know that name?"

"You acquired his father's ranch a few years back"

The name registered with him immediately. "He'd be about twenty now, wouldn't he? What's he been doing with himself?"

"Working as a bottle washer over at the Moose," Bookman told him.

Mr. Hagen closed his eyes. "Good God. Fine, but I insist on one of my boys driving the wagon."

"I've got that covered, too. Elmer has signed on to help me."

"Elmer?" Mr. Hagen barely managed to hold on to his tongue, but he did. "You assembled quite a team for yourself, Trammel. The town drunk and my ne'er-do-well offspring with three hostile prisoners."

"And me, sir," Trammel said.

"And you," Mr. Hagen said. "And I'd be a damned fool to doubt you just might be able to pull all of this off."

He surprised Trammel by holding out his hand to him. "Best of luck, Sheriff. And thank you."

Chapter 35

As the first light of dawn began to appear in the eastern sky the next morning, Smith had already saddled two horses and hitched up a team to an old wagon by the time Trammel, Elmer and Hagen got to the livery.

Hagen looked less than pleased by the two horses Smith had chosen. "Are you sure this old nag will make the trip to Laramie? Look more fit for the glue pot than the trail to me."

Trammel may not have known much about horses, but even he could tell these two were scrawny and just about at the end of their rope.

"They'll stay alive out of habit if nothing else," Smith told him. "And with all of this shooting going on, I ain't dumb enough to give you any good horses only to see them get killed. Or worse, that old drunk Elmer slappin' them to death with them straps."

Elmer climbed into the wagon box and took the reins. "I was handlin' teams twice this size before you was a thought, you old fool. Now get out of my way. I've got prisoners waitin' to get loaded."

As Elmer moved the wagon off toward the jail, Hagen and Trammel began checking their saddles.

The sheriff could not resist the chance to rib his friend a little as they tucked their rifles into the saddle holsters. "Sorry if I cut into your social calendar by volunteering you like that, Adam."

"Cut into it?" Hagen glared at him as he secured his Winchester. "You outright obliterated it. What got into you back there, volunteering me to ride to Laramie with you like that?"

"Figured it'd help pry your old man off your back," Trammel said. "He was hitting you pretty hard."

"I'd rather take a beating and be in bed than riding out with you and a wagon full of prisoners at this ungodly hour."

"No need to come if you don't want to," Trammel said. "Just point me in the right direction and Elmer and I will bring them in together."

"With your sense of direction and that old rum pot's memory? You'd probably wind up in the Yukon before you found Laramie."

Trammel felt a pang of resentment. "I'm a bit better at finding my way than that."

"I'm glad you think so," Hagen said. "You may be a hell of a man in a fight, but you're hopeless on the trail. But I have big plans for your celebrity, Buck, and I won't have those plans dashed on account of stubbornness on your part."

"I've got my own plans." Trammel slid the Winchester into the scabbard. "And they sure as hell don't include being famous."

"You'll take to it, don't you worry." Hagen stopped checking his saddle and looked at Trammel. "You know I planned on trailing out after you anyway, don't you? No matter what you said to Father in there."

Trammel was glad he was right about Hagen. He would never admit it, but he felt better having his old trail partner along for the ride. He decided it best to focus on the business at hand. "You sure you don't know anything about this Lucien Clay character?"

"I've only been in town as long as you have, Buck," Hagen pointed out. "But Father is right. If he sent five men to shoot up a town to free our fair madam, then he probably has at least ten between here and Laramie to cover their retreat. Since I'm the one who brought you here, I feel a bit responsible for you. I'd hate to see you get killed on account of my plans."

Trammel made sure the coach gun was secure in its scabbard. He may not have shared Hagen's low opinion of his skills on the trail, but he was glad for the company. "I never pegged you for the type who had a heart."

"Just keep it to yourself." Hagen began leading his horse from the livery. "I'm in the process of building a bad reputation for myself. Wouldn't want to ruin it."

A small, but intrepid crowd of townspeople had gathered in front of the jail to watch the wicked Madam Peachtree and her cohorts be loaded on a wagon and ridden out of town. Trammel had asked the townspeople to clear out the wreckage of the roof and dead horses, and he had to admit they'd done a damned fine job. Save for the bullet holes in the jailhouse wall, there was no hint that men had died at the site less than twenty-four hours before.

Never one for spectacle, Trammel had ordered

Elmer to bring the wagon to the back door of the jail, where Hawkeye brought out Madam Pinochet and March. Both of them had their hands shackled behind their backs.

When they were seated and secured in the wagon, Trammel said, "Good job, Hawkeye. Bring out the last one."

"Can't," Hawkeye said. "He hanged himself last night. Looks like March there gave him that blanket what hung between his cell and Madam Peachtree's."

Trammel reached into the wagon and snatched March by the back of the neck, pulling him upright. "Is that true?"

"It was his life," March said, "his decision."

"And your idea." Trammel released him with a shove, allowing him to fall back into the wagon. "It was certainly your blanket. You just got a couple of charges added to your record, March. I know it was your lady's idea, but you're going to be the one who pays for it."

"It was my idea!" March roared. "At least allow her the dignity of sittin' upright, not lying in the back of a wagon like some damned sack of grain!"

Trammel looked at Pinochet's prostrate black form and decided she did look a bit like a sack of grain after all.

She cursed in French and added, "You fools are riding to your deaths. None of you will make it to Laramie alive."

Hagen nudged his mount close to Elmer's team. "We're going to be taking some rough paths though the wood between here and Laramie, old man. There's a lot of tough customers between here and there.

Some damned uneven terrain, too, especially for a wagon. You sure you're up to it?"

"I've ridden through worse with hostiles hot on my tail hungry for hair," Elmer said. "I reckon I can handle this bunch. Just point out which way you want me to go, and I'll follow."

As Hagen laid out the path, Trammel saw how dejected Hawkeye looked over the prisoner's suicide. He didn't want the boy dwelling on it in his absence. "That man's death is not your fault, Deputy."

"It was my duty to watch him."

"It was our duty to watch him," Trammel corrected him. "And we were both busy preparing for this ride. Besides, the man tried to kill me. There'll be plenty of time and reason for regrets in this job. This dead man isn't one of them. Understand me?"

"Don't make it right, boss." Hawkeye said.

"Then we learn from it and move on." That was the last he intended to say on the matter. "I need you to keep an eye on things here in town while we're gone. We should be back by lunch tomorrow."

"And what if you're not," Hawkeye asked. "I mean, what should I do?"

"Don't worry," Hagen called out to him, his conference with Elmer finished. "My father will be more than happy to tell you what to do."

Hagen tipped his hat to them as he galloped off into the woods behind the jail. Elmer set the wagon team moving with a crack of the reins.

The grim procession of leading Madam Pinochet and her disciple March to jail in Laramie had begun.

Trammel and Hawkeye turned when they heard

a female voice say, "Weren't you going to come say good-bye?"

Hawkeye pulled off his hat as soon as he saw her. "Morning, Mrs. Downs."

"Good morning, Jimmy," she smiled. "We're also grateful that you'll be watching over us while Sheriff Trammel is in Laramie."

Trammel watched the kid blush. "You are?"

"Certainly. Anyone who the sheriff has faith in must be a capable man."

"But I—" Hawkeye looked at Trammel. "I mean, I'm nowhere near as good as—"

Trammel decided to let the kid off the hook. "It's been a long night, Deputy. Get some rest while you can. I'll be back tomorrow before lunch."

Poor Hawkeye was still bowing to both of them as he backed into the jail and slammed the door shut behind him. Trammel was glad to hear the heavy bolt slide home.

Trammel and Emily shared a laugh at the young man's expense.

"If he kept bowing like that," Trammel said, "I was afraid he'd break something."

Emily's smile faded as she looked up at him. "I'm worried you're going to do worse than break something in bringing that witch to Laramie."

"I'll be fine," Trammel lied as much for her benefit as his own. "I took down five men singlehandedly yesterday, remember?"

"How could I forget? It's all anyone is talking about. And the rumor mill has run the number up to ten as of this morning."

He imagined the number would be as high as

twenty by the time the drunks retold it that evening. "Five was plenty."

"You don't have to do this, you know?" She gently leaned against the jail and folded her arms. "Mr. Hagen could send ten men or more if you'd just ask."

But Trammel's mind was made up. "Mr. Hagen hired me to do a job, Emily. This is part of it. It wouldn't be right to have him help me. I don't just work for him. I work for the town. And if the people think I only work for him, then I'm no different than the judge or Montague or Mayor Welch."

"You've been in town less than a week, Buck," she said, "and you've already done so much. You don't owe anyone anything."

A part of him knew she was right. But another part of him knew she couldn't be more wrong. "Maybe I owe it to myself to try. For a lot of reasons you don't know yet."

"Stubborn." She shook her head. "In that case, you'd better make it back here in one piece so I get the chance to know more about what those reasons are. And more about the man they belong to."

Trammel felt himself blushing again. He simply touched the brim of his hat and pulled his horse about to follow Hagen and the prison wagon down to Laramie.

He looked back when he reached the edge of the trail and was pleased Emily was still looking at him. "How'd I look just then? Like a Westerner?"

"Like a New Yorker." She laughed, "But we'll work on it."

Chapter 36

Trammel caught up to Hagen and the wagon about a mile away from Blackstone. The gambler was leading Elmer and the prisoners on a crooked, uneven path over the tangled roots and uneven ground of the forest.

"How's it going?" he asked as he pulled up next to Hagen.

"Relax, Buck," Hagen smiled. "We're barely a mile away from town. But her ladyship here has already regaled old Elmer and me with dark tales of our impending doom. About how we'll both be gut shot before long and the last thing either of us would see would be her pulling the trigger." He looked back at the wagon. "I leave anything out, dearie?"

Young March comforted her as she responded with a string of curses in her native French.

Hagen was amused. "I'd translate that for you, Buck, but I think you've blushed enough for one day. Let's just say she didn't dispute anything I told you. Though, I must say, if I'm to be called a lying, double-shuffle jackass, French is just about the prettiest language I can think of to hear it."

"The last thing either of you will hear," young March added, "will be the sounds of your own screams."

Elmer cut loose with a stream of tobacco off the side of the wagon. "I'll be more than willin' to gag these two if you want, Sheriff. This here ride's spooky enough without her yappin' all the time. I don't care whatever language it is."

Trammel decided it might not be a bad idea. "Do it, but be quick about it."

The wagon driver's face brightened. "You mean it?"

"Just hurry."

Elmer threw the break and eagerly swung his legs around and hopped down into the wagon.

The prisoners began to protest while Elmer produced filthy handkerchiefs from his pockets to use as gags.

Hagen rode closer to Trammel. "I think Elmer was just joking, Buck."

"Well I'm not. These woods might be full of Clay's men. One scream from either March or Pinochet could bring the whole bunch down on us. The quieter they are, the better for us." Hagen looked like he had more to say on the matter, but Trammel wasn't in the mood to hear it. "Since you seem to know these parts better than anyone, you take point and lead the way. If not, take over the wagon and let Elmer do it. I want to make Laramie as soon as possible."

When they arrived at Laramie, Trammel got his first look at the town that had sprung up around the fort. Except for its size, it wasn't all that different from Blackstone. It had shops and liveries and hotels all bustling with people moving to and from the train station. Teamsters dropped off goods at trading-company storefronts, and people gathered in front of lawyers' offices and banks to chat about the weather and their crops and whatever else Trammel imagined people spoke about in towns like this.

All of them stopped whatever they were doing when they saw Hagen and Trammel leading Elmer and the prison wagon into town.

"I've been ridden out of this town in shackles plenty of times," Elmer told them. "But I believe this is the first time I've ever led someone in that way."

"Congratulations," Trammel said, eyeing the crowd for anyone who paid too close attention to them. This was, after all, Lucien Clay's domain, and the mystery man had sent a small army to free the madam. Now they he had brought them to his ground, Trammel knew anything could happen.

Hagen pulled off to the side of the thoroughfare and let Trammel and the prisoner wagon pass. "Continue on to the jail, Elmer. I trust you know where it is."

Elmer laughed and told him of course he knew, having spent many a night as a guest in one of its cells.

Trammel pulled his horse next to Hagen's. "What the hell do you think you're doing?"

"What I came here to do," Hagen said. "Become acquainted with the town's criminal element, especially Lucien Clay."

"But what if I need you for . . . something?"

"But you won't need me," Hagen told him. "It's your show from here on in, Buck. Just follow Elmer and his wagon to the county sheriff's office right up the street. You should be the one who leads Pinochet and

March into the jail. I'll drop back to a safe distance and cover your back, just in case this Lucien Clay or his men attempt to stop you."

Trammel rode past him, surprised by how much attention the two riders and the wagon were receiving from the people on the street. News of their arrival rippled ahead of them along the boardwalks like a wave along a shoreline until it crashed upon the rock that was the county jail. By the time he reached the jail, a man Trammel pegged for the county sheriff was already on the boardwalk, flanked by two of his deputies. The sheriff was taller and older than the other two, but all of them were well fed and bore the coloring of men who had spent a great deal of time in the sun.

Elmer had already thrown the wagon brake in front of the jail when Trammel stopped next to him. Neither man made an effort to dismount.

"You Sheriff Abernathy?" Trammel asked the man in the center.

"I am." His eyes shifted back and forth between Trammel, Elmer, and the two prisoners in the wagon. "And just who the hell might you be, big fella?"

"Sheriff Buck Trammel from Blackstone delivering a prisoner to stand trial. Mrs. Alexandra Pinochet and Mr. March, her accomplice."

"Madam Peachtree?" one of the deputies asked. "How the hell did—"

"Shut up, Johnny," Abernathy barked at him. He looked up at Trammel. "I hope you've got writs for these prisoners from Judge Burlington, boy, because we're not in the practice of taking other town's trash here, not even from Blackstone."

Trammel noted the rifles each deputy was carrying

as he slowly pulled Judge Burlington's writs from inside his coat pocket. He heeled his horse to move closer as he handed the sheet of paper down to him. "I was told to give these to you. Judge's orders."

Abernathy frowned as he opened both sets of papers and read them. He handed it to the deputy on his left and took a closer look at the woman prisoner. "You really have to lead her in here like that? Chained up and gagged in a wagon the whole rough ride to Laramie?"

"I just showed you the charges against her," Trammel said. "She tried to kill me personally and was responsible for several attempts on my life, one of them at the hands of Mr. March here. You can't blame me for being cautious."

Abernathy looked up at Trammel. His jowls had begun to sag with age, and he reminded Trammel of a bulldog. "I don't know you, mister. That star on your vest says you're the sheriff of Blackstone, so I guess that makes it so. It's up to a judge to figure out why you did what you did to Madam Peachtree and her friend here. That's what judges are for. But I do know King Charles, and I know his men ain't known for being subtle. Guess you might as well unhook her and bring her inside."

"That's your job, Abernathy, not mine." Trammel dug the key to the shackles and tossed it to Elmer. "Help the deputies take the prisoners into the jail. I'll cover you from here in case one of them tries anything."

"One of my men," Abernathy said, "or one of the prisoners, Trammel?"

Trammel let that one go. "Just be quick about it

because we're hungry. Got a place around here where me and Elmer could get something to eat?"

One of Abernathy's deputies began to say, "There's Olson's—"

"Shut up, Johnny," Abernathy said. "Climb up into that wagon there and help Milt here with the prisoners."

Trammel caught the exchange. "What's wrong with Olson's?"

"Nothing," Abernathy said. "It's a fine place, but there's a much better place right across the street called The Longhorn Saloon. Best steaks in town, by my reckoning. You can leave the wagon right here if you want. Come back for it later after you and your man here have had a meal."

Elmer clapped his hands. "Sounds downright affable to me!"

Trammel looked at Abernathy's belly and grinned. "Sounds like a hell of a recommendation. Thanks."

Abernathy helped March down from the wagon and handed him off to another deputy who had come outside, then Madam Pinochet. "Mention my name and you're likely to get a free glass of beer on the house."

Elmer climbed down on his own steam and walked beside Trammel's horse toward The Longhorn. "Looks like this day is shaping up to be quite somethin', ain't it, Sheriff?"

Trammel couldn't ignore the bad feeling spreading in his belly that wasn't from hunger. "Yeah. Something."

* * *

Trammel found a vacant spot at the hitching rail, and Elmer was kind enough to wrap his horse's reins around it for him.

Hagen was already up on the boardwalk, leaning against a post as he smoked a cigar. "Elmer, I've got bad news."

The town drunk frowned. "You mean I ain't gettin' paid for transportin' them prisoners."

"Not that," Hagen said. "I was just inside and found out this place only serves beer."

"Beer?" Elmer said as if the word itself was enough to poison a man. "What kind of place only serves beer?"

"The kind that doesn't want customers who get crazy on liquor, and the Longhorn here is one of them. Olson's down the street is a whiskey establishment. I think you'll be happier there."

Elmer looked up at Trammel for permission. "Go ahead, Elmer, but don't wander or get too drunk. We'll be needing you to drive that wagon back home tonight."

"Don't you worry about that, Sheriff. Feels good to be needed again." The town drunk of Blackstone shook Hagen's hand. "You saved me from an afternoon of disappointment, Mr. Hagen. I'm grateful."

The two of them watched Elmer toddle off in the general direction of Olson's, surely to be found somewhere amid the sea of buildings and people that was Laramie.

"You hear all that between me and the sheriff just now?" Trammel asked Hagen as he stepped up to the planking.

"Every word," Hagen said. "Saw that deputy's

expression, too. Johnny. I think they were all mighty surprised to see you'd made it here alive."

Trammel stretched his back. The ride from Blackstone may not have been long, but it was long enough to make him sore. He didn't know how the cowpunchers could spend so long in the saddle and not hurt for days. "Don't know why he'd be surprised. The trail was clear."

"The trail was littered with Clay's men. Twenty by my count."

"What?" Trammel took a step back, almost falling off the boardwalk. "You said it was clear!"

"I *told* you it was clear," Hagen explained. "Or rather, I told you it was clear for Pinochet's benefit. I didn't want her knowing her friends were around and trying something. Since there was no way of telling you without her finding out, I'm afraid I had to lie to you. I'm sorry about that, but I hope you'll understand it was for the best."

Trammel didn't know whether to thank Hagen or punch him. He knew he didn't like being kept in the dark about being so close to danger but understood why his friend had done it. "How come they didn't hit us?"

"Because they were watching the main road to Laramie, not the way we took. They were close enough in places, but were too busy with their cook fires and coffee to pay attention to what was happening behind them. I'm just glad we had Elmer gag them when we did or else it would've meant trouble."

Trammel didn't like the implication that they couldn't have handled themselves. "We've lived through scrapes before, Adam."

"When we had the element of surprise and suitable

cover." Hagen flicked his cigar ash off the boardwalk. "But all bets are off in a heavily wooded area, just like in the woods outside of Wichita, remember? The men along the Laramie road had us outgunned, out mounted, and outmanned by five to one. Those aren't odds anyone would take, much less a gambler like me."

Hagen smiled as he clapped Trammel on the shoulder. "Forgive me for lying to you? Please."

A part of Trammel knew he should be angry, but it was difficult to be angry with a man who had just saved his life. Again. "Just don't make a habit of lying to me, even if it's for my own good."

"You have my word, for whatever it's worth."

Trammel's stomach reminded him he was hungry, and he was eager to forget all about it. "Come on. Let's get something to eat. Elmer might need his whiskey, but I need food, and Abernathy says the steaks here are the best in town."

But Hagen didn't budge. "Laramie's a funny town."

Trammel sensed more bad news coming. "In what way?"

"Seems Laramie's town elders, in their infinite wisdom, passed an ordinance saying that a proprietor's name had to be clearly displayed on the front of each business. The Longhorn Saloon is no different." He waved his cigar toward the door. "Take a look at that sign and tell me what you see."

Trammel already had a good idea of what he'd see before he actually looked at the sign, so he wasn't surprised when he read: LUCIEN CLAY—*Proprietor*—1875.

The sheriff felt his anger spike. "Abernathy, that scalawag. Trying to set me up."

He was about to step off the boardwalk to storm back over to the jail and confront the sheriff when Hagen grabbed his arm. "That would be unwise, my friend. Think about what you'd do when you got there."

"Kick the hell out of him, for starters."

"That's right. And you'd cut through his deputies, too, like a hot knife through butter."

Of that, Trammel had no doubt.

Hagen continued, "And where would you be then? You'd have the entire town against you and a judge who's probably not going to be inclined to convict Pinochet or March even with all of the evidence we have, since much of that evidence is based on your testimony. The testimony of a man who had just killed or wounded the local constabulary."

Hagen's words did little to prevent Trammel's temper from beginning to rise. "There isn't a man alive who can say he made a fool out of me and I'll be damned if some dung-kicking sheriff from Wyoming thinks he got the jump on me."

"So prove him wrong," Hagen offered. "Not by beating him up but by showing how wrong he is." The gambler smiled. "And you can show him by going inside anyway."

Trammel was beginning to understand the way the gambler thought. "The element of surprise, right?"

"Do what the enemy least expects you to do, my big friend." Hagen pushed open the batwing doors of the saloon. "Come on. First round is on me."

"Wait a minute." Trammel stepped off the boardwalk and pulled his Winchester from the saddle. "I'm bringing a friend along with us. Just in case."

Chapter 37

The Longhorn Saloon was certainly larger than any of the saloons in Blackstone, but, to Trammel's thinking, served the same purpose.

A spirited crowd of gamblers and drovers and drunkards huddled together over whiskey and cards. No fallen doves near as he could see, but he was sure they were somewhere upstairs plying their trade.

The interior was plainer than Trammel would've expected. No fancy mirror behind the bar or paintings from back east. Just a bare wooden interior with dozens of tables filled with men looking to escape the pressures of frontier living for a while. A few soldiers on leave stood at the bar, trying to act more sober than they were.

All of them grew quiet when they noticed the big man with the star on his chest and the Winchester in his hand walk among them. Trammel took little notice of it. He was used to people staring at him before he was a sheriff. He saw no reason why it should be different now. He was more interested in allowing his eyes to adjust to the dim light of the saloon.

He had no idea what Lucien Clay looked like, and

neither did Hagen, if Hagen could be believed. He could be any one of the men looking up at him now or none of them. But Trammel needed to be ready in any case.

Trammel followed Hagen to a table in the darkened corner of the saloon. Men eagerly moved their chairs out of the way for him. Some of them even nodded up at him as they passed.

Hagen and Trammel sat in the corner chairs facing the rest of the saloon. From there, they had a perfect view of the front door and everyone in the place. There was a stairway that led up to the rooms, but Trammel noticed the balcony didn't extend behind them, only over the front of the saloon. If anyone tried shooting down at them from there, they'd be spotted.

Trammel waited for the din of saloon noise to rise again when he told Hagen, "I don't like being backed into a corner like this."

"Like I learned in the Point," Hagen explained, "sometimes you have to sacrifice maneuverability for clarity. No one can get behind us, so for our purposes, these are the best seats in the house."

Trammel looked over the saloon from beneath the brim of his hat. "Which one do you think is Lucien Clay?"

"I haven't the slightest idea," Hagen said. "Given the reception we received, I would have expected to see deference to his position. A clamoring around him of protection or some such thing. Why, at this very moment, someone may be dashing off to warn him strangers are about." He flicked his cigar ash on the floor. "But I'm sure the devil will show himself in some form or another if we just give him enough time."

Trammel kept his head still when he heard a commotion just behind them on the other side of the wall. Probably by the back door he had noticed when they walked inside. A large man with long greasy hair cleared the wall and headed straight for the bar. He was pulling up his suspenders as he did so, though his shirt wasn't tucked in.

The man's hair was in the way, so Trammel couldn't see his face, but he saw the gun on his hip plain enough.

The man yelled at the barman, "You see a big ass stride in here? Bigger 'an me, even? Name of Trammel?"

The big sheriff ignored Hagen's plea to sit still. He came out from around the table and shoved his way through the men and chairs between him and the bar. Men scrambled out of the way, forgetting about the cards they had been dealt and the money they had on the table.

The loudmouth at the bar didn't turn at the sound of commotion behind him.

Trammel stopped a good ten feet away from him. "I'm Trammel. Now who the hell are you?"

The big man slowly turned. Trammel didn't recognize him at first until he saw the filthy bandage over his eye.

Trammel heard himself say the name before he remembered it. "Hanover. You finally caught up with me."

"Glad you remembered the man you crippled," Lefty sneered. "And the man who's going to kill you for takin' my eye."

"You lost that eye to an infection," Trammel said, "not on account of—"

Trammel didn't have time to finish his sentence before Lefty's right hand slapped at his holster. The sheriff stepped forward and fired a loping left hook that caught Lefty in the jaw, snapping his head back as he sprawled back against the bar.

Trammel took the gun from Hanover's holster and stepped back. "That's enough, damn it. I didn't do anything to you except throw you out of the Lilly a couple of times."

He looked at the barman, who had pinned himself against the liquor shelf. "Get some coffee into this fool before he hurts someone." He opened the pistol's cylinder and spilled out the bullets into his hand. He tossed the gun to the barman, who flubbed it and let it fall to the floor. "And don't give that back to him until after his hangover is gone."

Lefty emitted a primal scream and leapt at Trammel, catching him dead center in the ribs.

He only managed to push the big man back a couple of feet before Trammel buried two hard right hooks into his left kidney. Hanover cried out before he crumpled to the saloon floor. Trammel reached down and grabbed Lefty by the collar as he dragged him out of the saloon, making a wide, crooked trail in the sawdust on the floor as he did so.

He pushed through the batwing doors and yanked Hanover to his feet, only to kick him in the backside and send him sprawling into the thoroughfare. He was surprised by how winded he was, but given Hanover's impressive deadweight, he realized there was a reason.

When he got his wind back, Trammel stood to

his full height and pointed down at Hanover. "I'm warning you for the last time. Go dry out someplace before you get killed."

Hanover spat a mouthful of blood into the mud as he got to one knee. "The only one dyin' here today is you!"

He reached under the back of his shirt and pulled a pistol.

Trammel drew his Colt and fired before the one-eyed man had a chance to aim, striking him in the left side of the chest. Hanover tumbled backward into the dense mud of the Laramie thoroughfare. He died looking up at a cloudless sky as the hole in his heart leaked blood into the mud.

Trammel looked at some of the people on the boardwalk gaping up at him. He was as surprised as they were. He had known Lefty and his men had been tracking him and Hagen from Wichita, but he thought they would have given up after their trail ran cold in Dodge.

Trammel ducked when a rifle shot from inside the saloon struck the doorframe next to his head. Wooden splinters pierced his skin as he dropped to the boardwalk and rolled away.

"I got him," yelled a man with a Mexican accent from inside the Longhorn. "I killed him for what he done to Lefty!"

Trammel ignored the pain as he got to a knee and saw a scrawny Mexican barrel through the batwing doors onto the boardwalk, a rifle at his shoulder.

Trammel raised the Colt and fired. The shot caught Chico in the temple. The impact sent him spinning as he fell. His rifle skittered to Trammel's feet. The people on the other side of the boardwalk screamed as the spray hit them.

"Chico!" screamed a man from inside the saloon. "Chico, are you hit?"

Trammel holstered his Colt and picked up the dead man's rifle. He checked the breech and saw there was at least one round in the chamber. Being more comfortable with a rifle than a pistol, he decided he'd use it instead.

He was beginning to wonder where Hagen was in all of this when a shotgun blast tore out the window above his head, covering the sheriff in glass. He felt some shards had fallen down his shirt as he dropped flat on the boardwalk. Another blast boomed, and a hole exploded through the saloon wall.

Trammel ignored the pain in his back and rolled until he was in a prone position under the batwing doors. He saw the shooter—a tall, rawboned man with a heavy beard—feeding more rounds into a double-barreled shotgun. Trammel fired from beneath the door and hit the man in the center of the chest. He staggered back but didn't fall. He didn't drop the shotgun, either. Trammel fired again; the round caught the man beneath the chin and sent him down for good.

A pistol shot struck the boardwalk next to Trammel's leg. Another sailed high above him. Trammel got his feet under him and somersaulted into the saloon as more shots peppered the doors and frame. The sheriff got to his feet just as the man put a shoulder into the doors.

Trammel slammed him in the head with the butt of his rifle. The man dropped the gun as he staggered back against the porch post. Trammel burst through the doors and hit him in the nose with the butt. The man fell back against the post, slumped to the boardwalk, then flopped sideways off the boardwalk. The look in the man's eyes told the sheriff he was dead.

Trammel ignored the crowd of people who had begun to swell around the boardwalk now that the shooting was over and pushed through the doors into the saloon.

His hands were shaking from the excitement and fear coursing through his veins. He glowered at every man in the Longhorn, but none dared meet his gaze. Blood streamed from the wooden splinters that had peppered his cheek.

He wanted the man who had been trying to kill him. He wanted him right now.

"LUCIEN CLAY!" he bellowed. "Show yourself, you coward!"

From the back of the saloon, a tall, swarthy man with curly black hair and neatly trimmed muttonchops wearing a red brocade vest edged through the crowd. He walked stiffly and with his hands away from his sides, though Trammel could see he was unarmed.

"I'm Lucien Clay."

"And I'm Sheriff Trammel." He tossed the rifle aside and set his hand on the Peacemaker on his hip. "You're under arrest."

Hagen stepped out from behind Clay, and Trammel could understand why the saloonkeeper was so stiff. Hagen had Trammel's Winchester stuck in the small of his back. "I'm afraid not, Buck. He had nothing to do with those men attacking you. They were customers, not employees. They got here yesterday looking for you. Rode up here clear from Wichita. They planned on riding up to face you in Blackstone once they shook off some trail dust with the help of Mr. Clay's lady friends." He dug the rifle barrel deep into Clay's back, causing him to almost cry out. "Isn't that right, Lucien? Speak now before the good sheriff here beats you to death. He's a force of nature when his blood is up, and I think you can see his blood is up now."

"He's right," Clay yelled. "Those cowpunchers came in here yesterday talking about how they were going to Blackstone to wipe you out."

Trammel's temper didn't abate. "And what about the men you sent to kill me in Blackstone yesterday? The ones you sent to free Pinochet?"

"Don't know anything about that," Clay said. "Or the twenty men your friend here says were waiting for you on the trail."

The room gasped when Trammel drew his Peacemaker and aimed it at Clay. "I think you're a liar."

Hagen stepped out from behind Clay and placed the Winchester barrel under the saloonkeeper's chin. "A fact I intend to find out soon enough, Buck. Now please, lower the gun and let me do what I do best."

Trammel froze when he heard three rifles rack behind him. Sheriff Abernathy said, "Holster your iron, Sheriff. What happened 'til now was self-defense. Shooting Clay would be murder. I won't cotton to murder in Laramie. Not while I'm sheriff. Now tuck that hog leg back where it belongs and do it real slow. I'd hate to have to shoot you, but I will if I have to."

Trammel slowly lowered the Peacemaker, then slid it back into the holster. He heard Abernathy and his deputies lower their rifles.

"Glad you saw clear to reason," Abernathy said. "Things bein' as they are, it'd be best if you came over to the office to make your formal statement."

Trammel slowly turned and faced them. Deputy Johnny swallowed hard. The other deputy backed up a step. Only Abernathy held his ground.

"You arresting me?"

"If I was, you'd be in irons by now. But I'll need your statement for the report, and I'd like to get it from you while it's fresh."

Hagen walked the distance between him and the sheriff and handed Trammel the Winchester. "Go with them, Buck. I'll be along in a minute."

Trammel was still mad at him for not backing him in the gunfight. "And just what the hell will you be doing?"

"Talking to Mr. Clay, of course." He looked back at the chief merchant of vice in Laramie. "We've a great many things to discuss, don't we, Lucien?"

Chapter 38

Lucien Clay's rooms made Adam Hagen jealous. It was a space fit for a king, though far too gaudy for a king like his father Charles. It had all of the adornments he would have expected to find in the saloon downstairs. Intricately carved wood around the fireplace, paintings of lounging naked women eating grapes, and more mirrors than he had seen in some brothels.

The whore on Clay's lap clipped his cigar and placed it in his mouth. She thumbed a lucifer alive with an elegant hand and lit it for him. Hagen had been forced to light his own cigar, not that it bothered him much. It was fine tobacco, rivaled only by the brandy Clay had offered his guest. Hagen realized he would have to adopt many of these trappings in his bid to shift the power of this territory from Laramie to Blackstone. The true power, anyway.

But despite the elegant atmosphere and the beautiful woman in his lap, Lucien Clay still managed to glare at him from across the room. "Now that all the nonsense is over, tell me what you want."

But Hagen was having too much fun to be rushed.

"Why so angry, Mr. Clay? I would've thought some gratitude would be in order after I spared your life just now."

"You mean that monster with a star down there?" Clay laughed. "Why, if he'd taken one step toward me, he would've been shredded before his next foot hit the floor."

"Yet he aimed a pistol at you and no one moved a muscle," Hagen observed. "Still, you were wise to keep your men out of it. It wasn't their fight, and they were smart to let it play out."

"I didn't have much of a choice," Clay said. "You had a Winchester at my back, remember?"

"Of course." Hagen flicked his ash on the rug, intentionally ignoring the ashtray at his elbow. "Another wise move on your part. A gunshot to the kidney is such a horrible way to die. You're a smart man, Mr. Clay. I think we can do business."

"Business?" Clay sneered. The woman on his lap caressed his hair. "Why in the hell would I want to do business with you?"

"Because I'm very good at what I do," Hagen said. "Because I've just cornered the opium market in Blackstone, and by the time I get back to town, I'll have every saloon owner in town giving me a piece of their business due to my close relationship with Sheriff Trammel."

"Blackstone isn't even a pimple on Laramie's ass," Clay said. "I pull in more here at the Longhorn in a week than that whole burg does in a month, and that includes the opium trade."

"Yet you tried so hard to free Madam Pinochet from Sheriff Trammel's clutches. A woman who ran a town that isn't even a pimple on the ass of Laramie, to use your phrase. Why is that?"

Clay told the whore on his lap to leave, which she did.

When they were alone, Clay said, "I don't like discussing business in front of my girls. And I've got no idea what you're talking about."

"Of course, you do," Hagan said. "You don't feed Madam Pinochet opium. The Celestials bring it to Blackstone first before it comes here. Fewer eyes that way. Less possibility of a shipment being stolen on a coach or a train," Hagen offered. "Less for you to worry about, too, what with this being the county seat and all."

Clay's mouth grew hard. "No law against opium, Hagen."

"But it's so unseemly," Hagen said. "And it's so much nicer when such nasty things are handled elsewhere, like in Blackstone. So close, yet just far enough away. It's a pleasant arrangement. Tell me something. Was it your idea or hers?"

"I don't know what you're talking about."

"Sure you do. I read all about it in her ledger."

Clay stood up. "How the hell do you know about that?"

"Know about the ledger?" It was Hagen's turn to laugh. "I not only know about it. I have it. And I know everything that's in it, including all of the money you owe her. And all of the money she pays off to everyone in the territory. Including you. And the good Sheriff Abernathy, too."

Clay's eyes narrowed. Hagen could tell he was a man used to being in control of things. He didn't like being on the pointy end of the stick, but he'd get used to it. He'd have no choice if he wanted to continue to operate in Wyoming. "How do I know you're not bluffing?"

Hagen had been expecting that. "Because most of it is written in blue ink, in French, and in the madam's own hand."

"God, you really do have it." Clay collapsed back into his seat. "What do you want?"

"For you and I to be friends, Lucien," he said. "For us to become friends, and if you'll give me a few moments of your time, I'll lay out a plan that will not only make us both happy but incredibly rich."

Trammel signed his name to the report Sheriff Abernathy had drawn up.

"You didn't even read it," the sheriff said.

"You wrote it down as I told it. I didn't have to read it. I'm sure it's fine."

Abernathy sighed as he took the paper from him. "You know this is an official document, don't you? A public document?"

"I've been a lawman before," Trammel said. "Of a fashion, anyway. I know how the system works."

"So you know word of what happened here will be in the papers. What you did and how you did it."

"I killed four men who tried to kill me in broad daylight," Trammel said. "I didn't expect it to be forgotten the next morning."

"There's liable to be an inquest," Abernathy went on. "You may have to come back to town to testify in open court. Would you be willing to do that?"

"Don't see why I wouldn't. It's part of the process."

Abernathy folded his thick fingers on top of the desk. "What I'm getting at here is that I don't want to have to go up to Blackstone to get you. I'd appreciate it if you'd come peaceable if and when you have to. I'd like your word on that."

Trammel grinned. "What's the matter, Sheriff? You don't think you and your men are enough to bring me here on your own?"

Abernathy leaned forward. "Boy, you just killed ten men in two days and hardly have a scratch on you except for them splinters sticking out of your face. Now, I know I could take you if I had to, but not before you and, most likely, some of my men got killed in the process. I'd like to avoid that, especially given that you're in the right here. So, I'm asking you for your word that you'll come back peaceably if you have to." He extended his hand to Trammel.

Trammel regarded the hand, then shook it. "Peaceable."

The sheriff tried to pull his hand away, but Trammel didn't let it go. "Peaceable as in you sending me to Lucien Clay's place without telling me about it first?"

Abernathy's jaw opened. "Now just wait a minute."

But Trammel's grip only tightened, making Abernathy wince. "He told you to be on the lookout for me, didn't he? Told you to send me into his place if I brought Pinochet to town."

Abernathy said through gritted teeth. "Damn it, Trammel, it's not as easy as that. Clay draws a lot of water in this town."

"So you set me up to get killed, didn't you? Not by those idiots who came at me just now, but by others he had sitting in the crowd." He squeezed the hand just a bit tighter, causing Abernathy to cry out. "That's why you knew I didn't take the road from Blackstone. Because you knew Clay had men guarding that road. That's why you made that crack about making Pinochet ride rough ground all the way from Blackstone, isn't it? Admit it!"

"He said he wanted me to point you out if you got to town," the sheriff winced. "That's all, I swear."

The two deputies rushed into the room with their pistols drawn.

Trammel looked at them as he squeezed the sheriff's hand even tighter, making the lawman shriek. "Drop those pistols or I shatter his hand and pull his arm out of the socket." He twisted the hand to the left, causing the sheriff to scream again. "Do it now, boys. Your boss is in a lot of pain."

"Do it, damn you!" Abernathy screamed.

Both deputies placed their pistols on the jailhouse floor and took a step back. Trammel motioned for Abernathy to get up and come around to his side of the desk. He took the sheriff's pistol from him before releasing him with a shove. The deputies scrambled to keep him upright as he cradled his arm.

Trammel held the sheriff's gun on them. "Back in the cells. All three of you."

Abernathy squinted through the pain. "What? Why?"

"How many men did Clay send to ambush us on the trail? And don't tell me the five I killed because I don't count them."

"About twenty," Johnny said. "At least that's as near as we can figure."

"And they'll be coming back to town now that they know I'm here, won't they?"

The second deputy nodded. "Mike Wilcox rode

out to tell them the second we saw you in town. And they're not those drunken cowpunchers you butchered, mister. They're twenty of the worst men in the territory. You'll be dead five minutes after they hit town."

Trammel glanced at the Regulator clock on the wall. "Which I take it will be any minute now." He looked at Sheriff Abernathy trying to flex feeling back into his arm. "Which is why you kept me busy giving my statement, isn't it?"

Abernathy didn't bother to deny it.

Trammel had heard enough anyway. "All of you, back in the cells like I said."

"You can't do this, Trammel," Abernathy said. "By God, it ain't right."

"Looks like I'm doing it." He thumbed back the hammer of his Colt. "Move. Now."

The three lawmen reluctantly slunk back toward the cells. Johnny tried to grab the ring of keys that was on the hook next to the door. Trammel squeezed off a shot that slammed into the wall just above the peg. "Keep moving."

When they got in the back, Trammel ordered all three of them into a cell. They grumbled as he locked the door.

Abernathy banged against the locked door and grabbed the bar with his left hand. "You'll be dead in a few minutes, Trammel. You'll never get away with this."

Trammel smacked Abernathy's hand with the butt of his own pistol. "Where have I heard that one before?"

Madam Pinochet's cackle cut through the air as

Trammel shut the door to the cells and locked it. He put a chair under the knob just for good measure.

The door did a good job of blocking out most of the cries for help from the deputies and the cackles from Madam Pinochet while he took stock of his situation. With Clay's twenty riders coming back to town, he knew he didn't have much time.

He threw the bolt across the jailhouse door, locking it. The door was too thin to withstand much of a barrage of rifle fire if it came down to that. The windows were small and didn't have shutters. An intrepid rider could easily toss a firebomb in that way, making a bad situation even worse for Trammel. At least the walls were thick and would provide some sort of protection for him.

He checked the rifle rack for weapons he could use. None of the Winchesters proved better than his own. At least they had plenty of ammunition, which would help. He remembered he'd used his Peacemaker during his fight with Lefty and his men back at the Longhorn. He dumped out the spent rounds and reloaded from a box he'd found with the rifles. He left the box of bullets on the desk for fast reloading if it came down to that.

He checked his Winchester Centennial to make sure Hagen hadn't used it during the dustup at the Longhorn. Fortunately, the weapon was still fully loaded. The sheriff's office had plenty of spare ammunition for the rifle as well, should he need it.

Going up against twenty men, he figured he'd be dead before he made it through a box, but it was nice to know it was there if his luck turned.

He looked up when he heard people shouting

outside. Then he felt the reason why they were shouting. The jailhouse floor began to shake beneath his feet as the twenty riders Clay had sent to watch the road from Blackstone came back to town.

It was time to make a decision. Would he hide in the jail until they came in to get him, probably after trying to smoke him out first? He might get the first bunch that came through the door, assuming he could see them through the smoke or hadn't choked to death by then.

Or would he go out and meet them—and his death—on his terms? Die his own way and definitely take a couple of them with him?

It wasn't a difficult decision for Buck Trammel to make.

He picked up his Winchester and threw the door open. He strode out onto the porch and set the butt of the rifle on his hip as he waited for the riders to reach town.

The first of the twenty raced past the jailhouse, while the others trailed behind at a slower clip. Trammel's grip on the Winchester's stock tightened as one after the other, men of all shapes and sizes filed past him without so much as a glance his way.

Are they surrounding the jail? Are they going to come back on foot after they livery their horses? Why not get it over with right now? I'm one man. They could ride past the building and take shots at me like I've heard the Indians do. Why aren't they stopping?

He gave a start when he heard his name called out from across the street. "Sheriff Trammel!"

He brought his rifle to his shoulder as he aimed at the direction of where the sound had come from. It was Lucien Clay. And Adam Hagen was standing next to him.

Both men were smiling, which didn't make Trammel feel any better. He lowered his rifle. "What do you want?"

"How are Sheriff Abernathy and his men?" Clay asked.

"They're back with the prisoners." Which wasn't a total lie. "Why?"

Hagen's laughter echoed across the thoroughfare. "Let them free, Buck. And if they're still able to walk, let them come over here. Mr. Clay and I would like to talk to them. Then get something to eat. You look all about done in."

Trammel slowly lowered his rifle entirely. He didn't know if he could entirely trust Hagen, given his apparently new friendship with the man who had ordered him dead.

But Hagen had never crossed him before. Besides, if there was any shooting to be done, it probably would've happened by now. "You mean it's over?"

He saw Hagen shove Clay, who yelled back, "It's over, Sheriff. No hard feelings. Now go get something to eat anywhere in town. It's on me. And don't forget to send Abernathy over. I've got to get him straight on a few things."

Trammel looked up at Hagen, who was positively beaming. "You all right?"

"All right?" Hagen clapped a hand on Clay's shoulder, who didn't look too happy by the gesture. "My friend, I've never been better. Now get those splinters taken care of. We've a fair piece of ground to cover tonight to Blackstone, and I don't want that getting infected."

CHAPTER 39

It was going on full dark by the time they saw the hint of lights from Blackstone on the trail. Trammel knew it wasn't much of a town by Laramie's standards, but he was beginning to think of the place as home. He remembered standing on the jailhouse porch in Laramie only a few hours before, wondering if he'd ever see this place again. Wondering if he'd ever see Doctor Emily Downs again.

The poultice the doctor in Laramie had placed on his face was beginning to itch something fierce, but something worse had been nagging at Trammel the entire ride back to Blackstone. It was Hagen's refusal to answer any questions about what had happened between him and Clay. Hagen's constant humming had only served to make it worse.

Trammel drew his horse to a sudden halt, causing Hagen to do the same. "What's wrong?"

"You've been too damned quiet and happy the whole way back here," Trammel said. "I want to know what happened."

"You already know what happened," Hagen said. "I saved your life. Again." He thought for a moment and said, "I suppose that's not entirely true. I saved my own life, too. I wouldn't have let you face those men on your own, and I would've been cut down right alongside you."

Even in the dying light of the day, Trammel could see Hagen's eyes flash. "Would've been a glorious end, though. Probably would've taken at least ten of them with us in the cross fire, but I'm glad it didn't come to that."

"That's what's been bothering me." Trammel leaned forward in the saddle. "Why didn't it come to that?"

"Because I was able to appeal to Mr. Clay's better interests as a businessman and a proprietor," Hagen explained. "I told him bloodshed was unnecessary and would be bad for business. Fortunately, I was able to convince him in time to send a rider and head off the men before they reached town." Hagen's eyes narrowed. "You don't look happy."

"Because I'm not. I don't care about whatever agreement you reached, but you damned well better not have made any promises on my behalf."

"None whatsoever," Hagen said. "Our arrangement was one of business and had nothing to do with you, except insofar as he agreed to stop all attempts on your life. I convinced him your death would serve no purpose now that Madam Pinochet was in custody. And now she'll be brought to trial, and justice will be served."

Trammel had never considered himself a smart man, but he didn't have to be smart to see what was really going on. He'd had the whole ride from Laramie to figure it out. "You told him you had her ledger, didn't you?"

"It came up in the course of conversation."

"And Madam Pinochet will go before a friendly judge who's in that ledger and a jury who'll bound to have a few people who were in that ledger, too."

Hagen smiled and shrugged, content with his silence.

But Trammel was far from content. He felt his temper returning. "That means she'll get out. She'll come back and cause more trouble in town."

"Oh, I don't think you have to worry about that, Buck. Our madam has outlived her usefulness as far as Lucien Clay and other prominent members of the territory are concerned. She won't be troubling us again, I assure you."

"She can still talk," Trammel said. "Cut a deal, maybe."

"Not much possibility of that, I'm afraid, when anyone in a position to offer her a deal is also in the ledger."

"She could talk about the ledger itself."

"Without the ledger," Hagen said, "there's no evidence. Just the word of a scared old woman without proof."

Trammel's jaw tightened. "But you have the ledger, don't you?"

Hagen nodded. "Which is the only reason why we're still alive. And it's the reason we're going to remain alive, because I intend on assuming her place in the order of things in this territory."

"You mean the opium." Trammel gripped the reins harder and his horse began to fuss. "And the corruption. All of it continues through you."

Hagen grabbed the bridle of Trammel's horse. "Careful, Buck. You're not enough of a horseman to know the animal can feel your every emotion and respond accordingly. I wouldn't want you to get thrown so close to home. Especially after all we've been through, even today."

But his temper was beginning to build. "I've got no intention of being the sheriff of a town with the worst damned opium house in the territory."

"And I have no intention of owning one. It'll be the finest in the territory, catering to the darkest desires of the most luminary people in this part of our growing country." An edge came to Hagen's voice. "And let's quit pretending that you've embraced the mantle of law and order all of a sudden. You're not some naïve plowboy like Hawkeye who thinks he's someone different just because he's got a tin star on his chest. I'd wager you've done your fair share of reprehensible things back when you were a policeman and, later, a Pinkerton. I admire a man who desires to change, but abhor a man who refuses to accept what he really is. And how things really are."

Trammel's hand dropped to his Colt, but he couldn't grab it. His hand was shaking too hard and he balled it into a fist to make it stop. "I want that ledger."

"And I won't give it to you. You're not going to take it back, either. Father might not have much use for me, but he won't take kindly to the man he hired killing his son, even a wayward son like me. You'd lose your position, if not your life, and then where would you be? Back wandering the great expanse of our country? Go back to Wichita and the waiting arms of the fair maiden Lilly? What welcome do you think Earp would have for you? What welcome do you think old man Bowman would have for the man who killed his sons?"

"Don't think I'm so easy to kill."

"Only a fool would think that, my friend, and I'm no fool. But you'll have to kill me in order to get that ledger back, and my death would only bring wreck and ruin to everything we have a chance to build. Me and my empire of vice. You and your yearning for respectability and the love of a good woman. And Emily is a very good woman indeed, Buck. She'll be yours one day if you want her bad enough, and I believe you do. Why throw that all away over a stupid ledger? You're not naïve enough to think handing it in would accomplish anything. Someone else would step in and make the payoffs in my stead, just as I've stepped into Madam Pinochet's place." Hagen leaned forward, too, bringing his face only a few inches away from Trammel's. "I'm not talking about death, my friend. I'm talking about the kind of life we both want."

Trammel pulled back on the reins, breaking Hagen's grip on the bridle. He wasn't sure if Hagen's grip had slipped or if he'd let it go. The mount fussed a bit before Trammel brought it back under control.

"I won't be in your pocket, Hagen. You break the law, you pay the consequences just like anyone else."

Hagen and his horse stood stock-still. "I wouldn't have it any other way. I take it, then, you'll refuse your share of the proceeds? It's a substantial sum, I assure you."

"I'll live just fine on what the town pays me."

Hagen sighed heavily as he looked up at the sky. "Such a beautiful night at the end of such a beautiful day. I'd hate for it to end on such a sour note. We've ridden too far together and through too much to be enemies now. Please don't be my enemy, Buck. I wouldn't like that. And neither would you."

Trammel's horse fussed again as the rage he felt coursed through him and into the animal. Everything in his body wanted him to rip Hagen from the saddle and pummel him for using him this way. For using him as a bargaining chip in whatever game he was playing against his father.

But he remained in the saddle, because everything Hagen had just said made sense. There would always be someone else ready to step to the fore and cater to the vices of men. It might as well be someone in his own town. Someone he could keep an eye on.

Someone he could trust to be untrustworthy.

Without another word, he brought his horse around Hagen and heeled it toward town. The cool night air quelled his temper considerably, and, the closer he got to Blackstone, he could see Emily had been true to her word.

He could see a candle flickering in her kitchen window, beckoning him toward a place he had never known.

Home.

CHAPTER 1

Glenwood Springs, Colorado

When Matt Jensen rode into town, he stopped in front of the Morning Star Saloon, then pushed through the batwing doors to step inside. Saloons had become a part of his heritage. There was a sameness to them that he had grown comfortable with over the years—the long bar, the wide plank floors, the mirror behind the bar, the suspended lanterns, and the ubiquitous iron stove sitting in a box of sand. He was a wanderer, and though his friends often asked when he was going to settle down, his response was always the same. "I'll settle down when I'm six feet under."

Matt considered himself a free spirit, and even his horse's name, Spirit, reflected that attitude. Much of his travel was without specific destination or purpose, but so frequently was Glenwood Springs a destination that he maintained a semipermanent room in the Glenwood Springs Hotel.

"Haven't seen you for a while," the bartender said

as Matt stepped up to the bar. "Where've you been keepin' yourself?"

"Oh, here and there. Anywhere they'll let me stay for a few days before they ask me to move on."

"I envy people like you. No place to call home, no one to tie you down."

"Yeah, that's me, no one to tie me down," Matt said in a voice that the discerning would recognize as somewhat half-hearted.

"So, here for a beer, are you?"

"No, I just came in here to check my mail," Matt replied.

"What?"

Matt laughed. "A beer would be good."

"Check your mail," Max said, laughing with Matt. "That's a good one. I'll have to remember that one."

"How's Doc doing?" Matt asked.

"You're asking about Holliday?" the bartender asked as he set the beer before Matt.

"Yes. Does he still come in here a lot?"

"Not as much as he used to. He's pretty wasted by now, just skin and bones. Sort of wobbles when he walks. Big Nose Kate is here though, and she looks after him."

"Is he at the hotel or the sanitarium?"

"Hotel mostly, either his room or the lobby."

"I think I'll go see him, maybe bring him in here for a drink if I can talk him into it."

"Are you kidding?" the bartender asked. "He'll come in a military minute. That is, if Kate will let him come."

"What do you mean, if she'll let him come?"

"She watches over him like a mother hen guarding her chicks."

"Good for her. Well, I'll just have to charm her into letting him join me."

"You're going to charm Big Nose Kate? Ha! You would have better luck charming a rock."

Matt stepped into the hotel a few minutes later and secured his room. Looking around, he saw Doc Holliday and Big Nose Kate in the lobby sitting together on a leather sofa near the fireplace. And though it wasn't cold enough to require a fire, one was burning.

As Max had indicated, John Henry Holliday was a mere shadow of his former self. Matt had met him in his prime, though even then, Doc had been suffering from consumption and had had frequent coughing spells. He had also been clear-eyed, sharp-witted, and confident. He was a loyal, and when needed, deadly friend to Wyatt Earp.

Big Nose Kate, Mary Katherine Haroney, was by Doc Holliday's side. Despite the sobriquet of "Big Nose," she was actually quite an attractive woman. Matt had asked once why they called her Big Nose and was told that it wasn't because of the size of the proboscis, but because she had a tendency to stick it into other people's business.

"Hello, Doc," Matt said as he approached the two.

"Matt!" Doc Holliday greeted enthusiastically. He started to get up.

"There's no need for you to be getting up," Kate said with just a hint of a Hungarian accent.

"Hello, Kate. It's good to see you here."

"And if Doc is here, where else would I be?"

"Why, here, of course. Doc, I was just over to the Morning Star and noticed something was missing.

It took me a moment to figure it out then I realized that it was *you*, sitting at your special table playing cards. How about going back with me so you and I can play a little poker?"

"Oh, I don't know," Doc said. "I'm not as good as I used to be."

Matt chuckled. "Yeah, that's what I'm counting on. I thought if we could play a few hands I might be able to get some of the money back I've lost to you over the years."

Doc laughed out loud. "Sonny, all I said was that I'm not as good as I used to be. But I can still beat you. Let's go." He began the struggle to rise, and quickly, Matt came to his assistance.

"You don't mind, do you, Kate?"

"Keep a good eye on him, will you, Matt?"

"I will," he promised.

Doc was able to walk on his own, but his frailty meant that the walk from the Glenwood Springs Hotel was quite slow. When they stepped into the saloon a few minutes later he was greeted warmly by all as two of the bar girls approached.

"We'll get him seated," one of the girls said as she took one arm, and the second bar girl took the other.

"Your table, Doc?" one asked.

"Yes, thank you."

After they were seated one brought a whiskey for Doc and a beer for Matt. Shortly after that two more men came to the table and a game of poker ensued.

They had been playing for about half an hour when Matt saw a man come into the saloon. He stood just inside the swinging batwing doors, surveying the saloon until his perusing came to a stop at the table where Matt, Doc, and the two others were playing poker. The man pulled his pistol from the holster and held it down by his side.

Matt had no idea who this man was, but it was pretty obvious that he was on the prowl. For him? It could be. He had made a lot of friends over the years, but he had also made a lot of enemies.

"There you are, you son of a bitch!" the man said. He didn't shout the words, but they were easily heard. Curiosity had halted the conversations when he'd first come into the saloon. With his raised pistol, the curiosity had changed to apprehension.

"An old enemy, Matt?" one of the players asked.

"No, gentleman. I'm afraid that one is after me," Doc said.

"Stand up, Holliday! Stand up and face me like a man!"

"I'm not armed, Hartman. In case you haven't noticed by my emaciated appearance, I am in the advanced stages of consumption, so you can just put your gun back in its holster. If you are all that set on seeing me die, all you have to do is hang around for a short while, and I'll do it for you. Your personal participation in the process won't be needed."

"Yeah? Well, I want to participate," Hartman said.

"All right. Well, go ahead and shoot me. I've no way of stopping you." Doc's voice was calm and measured.

"I wonder if I could intervene for a moment?" Matt's voice was calm and conversational just like Doc's.

"Mister, you 'n them other two that's sittin' at the table there had better get up and get out of the way. I come in here with one thing in mind, 'n that was to kill the man that kilt my brother. 'N I aim to do it."

The two others at the table heeded Hartman's advice and moved out of the way.

Matt stood, but remained in place. "Speaking as John Henry's friend, and on behalf of several others who I know are also his friends, I'm going to ask . . . no, I'm going to *tell* you to put aside any grievance you may have with Doc, and let nature take its course. Let him die in peace."

"Mister, I'm standin' here with a gun in my hand and you're tryin' to tell me what to do? Suppose I tell you I'm goin' to kill him anyway?"

"You'll have to come through me first."

"All right, if that's what it takes. Doc, I'm going to ask you to get out of the way for a moment," Hartman said. "I intend to kill you, but I don't want it to be an accident. When I kill you, it's goin' to be purposeful."

"Oh, I'm not worried about it, Hartman. I'm in no danger here. If you really are dumb enough to engage my friend here, you won't even get a shot off."

"What is he, some sort of fool? I already have my gun in my hand," Hartman said as if explaining something to a child.

"Yes, well, go ahead and do what you feel you must do," Matt said.

Hartman lifted his thumb up from the handle of his pistol, preparatory to pulling back the hammer, but his thumb never reached the hammer. Matt drew and fired. His bullet crashed into Hartman's forehead, then burst out through the back of his head taking with it a little spray of pink. Hartman was dead before he ever realized that he was in danger.

"My God. I've never seen anything like that!" said one of the other card players.

A buzz of excited chatter came from all the others in the saloon, and several gathered around Hartman's body.

"Gentlemen," Doc Holliday said, "can we please get back to the game? I plan to teach this young whippersnapper here a lesson he won't soon forget."